Richard Savage

For Life and Love

A Story of the Rio Grande

Richard Savage

For Life and Love
A Story of the Rio Grande

ISBN/EAN: 9783744661904

Printed in Europe, USA, Canada, Australia, Japan

Cover: Foto ©Andreas Hilbeck / pixelio.de

More available books at **www.hansebooks.com**

FOR LIFE AND LOVE

A STORY OF THE RIO GRANDE

" And Leavenworth lay dying, with his head upon my knee—
' Take these,' he sighed, ' to one, who long will wait and watch for me! '
Only a tress of woman's hair! A rose, dead many a day!
It was upon the sandy banks of the Rio Grande, where we lay! "

"OLD BALLAD."

BY

RICHARD HENRY SAVAGE

AUTHOR OF

"MY OFFICIAL WIFE," "THE LITTLE LADY OF LAGUNITAS,"
"PRINCE SCHAMYL'S WOOING," "THE MASKED VENUS,"
"DELILAH OF HARLEM," "THE PASSING SHOW."

FRANK TENNYSON NEELY

CHICAGO AND NEW YORK

RICHARD HENRY SAVAGE.

F EW of the recent American novelists have attained the success of RICHARD HENRY SAVAGE, whose dashing and romantic stories are to-day published in Germany and England as well as America. His experiences are as varied as the scenes of his works, and, save India and Australia, he is familiar with the entire route of the wayfarer in life. Student, traveller, soldier, author, and scientist, his forty-seven years have been marked by mental toil, physical hardship, and stirring adventure.

· The author of "My Official Wife" was born in Utica, New York, and as a lad, arriving in California in 1852, attended the first public school in San Francisco, being the youngest scholar in the first class of the High School. Taken to the wilds of Nevada County, where his father was a leading merchant, the youth saw, in its prime, the wild life of Bret Harte's heroes. Later, in San Francisco, he witnessed the Vigilance Committee's sway of 1856, and the final crystallization of California society.

His law studies with Edward Stanley and Sidney V. Smith, of San Francisco, were interrupted by the war. A commission in the California Volunteers was reluctantly declined by reason of his minority, and in 1864 he was entered at West Point, representing the San Francisco district. Already a fearless rider and a daring hunter, he soon excelled in physical exercises, taking a distinguished rank in his class, and was graduated in 1868 as Lieutenant of Engineers, the highest corps. He was a leading cadet . officer and led his class in law, literature, ethics, and several branches of science.

From 1868 to '71, LIEUTENANT SAVAGE served as *Engineer officer* and personal *Aide-de-Camp* of the heroic Gen. Geo. H. Thomas, who was attracted to the spirited young officer who had executed dangerous and difficult duties on the Western frontiers. From 1861 MR. SAVAGE had been writing now-forgotten poetry for the Golden Era, essays and newspaper work, and desirous of travel, he resigned from the army and visited Europe for two years.

Possessing the confidence of President Grant, he was given several diplomatic appointments, among which were a consular position at Marseilles and Rome, and later a commission to examine Mexican and Texan outrages By the choice of Gen. ,W. T. Sherman, he was named to fill the position of confidential and military secretary to Gen. Chas. P. Stone, in Egypt, and after *finally* leaving the diplomatic service, engaged in railroad engineering in Texas and later, practiced engineering in California.

Retiring from business in 1884, he resumed his first profession—the law — and cast his eyes toward the literary field in the intervals of seven years' travel and residence abroad. Domiciled to-day in New York City, in a home filled with the trophies of travel and adventure, the world-wearied writer has returned to his native State. With a marvellous memory, an untold fund of adventure, and a quaint library, the ex-soldier, abandoning society, finds his books and the companionship of his accomplished wife filling these days of quiescence. New York has drawn John Brisben Walker. Arthur Sherburne Hardy, and Col. Savage together, and they want to capture that brilliant and daring veteran Captain Charley King, (now on a two years' run in Europe), and reunite in the metropolis the quartette of the literary West Pointers of thirty years ago. It is strange that they have all been strikingly successful.

COLONEL SAVAGE is matched in social and personal experience by few men. His range has been from Siberia to the Red Sea, from the wilds of Central America and the plains to the Greek Sea and the Winter Palace. Tall, energetic, and animated, his conversation teems with memories of me of many lands and grades. It is hard to realize that Cortina the raide. William Walker, Lola Montes, and Billy Florence, are companion negative; with Pius IX., General Grant, Ismail Pasha, and Denis Kearney in one man's mind. From the frontier camp-fire to the Coliseum, from the Sand Lot to a palace ball, the traveller has threaded the mazes of a strange life.

COLONEL SAVAGE is an excellent speaker and his lectures at Yale College, the University of California, and other public institutions have been delightful. He eschews literary society and bohemianism, and stands alone— a firm believer in the romantic school.

In his mingling with great men, with a remarkable personal experience in the four quarters of the globe, and his acquaintance with cosmopolitan society, COLONEL SAVAGE stands high as a man of thought and action. Thrilling episodes in his useful and eventful life were his two thousand miles march in Arizona in 1869, before a rail was laid; his winter experience in 1870 in the great fastnesses of the Northern Sierras, with Pitt River and Modoc Indians on the Round Valley Survey; his lonely ride from Mangalile through the jungles of Honduras; his facing the terrific cholera pest in Japan and Corea in 1886, as well as the adventures on the wild Rio Grande border in

'72; and a desperate boat adventure in the Caribbean in 1890. His collection of personal and military relics is a museum, while his correspondence with the great men of the last twenty years is a sacred trust.

A treasured ornament of his sanctum is a superb silver bowl given to him by the Committee of Safety in San Francisco for services in aiding the suppression of the Kearney riots of 1877. His engineering record stands firmly from lighthouses on the Red Sea, and a railroad in Texas, to towering iron architectural ornaments of San Francisco. His essays, theses, sketches, and journalistic volunteer work, as well as speeches, would embrace several volumes and may yet be collected.

A distaste for criminal law and political manipulation caused him to adopt literature as a change. In his six published works, he reviews life experiences, "The Little Lady of Lagunitas" being a marvellous story of early California; "Prince Schamyl's Wooing," a scholarly Russian romance; "The Masked Venus" and "Delilah of Harlem," mirror the gilded intrigues of later years, and "The Passing Show" gives us seven thrilling stories of actual experience. A strong dramatic shade in several of these works forecasts their adaptation for the stage.

COLONEL SAVAGE is a type of the self-contained American, and equipped with extensive studies, a cosmopolitan acquaintance, a splendid linguist, has in view further foreign travel in his literary researches. A charming raconteur, a patient and dauntless traveller, he is known from the Neva to the United Service Club, and from the Nile to Edinburgh.

A splendid German and English appreciation of his works is evinced in their great sale abroad, "My Official Wife" being now in French, German, Swedish, and Italian. A uniform library edition in German is soon to appear.

In pursuance of future literary plans, this indefatigable author has placed the publishing of his entire works in the hands of Frank Tennyson Neely, of Chicago, who has achieved wonders with "The Passing Show" in the way of brilliant sales. His great success with this book has induced MR. SAVAGE to place in his hands all of his *previous* novels not permanently engaged, as well as his future books, thus removing his publication head-quarters from New York to Chicago.

By November 1st, Mr. Neely will bring out the most exciting and dashing of COLONEL SAVAGE'S conceptions, a thrilling and delightful border romance entitled, "For Life and Love," a story of the Rio Grande. Another maze of descriptive word painting, skillful plot, and a case where true love wins the race of life!—*The Chicago Herald, Sunday, October 8, 1893.*

CONTENTS.

BOOK I.

"LOVE THAT HATH US IN THE NET."

BOOK II.

THE RIO GRANDE COMPANY.

BOOK V.

THE LAST THROW OF THE DICE.   LOVE WINS!

FOR LIFE AND LOVE.

A STORY OF THE RIO GRANDE.

. BOOK I.

"LOVE THAT HATH US IN THE NET."

CHAPTER I.

JACK MANSON'S ORDERS—FROM THE "ROCKIES" TO
THE GULF OF MEXICO—THE DAY STAR!

"WHAT nonsense!" cried handsome Jack Manson,
as he hurled the book he had vainly essayed to read,
into the dim recesses of the room, now shadowed by
the dusk of evening. The offending volume fell, torn
and fluttering its leaves in vain protest, into a jungle of
instruments, surveying chains, saddles, guns, books, and
frontier gear.

Manson glared at the ruined romance, and, springing
from his couch, lit a lamp and carefully filled his pipe.
"'She Loved Another!' Well! suppose she did!"
he growled, as he gazed wearily at the rough interior
of the temporary Engineer Headquarters building at
Cheyenne. Pacing the room with uneasy strides,
Manson gazed from the uncurtained windows. The
September winds were blowing keen and chill from
the Rockies, far above him. Never before had the
bald, gray, stony hills looked so uninviting. Cheyenne

in 1872 was not an agreeable place of residence; for the horde of gamblers, thieves, and outcasts who followed the construction of the Union Pacific Road, still lingered to grace the society of Manson's temporary home. Wyoming, at this date, proudly boasted daily. robberies, "shooting scrapes," lynchings, and a more generally assorted deviltry than any division of the Union; with a slight polite reservation in favor of Texas. The outlook was unlovely!

"It's a bad case of the blues," muttered Manson, as he threw himself into a rough chair, and listened, vacant minded, to the rattle of the dishes in the adjoining shed, where Hop Wo, the Chinese Soyer, was preparing the usual feast of coarse food.

Frontier beef, canned stuff, i. e. preserved tinned goods, alleged bread and campaign coffee, were the usual garnishings of the mess table, unadorned by linen.

Jack Manson, as a division engineer on the Union Pacific Railroad, was finishing up the final professional work on the line, hastily thrown down from 1866 to 1868. In the fierce race between the Central Pacific and the Union Pacific to build the greatest number of miles and gain the largest national subsidy, Jack Manson had been the main-stay of the Chief. For six long years the young engineer had toiled with transit, level, and field-book over the unbroken prairies and through the rocky gorges of the mountain spurs. Sometimes working with rifle in one hand and the compass in the other, the young man was jaded and wearied with anxiety, fatigue, and danger.

Now the lines were to be rectified, grades reduced, curves enlarged, and all the real finishing work executed under his watchful eye. His mind had grasped the needs of the situation, and two hundred miles of the road were photographed in his brain.

" Anderson should be here now !" he murmured, rousing himself, as the moon-eyed Hop Wo silently spread
the frugal board. " I'll wait a little!" His head fell
on his breast in revery. He had sent his assistant on a
reconnoissance trip of fifty miles to examine a proposed
detour of the hastily patched-up road.

" I wonder if the Indians have got him," Jack
anxiously pondered. Sioux, Cheyennes, Ogallalas,
Blackfeet, Kiowas, and other murderous tribes had
amused themselves for years in harassing small parties,
butchering teamsters, and dashing unawares on the
scientists at their work. The young man's head
drooped and his eyes were very dreamy.

" Is this to last forever? " he murmured. The six
years since he left the Polytechnic at Troy were a mere
dreary waste of life. Dull days unmarked by aught
save the varied dangers of the Sioux country and the
arduous labor of his profession.

A rush and clatter of hoofs! Jack sprang to the
door and peered into the darkness. " Is that you,
Harry? " he cried anxiously.

" All right, Chief," was the cheery response, as
Harry Anderson strode into the room, now quite
inviting with its huge log-fire and the steaming supper.

" Come in, Allison, when you've put the horses
up," said Harry, as he threw off his pistol-belt and
unbuckled his spurs. The guide disappeared with the
tired steeds, and, after a hearty greeting, the two young
men attacked the waiting repast.

"Anything special, Harry?" queried Jack, as he
heaped a plate for the hungry rider.

"Not much," said Harry, between bites; "we hid in
an arroyo from a little war party of young bucks—
about half a dozen. Allison wanted to try his Winchester. I wouldn't let him. We were fired at in

the cañon behind Bald Peak. Road agents, I guess! Probably took us for a couple of deputies hunting horse thieves!"

"How about the line?" queried Manson, with some interest. Anderson swallowed a cup of coffee and slowly replied:

"Very good; we can save that heavy grade on the divide and go around, well protected from land slides and floods."

"Excellent!" cried the overjoyed Manson. "Harry," said he, "If I leave nothing else, I wish to show the Chief our division in first-class trim, when he comes over the road. I'll look over the notes and sketches by and by." Silence reigned until the hungry assistant had revenged himself for the three days' bivouac privations.

Pipes lit, by the blazing fire the two friends awaited Allison's return. They were types of manhood, yet differing widely.

Jack Manson's five feet ten inches gave his well-knit frame a certain dignity. Crisp, curling brown hair shaded his sunburned brows, beneath which a pair of clear blue eyes sparkled with the fire of youth. The straight nose, firm mouth, and square-cut chin made him the ideal of a resolute Anglo-Saxon, in the American edition. Quick, lithe, and neat-footed, his whole being exhaled energy and decision.

A sweeping mustache, worthy of a trooper, gave an air of frontier dash to the man whose thoughtful brows bespoke the mathematician, while Harry Anderson, stocky and sturdy, with crisp, curling black hair, a flashing, truculent eye, and a heavy chest with rounded shoulders belted with muscle, was a representative of that stubborn cross, the Scotch-Irish.

The night winds rose and howled around the rude

dwelling. Jack Manson's eyes were fixed on the fire and a wistful shade crossed his face. For, in the utter loneliness of six years, the sights and scenes around had grown weary and distasteful.

Manson lifted his head as Allison, the guide, strode into the room. " Well, Allison, you brought back all your hair, I see!" cried Jack, as he motioned the scout to the modest feast.

" So we did, Cap," answered the lank six footer, as he dropped into a chair and vigorously attacked the remains of the supper. " There would have been bald spots on our heads if those young braves had caught us in the arroyo. I hate to run before an Injun," he remarked, with evident disgust. "Here, Hop Wo!" he cried, and smiled approvingly as the celestial poured out a pint of steaming coffee.

Allison, clad in a fringed suit of Indian tan buckskin, was belted with his heavy pistols and a bowie-knife of formidable dimensions. Filling his pipe, he drew up with easy familiarity to the fire. " Thar's entirely too many of these young Sioux bucks knocking around in the hills now, Cap. You ought not to send less than five or six men out, now. You may get used to these devils, but they are always on the scalp hunt! They follow for fifty miles and make a run in when you're off your guard."

Manson smoked reflectively. " I will get up a half-dozen good fellows from the big camp," he said. " I think you are right."

Allison relapsed into silence and finally, knocking out his pipe, said: " I'll wander over to town and look in at the express and telegraph office." With a nod, he disappeared in the darkness. After a half-hour's discussion of Anderson's rough notes, Manson said kindly: " Harry, you turn in! You are tired! I'll sit and smoke awhile."

Silence reigned in the rude shelter as Manson dreamily gazed in the fire. An intense weariness, a feeling of desolation came over him. There was a warm strain of sentiment running through Jack's nature. The great logs crackled and fell into coals, little blue and red flames danced above the glowing coals. Young in years but old in experience, happier days came back to him. He could see again the wooded hills and green slopes of the Mohawk Valley, with the river flowing gently to join the blue Hudson. His home, his early friends, his school and college days came back.

In the lonely Western cabin, the young engineer lived over again the sad days when Colonel Manson was brought home from Spottsylvania, with the regimental flag wrapped around his coffin.

The gentle mother who followed her dead soldier to the land of shadows came back once more, and he could hear again her last appeal to grim old Mark Manson, his uncle, "Take care of Jack, Mark! He's all alone now!" The young man could see his stern uncle, standing with a suspiciously moist eye, by the pale woman, waiting for the summons, and hear him say again, "I'll make a man of him, Helen!"

A great log fell down and broke in crackling fragments; Jack rose and trimmed the fire. He sighed as he gazed at stout Harry Anderson, sleeping like a child. "He does not care," bitterly thought Jack. "But I was made for better things than this!"

"True," he soliloquized, "Uncle Mark educated me, has stood by me, and between him and my work, I have gained promotion! But there's another life than this. Home, friends, books, the thousand delights of civilization, and—and—" the young man's mind drifted away into a dream of fair women. The wine of life was stirring in the handsome fellow's veins. "It's a death in life," he growled. "I have not seen a woman I knew for years." He ignored the several Indian princesses of note he had met. "Brave Rainbow," "Moonlight Shadow," and "Bounding Antelope," daughters of war chiefs, were young Sioux rosebuds somewhat peculiar in their habits. "Brave Rainbow" was far too fond of firewater; "Moonlight Shadow" would slyly abstract anything lighter than an army wagon, and "Bounding Antelope" he had seen the day before, "al fresco," calmly lunching from portions of a dead army mule.

"Not up to the ideal of Pocahontas or Minnehaha," Manson sneered. As for the pale anæmic frontier women, they were draggled children of misery—vainly wandering to and fro with their uncouth liege lords. Saddened, hopeless drudges, were these poor feminine pioneers. Occasional glimpses of weary, dusty, cross-looking women tourists, sullenly gazing from car windows exasperated the impressionable youth—for it was before the days of vestibuled luxury, and feminine graces were but feebly affected by the tired, jaded travellers of that day.

As for the shrill-voiced, unabashed "beauties" of the ambulatory settlement following the railroad, they were merely "wrecks on error's shore." They were house-less shadows, flitting specters, these wild-eyed, battered Mænads, flaunting the crimson flag of vice, with no rosy charms to beguile.

"I would like to see a sweet bright woman once more," he muttered as the fire sank low. A child of care, early thrown on his own resources, Manson felt that he was alone in the battle of life, with no tender eyes following his pathway in the conflict. His youth was hard and lonely, his early manhood a social blank.

"Will it ever end! Shall I lay my bones down in these gray hills!" He gave a stray log a kick, and sought his fur-decked couch.

Before his eyes closed, the door was thrown open. Allison strode in, bringing gusts of night wind with him, setting the dying embers flaring. "Telegram for you, Cap! Answer immediate! I'll saddle my horse and ride down with your answer to the station. Office in town shut now. I'll be back in five minutes." The sturdy guide cheerfully stalked off to toss the saddle on his jaded pony.

By the gleam of the one kerosene lamp which the palace of science boasted, Manson read the words flashed over the talking wire. He sprang up with a shout which aroused even the tired Anderson, who growled: "What's up, Chief?"

Manson stood by the table, the paper fluttering in his hand. He devoured it over and over again. Its laconic words thrilled his very heart. He handed it to Anderson without a word. The missive needed no explanation. It was dated New York, September 8, 1872, and its fateful contents were:

"Turn your division over to Anderson, promoted. Settle your accounts with Chief Engineer at Omaha. Come here at once; want you to go South. Draw for funds, if needed. Answer."

The signature was that of the potent railway magnate, steamboat king, and financial prince, Mark Manson.

Jack threw himself in a chair, and said quietly, "I congratulate you, Harry. That means two thousand a year increase to you."

"When will you go, old man? By Jove! This is sudden!" ejaculated Anderson, still half asleep.

Manson's flying fingers traced a few lines with nervous eagerness. He tossed it to Anderson. The overjoyed, newly-made Division Engineer read:

"Leave on to-morrow's train. Report forthwith. No funds needed."

As Anderson's eye scanned the last word, the clatter of hoofs announced Allison, who grasped the despatch and dashed away in the darkness, his horse striking fire from the flinty float rock, with his armed hoofs.

There was an end to sleep. With the aid of sundry candles, and the glaring kerosene, Manson began throwing together, in a pile, such traps as he proposed to save from the flitting.

" The train comes along at 7:30," said Manson, as he stuffed his private papers into his trunk and tossed in at random the few belongings he was encumbered with.

" You can give me a memorandum receipt, Harry, for the instruments and records. Send your full papers on to New York. Keep all this trash here. It will be of some use to you."

Anderson nodded and with his executive dash, roused the son of the Flowery Kingdom and announced the early departure.

When Allison, wearied and chilled, entered the room, he was visibly affected by the news, and even more so by the present of Manson's riding gear and formidable armament.

Over a reserved bottle of good Bourbon, the three companions of many dangerous ventures held an impromptu carnival of frontier jollity.

The stars were low in the west, and the genial volunteer orchestra of coyotes was waking the echoes of the surrounding hills—a hint of daybreak—when

Manson threw himself down for two hours' sleep. He tossed uneasily in the wildest dreams.

It cost Jack a heart wrench, as four hours later he wrung Anderson's hand, when the screech of the locomotive warned the friends of the parting hour.

"God bless you, old boy! Go on up to the top!" cried Jack, as the elated Anderson essayed vainly to say "Good-bye." Six years of toil and danger had knitted closely their bond of brotherhood. Allison, loose-jointed and laconic, grasped the young traveller's hand with the grip of a vise.

"Good-bye, Cap!" he heartily said, "Yer as squar' a man as ever straddled a horse! When ye've got a pretty wife, you'll be over here in a director's car. Don't forget the boys!"

Hop Wo, with forethought, presented sundry dainties, and grinned an approving adieu as he pocketed a bright twenty-dollar piece.

The tired eyes of Manson closed in slumber as the train tore along, past the unbroken sameness of the rolling hills, and in the young man's dreams a haunting sense of curious expectancy kept his nerves in feverish unrest.

In half-waking hours he experienced a delicious sense of restfulness, as he noted from hour to hour the old familiar scenes of storm, toil, privation, and danger flit by.

Memories of friends dead, of unnoticed hardship, and lonely hours came back as the familiar names, Sidney, Ogalalla, North Platte, Plum Creek, and Grand Island sounded on his ear. In two days he glided over the thousand miles over which he had trudged, transit on shoulder, revolver at belt, for six weary years. It was only when the red banks of the Missouri, crested with Omaha's straggling houses, appeared in front,

that he turned his tired head and said, "Good-bye, Mr.
Sioux Brave and Mrs. Sioux Squaw! May we never
meet again."

Two hours of the next morning sufficed to settle his
accounts. The grizzled Chief of the Trans-Continental
Line handed him a testimonial, his arrearages, and a
check for one year's pay.

"General, I do not understand this," said Manson,
his cheek flushing; "I do not ask for presents."

"Take all you can get in this world, my boy!" said
the busy ex-general, now Chief Engineer of the Union
Pacific.

"Don't be so bashful! Did you ever hear of the Credit
Mobilier? This is some of their loose funds—a little
fragment. It's orders from headquarters anyway."

Manson winced, for well he knew that silent old
Mark Manson was the arch high priest of that
mysterious body. He pocketed the check and declined
the general's plea for a parting dinner.

"I must hasten along," he said, while returning
thanks. " By the way, General, do you know where I
am to go? "

The general's steady gray eye almost condescended
to a wink. "Did you ever know Mark Manson to tell
his business? "

The young man was fain to wait for the answer at
New York.

" By the way, my young friend," said the chief, as
he grasped Jack's hand in farewell, "don't forget to
visit the tailor's in Chicago. A man may be a swell in
Cheyenne and yet cut a strange figure on Broadway."
The old engineer laughed heartily as he swung Jack
around before a mirror.

Manson joined gleefully in the burst of merriment.
"By Jove!" he cried, "I thank you. Now I remember,
even here people stared at me."

For his handsome face and splendid physique made
a medley of frontier garb—soldier's uniform and picked
up "store goods"—seem ridiculous.

"You will see hosts of pretty girls in Chicago and
eastwardly," the chief chuckled. "They would take
you for the 'Whirlwind of the Prairies' or 'Deadwood
Bill, the Man Eater.'"

Light-hearted and happy, Manson crossed the muddy
Missouri. Two days in Chicago sufficed to restore him
to the outward semblance of civilization. His face
seemed strange as he gazed at the splendor of raiment
unaccustomed in use for six weary years.

Save the ruddy brown of his cheek and the stern,
almost careworn expression of his features, Jack was
now the "every-day young man" as he sought the
easy Pullman for the final stage of his journey. No
trace of his frontier life lingered with him save a
nervous distrust of the crowded sidewalks and a longing
to take the middle of the street. He had conquered his
habit of looking to right, left, and rear for concealed
foes in ambush, but was forced to admit the danger of a
fusillade of admiring eyes from the milliner stores and
corner shops. Women in all their charming variations
of dress, feature, and diverse attractions made Chicago
seem a sort of brick-and-mortar Eden. With a sigh of
relief he saw the Lake City fade away behind him.
The fresh breeze from the water served to brush away
his olden cares. Jack, having announced his arrival in
New York by telegraph, felt a keen enjoyment in
yielding to a destiny pointed out by the stern old Crœsus
who waited for him.

Hourly his spirits rose, and, as the fragrant clouds
from a Cabaña hovered round him, he ruminated:

"Down South, even Kuklux and Cowboys can not
be worse neighbors than the long-haired Sioux or the
Cheyenne dog-soldiers."

On past the roar of Niagara, down through the lovely Mohawk Valley (his head resolutely turned away from the hills hiding his old home), past his boyhood's Alma Mater, and dashing along the unrivalled shores of the Hudson, Manson swiftly sped, eager to know his final orders. The car was filled with travellers, eagerly discussing the great presidential election impending. The burning question of the hour was the selection of the hero of the sword, the taciturn Grant, or the eccentric veteran field-marshal of the pen, Greeley, to preside over the councils of the country for four years.

High waxed discussion in the smoking-room, and the wearied engineer sought the interior of the car.

Nearing the Highlands, a merry delegation of fair college beauties from Vassar joined the train at Poughkeepsie. Maxwell was checking his curiosity as to the future by poring over a thrilling romance, a weird tale of love, one of those heart-moving narratives whose sole excuse of being is that "He who runs may read."

The sound of a woman's voice awakened him from his listless day-dream over the florid pages of the novelist. Sweet and low, thrilling in its soft earnestness, it seemed to pierce his very heart. In uneasy resistance he lingered a few minutes. In a few moments the simple artifice of passing in and out of the car gave him an excuse to gaze upon the unknown whose accents moved him so strangely.

Mr. Jack Manson was conscious of a strange new feeling in his heart as he turned and stole a glance at the woman he listened to.

There was no mistaking the indications. Two sisters, emancipated from the guarded bowers and academic shades of Vassar, guardian of these lovely voyagers— a middle-aged lady of irreproachable manner, dress,

and composure. The elder girl, tall, with dark eyes
and a sweet serious face, was gazing fondly at the animated Hebe whose voice had wakened the lonely
echoes of his heart. The calm brows of the elder
sister, shaded by silken brown tresses, were worthy of
a St. Cecilia. Stealing a glance at the younger stranger,
Manson whispered to himself, " A dream of beauty!"
And so the fair unknown was. Bright and eager, she
was wondrously lovely. In her witching deep-blue
eyes the light of womanhood's spring-time sparkled.
The exquisite symmetry of her form aided the charm
of the sea-shell's magic tints shading her fair face.
Manson trifled away a few moments and quietly
reseated himself. As he passed the unknown beauties
he felt his cheeks burn, for one keen flash of the blue
eyes told him instantly that his unconscious admiration
had been observed.

Jack Manson dropped humbly in his seat and
feigned to diligently devour the unfinished story of
"pride and passion," which fortunately concealed his
sudden confusion.

Still that velvety voice, thrilling every fibre of his
being! "If I were a free man," he mentally resolved,
"I would follow that girl to Greenland to be near
her."

With clash and roar and screaming whistles, the train
drew into the great Empire City.

"I'll have a last look at this rosy fairy," the young
traveller decided, as he sprang off the car and awaited
the leisurely departure of the ladies. The shouts and
bustle of a great station confused him and he gazed
around in sudden helplessness. His eyes roving over
the joyous groups rested at last upon a tableau which
chilled his pulses like an Arctic blast.

The graceful head of the blue-eyed enchantress was

resting on the breast of a tall, stalwart young man, her rounded arms were twined around his neck.

Jack Manson gasped and almost dropped his "sac de voyage."

"Great Heavens! She's engaged! This closes this chapter and the book forever!" Manson was rooted to the spot, and gazed vacantly at the only energetic demonstrations of affection he had seen for six years.

He started in surprise as the eager stranger fondly embraced the St. Cecilia with equal fervor.

"Can he be engaged to both of them?" was a hideous flash-light thought, smacking of Mormonism. The gentleman from Cheyenne was further astounded to see this universal kisser salute the dignified and still handsome duenna with a judiciously graded fervor.

"Affection mingled with respect!" Jack decided. "I'll have a peep at that youth's face! He seems to be a 'persona grata.' By Jove!" Manson thought, with an inspiration which made his heart bound, " he may be only a brother! He hugged *both* those girls." And, moving sidelong in apparent abstraction, Jack, the sudden prey of roguish Dan Cupid, glared on the happy man whose florid affection galled the impressionable traveller.

Manson made one bound, as he dropped the satchel from his hand—his surprise found vent in words:

"Jimmy Leavenworth! By all that's holy!"

Extricating himself from his fair captors, the party addressed turned his head sharply, and sprang forward with outstretched hand.

"Jack, my dear old boy, where did you come from?"

Manson drew a great breath of fresh air, and pumped out the words: "Cheyenne. And you?"

The calm eyes of St. Cecilia were fixed on the excited pair. The rosy Hebe levelled a furtive glance at the handsome interloper, and the duenna lifted her eyebrows in interrogation, as their escort said:

"Why, from Texas, of course! I came up here to take my sisters home."

The solid asphalt billowed under Jack's feet, as he vacantly remarked: "Oh! I see! Certainly!" And his wandering eyes rested upon the graceful young beauty before him, whose eyes dropped strangely under his ardent gaze.

Leavenworth, suddenly recalled to the duties of the moment, most ceremoniously said: "Mrs. Marshall, permit me to present my classmate at the Polytechnic, Mr. John Manson."

Jack's low bow was worthy of a Spanish grandee. "Must conciliate the duenna," his startled brain flashed out.

"My sister Alice, Mr. Manson," continued the over-joyed Leavenworth. Jack's composure had returned. He bent in stately homage. "My sister Katie," concluded the Texan master of ceremonies.

Jack Manson raised his eyes to the sweet face and for a moment he gazed into that mirror of loveliness. A bright-red danger-flag burned upon the pretty girl's cheeks as she greeted the stranger knight. The rosy Hebe rippled out in merry laughter: "We were travelling companions, were we not?"

"By Jove! She did notice me," thought Manson his pulses throbbing.

"Where do you go, Jack?" hurriedly cried Leavenworth. "We are at the Fifth Avenue. Come down there. I must have a long talk with you."

With deceitful meekness, Mr. John Manson, inwardly dissembling, drifted with the tide of his good fortune, and in the carriage in the growing dusk was strangely silent. Katie Leavenworth's fair head was resting on the cushions. Her tired eyes drooped and her gracefully moulded arms were resting, with the delicately gloved hands clasped. " A sleeping fairy princess," thought the man who gazed upon her virginal beauty.   .   •

The sparkling stars were peeping through the evening shadows as the little circle assembled in the salon of the Fifth Avenue. Leavenworth and his fair sisters, with Manson, awaited Mrs. Marshall who glided into the drawing-room, followed .by a third Grace, a surprise to the mystified Jack who rehearsed his Chesterfieldean bow, as he was presented to Miss Gertrude Marshall of Virginia.

The reflection of Jimmy Leavenworth's face in a mirror gave keen-eyed Jack Manson his cue.

" Here is the ' one fair woman ' who will rule the gallant Texan! " It was even so. A few moments sufficed to inform Manson of the sisterhood of the three beauties, long immured in the friendly shelter of Vassar College.

" I think Jimmy's visits were half for his sisters and largely for the sweet Virginian," mused Manson.

The engineer was right. In several journeys North, Jimmy Leavenworth had been swept far over the outer edge of indifference into the sweeping maelstrom of love. Gertrude Marshall mingled in her calm, finely chiselled face the mental firmness of her distinguished father, who died under the Stars and Bars at Malvern Hill, with the youthful graces of her gentle and refined mother. Liquid gray eyes, a Greek brow, and lips as delicate in tint as the spring wild rose, were elements of a great beauty bespeaking the high soul and the stead-fast mind. A nameless air of poise and fixed purpose marked her as a daughter of the Old Dominion.

With quiet dignity Mrs. Marshall presided over the

dinner, which was only interrupted by the rattling cross-fire of question and answer between the lively college chums, so long parted, and the merry chatter of the three emancipated rosebuds of Vassar.

Jack Manson was recalled from a dream of unhoped-for delight by Leavenworth's question:

" Where do you go now? "

" By Jove, old man! I don't know, myself! " said Jack. "I must see my uncle and find out."

He briefly explained his sudden change of base. " I will take a coupé and run over to Gramercy Park and report." The engineer concluded: " Wait for me in your room and we will have a long talk to-night."

"When do you go South?" said Manson uneasily, with a furtive glance at the glowing face of the imperious little Texan rose.

Leavenworth laughed as he gaily answered: " I have to wait two months till the election is decided, and also close up some important mail-contract business for my father in Washington. He has numbers of freight, mail, and supply contracts with Uncle Sam. I shall take my sisters down to Mrs. Marshall's place at Fairfax Court House, and when October comes give them a month in Washington before they return to Rancho San Miguel."

" Laus Deo!" mentally ejaculated Jack Manson. " If I can find Fairfax Court House on the map, I think I will pass through there on my way to Dixie's Land."

The ladies acknowledged Manson's request to be excused with frank kindness, save the rosy Hebe, who dropped her eyes and demurely said " Good-evening," as Leavenworth escorted Jack to the corridor.

"Is he not just splendid?" said Gertrude Marshall, with unwonted animation, as the two tall comrades disappeared.

"Who?" said Katie Leavenworth, with a careless toss of her pretty head.

"Why, Mr. Manson, of course!" answered the daughter of Virginia.

"I hardly looked at him," replied the unabashed child of the Lone Star State, yet in her own heart Katie knew she was fibbing to a degree.

When Jimmy Leavenworth shook hands with Jack, he whispered, "Is she not lovely?"

Jack started, but firmly answered: "She's the sweetest girl I ever met in my life." Leavenworth continued: "Her family is one of the oldest in Virginia."

"Oh, yes, I see!" cried Manson, with singular abstraction, as he darted away. "I'll be back in an hour, Jim," he cried from the elevator.

"That love-sick youth thought I meant his Virginian heart's-ease. By Jove! I suppose he does not know how much lovelier his little sister is than the scion of Pocahontas. Blind! yes, blind!" So sagely ruminated Jack, as he swiftly sped toward the stately old mansion of the autocrat of twenty great enterprises. His heart was beating with anxiety and curiosity, as the butler, with obsequious respect, ushered him into the library. He was evidently expected.

"Mr. Mark Manson awaiting you, sir," said the functionary, with a glance at the card.

Seated before a fire of hickory logs in his favorite den, surrounded by the wit, wisdom, and lore of centuries, gray, hawk-eyed old Mark Manson was calmly enjoying the very best cigar that the Cuban plantations could furnish. He turned; one glance was enough.

"Jack, my boy, I am thankful for your promptness. Sit down and let me have a look at you." Offering his own cigar-case, the old millionaire, a veteran wizard of finance, keenly eyed his nephew.

"Looks like Helen," thought the senior, with a
shadow of a sigh as he thought of his dead sister and
his own lonely life. Wifeless, childless, and doomed to
keep in the race for wealth to the very last, Mark
Manson's heart was locked in a rugged breast. He had
every secret detail of the young man's career for the
long years of his probation.

"I guess he has grown up a man, after all. A fine
fellow!" thought Mark, as he rang for his choicest
Madeira.

"Where are you staying, Jack?" the magnate
queried. "It's a lonely house, but you are welcome
here."

"I have an old chum at the Fifth Avenue, Uncle,"
said Jack; "Jimmy Leavenworth of Texas. I have not
seen him since we were graduated. I would like to be
near him a few days."

A lightning flash gleamed in Mark's eyes. He
calmly said:

"Son of old Si Leavenworth of Rancho San
Miguel?"

"Yes, sir!" promptly answered Jack, as his eye
roved over the solid grandeur of the old mansion.

"How long will he be here?" queried Mark. Jack
briefly related Leavenworth's plans.

The old man mused as he poured the priceless wine
for his guest.

"You will need a few days' relaxation. You look
tired. Come over and breakfast with me to-morrow at
nine, and I will give you your marching orders," he said
kindly. "I know you want to talk old times over with
your friend. Want any money?" The capitalist eyed
Manson critically.

"No, sir; thanks. I have all I need," Jack simply
said. "Your generosity has made me easy in funds."

The old man lifted his eyebrows in surprise. "Well, youngster, I'll say good-night. Be prompt to-morrow. I have a lot of director's meetings. I suppose you would like to know just where you are going."

"Yes, sir;" answered Jack Manson, with a beating heart.

"Well, my boy, you are going down to Western Texas, to build me a railroad. Make friends with your old chum, for his father is the king of the frontier, and I have extensive landed interests there with him." Jack's heart bounded in his bosom.

"How do you like the title of Chief Engineer?" said the hawk-billed old financier.

"I will try and do my duty, sir," resolutely replied Manson.

"That's right, Jack! Now be off, my boy. I'll give you your general plan to-morrow. I want you to go to Washington and see Senator Steele. He's in with us. I'll be down there next week. We do not want to break ground till we know who will be President. The election of Greeley would paralyze our finances and stop all enterprise. We want no theorist, however honest and kindly. We want a strong man. We must have Grant. Now Steele knows that country, he can post you. You are in my pay, sir, from the day when you left Cheyenne. Take a little relaxation. I wish you to cultivate Senator Steele and your young friend Jimmy. It's a fortunate meeting, Jack, a very fortunate meeting! Good-night, boy!" the old man said, as Jack rose. "Keep this to yourself for the present!"

"Sharp nine!" was the last injunction of the gray schemer.

His words fell on unheeding ears, for as the great door clashed behind him, Jack sprang into his coupé and every click of the wheels seemed to echo a name grown strangely, suddenly dear. The refrain was " Katie! Katie! Katie!"

A grateful but astounded cabman glared in wonder at the five-dollar bill pressed in his hand, as Jack darted into the office of the Fifth Avenue.

"That chap's a lunatic, or in love!" the Jehu reasoned. " He's not on his wine. I guess it's love!"

Cabby was right. The subtle philtre of love was moving in the veins of man and maid that pleasant night, for Jack's secret joy made his eyes dance.

"I shall be near her," he thought with exultation.

Dainty wilful Katie's blue eyes closed, in deep, yet happy, slumber; for she whispered, " I would not let Gertie know I did look at him; but—but—Jimmy's friend is so manly, so pleasant," and, with a gleaming silver arm for a pillow, the heiress of San Miguel slept the calm unbroken sleep of innocence.

Late into the night, the reunited collegians recounted their adventures in the swiftly flying years, and when they separated, the magic spell of youth, high hope, and budding affection brought dreams of the Greek-browed patrician girl to the hawk-eyed Texan, and Jack Manson's midnight hours were blessed with thoughts of the rosy fingered Hebe of the deep-blue eyes.

The silent stars, sweeping to the west, sparkled over them as the invisible web of love, spun by the good fairies, knitted together four young hearts beating high with hope.

CHAPTER II.

IN WASHINGTON—WAITING FOR THE NATION'S CHOICE
—JACK'S NEW FRIEND—THE EMPRESS.

HANDSOME Jack Manson was aroused from the happy visions of his first night in New York by a vigorous onslaught on the panels of his door and the ringing voice of the Texan. Rubbing his eyes, he was forced to gaze on Madison Square in its glory of late summer, to realize that Cheyenne and the Black Hills were now only memories of a stormy past.

" Thank God! Katie is not a ' sweet dream of a summer night.' " He sprang to the door and admitted Leavenworth, whose usual reveille was the mocking-birds' song at daybreak, on the distant Rio Grande.

" Jack," said the Texan cheerfully, " if we can meet at luncheon, let us drive the ladies to the park this afternoon. Try and steal a few days from your affairs. I will shape our plans by yours."

Manson was already making his toilet with more raffiné solicitude than he had known for years.

" I suppose she thinks I look like a returned miner or a waif of the prairie," he thought.

A singular interest in his personal decoration was born of his desire to shine under the speaking glances of the dark-blue eyes which had haunted his pillow.

In his heart of hearts, Jack felt another man born within him, and fancied that beyond the nearest mile-stones of his life, the goddess of a day's love beckoned him to her side.

As the bells struck nine, the doors of Mark Manson's home swung open to receive the young engineer.

" Very good, my boy!" said the host, as he cordially greeted his visitor. " I like promptness." The financier was already equipped for the labors of the day, and a huge pile of journals, and dozens of opened letters proved his use of the morning hours. Ringing a bell, he curtly said: " Take all these to Mr. Walton. I will give him briefs of the answers before I go down town. Let no one disturb us. Now, Jack, to breakfast."

Seated at the well-ordered table, Mark Manson was the typical energetic human fly-wheel of a score of great enterprises.

In twenty minutes the old man drew back his chair and lit a cigar.

" Now, my lad," he began, as he gazed approvingly at the fresh, manly face of his bright-eyed nephew, "I am going to repose a great trust in you. I am going to send you down to the Rio Grande to represent me with full power. I wish you to cultivate young Leav-enworth, and find out all you can about that border country. Some years ago I bought an interest in several large ranches west of the Nueces. Senator Steele has an interest, Si Leavenworth, this boy's father, has another, and—one other person," he said cautiously.

Jack Manson could hardly restrain the wild exultation of his lover's heart. This road of the future led him onward to the newly crowned divinity. Mark resumed, gazing at the smoke wreaths floating around him:

" There are other interests of which you will learn later. This election is all important to us. A great secret movement is contemplated. It all depends on the voice of the people at the November election. I do not share all the hopes of my associates, but I have an enormous sum of money at stake. I can not go there; you must represent me. I will be frank with you; Steele is a 'carpet-bag' senator (you know his State), and I have found him deceitful and dangerous. He does not know that I distrust him. He is a smooth scoundrel and, unfortunately, is the necessary medium of communication with our fourth partner, who must be nameless for grave reasons. I wish you to watch him like a lynx till I order you down to the Rio Grande. I will give you a letter to him. Be very circumspect. You shall have my whole confidence, but only after I come to Washington. He must think that you go down merely to look at the lands. Leavenworth's acquaintance is a godsend to us. You can visit the Rancho San Miguel and, later, make a tour from El Paso to Point Isabel. That will post you thoroughly."

"As for old Si Leavenworth, he is indeed a strange character. He went to Texas in 1846 as a camp follower of General Taylor and a deck-hand. He is cool, sly, desperate, suspicious in business, and yet hospitable and liberal. He has dozens of active schemes in which I am not interested. I think, however, that Senator Steele is. Old Si uses Steele to handle his relations with the Government, as he was a noted Confederate. Strange man Si. His tough old body is scarred with bullet and knife wounds, and he is as fearless as a Sioux brave. His education is that of hard experience, and he is a very Machiavelli in cunning. He has the ablest advisers, and has gathered around him, from the Nueces to the Rio Grande, some remarkable adventurers. You will need all your prudence down there. His wife is an educated woman of exemplary character, a clergyman's daughter. What's the boy like?" said the financier, ending abruptly.

"Jimmy is twenty-five. He was a keen, bright student at the Polytechnic. His father wished him practically educated. He is tall, wiry, with a cold gray eye, thin featured, and the straight Southern hair.

A splendid athlete and rider, good tempered, the soul of honor, and neither wild nor foolish," replied Jack. "He will be a couple of months settling some mail contracts and business for his father at Washington."

"Excellent!" said Mark Manson decisively. "That clears all up. Now, I've got to go down town. You can tell young Leavenworth now that you are going down to look at my lands. They are all undivided. He naturally will ask you to visit San Miguel. Conform to his movements. You must stay here with him and take it easy. Come over and dine with me every other evening. I will give you a check book and carte blanche on this matter. I'll have Walton give you my private cipher. Cultivate Leavenworth and watch Steele. We are thinking of a railroad, if Si Leavenworth is successful at Austin with the franchise. You can stay around Washington until the people make a President. I will hear from Si Leavenworth through Steele, and give you your final orders at Washington. By the way, do not write me from Washington. It is too risky. Use the wire and my cipher. What are the young girls like?" the old man queried.

Jack's voice was strangely cold in accent, as he said, with assumed carelessness: "Nice girls, well bred, well educated. Vassar College graduates."

The old man nodded and rang for his carriage. As he grasped his hat, cane, and gloves, he said kindly: "Now, boy, amuse yourself a little. You may run up to the old home if you wish; I have bought it for you and placed it in your name. There's a farmer living there. I have written him that you are here." The young man felt a choking in his throat as he pressed his uncle's hands.

"It is only right, boy; you have done your duty." Jack Manson gazed after the departing carriage, as the veteran threw himself back, murmuring: "Fine fellow, looks like poor Helen!" And over the old man's mind floated memories of the far-away days when he had played with his bright-eyed sister by the placid Mohawk. While he scanned his morning papers, swiftly swinging down to the day's battle in Wall Street, Jack Manson sought the Fifth Avenue in secret joy.

The Texan was in waiting, pacing the marbled-tiled hall, the rallying place of a generation of statesmen and heroes. Manson sprang forward impulsively, and cried: "It's all right, Jimmy! I am going down to the Rio Grande to inspect my uncle's lands and watch his affairs there."

"Glorious!" rejoined his friend. "We will show you the prettiest stretch of land in Texas. And you will say the Nueces Valley is the garden-spot of the world. Let us go over in the park and have a cigar. These brick walls stifle me," rejoined Leavenworth. "I prefer the open prairie, and the canopy of Heaven for a spangled bed curtain!"

"By the way, Jack," said the Southerner, "I have secured the carriages. Mrs. Marshall is timid. I have a landau for four, but I ordered a rattling double team. You can drive Katie."

Manson concealed his sudden emotion, and was eminently successful in his ruse. The unconscious carelessness of brotherhood was his effective protection.

Seated at ease, Manson felt impelled to probe Mr. James Leavenworth's heart a little.

"Miss Marshall is a charming girl," he casually remarked, gazing at the passing throng.

"She's the sweetest woman on earth," cried the enthusiastic Texan, whereat Jack inwardly added "save one," as he nodded his head attentively.

"Why don't you marry her, Jimmy, and settle down?" Jack slowly said, looking him fairly in the face.

"I'll tell you," mournfully replied his friend, nursing his cigar.

"Mrs. Marshall is one of these rare Virginian women whose quiet pride is measureless. They are of the very finest strain of the old blood. Now, Jack, my father is a self-made man of the humblest antecedents. But he is an old hero—a wonderful man. Mrs. Marshall has never met him, although her husband was father's lawyer here, before the wretched war. My mother is a woman of early education and refinement. I do not wish to risk a refusal, and I can not bear to lose that darling girl. I hope she can come down to San Miguel and learn to know my people. But the border is too wild yet. The Rio Grande frontier, west of the Nueces, is filled with roving scoundrels, broken down stragglers of the two armies, deserters, horse thieves, and Mexican desperadoes. We have a strong force at San Miguel, but travel is very dangerous. When the situation clears a little, I hope to have Mrs. Marshall and Gertie visit us. I feel more at home on my own chosen ground," said the young prince of the frontier.

"All will come around in the right way," said Jack. reassuringly, as he thought selfishly of Katie.

"Your sisters should be a great help in this delicate matter," he concluded.

"Alice might be!" dolefully replied the lover. "As for Katie, she is a witch of delightful mischief. She already enjoys my suffering. She is a born flirt and coquette."

"That is a nice prospect," groaned Manson, with a sinking of the heart.

The two friends sauntered over to the hotel. Manson

critically examined the charming countenance of the
blue-eyed witch at their merry luncheon, and was forced
to admit in his heart of hearts, that the divinity was of
a singularly variable disposition. Late in the afternoon,
as Jack turned the horses' heads homeward, and under
the trembling, leafy arches of the unrivalled Central
Park gazed on his enchantress, he decided to lock his
ardent feelings in the breast of a Stoic. For, even on
their arrival at the hotel, her only response to a cautious
announcement of his Texan journey, was a careless
rejoinder, "I suppose you will come some time to San
Miguel—to see Brother Jimmy."

Not a single word on her own account. Manson
vowed in his heart of hearts that the merry heiress
herself should ask him before he set foot on the baronial domain!

Pleasant days sped by, leaving the engineer in a
bewildering day-dream.

"It is a chase of the fleeting rainbow," Manson
groaned. "That girl has no heart." It was undeni-
able that handsome Jack was en rapport with stately
Mrs. Marshall, the Greek-browed Gertrude, and was
daily knitted closer to St. Cecilia Alice. He did not
dare to dream of Katie's defensive tactics as only a
"sweet piece of bashful maiden art."

With solemn courtesy Mark Manson had visited the
ladies, welcomed the young ranchero, and opened his
mansion for a ceremonious feast in honor of the
impending departure.

Possessed of his final instructions, the cipher, and
fully advised as to his relations with Senator Steele,
Mr. John Manson was happy to escape his keen-eyed
uncle's watchful glances, as the train drew out for
Washington.

"I will see you in ten days," was Mark's good-bye.

" Make friends with these people, they will be useful later." Manson's effort at cultivating the flowers of "friendship" with the blue-eyed divinity ended in a profound gloom, arising from a sudden determination to lock his secret in his breast and suffer silently. His manly pride was piqued.

"I will not let her see my agonies, at any rate," he decided, with wild ideas of revenge.

As the great dome of the Capitol rose before them, Jack, with calm courtesy, bade his friends adieu. "I must leave you here. My business will detain me for some time in Washington." Leavenworth, Miss Alice, the gentle Gertrude, and even Mrs. Marshall, protested. The Virginian matron, with a cordial smile, earnestly bade him a prospective welcome to Fairfax Court House. The only silent member of the coterie was the dainty Katie, who was diligently studying external objects from the window.

As the train halted, Manson skillfully possessed himself of the blue-eyed queen's small belongings, and trudged along to the carriage with the demeanor of a Trappist. Miss Mischief never lifted her eyes! Manson could feel his heart beat in indignation.

"Absolutely without feeling," he growled, and it was in no pleasant mood that he arranged the small articles in the carriage, already tenanted by the others. With a stiff bow, Mr. Jack Manson said good-bye to the undaunted coquette, who lingered a moment ere she entered the landau.

A glance of merry amazement kindled the sapphire depths of the wonderful eyes. Miss Leavenworth offered a slender gloved hand. "You will come to Fairfax and see Jimmie," she whispered, with a frightened glance. She feared that her coldness had been only too effective!

"I will meet your brother here later, on business,"
rejoined the desperate lover, whose heart was anxiously
tugging at its strings. "Then come and see *me!*" the
wicked maiden faltered, with one sweep of the silken
lashes.

Before the astounded Jack could find words, the
Rose of Texas lightly sprang into the carriage, and ten
yards away waved a merry farewell with a filmy
kerchief.

"That young girl needs discipline," muttered Jack,
as he stood rooted to the spot, with the insidious invitation ringing in his ears.

Yet his heart was very light as he bestowed himself
in a pleasant suite of rooms at the Ebbitt House.
"Château qui parle, se rend toujours" is an old proverb,
and Mr. Manson decided upon a regular siege by
gradual approach. "If I betray my feelings, this
damsel will take all the advantages of my thoughtless-
ness. 'La belle dame sans merci.'"

With serious mien Manson entered the parlors of
Senator Steele, next day, at the Arlington.

The great man welcomed him with effusive cordiality.
Senator Steele bore easily his fifty-five years. Smooth,
cool, adroit, and with a furtive expression of his round
light-blue eyes, calmly caressing his flowing beard with
a bediamonded hand, his well-kept figure and general
air of ease bespoke the prosperous politician.

"Just a little *too* smooth," thought Jack, mindful of
Mark Manson's caution.

"I am somewhat busied with this exciting campaign,
my dear sir," began Steele, with a wave of his pudgy
hand, "but I will be happy to be of service to you. I
have heard from your uncle and, as you have leisure,
will go through the Texan situation in a day or so. I
unfortunately have business of importance this after-

noon, but will give you all the time I can." Manson
bowed in acknowledgment. A half-hours' conversation informed the senator of Manson's history.. The
statesman was awakened by the mention of Jimmy
Leavenworth's name.

"Rising man, sir. Has marked ability. We hope
to see him soon in Congress. Alas! Western Texas is
hopelessly democratic. I shall do my best to entertain the party on their arrival."

Further flourish on the part of the smooth statesman
(who was secretly studying the young man's face) was
cut short by a card sent in.

"Ah! Very timely. Show the gentleman in. I
wish to present you to an intimate friend. You may
meet him on the Rio Grande. He is a man of note in
Mexico, though American born." When the visitor
entered, Senator Steele greeted the new-comer with
friendly familiarity.

"Mr. Manson of New York, my friend, Mr. Ramon
Maxan of Hacienda Maxan."

The two young men greeted each other. Ramon
Maxan was evidently at home.

Manson, accepting a cigar, studied the new-comer.
Of elegant mien, gracefully and powerfully built,
Ramon Maxan's olive cheek, restless, brilliant black
eye, dark hair, and drooping jet-black mustache, as well
as his soft, semi-foreign intonation, betrayed the Louisiana Creole. Carefully dressed, and of cosmopolitan
manners, he was versatile and most winning in address.

Half an hour later the young men left the senatorial
sanctum together. Their host, in parting, said heartily:
"Ramon, you must show the local lions to my young
friend. It is his first visit to Washington. By the
way, take him to call on Mrs. Smiley. I am to dine
there to-morrow night. Mrs. Smiley would be happy,

I am sure, to have Mr. Manson join us. I could then have a quiet chat with him." A meaning glance scintillated in the pale fishy-blue eye of the "carpet-bagger."

Just a tremble of Maxan's long black lashes indicated his response, for he cheerily said: "Certainly. And I claim Mr. Manson for a dinner this evening at the Club. As he is going to be a Texan, I can post him a little."

Manson accepted the proffered courtesy and left the smoothly smiling senator beaming at his open door.

"Let me see," said Maxan, consulting his watch, "It's now three, Mr. Manson. I will call at your hotel at half-past four and we will drive out and also pay our respects to Mrs. Smiley, a charming hostess."

Jack acknowledged the courtesy and betook himself to an hour's correspondence. He would have been surprised to have seen Ramon Maxan swiftly retrace his steps to the Arlington.

"What's that d——d fool coming bothering here for?" said the Creole, as he smartly closed the door of Senator Steele's room. The old fox was expecting his return. Maxan threw himself in a chair, after liberally patronizing the cognac flask, on the richly spread sideboard, and critically choosing a fresh cigar.

"I don't know, Ramon," said the senator, now alert and with none of his official soapy manner. "He is old Manson's only relative and heir. I am afraid of that old skinflint. He will be down here in ten days. Now he must not stumble on our outside operations! Mark Manson does not know what the Rio Grande Company really is. He went in on old Si Leavenworth's advice. If this fellow has any brains we can't hoodwink him long if he stays on the Rio Grande. We need old Manson to place those railroad bonds in New York

when we get the franchise. You must cling closely to
this fellow. He's been on the plains. Let the Smiley
make a running on him, and when these young Leavenworth people come over, you must cultivate the whole
party. Mrs. Smiley can watch the girls and you can
keep an eye on Leavenworth and Manson. They
were college classmates. Now give 'the Empress'
the tip this afternoon."

"All right!" snakily said Maxan. "If this green-
horn should be plastered on the road as an official, it
might stop our private use of the 'bonded goods
privilege'!" A dark wicked look glittered in his uneasy
eye.

"I'll put him out of the way down there, if he noses
into our secrets," the Creole fiercely cried.

"Yes. That's so. Everything goes on the Rio
Grande," said Steele, with a vicious leer, "but only at
the last. Old Mark would raise an awful row."

"Row or no row, he's a dead man if he fools with
our inside matters," the Creole cried. "I half suspect
the old man of setting him on us as a spy. Well, I'm
off. I'll post Milly Smiley about him. She'll keep an
elastic string on him."

Maxan seized hat and cane and darted away to bring
up his horses. Honest Jack Manson was all unconscious
of the webs ready to entangle a buzzing stranger fly.

In friendly discourse the young men rolled over the
noiseless pavements of the great centre of national cor-
ruption. The broad avenues were already lined with
the ambitious home palaces of those whom the war had
enriched. Washington was already seething in the
preliminary excitement of a "boom."

With the easy familiarity of an old "habituè," Maxan
pointed out to Manson the remarkable features in still
life and the street throngs.

"You are almost to the manner born," said Jack, admiring the splendid team of bays and Maxan's magnificent skill in driving, as well as his thorough local knowledge.

"Hardly. Yet Washington is a second home to me," rejoined the Creole. "My father was one of General Taylor's officers in the Mexican War, and at the close of the war married my mother, a descendant of the old Conquistadores. So, though my father was a New Orleans man, I am, by reason of my birth and Mexican estates, practically a Mexican. I was educated in Paris, and I am a mélange of Frenchman, Southerner and Mexican. I am equally at home in the three countries, and their languages are all born in me. Here I have spent half my time, for in the throes of Mexican revolution, Señor Romero, our able Minister, has been my best friend and adviser. He was a friend of my father's youth. Yet I prefer the vales and fastnesses of the 'Zona Libre.' The high ground is the garden of the world. I yearn to return. Business will detain me until Congress meets here, I am sorry to say."

"What is the Zona Libre?" asked Manson, with interest.

"The three states of Nueva León, Tamaulipas, and Coaguila, lying on the 'Rio Bravo,' or 'Rio Grande del Norte,' as you call it, are exempted from all customs duties, and goods in bond from the United States or Europe are freely distributed there to be used in these three Mexican frontier states alone. There is an enormous import trade from the United States and Europe."

"What is the object of this exemption from your heavy duties?" asked Jack. "I have understood Mexican customs laws are onerous and marvels of red tape."

"The real object, my dear sir," said the fluent Creole, "is to make it advantageous for our people to settle these three open states thickly, and thus form a barrier to American aggression."

"There is no immediate danger of that," Manson remarked.

"Wait and see," replied Maxan. "General Grant will be triumphantly re-elected. He may draw his all-conquering sword again. No one can tell what military ambition may do. Mexico will fight though to the last man! We quarrel among ourselves, but our motto is, 'Muerte à los estrangèros.'"

"Is this Zona Libre not a demoralizing feature?" Manson said, after a pause.

"Certainly," said Maxan, flicking a bee off his pet horse's back with a neat cut of the whip. "Every man, woman, and intelligent child in the Zona is a smuggler. The land swarms with desperadoes. Besides, the officials are corrupt, and the export tax of eight per cent on Mexican silver dollars is avoided by smuggling them out. They are now at a premium for the Chinese and Japanese trade. Moreover, Bagdad, at the mouth of the Rio Grande, was the port of reception of fifty million dollars' worth of Confederate supplies and the great shipping point of rebel cotton for Bermuda and Havana."

"Did not our fleet stop these blockade runners?" said Manson, naturally.

"My dear friend," the Creole smilingly replied, "I have seen piles of Yankee stores, a half mile long, lying there marked 'Q. M. D.' and 'A. C. S., New Orleans,' which were exchanged by Yankee commanders for our good cotton at Bagdad. Money made strange friends in the great war."

Manson was astounded as Maxan continued · "The

unwritten history of the secret relations of some
Union and Southern commanders and officials would
tear some national reputations to tatters, if exposed.
Great 'loyal' merchants in New York, Boston, and
Philadelphia slyly aided this nefarious traffic, and they
were, in some things, our surest agents of supply.
Naturally, my sympathies were with secession. Now,
not to weary you, both sides of the Rio Grande are
thronged with outcast fugitives from both the great
armies, negro deserters, criminals, and the riff-raff of
the world. These people would welcome any conflict
between the nations. The proud, dissatisfied Southern veterans would pour into Mexico at the first slight
cause."

"But enough of the Rio Grande. If you stay here a
couple of months you will see what Washington life
really is. Already the harpies gather. The taint of
the war lingers. Fifty thousand idle negroes float
around the suburbs. The old residents are poor, or
proudly reticent if high in society. A wild horde of
office-seekers, schemers, reckless military men, lobby-
ists of both sexes, claim agents, politicians, and sharpers
will throng the town the moment General Grant's
election is assured. Disgraced officials, sly go-betweens, and swarms of the volunteer officers, anxious
for place, will wear out the very paving stones here.
The President's receptions will be human menageries,
and the society houses open will be besieged by well-
dressed adventurers, men and women, who will not be
put *down*, and who can't be put *out*. 'Fox and Geese'
will be the national game played here for the next four
years." He paused.

"Can not the President stem the tide?" Jack questioned. "He is strong-minded."

"I fear not," Maxan answered. "General Grant is

a man of the people. He is singularly loyal to old friends. Though taciturn, he is very approachable, and the pressure on him will be tremendous. He is a pillar of unsuspecting honesty. He will be only a human buffer between this crowd of pirates and the treasury door. The schemes are not all in vulgar hands. Great names lurk behind many of these insidious movements. It's the wildest hurly-burly on earth to-day, and Washington will be the luxury-loving Vanity Fair of the world for four years. These people do not merely arrive. They will *storm* the city. But, here we are, at Mrs. Smiley's."

"Who is Mrs. Smiley?" asked Manson, with a cordial interest.

"Ah! Now we have a congenial topic," smiled Maxan. "Mrs. Milly Smiley is the handsomest woman in Washington. Born a Southerner, to her beauty, she adds every accomplishment. Her first husband, a gallant Confederate officer, was killed in the war. He never returned. She was left a mere girl widow. She ran the blockade to avoid the social situation at New Orleans, and after several years abroad married an enormously wealthy American named Smiley, who died, leaving her his immense wealth. Her talents have been heightened by the years of foreign travel and her home is the rallying spot, the social oasis in this desert, for the diplomat, the cultured, and the cosmopolitan."

Maxan was moving his horses easily around the square.

"She is an intimate friend of Senator Steele?" inquired Manson thoughtfully.

Maxan started and gave the horses a cut. "Did he say so?" the Creole sharply said.

"Oh! Not specially. I only thought he spoke of

her with some enthusiasm," remarked Manson with a slight astonishment at Maxan's manner.

"Ah! Yes. I see," slowly said the Creole. " The fact is," and he lowered his voice confidently, " her house is one of the few here where a dignitary can visit or dine without his words being repeated, or politics being served up with the soup. Steele is a widower and very cautious. He is at home here." And Maxan lightly sprang from the carriage.

Jack Manson's brain was teeming with the flood of information poured into his ears. He mechanically followed his new friend into a magnificent hall, and entered a drawing-room replete with the garnered gems of art, taste, and the spoils of foreign travel. An air of decorous respectability hovered over all, from . the stately old colored butler, a relic of slavery days, to the neat-handed maids flitting noiselessly about.

" Miss Smiley will receive the gentlemen very soon," announced the major-domo, with profound African salaams. A curious feeling pervaded Manson's mind as he gazed upon this dream of luxury. Conscious that his voluble friend was watching him, his thoughts flew away to Arundel House at Fairfax, as Gertie Marshall had described. He could almost see the simple grandeur of the old mansion with its stately pillars, its smooth lawns, and the " romance of the old " clinging to every gray oak and weather-beaten landmark of the " great days of the Mother of Presidents." His heart pictured the blue-eyed goddess (the refractory one) tripping over the fragrant blossoms of the " sacred soil."

Jack Manson had no gift of second sight, yet there was a gorgeousness (even if restrained by taste) which jarred upon his present mood in this newly gilded jewel-box, velvet tapestried and decked with costly adorn-

ments.   Little did he dream that cabals and coteries of
desperate men often assembled quietly in this sumptu-
ous, quiet retreat.   He was too innocently unsuspecting
to imagine that in a retired salon, statesmen and money
lords wooed the goddess fortune over the painted cards,
that thousands changed hands nightly " in the season,"
and that dark schemes were perfected, reputations
smirched, votes bought and sold, and the devil's work
silently and expeditiously dispatched, here under the roof
of the imperious beauty of the hour.

Not being a prophet, Manson could not dream that
Mildred Smiley was the enchanting Egeria of that servant of the people, a modern Numa, Senator Steele!

Before Jack's eyes had catalogued half the prominent
features of the splendid retreat, Mrs. Milly Smiley
silently glided into the room.

Ramon Maxan was instantly on his feet, and on greeting the peerless woman who was now the living
accentuation of the pervading idea of the beautiful,
presented Mr. John Manson of New York.

Jack, in bewilderment, bent over a blue-veined hand
sparkling with nonpareil treasures of India's mines.

" You are welcome, sir, as Mr. Maxan's friend, and—
for yourself," said the regal hostess.   Her rich voice,
with a thrilling undertone, moved Manson like the
wind harps of the forest.   In five minutes Jack Manson
was within "the danger line".   As Mrs. Milly Smiley
gazed frankly at the neophyte in Washington society,
his eyes fell.   He was only conscious of an imperial
presence.   Reclining in an easy chair, attired in a
masterpiece of the Worth and Pingât school, the
attitude of this modern Venus was seductive, enticing,
inevitable.   The exquisite curves of her faultless form,
the nameless grace of each pose, were accentuated by
the wonderful loveliness of her face; liquid, dark, soft

shining eyes, and the nobly poised head crowned with lustrous masses of silken hair, black as a raven's wing, betokened a Southern queen of the realm of beauty. " The most perfect brunette I ever saw," thought Jack, as he drew his breath.

When Ramon Maxan gracefully delivered the message of Senator Steele, the hostess bent her wistful, tender eyes, with an unconscious fervor, on the impressionable Manson.

" This is a double reason why I shall claim you as my guest. Senator Steele's name is an ' open sesame' to my house."

When the young gentlemen rose to terminate the "visite de ceremonie," Jack Manson could not help turning his head to gaze upon the living marvel once more.

Standing, with a few roses in her hand, carelessly caught up from a Sèvres vase, Milly Smiley was an unspeakably magnificent ideal of the dark beauty of the Magnolia Land.

Manson was thoughtful and silent as his versatile Mentor drove to the Club. He replied briefly to Maxan's comments upon the lovely woman they had left. Her siren charms at once dazzled and oppressed him.

Ramon Maxan was a charming host, a modern Brillât Savarin. The open-hearted young engineer lost all reserve, and before the coffee and cigars, the Creole was possessed of the entire social plans of the circle at Fairfax Court House.

" I should be delighted to meet Mr. Leavenworth and the ladies," Maxan politely said. " I know of Si Leavenworth, whose name is a watchword from St. Louis to the City of Mexico, but I have never met him personally. His son, I think, I met casually at the

Crescent Club in New Orleans, several years ago, but he would perhaps not recall it. He is a rising man, by common report."

Jack Manson was far along on the highway of friendship when the parting hour came.

" Till to-morrow," said the Creole, laughing a good-night. "Don't lose your heart to Mrs. Mildred Smiley. She is an untamable falcon. She soars high. She has even refused a Cabinet Minister."

"No danger," replied Jack, good-humoredly. " I have my fortune to make."

" Nonsense, Manson. Your uncle's wealth will fall your way, surely," incautiously said the Creole.

Jack eyed him curiously and muttered the old proverb about "dead men's shoes."

Ramon Maxan was gone, leaving Manson confusedly murmuring, " He seems to know a good bit of my private affairs."

As Jack entered his apartment, he recalled himself. " Certainly, Maxan would surely hear that from Senator Steele. That is perfectly natural."

Still oppressed by the overpowering tropical beauty of the witch of night, Manson lit a cigar, and turning out his lights gazed at the stars twinkling down on the Mecca of his hopes at Fairfax Court House. Gertie's word pictures made it almost familiar ground.

" I will go through this dinner, confer with Senator Steele, and then despatch to Uncle Mark, then, then," he said with determination, " I will run over to Fairfax and see Jimmy." Honest Jack closed his eyes without acknowledging that two gentle deep-blue eyes were the duplex magnets drawing him to the " sacred soil of Virginia" and that "Katie " should have been substituted for " Jimmy," in that expression of a settled purpose. Those far-away blue eyes closed that night at Fairfax in gentle sleep, as the fair Texan murmured: "It's so quiet here; I hope Mr. Jack Manson will come to see Brother Jim." The gentle dissembler dared not give expression to the thought and wish of her heart.

Mr. Ramon Maxan, pacing the silent street, said to himself: "I will get into this friendly circle. The girls are said to be lovely. Rancho San Miguel would be a safe retreat if the Rio Grande Company gets into trouble, and particularly if I owned a third of it.

"Yes, decidedly it's a good scheme," said the Creole, as he contemplated his graceful person in the mirror on retiring. "I flatter myself I can walk around this Western stranger. But I must have Milly's help. By Jove! I don't know how the 'Empress' will take it. She's a tiger! Nonsense! Steele has her in his power. He must stay in with me. If they build this road and I can marry one of these Leavenworth girls, I can be the King of the Zona Libre.

"I must cut in between Manson and young Leavenworth. It must be done. If I can not, a machête will do the work while this tenderfoot explores the mésas and thickets of the Rio Bravo.

"By heavens, I have it! Ximenes is down there. I'll put Joaquin on his track, and if Mr. Jack Manson wont move out for *me*, I will move *him* out! Another frontier tragedy."

With a devilish mocking smile on his thin fine lips, Ramon Maxan closed his eyes with the cheering consciousness of a good day's work. "I'll make the 'Empress' keep him away from those girls," was the Creole's last thought ere he slept.

CHAPTER III.

THE COURSE OF TRUE LOVE—A SNAKE IN THE GRASS —CREOLE WILES—A VIRGINIAN HOME.

JACK MANSON pondered over the previous days' varied experiences, as he leisurely dressed, and sought the half-deserted streets next morning for a breath of fresh air.

Devoid of manufactures and any real " raison d'être" the city of Washington is an assemblage of ill-assorted human abodes clustering around the various strong-holds of the Federal Government.

Appropriately, the Capitol is the central point, and clustered around the Treasury and White House are the lairs of the hungry army besieging the mythical Uncle Sam. Great hotels fencing in the White House and Treasury are the outworks of these besiegers; luxurious mansions mark the resting place of the suc-cessful; straggling apartment houses afford shelter to the temporary reinforcements of the besiegers, and the faded rows of neglected houses, all placarded " Rooms to Let," shelter the humbler schemers.

Georgetown and the suburbs are crowded with the modest domiciles of the patient, inert body of men and women toiling along in the unambitious lives of de-partment clerks. Hurry is unknown. All that is local is colorless, faded, dejected, and humdrum. A few of the old families, behind their seldom-opened doors in doleful chorus, mourn the fabulous days when "Wash-ington society was select." It must have been in some prehistoric age!

All the local life, all the stir and dash of the hour is brought in by the eager, ardent, never-tiring plotters, schemers, " agents," and office-seekers, who " move in a mysterious way their wonders to perform." The

local population nave simple occupations. The rather
shabby men haunt the hotels in eager search of visitors to
be plucked, or aided " for a consideration." The women
wander, in the season, from one open reception to
another, neatly making vacuums in the punch bowls, and
furtively descending on the beaufet refreshments like
veteran crows upon a field of tender corn sprouts.

All things mundane take on peculiar characteristics
in Washington. The lazy, chattering, easy-going negro
servants, the antique vehicles of hire, the peculiar rem-
nants of all classes of merchandise, ill-assorted and
meager, the crowds of Munchausen union veterans, the
circles of sad-eyed, resentful Confederates, the summer
lethargy from April to November, and the condensed
local excitement from early winter to the end of
March; all these things are peculiar to the capital of
our beloved country.

Boarding houses (human man-tràps) have been organ-
ized upon a shadowy commissary system, in mute
protest against substantial creature comforts. The dim
crepuscular lights of their antique "parlors" hide lurking,
faded, single females of judiciously varied homeliness,
but full of haughty pride. In these spectral institutions
the sombre-clad " landlady " receives her weekly dole,
with a mute protest against the disgrace of being paid,
in the faint hope that the idea of being " simply enter-
tained " may prevail! The foreign diplomats, from the
haughty Briton to the modest Haytian, mingle, with an
air of distinct superiority, in the alleged " maddening
whirl," and numbers of superannuated army and navy
officers haunt the clubs, growl at their insufficient re-
wards and consume vast quantities of "strengthening
beverages," while the cloud of younger men of both
services jauntily skip in the mazes of the German, toil
with the harmless weapon of tennis, report at dance,

dinner, and tea-fight with military promptness, and occasionally (by a wild dash) swoop down on the unwary and carry off a red-handed Western heiress or some lively widow, whose golden tokens of the " dear departed " may gaily furnish forth the marriage feast.

Slightly below this glittering throng, moving before the dais of " high society," the ambitious masculine clerk apes (when unemployed) the "fin de siecle " swell, and the pretty pushing feminine employee, keen-eyed and fun-loving, cuts out her prize often from under the social guns of her more fortunate sisters!

Shifting, ebbing, moving without law or apparent cause, from year to year, the familiar places soon know these strangely assorted faces no more. But a general air of Micawber-like hopefulness pervades the unemployed.

There are shadowy legends that, by waiting, sundry tough-nerved souls have " dropped into something," *not* the Potomac! The star of hope flickers feebly, yet it always flickers. A distinct stratum of Washington society is the returned Senator and Representative. Alas! Hotel clerks know them not; their tables are no longer littered with invitations; pretty faces do not beam meaningly from carriage windows, and they are no longer buttonholed by eager suppliants, suggesting a " private room and a cold bottle."

Furtively darting around corners, and appearing mostly at nights, are the guerrilla classes—principally discharged clerks, ejected office-holders, broken officers of the services, and the omnipresent man with a claim for "clams furnished the blockading fleet at Charleston" or "shoe-strings for the Army of the Potomac."

At recurring periods of four years, the ignominious flitting of the retiring President occurs, and he who came in, escorted to the Capitol by a motley procession of tinsel-clad clubs, negro Knights Templar, Bungtown Rangers, and faded-looking, patched-up battalions of Regulars, awed by the ferocious militia in the rear, and sundry visiting Governors in unromantic cylinder hats, slinks away, grip-sack in hand, and with untold bitterness in his heart. "None so poor as to do him honor!" No wheezy German bands blare out, "Hail to the Chief," as he steals into the railway station and buys a ticket to his home. The iron has entered his soul, for his "pass" is cut off—he is a discrowned Cæsar! The Prætorian guards of the country have made a new king. "Le roi est mort! Vive le roi!"

These things occurred to Jack Manson, in a fit of philosophy, as he wandered through the early morning streets. Here and there, lazy negroes dragged along to market, tired barkeepers arranged the "decoctions" for the dull day, and a few workmen in a limp, uncertain fashion, ambled along on some supposed daily tasks.

"Queer place! Everybody asleep!" remarked Jack as he sought the hotel. The gorgeous clerk tossed him a letter, with an air of easy superiority, and listlessly, from mere ennui, invited the stranger to have a "morning cocktail."

"Very quiet here!" said Jack, led, like a sheep to the slaughter, to the Temple of Bacchus!

"Wait till Grant's elected! You will see things hum here," carelessly replied the clerk, "we will scalp from the crowd in five months enough to live the other seven on! Everybody loafs in the off months in Washington."

Jack tore open his letter. His heart lightened. "So Jimmy will be here in two days and take me over to Arundel House." Manson was almost gay as he escaped from the indolent clerk. During his breakfast he thanked the fickle goddess of fortune that he could, with due dignity, visit Fairfax Court House. "I will pretend that I am dragged over there by Jimmy. I will *ignore* Katie. By heavens! I'll make love to St. Cecilia Alice!"

On second thoughts Jack abandoned this as too dangerous. He resolved ways and means of "disciplining" the blue-eyed cruel one, and was still hazy in his ideas, when he dismissed the all-important subject and sent a cautious cipher despatch to Mark Manson.

"I will take one of these antiquated vehicles and systematically explore this half-peopled wilderness of the national official caravansary. I can worry out these days looking over the public buildings, and the dinner and Maxan, with Senator Steele's interviews, will exhaust the evenings till Jimmy comes," he thought, as he rolled away; for he was anxious to see the last person known to him who had seen the wilful maid of his heart.

Ramon Maxan's heart was troubled as he sent his card in at noon to Mrs. Mildred Smiley, yet his smiling face and irreproachable attire marked only the man on pleasure bent.

"I would sooner face a dead shot at ten paces than have an out and out scene with Milly," the Creole soliloquized, as he caught the soft, swishing rustle of her robes, when the beauty descended the stairway.

"Better have the breakfast first, and the conference later," thought the wily Creole.

With simulated passion he sprang to the side of the "Empress," never more radiant, her eyes lambent with a strange light, as she closed the drawing-room door.

Her head rested on his breast.

"It is an age since I have seen you, Ramon," the woman passionately said, "at least alone. Old Steele is such a bore—the old jackal," she snapped out.

"True, darling," murmured Maxan, "but he is absolutely necessary to us. The low beast has a clear interest in the 'inside deal' of the Rio Grande Company. It is only through him that we can manage the Government and control"—he bent his head and whispered a name in her ear. The beauty nodded.

"You are right, Ramon; but I despise him so!" the beautiful sorceress said, twining her arms around him.

She started as a hand was laid on the folding doors opening into the superb dining-room. "Let us breakfast," Milly Smiley cried gaily, leading her dark-eyed lover to a feast of her most thoughtful selection.

In merriest mood the two conspirators pledged their stolen joys of the past, the sweets of the present, and a rosy future. Milly Smiley was to-day the untrammeled fond and loving woman. Not the "Empress," but the favorite, anxious to captivate, to delight, to enslave her romantic adorer.

Resolute as Maxan was, he felt his heart beat nervously as the coffee and cigarettes marked the close of the happy hour.

"It must be done, for both our sakes," he reflected.

Drawing forth a cabaña, he threw himself in an easy chair, for the adventuress, reclining on a divan, was daintily toying with a cigarette, complacently eying her own lovely hands and playing with her priceless rings.

"See here, Milly," Maxan slowly began. "I have something important to say to you." The sound of his voice made the woman start. It was hollow and strangely unfamiliar. She half rose and almost screamed:

"You are not going away, Ramon?"

"Don't be silly," he sharply replied. "It might be easier if I were to. I have a hard campaign ahead for both of us."

"What is it? Don't trifle with me!" the excited beauty cried.

"Listen to me, then. You shall know all," the Creole began. " You saw that young fool last night? "

The woman nodded eagerly.

"He is smart enough at his railroad trade," said Maxan, with a sneer. "Old Mark Manson has no other heir. This boy is alone in the world. The old Shylock has started him off to Texas to dig up all about his Rio Grande interests, and to build that road, so vital to us, from Corpus Christi to Laredo. Now, old. Manson knows nothing of our 'secret operations.' He gets no dividends on his fourth share from that. Only Steele, Si Leavenworth, and No. 4," he said, with a meaning wink. " I get half the income of Steele's secret interest, but am forced to trust to his honor. You know what that is." He paused.

"I do—well enough," said the recumbent sultana, her bosom heaving.

"It's a queer thing. We must have old Leavenworth to run the franchise, the Texan legislature and courts, as well as the customs officers. He owns all the steamboats and wagon trains. We require Steele to 'square' the Treasury Department and hoodwink the President and No. 4. Steele, although he is only a 'carpet bagger,' will dictate the new Federal appointments in the Gulf States. General Grant is honest and unsuspecting, but the party will force Steele on him. The old devil really has good humor and self-control. Mark Manson is absolutely necessary to the floating of the railroad bonds and getting us iron and rolling-stock. We will divide the land in four equal shares, but Mark has never met me. I have never even seen him."

"I am the only man in danger! If there is any break, that little Indian devil of a Colonel—Mejia—who

commands the Mexicans on the Rio Grande, would
have me shot in ten minutes. He is as wily and stern
as old Benito Juarez. So is Romero. Now even this
Jack Manson may not be the ordinary every-day fool.
He has been six years on the Union Pacific and he
is up to ' Credit Mobilier ' and all that. Old Manson
has many schemes, and has his spies and agents everywhere. The only place where he can't break our lines
is with A. R. Chisholm & Co. of New Orleans. With
their branch houses at Brownsville, Matamoras, the
Corpus Christi Bank and Monterey, our 'inside work'
is safe and the money will be divided squarely. Chisholm is a cousin of * * *, and Maxan again whispered
the name of 'No. 4.' As long as No. 4 keeps his place,
we are safe. Si Leavenworth, Steele, No. 4, Chisholm,
and myself *must* trust each other for life and death; but
I have to look to my safety. I must hook on where
they won't dare to hurt me. While we control the
customs officers on both sides of the Rio Grande, our
secret trade is a gold mine. But I must make a decisive
move. My hacienda and rancho would go, if they shot
me! You would be stranded."

"What do you mean? What is it that you *must* do?"
faltered the frightened woman, as she rose and paced
the room in excitement. "What do you fear?"

" This Jack Manson is a heart brother and college
chum of young Leavenworth. They will be here with
his sisters till after election." The Creole briefly
recounted Jack's unreserved disclosures.

A growing fear haunted Milly Smiley's passion-
tormented heart. She felt her love slipping away from
her.

" Go on," she said, in a strangely muffled voice.
The mantel clock ticked noisily away. The silence
was unbroken till Maxan, gazing uneasily at the

"Empress," whose face had unconsciously hardened said slowly:

"I must cut in between young Manson and Jimmy Leavenworth. Manson will hang around Rancho San Miguel. Jimmy does not know all, but Jack will pick it up bit by bit, and old Manson will come down on us for back dividends, and he may pull out of the railroad and break us all up. *No. 4 could not stand it!* Disclosure would ruin him and also Steele. I would lose my life. The only safe ones would be Si Leavenworth and that old New York skinflint."

"I must capture Jimmy Leavenworth, break that friendship with Manson, and play for safety."

"How?" demanded Milly, with a wildly ocating heart.

"You must help me, Milly," said Ramon, with his eyes averted. He dared not face the "Empress" in her coming wrath. "You must make your strongest running on this boy to-night. Make him your slave. Drive all thoughts of every other woman out of his head."

Milly Smiley stood like a tiger at bay!

"And you, your part?" she hissed.

"I must marry the Leavenworth girl—the one this boy is wild over—her name is Katie."

Springing to the table, where the rich half-tasted feast was spread, Milly Smiley grasped a wicked-looking knife.

"If you do, I'll drive this tnrough your heart! By the God who made me, I'll kill you, and kill myself next!"

Ramon Maxan bowed his head before the whirlwind of a wicked woman's wildest rage.

"Then I have to leave all, and sneak off to Europe like a whipped cur," said Maxan bitterly. Gently grasping her hands, he drew her down beside him. The maddened beauty burst into tears.

" I can not give you up, Ramon. You do not know what you ask me. You are my whole life."

Five minutes of pleading and suing brought a lull in the tempest. Ramon tenderly held a brimming glass of the richest Burgundy to the pale lips of the " Empress."

" Listen to me," he said softly. " Manson is an open-hearted fellow. I divined his love for the younger girl, Katie, from his tell-tale face. The only way I can oust him from his friendship with Jim is to gain this girl's heart. You can handle Manson. No man can resist you, at your best," the Creole said artfully. She smiled faintly with trembling lips! " If I marry this girl I get a third of Rancho San Miguel. Si Leaven-worth must protect me, and he has Steele in his power. I will have a haven at once, and then I can defy Mejia. Old Manson will have abundant money and it will tie the whole system together."

" I swear to you," he cried, dropping on his knees, " Milly, I swear to you that I will leave this half-grown school girl down there in her mesquite groves! I will take you to Europe. You shall have a queen's luxury, and *her* money, *her* protection, will guard your real interests. You can come down to New Orleans any time you wish. I can run over at will, for I have all the ' outside secret business' to handle. You know, my beauty, that I could not marry you safely. No one has ever seen Smiley, whose name you bear. "

The imperial fair one winced, though her face was buried in her hands.

" It is the only way out, my darling," the pleading tempter whispered. " It opens life and love, the future to both of us. Old Steele will not be your jailer then, and I will fight for your freedom. I will give you my whole life! I wish you to stay here and fight this game through with me."

He continued: "When we have the land grants safe, and the government business controlled, I will have a clean half million as my share, and I swear that I will settle half of it on you! I will have the secret dividends also. If you will work with me, I can control Si Leavenworth, Steele, and, through him, No. 4. We three can outvote Mark Manson, and keep the ambitious youngster from controlling the new railroad. If you will not be reasonable, I shall have my revenge at least. I will put this young fool out of the way on the Rio Grande. He never shall marry that girl. D—n the girl! She's only a chit of a boarding-school miss, but she is the key to the situation. I have a fellow (one of my own), Joaquin Ximenes, at Rancho San Miguel. He is a cool desperado and a spy. If this youth goes down there, he will 'fix him,' or lead him into ambush. I don't want to kill him myself (unless we quarrel), for old Manson would kick, but Joaquin will attend to his little case," said the Creole grimly. "We had a treasury agent poking his nose in down there last year. He started from Brownsville to Corpus Christi with his report. He was killed by 'marauders'!" sneered Maxan. "All the same, Ximenes handed me the report and all his papers. He piously kept the other valuables for himself."

"Now, Milly, *will* you be reasonable?" Maxan's voice trembled from excitement. The "Empress" threw herself sobbing in his arms.

"And you will never desert me?" she said, gazing at him with flaming eyes.

"Never—by the God above us!" protested the Creole. Milly Smiley pressed burning kisses on his lips.

"Then watch me at dinner," she said, with an ominous pride in her accents. "Leave me now, Ramon! I must look my very best to-night," and she smiled through her tears.

"One word more," said the Creole, drawing her to his bosom, for the victory was his; "Senator Steele will bring this whole party to you. I wish you to use carte blanche in entertaining the ladies. Be careful of Mrs. Marshall and her daughter. They are quiet, haughty Virginians. Do not be too familiar and eager with them. They are as proud as they are poor. But as to the Texan girls, lavish all your arts on them. Draw them away from Mrs. Marshall, she is very quiet. The girls love pleasure naturally. Wind your webs around Katie Leavenworth's heart and get her whole confidence. Your friendship will flatter her. I will come here and meet her and I will have Steele keep young Manson off on business pretexts. Before she goes to Texas she must be my promised wife." In ten minutes, Maxan, with a light heart, turned his horses toward the Soldiers' Home, and Milly Smiley decked herself and arranged the feast of the evening to ensnare a new lover in order to keep an old one. For the simple girl to be deluded she had neither pity nor sympathy! "Ramon's will must be my law," she thought, as her dark lover's face came back to her.

"I could not marry him, it is true, but he shall be *mine till death!*"

While Jack Manson rested at his hotel and Milly Smiley deftly arranged her plan of campaign for the evening, Senator Ezra Steele complacently listened to Ramon Maxan's partial confidences.

"I think, Senator, I will be able to get pretty close to this young man's inner thoughts. I wish to bring all our guns to bear socially upon this party. They are

all coming here soon. Jimmy Leavenworth has a
penchant for the Virginia girl. Mrs. Marshall will
probably come here to the Arlington and matronize the
three 'rosebuds.' Nothing more likely than that the
two chums will stay at the Ebbitt. Now you can do
much, in your high position, to occupy and distract Mrs.
Marshall. The 'Empress' will make special running
on these Texas girls, and your efforts will draw off Mrs.
Marshall's watchful eyes. Milly will twist this frontier
engineer around her fingers in a week. I flatter myself
I will captivate Mr. Jim Leavenworth and cut Manson
off from the girls and the young man. Miss Gertie Marshall will be the only person the Texan will watch
closely.

"By the way, we must be a half-hour late at dinner
to-night. Milly will be in her best war paint and I
think she will make young Manson's head whirl in that
tête-à-tête. I will come over for you," said Maxan,
in adieu.

Mr. Jack Manson, after a careful toilet, bethought
himself of the little duties of that society so long denied
him. An exquisite basket of the choicest flowers preceded him to the residence of the graceful hostess.

"I must confer with Uncle Mark," thought Jack, as
he sauntered in the cool of the evening to the residence
of the Louisiana beauty. "Senator Steele and Ramon
Maxan are very different natures; yet both are evidently
in confidential intimacy with Mrs. Smiley. Can it be
mere social friendship which knits them together? I
will confide in Uncle Mark. He seems to know everything by intuition!"

When ushered into the drawing-room, Manson found
himself alone. His eyes roved over the beautiful surroundings and, half abstracted, he started up in surprise
as the hostess glided quietly into the room.

The young man's face expressed the astonishment and delight he could not conceal. For Mildred Smiley was wondrous fair, her imperial beauty heightened by the exquisite robe and the flashing diamond stars gleaming in her hair. On her shapely neck a necklace of gems (a prince's ransom) glittered, and Jack noticed the loveliest blossom of his offering, nestling on her sculptured bosom.

"Thanks for the beautiful flowers, Mr. Manson. They are really superb," the châtelaine said gracefully, as she motioned her visitor to a seat. She glanced furtively at the rose in her bosom. In the gloaming, the soft half-light, with the wonderful eyes beaming upon him, Jack fell under the spell of the enchantress whose art was the highest and most delicate. Unused to the persiflage of society, ardent and sincere, Manson yielded to the gentle guidance of the woman by his side.

Milly Smiley's witcheries melted the reserve of Jack Manson's nature like wax under the summer sun. The "Empress" swept the harp strings of men's souls like the forest breeze waking the Eolian chords.

"So," the lady remarked, "your friend, Mr. Leavenworth will be here to-morrow! Pray, bring him to see me. Is he like yourself in nature?" Milly's implied compliment touched Jack. "Ramon must know of this arrival at once," the temptress thought.

Jack Manson, under the spell of siren eyes, half regretted the coming of the expected guests. As the hostess rose, she whispered to the man around whose heart she was weaving her subtle web: "You must come and see me often. Come alone! I am always at home mornings after ten. You must let mé show you the beautiful environs. For I pride myself on my horses!"

Manson bent over the slender hand, daintily offered, and kissed it chivalrously.

"We are friends, are we not?" Milly Smiley archly said, as the imposing form of Senator Steele appeared at the door, followed by the dark, graceful beauty of the Creole.

The dinner was a masterpiece of the refined luxury of pleasure-loving Washington. Senator Steele took on a temporary dignity and air of the "haut-ton" in deference to the æsthetic background and his desire to shine before his Egeria. Maxan's cosmopolitan accomplishments made him easily the star of the little circle. He gracefully drew out of Manson the fact of Leavenworth's arrival.

Senator Steele was apt at his cue. "It will afford me great pleasure to offer the usual courtesies to Mrs. Marshall and the young ladies. Her husband was an eminent man; I knew him well as Judge Marshall, and I am glad I was spared meeting him as Colonel Marshall of the C. S. A."

Steele heaved a sigh. He had been a judicious warrior of the great Army of the Union, in some apocryphal staff appointment which kept him with whole bones, full pay, and an unsoiled uniform.

The "Empress" gently added her prospective welcome to the expected visitors. When the superb feast was ended, Maxan adroitly separated himself from the senator and Manson. His foreign courtesy prompted him to seek a corner of the drawing-room with the radiant hostess.

The butler ushered Steele and his young neophyte into the smoking-room "à la Turque". Ezra Steele, reclining in an easy chair, sipped his coffee and enjoyed a regalia while deftly sounding Jack Manson's mind.

"I expect your uncle soon, in fact in a very few days. We will go over these railroad plans and I shall defer much to your practical views. Cultivate

Maxan; he is a man of great influence in Mexican circles and can largely aid our future enterprise. If there
is no accident in General Grant's re-election, you will see
stirring times below. A great local development, sir.'

For an hour, the sly old Judas carefully probed every
depth of Jack Manson's honest open nature.

"He is all right," thought the senator. "We can
handle the boy easily. Still I must keep on the best
terms with him and thus win young Leavenworth's confidence. These two friends will hoodwink each other."

Glancing at his watch, the statesman remarked: "I
regret I must now leave you, but you must bring your
college comrade to me at once, on his arrival."

Leading the way to the drawing-room, Senator
Steele artfully reminded Ramon Maxan of a joint
appointment.

The laughing lady of the enchanted castle claimed
Jack Manson as a knight in attendance, and the midnight hour was near when her visitor bent over the
lady's hand in ceremonious adieu.

"To-morrow, dear old Jim arrives!" Manson thought,
as he paced the now deserted street homeward, and a
vision of the bright-eyed Hebe dissipated the glamour
of Milly Smiley's royal beauty. "She is, however,
a queen, a wonder," the stranger mused.

Before the easy-going denizens of Washington were
attacking the tedious hours of the next day, the two
college friends were reunited.

"I will stay a day with you, Jack, but am under
orders to bring you ' by force of arms ' back to Arundel."
Manson's cheek reddened slightly.

"Whose gentle commands are laid on you?" he
asked.

"Oh! Mrs. Marshall, Gertie, sister Alice, and all,"
the bright-hearted Texan gaily answered. "Ah! Yes!

Katie said she supposed your visit was for me, but she too hoped to see you."

In friendly converse the chums made eager plans for the future, and Jack Manson revelled in Leavenworth's graphic word-pictures of life in the border land.

The card of Ramon Maxan put an end to these confidences. In an hour the three young men were seated in Senator Steele's snug lair at the Arlington.

An "entente cordiale" was at once established, as the business associations of his father caused the young frontier magnate to open his heart freely to Senator Steele.

Before the party separated for a dinner at the Club, Senator Steele's stately offer of courtesies was pleasantly accepted. The evening hours brought the new-made friends to the hospitable doors of the "Empress."

When the trio returned from the presence of the Fair Ladye, there was a quiet smile on Ramon Maxan's thin lips. Off-hand Jimmy Leavenworth had warmly invited him to Arundel House as a future visitor, and Mrs. Milly Smiley's kind proffers of attentions to the ladies pleased the gallant Texan.

With rare tact, Maxan deferred his Virginian visit for some days. " I must not go too fast," he thought, " but I will lay odds that the 'Empress' and Steele, with my humble efforts added, can handle this situation."

"Remember Leavenworth," Maxan cried gaily in adieu, "you will find Hacienda Maxan's latch string always out, and I will look you up at Rancho San Miguel."

"We will all meet on the Rio Grande. In the mean time let me do the honors here. You can pay me off later in true Texan style!"

Jack Manson's business weighed lightly on him now.

A despatch to his uncle announcing his temporary absence and telegraphic address closed all, leaving him free to effect the peaceful invasion of Virginia. Manson counted the hours till the train drew out from Alexandria the next afternoon. Manson's heart beat wildly as, stepping from the cars at Fairfax Court House, he saw once more the bright-eyed Hebe who had haunted his uneasy dreams. The antique travelling carriage, in faded grandeur, and the aged African driver were characteristic of the Old Dominon. Sweet Gertie Marshall's fair cheek took on a brighter shade of rose as Leavenworth sprang to meet her. With stately deliberation, Jack Manson approached Miss Katie.

The premeditated programme of "discipline" was at once abandoned by the young engineer as the Texan belle demurely remarked: "It was so kind of you to come. I suppose you can finish your business with Brother Jimmy here at leisure." The carriage was soon under way, driven in solemn fashion through the long street of sleepy Fairfax Court House, where the first cavalry outpost dash of the war occurred.

Jack Manson bit his lip to avoid bursting into laughter. As the rolling ground was reached, Leavenworth and Gertrude were deep in a murmured conversation. Manson was conscious that the keen-eyed Katie was searching his very soul. His delighted eye rested on the beautiful landscape, its fair extent now smiling in peace and plenty. The evening shades were creeping into dells and stealing over the wooded hills.

Nature's fairy touch had hidden the ravages of war. The tired feet once plodding the ancient roads had been resting by thousands, for years, under the "sacred soil." Stealing a glance at sweet Katie, Manson in courteous terms sought news of Mrs. Marshall and sister Alice.

"They are anxiously awaiting your arrival," the fair one with the golden locks answered.

"And you?" said Jack, with a wild dash into sentiment.

"Oh! I came only to meet Brother Jimmy," the wicked maiden demurely said.

"Most certainly, I see," replied Manson, sinking into a renewed despair. He glued his eyes to the witching scenes of dying day and deepening shadow, as the horses trotted along toward Arundel House.

Miss Katie eyed her dejected companion curiously. "You are fond of nature, Mr. Manson?" There was a roguish ring in her words.

"I am tired of still life," mutinously replied Jack, watching her pretty little foot tapping nervously.

"*That girl has temper*," Manson muttered, down in the depths of his being. He was permitted to indulge his fondness for "still life" until, with a flourish, the carriage, sweeping through noble groves of old oaks, past copse and hedges, on through the stately old-fashioned gardens, drew up before the imposing Doric portico of Mrs. Marshall's pre-revolutionary home.

The graceful hostess, with "St. Cecilia," greeted the young travellers. Manson, with the grave courtesy of a Sir Walter Raleigh, assisted Miss Katie to alight.

The fairy Hebe flitted to her bower with a pretty nod of her head, followed by a heartfelt sigh from her baffled adorer.

Manson's eye roved over the quaint old three-storied mansion, whose solid walls gleamed white among its embowered oaks. The grand old hall was rich yet in relics of family grandeur, spared even by the ruthless spoilers of the Civil War.

It was a merry circle which gathered around the simple home table. Mrs. Marshall's gentle dignity was a foil

to the ringing laughter of the younger convives. It was
the first outburst of natural merriment since Colonel
Marshall had been brought home from the field of
honor.

Under the guidance of Gertrude, Jack Manson
explored the nooks and corners of the seat of the
Marshalls, on whose walls worthies and beauties of
past generations still looked down in bravery or sweet-
ness. The romance of the old still lingered, clinging
to the stately rooms, within which the loyal sons of
King George had toasted " Church and State;" where,
later, the revolutionary blue and buff had swaggered
bravely, and in recent sadder days, the gray-eyed
chivalry of Lee, Jackson, Jeb Stuart, and Ashby had
pledged the "Stars and Bars" to bright-eyed girls, clad
in the "red, white, and red" of the Southern Confederacy. The ancient halls seemed filled with whispers of
days long dead and gone, and the accentuation of pathos
was the simple portrait of a handsome lad in Confederate gray in the place of honor on the drawing-room
mantel.

" My brother," softly said the Greek-browed Gertie,
" killed in Pelham's Horse Artillery, at Yellow Tav-
ern."

Raising her eyes, the Southern maid, with fond rev-
erence, whispered " My father! We lost him at Malvern Hill."

The crossed swords of sire and son hung between the
pictured faces of the victims of the delirium of " 61."

Joining the group on the portico, Jack Manson, in the
witching moonlight, drew near to the sweet stranger
who had stolen into his heart of hearts.

Leavenworth had gaily recited the glories of Mrs.
Mildred Smiley's home, the hospitable proffers of the
statesman, and the offered escort of the romantic Creole.

"By all means!" said Mrs. Marshall. "I should be happy to receive your friend, Mr. Maxan."

A general council of war decided upon a visit to the Capital City. "Mr. Manson," said the widowed hostess, "I shall leave it to James and Gertrude to pilot you around the country. We have still good horses—there are charming rides. Pray consider this your home."

As the gentle lady withdrew, Jack Manson ventured an approach to the "maid who needed discipline." "Do you ride, Miss Katie?" he asked with interest.

The merry laughter of the Texan Rose rang out as musical as the carol of a bird.

"A Texan girl asked if she rides!" Katie regained her composure with difficulty. "I will pardon you, sir," the beauty said, rising with mock dignity, "on condition that you report as escort to-morrow at nine! You can then indulge freely your fondness for landscape effects. You will see nothing but prairies in Texas. Prairies, sir!" cried the merry girl as she vanished.

The abstracted Leavenworth roused himself from his tête-à-tête with Gertrude to plan the future use of the sunny hours before them.

Happy days, merriest hours glided gaily by. Four days later Jack Manson and Katie Leavenworth, returning from a sunny morning gallop, saw Ramon Maxan standing on the portico of Arundel House. His dark impassioned eyes gleamed as Jack Manson presented the handsome Creole to his lovely Amazon. The golden morning sunlight flooded the eastern front of Arundel and the coming guest's shadow fell dark across the threshold of the old Virginian home. "Was it an omen?" Manson started in surprise.

"I have business as well as pleasure in view!" said Maxan, with ready aplomb. "Senator Steele desires greatly to see Mr. Leavenworth on an important matter, and I availed myself of the invitation transmitted through Mr. Leavenworth to pay my respects." When the daughter of the house and the frontier prince returned from a morning drive, Mr. Ramon Maxan made his début in Virginian circles. With restrained and artful courtesy he indicated his return to Washington in the evening.

Mrs. Marshall's quiet welcome was characteristic of Southern hospitality.

The family visit to Washington was definitely settled for the next day.

"Those mail contracts need my attention," said Leavenworth to Jack Manson, "so we will go up now."

While the three men drove to the station the woman congress of Arundel busied itself with the romantic Creole. Katie alone was silent; her thoughts were busied with inventing new schemes to torment "her loyal knight, Jack."

"His manners are charming," was the favorable comment of the conservative hostess on Maxan, "and yet I have always feared the close acquaintance of people of mixed blood." The lady of Arundel, with a mother's intuition, had noted Maxan's eager glances drinking in the unconscious Katie's beauty.

While Leavenworth and Manson drove home, Ramon Maxan, thoughtfully reviewing the day, murmured, as he dreamed over his cigar, his easy nature lulled with the click of the flying wheels:

"Caramba! she is a young goddess, this Señorita Katie. She must be mine. She shall rule at Hacienda Maxan. And yet, Panchita is down there!" His eye grew steely in its restless glitter. "Madre de Dios! I must get rid of her." He gazed at a picture in his pocketbook. "I can bully and hoodwink the 'Empress.'

But Panchita!" He fell into day-dreams and plot-
weaving until the lights of Washington twinkled
before him.

————

CHAPTER IV.

FOXES IN COUNCIL—SNARES FOR THE UNWARY— CRŒSUS AND THE SENATOR.

"MADAM, allow me to welcome you to Washington,
I am delighted to meet you!" said Senator Ezra Steele,
in his grandest " parade manner," as he ran the gauntlet of introduction to Mrs. Marshall's coterie at the
Arlington.

For the three bright-eyed beauties were a sweet guard
of honor to the gentle Virginian matron, and were assembled at this pleasant formality; the young men also
appeared in evidence.

The city of Washington was rapidly filling up with
excited politicians. Election excitements stirred the
capital with wildest rumors, and the preliminary throes
of the great struggle of 1872 were being felt. The
hotel corridors were thronged day and night.

" I hope you will permit me to show you the later
lions of Washington," the senator genially remarked.
" I shall have to deprive you of Mr. Leavenworth's
escort for a while, as his father's department business
may continue for many days. We are associates in
many affairs. I shall leave it to Mr. Manson and my
young friend, Señor Ramon Maxan, to aid and guide
you. Though the season is not open, there is still much
to interest."

Mrs. Marshall accepted the senator's courtesies and
Ramon Maxan's eyes gleamed with a newer fire, as
he gazed on the radiant young beauties by her side.

Jack, in the three days since Maxan's visit to Arundel House, had been awaiting the coming of Mark Manson, whose telegraphic announcement of arrival was just received. So, happily, the new friends journeyed on to Washington.

The hotel register at Willard's bore the name of A. R. Chisholm, New Orleans. In a lull of the ceremonial conversation, Senator Steele found time to confer a few moments with Manson.

"We will probably have a meeting of the Rio Grande Company to-morrow afternoon. I hold one proxy. Your uncle telegraphs me his arrival to-night, and your friend Leavenworth received his father's power of attorney from me this morning. So, my young friend, you must be content to let Maxan escort the ladies for a day or so. We will take up the railroad matter, for time presses."

Manson was willing and anxious to learn the full details of his trust. While Jack conferred with the Texan, Senator Ezra Steele requested permission to bring Mrs. Mildred Smiley on the morrow to meet the visiting circle from Arundel House. This delicate bit of feminine diplomacy arranged, the statesman took his leave, followed by the brilliant Creole. This last gentleman was a past master of the art of "squiring dames." His floral offerings already ornamented the spacious apartments of the ladies.

"My services are yours to command, madam," he said in parting. "I hope my horses may please even a Virginia lady."

As the senator's footfalls died away in the corridor, the widowed patrician woman gazed wistfully from her windows on the far distant dome of the Capitol.

"I am sadly changed, or the times are greatly

altered." Mrs. Marshall recalled the embryo Washington of her girlhood and her early married days.

Senators, august, revered, and brilliant, returned to her mind from a dead and forgotten past. Knightly Clay, grand Webster, the mighty Calhoun, courtly Preston, great Benton, and a host of national leaders. Foote, Gwin, Crittenden, Breckinridge, and all the vanished heroes of the forum passed in shadowy review. The still sorrowing woman turned away with a sigh of sadness.

"He seems pleasant, this man, yet— yet——" She thought bitterly of the fate of the eleven wayward sister States under the reconstruction government. The vulgar thronged in these halls of state; adventurers posed as governors, senators, and representatives, aliens to the States they ruled, and pigmies by the side of the august shades she invoked. Winifred Marshall knew, at last, the helplessness of the South under the armed heel of the stranger. The avalanche of the "Reconstruction debts" of nine Southern States already aggregated two hundred and ninety-two millions of dollars!

There were more grinding losses than the dead on the field, greater sorrows than defeat, and a cup far more bitter than the humiliation of Appomattox still fated to be the lot of the Southron. For it was before the blush of the bright dawn of the new era in which the regenerated South was destined to proudly move onward and upward, and even with fidelity to old State traditions, with reverent affection for the "loved and lost," to nobly keep time in happier days to the march of the Union, consecrated anew with the chrism of warrior blood.

"Alas! The re-election of the Soldier-President binds us down for four years more," she murmured. Turning her eyes fondly on the group around her she thought: "I must try to make them all happy. They are in the morning sun of life. I walk even now in sunset shadows."

The two young men briefly arranged for the duties before them, and the social exploration of Washington was commenced for the three graces, whose eager hearts were happy in venturing out on society's wave-tossed bosom.

In the same giant hostelry, Ezra Steele held a council of war with Maxan before seeking the "Empress" on his social errand.

"Now, Ramon," Steele sharply said, "our inside circle is all here. We will have the *open* meeting first, discuss the railroad scheme, and close up the annual business to September 1st."

"Old Mark will put his nephew into the directory, I suppose. Young Jim will have his father's power of attorney, and I will act for partner No. 4." "So we will get old Manson quietly out of the way and back to New York. I fear that cool old skinflint. He can look through a grindstone. Then, when he is disposed of, we will have our *secret* meeting and divide the proceeds of the season's work. The others are all near here. I sent cipher telegrams to them to go to Barnum's Hotel, Baltimore, till I telegraph for them."

"Who is up here now?" said Maxan, all alive.

"Well," said Steele, as he took a toss of cognac, "Don Patricio from Monterey, Beriah Mott from Corpus Christi, Chisholm (who is already in town), and that Danish lawyer of Leavenworth's, Colonel Nordenskiold. The collector's brother from the Rio Grande represents him as well as John Park and Jerry Mulvain of Brownsville and Matamoras. So, you see, we have a full house!" The old schemer laughed softly.

" We will push ahead openly on the railroad and transportation matters. That will do until this election is safe. It looks even a little doubtful now, but when the General is re-elected, I shall know in a day or so if No. 4 keeps his place in the government."

" Then we will get rid of this young engineer by sending him out on the surveys. I will make old Leavenworth watch him and we will put two or three men in his party who will keep him hoodwinked and off our working lines, in the secret matters. When he goes out on the exploration and survey work, you had better have your fellow Ximenes stick pretty close to him, and have a couple of trusty riders to carry you the news and take your orders. You must hound this interloper down, but not too openly. I will get him away from here the minute that the election is safe. You must follow him up secretly."

"All right," snarled Maxan, "if he worries us he will lie some day under a mesquite bush with his throat cut. He shall not cross my path and live." The Creole's brows wrinkled in the grim horseshoe of the assassin.

" Easy, Ramon," earnestly answered Steele. " Not a blow till I direct!"

" Very good. I have got it in for him though," the half-breed replied with a malignant scowl.

" Now I am off to Milly. She must give these people a formal dinner, and as soon as Mark goes away, a reception. The town is half empty, but they will not know the difference."

" Both of you must cleave to young Leavenworth. Cut him off from Manson! Let Milly occupy the Virginia dowager's leisure hours, and also make Manson her admirer."

" You are right! That's the game!" said the Creole,

"I'm off now for a drive."

"Jack," said Leavenworth, as the friends walked over to the Ebbitt, "I have very important affairs to represent my father in here. I do not care to be thrown always against Senator Steele. He is a little *too* smooth for me. Now if I take a room here at the Ebbitt near you, I can spend my days with the ladies, and we can confer in quiet nightly. I can keep the senator at arms-length, as our family party has already a tête-à-tête table. He dare not intrude there."

"Moreover, Maxan is a shadow of the senator's. I know that my father has confidential business with Steele, but I will not have it leak into the knowledge of this Ramon Maxan. It is two to one always, if I confer with them in Steele's rooms. I may need your advice, and your uncle's through you. Ramon Maxan seems to be high up in Mexican councils, and my father's business is naturally antagonistic to the border Mexican interests. The half-breed is a pleasant fellow socially, but I think that he would be a dangerous confidant.

"Now, your Uncle Mark will be here at six. I will take the ladies to the theatre to-night, for you will wish to confer until he is done.

"Remember, if we hold your uncle's and my father's interests together, we can always checkmate Steele and No. 4."

The Texan selected his room and speedily sought the Arlington, only three squares distant.

Jack Manson felt a strange sense of relief as he welcomed Mark at the station when the New York train swept in.

After a deliberate dinner, the old capitalist settled himself in his rooms, and, drawing out a little note-book, gazed at Jack over his cigar.

"Now, sir, your report; tell me all."

The engineer detailed his varied experiences social and business, up to the very hour.

Not a word escaped Mark, who jotted down a brief note now and then.

"Very good!" the man of millions remarked, as Jack concluded. He asked a few pertinent questions as to the brilliant Creole. His brow was clouded with thought when Manson finished his answers.

"I can not see the reason of this close connection with Steele. Some of his many schemes, I suppose." Mark cross-examined the young man as to the fascinating Mrs. Mildred Smiley.

"Now what can such a woman be doing here?" the old man mused, and dashed off an entry or two. Jack's evident enthusiasm for the fair "Empress" did not escape the veteran's notice. "You are not falling in love with this fascinating stranger?" Mark Manson queried abruptly, as frowns wrinkled his brow.

"No, sir!" rejoined the younger man emphatically. But his cheeks were redder than usual! His heart secret was safe, however, for as a knock sounded at the door Mark Manson snapped his note-book clasp and called "Come in!"

The brief entries in his memorandums were:

"See Marshal Ritchie and get private report on Maxan and Mrs. Mildred Smiley."

"Watch Steele and Maxan."

"Ah! Senator," cried Mark heartily, as Ezra Steele followed his card. "Glad to see you." The statesman was soon at his ease. Jack Manson's keen eye noted the absence of Steele's "official manner." The "carpet-bag" senator was serious, deferential, and even manly in his intercourse with the man of millions.

"I will take a look through the offices," said Jack, leaving the seniors to their conference.

"Come back in a half-hour," the New Yorker said, nodding. Manson waited till he observed the senator's departure and rejoined his uncle.

"Well, boy," Mark said, as his nephew entered the room, "we will have our railroad meeting to-morrow at four. I must go over and see your friends before then; I have some local business. Tell young Leavenworth I wish an hour with him alone. Bring him in to-morrow; we'll breakfast here. By the way, Senator Steele asks us all to dine to-morrow on behalf of Mrs. Smiley. I will stay over as I wish to meet that lady, and also this influential young half-foreigner, Maxan. I am satisfied with you; you have been prudent. Keep your eyes open. Distrust *every one* here!"

"Why so?" honest Jack queried. "I have seen no underhand work here."

"Precisely!" calmly rejoined old Mark. "That proves how well 'Secret Washington' guards its picket lines. The political head of the government is only an automaton, pushed forward by the ruling party, and pulled by factions to right and left. 'Secret Washington' begins with a slight political grip of the Supreme Court, and a distinct hold on some of the Cabinet. The official household of the President has several members of this silent cabal. Heads of departments and chiefs of disbursing bureaus are under a continual fire of intrigue, and I am told that in the Senate and House are purchasable men on important committees, often leaders of the opposing forces, who can make or block any game. They take a graduated toll of all beneficial private movements, and it has been my experience of forty years that change of party does not affect the inside workings of 'Secret Washington.'

"The twenty thousand mere hangers-on amount to nothing. In the 'Secret Washington' these men of power keep eacn other's guilty counsels. All is externally decorous. If you have no special business to further here, you are only welcomed to a walk through the receptions and a glass of 'alleged' punch. You may dance and drive and flirt and yet *see nothing!* But in private houses, in select clubs, in exclusive hotels, the varied members of that great octopus, 'Secret Washington,' reach out and grasp all prey worth seizing. Wine, cards, suppers, pretty and approachable women, discreet ex-officials, and suave corporation lawyers; all these means are quietly used to hoodwink the man who must be led to understand 'addition, division, and silence.' These people of power know that their risk is great. They always take their pay in advance with greedy hand. Look at 'Credit Mobilier!' Its scandals pulled down several men of national reputation. The outsiders scarcely suffered. All in all, the cheapest way is to buy the *right* men, buy them *at once*, and keep them *bought* when you have paid the price. All these 'carpet-bag' senators and representatives will be swept away when the adroit Southerners regain full power. Therefore they fill their pockets now 'to make their calling and election sure.' One word, Jack. Be on your guard socially. Have no compromising correspondence. *Say* what you wish, to man or woman, *alone*, here, but *no letter-writing*. Now, good-night! Report on time."

The old man mused as Jack wandered to his room somewhat astonished.

"I'll get out early and see Police Marshal Ritchie to-morrow," mused Mark, as he sought his couch. "He will dig up these two life histories for money. Yes, money—money will do anything in Washington, if—if judiciously used." The old man's comments died away as he dropped into a heavy sleep.

"Well, Mr. Leavenworth, what news have you from your father?" queried the financier, as he eyed the young man at breakfast in his rooms next day. Mark Manson had skimmed the financial and political columns of the latest journals, and, up betimes, had disposed of a dozen letters arriving in the night mail.

"All is going well on the Rio Grande, sir," answered the Texan. "There's a great deal of excitement about this presidential election on the Mexican side. The borderers fear an annexation of the three States of Zona Libre."

"Nonsense," cried Mark. "Grant is a man of peace; but the real advance will be the projected railroads. In ten years there will be a railroad to Guaymas and Mazatlan on the west; one from Denver and El Paso to the City of Mexico; another from Eagle Pass to the table-lands, and a vitally important road from San Antonio to Laredo, tapping the Zona Libre. Now, we must push our cross-road from Corpus Christi to Laredo and make the first connection. We can control the Gulf trade with Eastern Mexico. How about the franchise for our company?" Mark's voice was eager.

"I had letters yesterday from my father, under seal, and here is one for you." Leavenworth produced it. "I have my father's power of attorney. The franchise is passed and signed by the Governor, but it is in my father's own name, with a few of his subordinates as directors."

"Why so?" demanded Mark Manson, his eyes flashing in angry surprise.

The young Texan calmly answered: "I think you will find the explanation in your letter. Father wrote me that it was done to avoid sectional feelings and to keep Northern names out until the bill was safely signed. The others can then resign to suit you and father."

Old Mark growled: " I see, yes, I see." Tearing open his letter, he read it with care. His face brightened.

" You are right, Leavenworth," the capitalist said. " Now, I will release you both till two o'clock. I will pay my respects then at the Arlington. Remember, the meeting of the company will be here at four sharp. I need you both."

Jack Manson, light-hearted, escaped to select a floral offering for the delightfully provoking Hebe, which should eclipse even Maxan's tribute. Mark Manson read his partner's letter over with great deliberation.

" Yes! It is a strong hand to play in this game. Si Leavenworth *is* a genius. Putting his son and Jack with himself and myself in as directors, we can absolutely control Senator Steele and No. 4. We will have four of the seven directors. We can hold back the land division for years, and make Steele and the hidden partner handle the government through No. 4. Old Si offers to assign the whole franchise, in trust to ourselves jointly, to secure my money advances. 'Further details to my representatives.'

" Mr. Jack, you shall go down the moment the election is decided. Now, for Ritchie."

Mark whirled away in a coupé, and in fifteen minutes was closeted with the Marshal of Police for the District of Columbia. Ten minutes of earnest conversation concluded the affair.

" I am already almost in a position to report," said the Chief, with the deepest attention to every word. "But how long do you stay here, Mr. Manson?" he queried.

" Till to-morrow night, ten train," sententiously said Mark.

" You have carte blanche. Give me all the inside

facts. I'll meet you at Wormley's at nine to-morrow evening. They will show you to my room at once. I'll post the chief steward. Now, I will put two or three good men on this at once," said Marshal Ritchie.

" Want any money? " said Mark.

" Not till I earn it," replied Ritchie, with a quiet smile.

" That's the talk," briskly said Manson, as he rose to leave.

" Now, Brother Steele, I think I can watch your running mates while the boy is in Texas," Manson mused. " Yes, I have the whip hand, and must keep it! I can handle this with old Si if no foul play comes between us.

" To the Arlington," commanded the financier, now well satisfied. As the coupé reached its destination, Mark Manson's way was stopped by a superb carriage. The financier started as Ezra Steele obsequiously assisted a wonderfully beautiful woman to alight. The elegant dark-blue carriage, the splendid Kentucky chestnuts, the stylish trappings, and faultlessly liveried servants were quickly noted.

" By Jove, the fair unknown does the thing in style. What is the game now on the table? Never mind, I'll soon get the key to this enigma," growled the financier as he sent in his cards.

With graceful dignity Mrs. Mildred Smiley met Mark Manson, after his general welcome had subsided. Nothing could be more cordial than her personally expressed invitation to dinner. Half an hour later, Mrs. Smiley's winning manners had achieved a decided conquest. As Mark Manson took his leave, he was followed by Mrs. Marshall and the fair visitor, departing for a round of sight-seeing, with the lovely Katie and Señor Ramon Maxan as general cicerone. There

was a grateful flash in the Creole's eyes as he thanked
Milly Smiley for her successful diplomacy.

An afternoon gained in which to push his careful
approaches to the unguarded citadel of the heiress' heart!
Well he knew that the "Empress" would thoroughly
occupy the placid Virginian widow.

Jack Manson chafed in vague unrest, as he awaited
the conclusion of Leavenworth's long private conference two hours later, with the New York magnate.

"I am thoroughly satisfied to go ahead with the
road," Mark announced, as his nephew joined them.
"Jack, you can run up to Baltimore with me to-night.
I can confer with you on the road. I find this young
man has a clear head for business," he said approvingly,
"and you two should work well together. You must
go down there as soon as election is over. By the
way, neither of you need go into details with Steele
or this Maxan. After our meeting, I will write my
views in full direct to Rancho San Miguel. Mr.
Leavenworth writes me that his lawyer will be ready
at Corpus Christi to give you all the general data and
explain the scheme in full.

"You can jointly study the matter here till Novem-
·ber 1st, and Jack, you had better come over to New
York during the last week and select your outfit and
instruments. I will have the inside views of the election by that time. Be here at four; I must go over and
see the President."

The alert old schemer departed for the White House.
Four o'clock found the representatives of the embryo
railroad in formal session.

Senator Ezra Steele, with his confidential secretary,
Mark Manson, grave and watchful at the head of the
table, Leavenworth, as his father's representative, with
papers and accounts ready, and Jack Manson eager to

learn of his future business. An hour's careful discussion and examination of papers sufficed to place upon the records the powers of the younger men and a resolution for a formal meeting of organization at Corpus Christi. Mr. John Manson's appointment as Chief Engineer was duly made, and the accounts of the undivided rancho, bands of cattle in joint ownership thereon, and transportation contracts of joint interest were passed upon and audited.

"Not so bad, Senator," said Mark Manson, as James Leavenworth read the final report of his father, authorizing each interest to draw on A. R. Chisholm & Co. for eighty thousand dollars each, as the yearly revenue of the four shares.

"Wait till we sweep in the Zona Libre, Mr. Chairman," hopefully remarked the statesman.

In closing, Mark Manson announced the fact that the franchise was secured, the bill having been duly passed. "It is the intention of Mr. Leavenworth to assign the franchise and lands jointly to himself and to me, on the completion of the organization, as required by law in Texas."

"Why so?" demanded Steele, his cheeks flushing in surprise. "Ah! we must have a legal directory of seven," Mark answered firmly—"Leavenworth, his son, Mr. John Manson, and myself. You can name three, probably Chisholm, yourself, and anyone you name down there."

"But it is hardly fair," protested the wary senator. "You have the balance of power, and you tie up the lands we earn."

"See here, Senator," said Mark, almost sharply, "Leavenworth is land and cattle poor and has much money tied up in his Rio Grande steamboat line. He needs all his capital. You, I presume, are taxed heavily

to handle the legislature of your State and effect your
re-election, as well as for strict party contributions."
He paused. "That's true!" replied Ezra Steele with
a groan. "Half this year's dividend goes for that, and
my personal expenses here are enormous." He secretly
thought of the "Empress," a veritable money devourer.

"Well! No. 4 (your proxy giver) can not openly
raise funds, now, you admit. I am left to procure alone
three millions of dollars to build this two hundred
miles of railway. I can get the funds in New York,
but the control must be in my hands. I insist that each
of my enterprises shall stand on its own bottom. Mr.
James Leavenworth here has a duplicate of his father's
letter to me, agreeing to this. I authorize my nephew
to draw on me for all the preliminary expenses up to
two hundred and fifty thousand dollars. I'll advance
this without interest. When my nephew has ridden
over the line in reconnoissance, and conferred with
partner Leavenworth, on completion of the organization and assignment of the franchise, I will put up
sixteen thousand dollars a mile for the road, and also
send rolling-stock down on my own credit. But we
must be unanimous. Otherwise, we stop here. I must
see my way clear!"

Senator Steele sighed and yielded with good grace!
In ten minutes a resolution spread on the records
closed the day's work. "We can begin work on the
road by January 1st, thanks to your Texan climate,"
said Mark Manson in conclusion. "There will be three
of us here—you, No. 4, and I. When Congress adjourns
you can run over to Texas, after going South, and I
will confirm anything jointly signed by Leavenworth,
you, and my nephew."

"That is fair," said the mollified senator. "Now,
gentlemen, to dinner!" The formal meeting broke up.

Mark Manson, well pleased, awaited his social début at the exquisite palace of the " Empress," and prepared for his departure. " After I see Ritchie, I am all ready for the trip."

Senator Steele quietly slipped down to the general telegraph office.

" The old pawnbroker," he muttered; "this is his day, ours is to-morrow. There'll be a vacancy soon in that directory, and Maxan shall have it. That will give us the balance of power." He dashed off a despatch to Baltimore, which called together the secret confederates. Its words were simple.

Be here at eight to-morrow evening. Bring everybody. Carriages for you at the station. M. leaves to-night.

" That will do," chuckled Steele, " I will have them all out of town and scattered, by daylight, save Chisholm. Young Leavenworth must not meet his father's lawyer here. I will checkmate you, Mr. Mark Manson. If this election goes right, I will see that the Federal officials and judges west of the Nueces River are all our own people."

The evening hour reunited the circle at Mrs. Smiley's table. In a blaze of light, the grand room was embowered with choicest flowers, sweet music softly stealing in from a hidden orchestra, and there the " Empress" welcomed her guests. The tables sparkled with crystal and plate. To sweet Katie Leavenworth, in the eager enjoyment of a novice, the scene was a fairyland.

Jack Manson's eyes shone tenderly as he gazed on the unconquered darling of his heart in her ravishing toilet.

Her loveliness in the rich robes was a revelation. The ardent young engineer marvelled at the superb beauty of the animated Rose of Texas. The brilliant hostess, with Mark Manson and Mrs. Marshall on her right and left, assiduously labored to charm the quiet Virginia widow. Mark Manson's keen eyes glanced often around the table. He made a mental note of the graceful adroitness with which Mrs. Smiley parried the few but pertinent queries of Mrs. Marshall as to her family connections in the historic circles of the South.

"Fights shy, smart woman!" ruminated the capitalist.

He did not fail to note Ramon Maxan's carefully modulated devotion to Katie Leavenworth.

Senator Steele was exhibiting his "grand cere-monial" manner to Miss Alice Leavenworth, and Jack Manson, with frank kindness, watched over Gertrude Marshall, save when his roving eyes would stray across and note the flushed cheeks of the woman he was daily learning to love more. Maxan's musically soft utter-ances reached only the beautiful partner whose attention he engrossed.

"Very neatly done," thought Mark Manson. "The hostess is making smooth the Creole's path. We will see! What's her motive?" and his gray eyes were keenly alert under the bushy brows. "This a sort of queer social triumvirate," the old man concluded.

"Ritchie may give me the points!"

The musical chime of the ormolu mantel clock recalled Mark Manson as the hour of eight sounded. In a quarter of an hour the capitalist accompanied the ladies to the drawing-rooms.

"I regret my early departure, madam," he said, as he thought of his appointment.

"Pray give me a few moments," replied the hostess, indicating an alcove.

"Now what's the game!" thought Mark.

"In my isolated position I have occasional business in New York in financial circles. Might I, at some time, should I need it, trouble you for your experienced advice?"

"With pleasure, madam," rejoined Mark, as he quietly ruminated: "I can watch her thus from time to time." Carefully presenting his residence and office cards, Mark summoned Jack to his side.

"I regret to take one of your guests away, but I have some private business to close with my nephew."

Jack Manson's hurried adieu to fair Katie and cere-monious leave-taking of the radiant hostess left him free to join his uncle, already in the carriage. The last glimpse of the drawing-rooms showed him Ramon Maxan at Katie's side, bending on her his brilliant eyes in undisguised admiration.

He joyously thought: "To-morrow I am free and I will keep this ardent stranger from her side."

The carriage drew up at Wormley's. "I have to see a man a few moments here, Jack," said his uncle. "Wait at my room, and we can have a chat as far as Balti-more."

"Well, Chief?" said Mark, as a steward showed him into a private room. Marshal Ritchie was awaiting him.

"There you are, sir!" answered the one man who held the social and private secrets of Washington in his unofficial note-books. He handed a concisely written document to his visitor. Mark Manson's stern face never changed a line as he eagerly ran down the sen-tences.

"Very good," he said, depositing the paper in a long pocket-book. He calmly spread out a check and seized a pen.

"How much?" was his laconic query. The official pencilled three figures on a blotting pad. Manson dashed off a check for five hundred dollars, to his own order, and endorsed it.

"Cash that at the hotel office, your name will not appear then on the voucher. I may need you again. By the way, keep an eye on those two, up to November 15th or December 1st. I will send you the same amount in currency on receiving your final report." The Chief bowed his thanks, and before he could speak Mark was half way down the stair.

Leaning back on the cushions, the old fox communed with himself as he sped to his hotel:

"As I thought—she is a high-class adventuress, equally intimate with Steele and this Maxan, a strong influence behind her. Her hospitality is inspired. The motive? I have it. Cutting off the Leavenworth influence from me, Steele and No. 4 could control the company and the road." The dinner incidents returned to him. "And Maxan, in Steele's interest, stalks the brother by making love to the sister. I'll warn Jack and break that up."

The carriage halted. Ten minutes later, the uncle and nephew were speeding to the railway station.

"Jack, my boy!" began Mark, as the lights of the capital receded, "There is some underhanded work under way."

The younger man gazed attentively at his principal, in the seclusion of their state-room.

"What do you mean, uncle?" he eagerly asked.

"I think you will need to keep your eyes open and be on your guard here, socially, as well as in my business. There is a mysterious connection between Steele, this dashing Creole, and the handsome hostess. I will not tell you all yet. You shall be posted before you leave. Keep cool. Do not give Steele your confidence. Be perfectly courteous with Maxan and see as much of him as you can. He is a nervous, brilliant fellow of tropical impatience. Cool and steady, always be on your guard, and let him do the leading out! He will surely commit himself.

"All three show a little too much interest in the Leavenworths and Marshalls. The air is full of ripening schemes only waiting the election triumph. Your whole career in Texas rests on your keeping nearer to young Leavenworth and his sisters than this Mexican ranchero. He's a romantic feature, my boy. Cling closely to your comrade. Join in all the general hospitalities and break up any tête-à-têtes between Maxan and Miss Katie.

"If anything occurs of great importance, come at once to New York and see me. I will write you through my bankers here, so there can be no spying. Don't antagonize Steele. I need him till after the legal organization of the road.

"Then I'll keep the whip hand," said Mark grimly. "Now, here's Baltimore, boy. Don't forget." Jack pressed his uncle's hand.

"I'll not forget," he answered, as he sprang off the train.

BOOK II.

THE RIO GRANDE COMPANY.

CHAPTER V.

THAT MYSTERIOUS COMPANY—A PAPER RAILROAD
—THE SECRET MEETING—ILL-GOTTEN GAINS—
MILDRED SMILEY'S FALSE LOVER.

"I THINK I will follow Mr. Ramon Maxan's trail pretty closely now," remarked Jack Manson, as he sauntered out of the Ebbitt, in all the glory of a faultless toilet next morning.

"That florid caballêro must be up early to outwit me to-day," mused the new railway director as he entered the florist's shop.

"I want a splendid basket of flowers—your best. Something like that," said Jack, approaching a beautiful corbeille just finished, glowing in its superb freshness of vivid color and wealth of perfume.

The direction of the note could not escape him. "Miss Katie Leavenworth. The Arlington."

"By Jove! He *is* wide-awake! It may yet be more than a 'battle of flowers' between us."

Manson's quickness of manner and reckless liberality was not lost on the florist.

"That's No. 2," joyfully cried the smug German as he pocketed a ten-dollar bill. "I wish the young lady more lovers—all *baskct* men!" chuckled the trades-man, as he bent over his roses. "I will send this lad's over first, for the other fellow looks like a handsome gambler."

Jack's tall form had vanished up the staircase of the Arlington before a single rose was broken, but *his* basket soon followed him, by a neat transference of notes.

At the piano in the salon, sweet Katie met her visitor with the flush of life's spring on her bright face.

A wild thought made Jack's pulses bound. "Shall I speak now?" His throbbing pulses were far quicker than his words.

Some guardian angel of prudence whispered "Wait!"

Reflecting upon the virtue of punctuality, his strategy was victorious in gaining the young nymph's consent to share a morning ride.

"I will be ready when you bring the horses. It is a day of days for a drive," cried the happy girl, as she thanked him for the lovely flowers.

Half an hour later, as Manson tossed the reins of a nonpareil pair of horses to the waiting negro, Ramon Maxan was standing with the Texan heiress in the drawing-room of the hostelry as Manson entered.

A dark gleam flashed from the Creole's eyes. "I regret an engagement," said the fair Katie, with a glance at Manson which was a mute appeal for departure.

The unsuspecting Jack, happy at heart, failed to note the coldness of the greeting his rival accorded him.

In leaving ceremoniously, Ramon Maxan's quick eye caught a view of the prancing steeds below, as well as noted the duplicate floral offerings displayed on the centre table.

Behind the plate glass of the reading-room, his fierce black eyes rested on a choice rose nestling on Katie's breast as she merrily waved her hand in adieu to the ladies on the balcony.

"Madre de Dios! I swear I will have a drop of that Yankee cur's heart-blood for every speck of color in that rose." He stalked, with gloomy brow, to the hotel café, as the thoroughbreds darted away.

"Ah! I'll break up that family party yet. If I can get that girl in my power, she shall wait on Panchita. Curse them all!" He clinched his teeth as he set down his glass.

"I will dog that fool over the border. If Ximenes can not fix him, Ramon 'El Jaguar' must do it himself."

Out beyond the now rising stately palaces of the "later set," over the hills and far away in happy unconsciousness, Jack Manson drove, followed by Maxan's curse.

At his side, Katie Leavenworth, in awakened interest, listened to stories of the Far West where the Sioux crouch behind the sedgy grass of the Platte.

Her cavalier feared to linger on nearer topics, but his heart was beating high. He artfully disclosed his final orders for Texas.

"That will be delightful!" merrily cried the fair maid. "You will like Texas! Jimmy can show you horses there! Not tame horses,—our prairies are the world's riding school!" she proudly added. "And such brave men! You will like them. They will give you a hearty welcome."

"And you?" said Jack, his eyes meeting hers with an expression which made the rich blood mantle her cheeks.

"Oh! certainly," calmly replied the girl, suddenly interested in a glimpse of far-off scenery, "I shall do the honors of San Miguel with pleasure, for Brother Jimmy's sake."

The mischievous words implied a grave doubt.

"And for my own sake, too?" persisted Jack.

"We will see. If you make a good Texan, I may even go as far as that," answered the pretty tease, looking frankly at him with wilfully solemn eyes.

"I hope I will be a pretty fair Texan," said Jack, as he gazed between the horses' heads.

"They are the bravest, most generous men in the wide world," replied Katie, with an air of great decision.

The rosy hours chased each other all too quickly for Jack's ardent heart. For he dared to dream that his friendly little monitress would aid him in the dim future, to become "a good Texan."

As the tired steeds drew up before the hotel, Manson had gained new love of the great border State from the romantic girl.

"I feel that I am quite a Texan already," said Jack meaningly, as he escorted the damsel to the door. "You must wait a long, long time yet," was the last bit of wisdom falling from Katie's rosy lips.

While Jack and his new fellow-director sat and smoked after their dinner, a strange coterie had gathered in the retired rooms of Milly Smiley's palace. There was no sign of festivity. Although a richly-furnished sideboard tempted the wine-drinker, and the blue smoke of Havanas clouded the air, there were no servants present.

Mrs. Mildred Smiley meanwhile ornamented her box at the theatre, and only a circle of stern, resolute men gathered around a long table littered with papers.

Dissimilar in speech, garb, and manner, the varying dialects and off-hand gestures of the speakers suggested a band of modernized pirates. Beard and hair worn at will, and the quaint garb of the Southwest gave a semi-rustic appearance to the gathering.

But one common thought animated all these men!

Gold! Easily gained—the fruit of sly conspiracy, open adventure, cunning fraud, concealed crime, and coldly plotted violence—The King of the World! Gold!

It was the inner cabal of the mysterious Rio Grande Company.

At their head, the glow of avarice kindling his faded eyes, watchful Ezra Steele presided, mindful of his sen-atorial toga. Papers, schedules, accounts, and vouchers lay before him, the carefully guarded returns of the other conspirators. Ramon Maxan, a hungry look in his dark, eager eyes, sat beside Steele and made private notes in a long memorandum-book.

Behind the glasses around the board, were ranged five eager, watchful listeners of Steele's cold sentences. For the different leaders of a huge nefarious traffic were now " reporting results " to the man who covered their deeds at the national capital.

Chisholm, a lean wolfish-faced New Orleans banker, with straggling mustache and shrunken shoulders, was an " unreconstructed " secessionist. Cool and wary enough to guard his own head, he had lingered after General Mansfield Lovell left New Orleans helpless under the guns of Farragut's fleet. Chisholm soothed his heart wounds by illicit operations in cotton, dallying also with the foreign consuls and directing covert trade between the rebels of the Gulf States and the thieving U. S. volunteer quartermasters during the occupation. Rich, haughty, and implacable, he was silent and skilful in his arts. An accidental connection by marriage with the secret partner (No. 4) gave him great power in the company. His knowledge of the Spanish Main, his comradeship with smuggler and blockade runner, and his alliances with the land pirates of the Rio Grande made him invaluable.

While his credit and financial ability were remarkable, his well-conducted business house, and his membership of the Crescent Club placed him on a high social pinnacle.

Thoroughly en rapport with the "carpet-bag" governors, the inner Custom-House ring, and possessing mysterious powers over the mails and telegraph systems, Chisholm's drafts covered many queer transactions, whose inner details were only explained by the trebly protected ciphers and broken correspondence of message and letter.

A living link between the Knights of the Golden Circle, the Kuklux Klan, the brummagem State Government, and the National Capital, he held in his power Senator Ezra Steele and Partner No. 4, for the one filled a national place at his sufferance, and smooth Senator Steele could only obtain his secret dividends through Chisholm's innocent-looking banker's drafts.

Not an operation, from buying a newspaper, wrecking a railroad, "removing a man," or bribing a judge or jury, could be devised in which the sallow, linen-clad banker was not an expert.

Cautious in speech, sparing in his use of liquors, he was a desperate gamester, a veteran duelist, and as deadly as a rattlesnake blinded with summer heat. He was the depositary of the secret revenues of the inner clique.

Near the banker sat Don Patricio Foley of Monterey, an oily, round-faced, cunning Irishman; a veteran of Zona Libre adventures, the trusted agent of the defunct Confederacy in smuggling cotton out via Bagdad and Matamoras during the Civil War.

A jolly hypocrite, a free liver; his splendid eyrie near Monterey was visited by the priests of Mexico, now expelled from their livings. It was the rallying place of revolutionist, bandit, and smuggler.

A dinner, "tertulia," or "fandango" always awaited
the welcome guests. Horses, guides, guards, and outfit
were there available, where a thousand "peons" toiled
with his flocks, herds, and tropic fields.

Don Patricio's children reflected his pride and the
faded beauties of their Mexican mother, Doña Anita,
whose dowry was the splendid hacienda.

In close conference with the Mexican-Irishman sat
a tall, military-looking man, whose foreign air was not
all hidden by the semi-frontier garb he wore. Olaf
Nordenskiold was a Dane. His eagle eye and beak-like
nose gave him the air of the "rapacidae." For years
he had been the leading lawyer in Western Texas.
Thanks to a fatal duel at Gibraltar, he left the Danish
navy without the king's permission. Gaining shelter at
New Orleans, he became an intimate of Chisholm, and
attained prominence in New Orleans circles by studying law and his marriage with a rich Creole heiress, who
was captivated by the university polish of the bold
foreigner. A fatal political affray before the war sent
the Dane, with fresh blood on his hands, to Western
Texas as a noted refugee. Throughout the war of the
rebellion, the wandering lawyer, now a widower, used
his many-sided skill in directing the Rio Grande blockade running, smuggling in of supplies from Liverpool,
via Bermuda, and cotton exchanges with England.
Chisholm furnished capital, old Si Leavenworth protection and transportation, and Don Patricio Foley
Mexican aid and financial co-operation.

It was easy for the Dane, as Si Leavenworth's
trusted counselor, to carry on, after Lee's surrender, the
money-making work of the old associates.

It was his fertile brain which evolved the neat trick
of dividing a great balance in Fraser, Trenholm &
Co.'s hand lying at Liverpool at the "surrender," several

ship-loads of cotton at Bermuda, and funds and stores in Mexico in Foley's hands between the four associated rebels at the close of the war.

They became residuary legatees of the Confederate States of America! Nordenskiold's share was deducted as counsel fees. After this great windfall, he suggested a continued robbery of the two governments of Mexico and the United States. Far safer it was for Si Leavenworth, Chisholm, and Don Patricio to leave the active guidance of this dangerous traffic to the Dane than to expose their local respectability. Having easily obtained amnesty through Senator Ezra Steele, the Danish go-between was now free to practice his legal arts at the State and National capitals and to cover the deeds of the three, now protected in secret by Chisholm's "loyal" relative partner, No. 4.

Matchless before the courts in intrigue and influence, the refugee lawyer, in his favorite haunt of "Joe Garcia's saloon," at Corpus Christi, safely handled those relations with bravos, cattle thieves, "regulators," desperados, and other agents of the upper Rio Grande thieves, which would have brought any other man before "Judge Lynch."

Co-operating with smooth Don Patricio, the Dane's rancho in the interior and bachelor home on the blue Gulf sheltered the rich fugitives of Mexican anarchy.

Strangest of all, even in his cups, in long nightly battles for fortune behind the painted cards, and in wild dissipation, Nordenskiold's professional faith was kept inviolate, and his stern self-repression safely guarded the dark secrets of a thousand swindles and a hundred desperate crimes.

Purveying to the vices of others, he calmly enjoyed his intellectual superiority and watched his puppets move on to fortune, ruin, or death, without a sigh or a single regret.

At the lower end of the table, Beriah Mott, the local money agent of Chisholm at the mouth of the Rio Grande, a bluff, resolute ex-rebel, smoked as he gazed on Bill Rains, a raffish-looking Deputy Collector of Customs, who was the agent of two of the great merchants of Brownsville, Texas, and Matamoras, Mexico, who conducted the foreign business and correspondence of the mystic company.

While the syndicate worked noiselessly, John Park and Jerry Mulvain (Bill Rains' partners) visited Havana, New Orleans, Europe, or the City of Mexico, in the open operations of an extensive trade, apparently honest.

" We've nearly all the professions except divinity represented here," said jolly Don Patricio as Senator Steele rapped the assemblage to order, and he set away his empty punch glass with a sigh.

In order, the secret agents gave in their reports of the private operations of the year.

Every eye kindled as the record of the different departments cheered the devotees of the modern Golden Calf.

Don Patricio Foley, with a grin, handed out the invoice returns of a shipment of arms and munitions smuggled into Mexico to aid an aspiring secret revolutionary general. Checking off from a list, he tossed to Chisholm a bundle of accepted drafts on American bankers.

" That's a good job, gentlemen!" he chuckled. " To swindle Uncle Sam out of the transportation to New Laredo from New Orleans, and the Mexican general government out of these funds to pay for them. General Rocha had 'custom-house certificates' issued and his friend Ceballos cashed them in clean silver dollars from the general funds. I'll take a receipt on account for these. Mr. Beriah Mott received the silver through his agent at Laredo."

"Yes," broke in Mott, "and my Laredo man got free transportation and a guard of soldiers to San Antonio for the silver. He gets a pass on our steamers and his commission you will see in my accounts."

"Very good," beamed Steele. "Now, Mr. Nordenskiold, what have you to offer ?"

"I have the accounts here of all the shipments of the year of cigars, cognac, silks, and velvets, as well as ordered goods coming over by Bagdad and the Zona Libre. Here are Park and Mulvain's returns. Mr. Rains has their final account, and I have deposited our balance with Mr. Chisholm and have his certificates of deposit.

"All these goods have been hauled to the railroad or their shipping point in army transportation going back empty, for which Si Leavenworth arranged, on the sly, with the government freight agents.

"Here is a return of the Mexican stock which was run over to my ranch and to San Miguel, and a receipt from Leavenworth of its value. I will give you mine now. It has been a great year for stock and we have had no serious trouble in the courts."

In the general buzz of congratulation, with twinkling eyes, the chairman addressed Chisholm:

"Here are my reports of New Orleans operations," quietly remarked Chisholm. "We have handled several shipping ventures, half a dozen 'bonded cargoes' out, all successful. The receipts and insurances are all tallied up," said he, handing Steele a statement. "I have paid the New Orleans custom house the usual commissions. I have here the account of expenses at Havana, Tam-

pico, and Key West. Mr. Rains has paid the amounts
due our agents on the Gulf, and 'squared' the Special
Treasury Agent on his annual visit!"

In an hour the whole field, from Hamburg, Havre,
and Liverpool, to Key West, the Spanish main, and
Mexico, and the Gulf and New Orleans operations, was
covered.

Rains and Mott followed Chisholm's rapid and
accurate calculations of individual balances.

The hawk-eyed Dane, with the senator, audited and
approved, while Don Patricio nodded affably at the
conclusion of the labors.

While Chisholm prepared a series of drafts and
checks, the latter-day bandits sipped their wine, and
over their cups enjoyed their smuggled Cabañas.

"I have dated all these drafts and checks variously,
and used my New Orleans forms. We have had
time," said the banker, "to figure this all up at Baltimore. If there is any discrepancy, you can give each
other currency or your own checks."

Mott received and receipted for the funds of the
absent Park and Mulvain. The silent lawyer carefully placed the moneys of the King of the Border in
his pocket-book, ready to meet Si Leavenworth's drafts,
and Chisholm reserved the secret dividend of the
unnamed "No. 4."

"If we are all satisfied, let us proceed to consider the
projected work of next year," remarked the "carpet-
bag" senator, as he folded his own drafts carefully and
placed them in a pocket-book. His smile changed to a
grave frown as he caught the glittering eye of Maxan,
fixed upon this manœuvre. While the others rejoiced
in a dividend of one hundred thousand dollars for each
principal share in the confederation of secret thieves,
Steele noted Nordenskiold and Chisholm in grave conference.

His own position suddenly was made clear to him. "I have played the fool as regards old Mark Manson. Here are Chisholm and Nordenskiold, each backed by *No. 4,* and Si Leavenworth. They are safe. I have to divide my private earnings here with Maxan. I would have been stronger if I had let old Manson in at the first!

"Sooner or later, all the reconstruction officials will be dropped. I must finally lose place and power. I have only Maxan behind me. He is safe in his Mexican hacienda fortress. I must now divide this money with him. With the railroad franchise in the hands of Leavenworth and Mark Manson, I am a mere incumbrance. But if Grant is re-elected I have a new lease of power. I will then be useful." His brow lightened up.

"I will make Maxan sweep this young Manson from my path. If they should kill each other over the girl, so much the better! If Maxan puts Jack Manson out of the way, I will help on his marriage with the heiress, and Maxan can handle Texas, while I cling close to old Mark here. Yes! I will get double work out of Ramon—young human tiger as he is—he already thirsts for Manson's blood!"

These mental reflections were cut short by Chisholm, who addressed the Chairman:

"Gentlemen, I must hasten back to New Orleans. We are on the eve of election. Tumults, riots, and bloodshed are feared below. It is useless for us to risk any daring new operations till we know who will name the Federal officers around the Gulf and on the Rio Grande, for the next four years. We are likely to have two governors, two legislatures, and a general conflict. I suppose the d——d Yankee bayonets will decide it, for I fear that General Grant will be the next President."

" Now," said the banker fiercely, " let us be watchful.
I will guarantee to handle the whole New Orleans
situation.   All the official people down there are easily
approachable," he sneered.   " I move that Senator Steele
directs the policy here through No. 4 and Mott.   You,
Mr. Nordenskiold, can handle the Gulf business, and
in a month we can prepare for our spring operations
from the West Indies and on the Rio Grande.

" You need no advice but old man Leavenworth's, and
you have always your cipher and telegraph code to
work with.

" I suggest that we leave all European connections
with Don Patricio.   I will telegraph him of Grant's
election at once."

" That's right! " cheerfully cried Don Patricio.   " I
will see Park and Mulvain as I go down to Monterey.
They can notify their agents in Europe of our wishes."

" Gentlemen," said the chairman, " If there is no
different opinion this will be our course then."

There was a murmur of approval.

" I will go down with you, Don Patricio," spoke
Maxan, who had so far held his peace.   " We can see
Collector Rains at Brownsville.   He can have the
troops scattered chasing raiders and Indians, and you,
Bill," the Creole continued, " can post your Inspectors
who are not in with us, at out-of-the-way points, so as
to leave us safe crossing-places for our goods, silver, and
stock."

" One word," broke in Beriah Mott, as he noted
symptoms of a breaking up of the conclave.

" We should separate at once.   Some fool of a newspaper reporter might chase us down on account of a
supposed political ' deal.'   Before we meet again I
presume this railroad job will be well under way.   I
do not like young Jack Manson coming up to the front

in that. Northern men are not exactly popular yet
with us," growled Beriah Mott, " and there are men
on the border jealous of that neat job of yours, Nordenskiold," he concluded, turning to the lawyer.

" We must let him run things until his uncle has
floated our bonds and we get the iron and rolling-
stock, as well as the construction funds in specie down
there. I will see that it never goes out of the country,"
Mott was answered, and the circle nodded approval.
"And if he meddles, Caramba! I will see that *he* never
goes out of the country," snarled Ramon Maxan, as his
black eyes flashed ominously.

There was a general glance of surprise at the speaker,
but the coterie dropped the subject as they served themselves at the sideboard, and a general leave-taking
began.

"Ramon will fix the Gringo," chuckled the Danish
duelist, who was not averse to seeing any local influence,
nearer than his own, cut off from the wary King of the
Frontier.

Daylight, streaming through the silken curtains
shading Millie Smiley's beauty sleep, lit up the different
paths of the conspirators.

Chisholm and Don Patricio journeyed toward New
York, in decorous moneyed gravity; the others were
speeding along to their now ready pleasures.

On the ground, awaiting the official news from the
White House, Ezra Steele and Ramon Maxan finished
a night of quiet inner plotting.

Once safe in his rooms, Ezra Steele threw off his
adroitness. He was jovial and happy as Maxan joined
him. The statesman had shown himself a few
moments in Milly Smiley's box, to prevent suspicion
and to whisper to her:

" You can send home that bracelet from Galt's,

Milly. It's all right. I will bring you the currency to-morrow!"

A wave of her fan, as the music of the orchestra rose and swelled, and a lightning flash of her incomparable eyes rewarded him.

This little episode was unnoticed by the dozens of paired-off actors in other schemes of projected villainy centering in the defrauded National Treasury.

But the tiger of Tamaulipas was pacing Steele's rooms as the senator entered. He had drunk a new fire stronger than the cordials, whose fiery drops fed his rage. The light of a deadly jealousy flamed in his eyes.

Where they were seated, as Steele puffed his cigar, curiously watching Maxan, the strains of Katie Leavenworth's voice floated in at the open window.

"She is singing to that Yankee fool," snarled Maxan. "I saw them. While I have been with you to-night, he has lingered with her. Sèa por Dios! I will do the job myself! And that ass of a brother—let him once cross the Rio Bravo, he shall remember this night!"

"Now, Ramon! Be half sensible," said Steele calmly. "Take this easily. I wish you to follow my advice. I will give you your money on *one* condition!

"You must go down immediately to New Orleans. Stay around there with Chisholm till this family party arrives in two weeks. I will telegraph you. Control yourself. Be friendly with young Leavenworth and watch both him and Chisholm. I want to know their every movement. Get your state-rooms on the Rio Grande steamer before these people do. Then you had better go on to your place, and stop at San Miguel as you go homeward. I will send you some letters for the old man.

"You can make your 'arrangements' (he shuddered slightly) as you go from San Miguel to your place, and don't act till you are apparently at home, far beyond the Rio Grande.

"After Jack Manson leaves San Miguel, you can strike him down wherever you can. You tell me that this Joaquin is trusty." Steele paused.

"To the death," Maxan answered, pausing in his panther-like strides.

"Then he can waylay him, or deliver him into your hands. Follow my advice. Manson will not suspect you. Keep friendly with the two Leavenworths, and when this meddler is out of your way, you can enjoy the inheritance he schemes for now, and be the King of the Zona Libre. But have no trouble with him till he leaves the Rancho for the border."

"You *are* right, *mi amigo*," said Ramon, dropping in a chair. "When shall I go?"

"Take a day or so to settle your affairs, and be at the St. Charles before Chisholm arrives. Now, let us both look over these money matters."

After Steele had drifted into the land of dreams, Ramon Maxan walked the avenue, watching the lights in the drawing-room where a happy circle jested, ignorant of the espionage of the Creole assassin.

"Steele is right, after all," the prowler concluded, as he turned toward the Club. "I will announce my departure to the men at the Club. I must say good-bye to Milly, and Panchita must be not forgotten.

"She, poor devil, a few bits of finery will content her, but the 'Empress'! Can I trust her to watch this old fox and play fair? I suppose we shall have a scene!" the complacent Lothario mused as he entered the club-house.

It was excellent judgment in Ezra Steele to restrict

his visits for a time at the home of Milly Smiley. " I
have a national position. I must not be too openly
identified there. And this young fire-eater can make
his farewells undisturbed. When he is safe over the
Rio Grande, I can knit up a new friendship with Manson. In the mean time I will do a little party scheming
at the White House and rivet my claims for Southern
patronage tighter until the election is safe."

It was therefore in undisturbed tête-à-tête that the
Creole lingered near the siren who clung to him!

Mildred Smiley gazed out on the theatre of her
victorious intrigues, tired of politics, and of the unending
daily scheming of her life. Her Southern nature was
piqued into a real exaltation by the graceful and impassioned Creole.

" You really leave to-night ? " the " Empress " whispered as the shaded lights fell on her resplendent beauty,
after an hour of serious conference.

" I *must* go, mi querida," answered Ramon. " I am
waited for at the City of Mexico and New Orleans.
Now, let me play this little game out on the Rio Grande.
I will be yours as I have sworn, and you shall reign
over my heart far beyond the sea."

In spite of the wrecks of fairest hopes strewing her
past, the woman half believed him, as her head rested
on his breast and his murmurs allayed her first sus-
picions.

When Ramon Maxan unwillingly departed, his last
act was to give the woman whose aid was so essential to
his future relations with the senator, a cipher address in
an envelope.

"Keep this for yourself alone. Write by the Mexican mail as directed there. The code we have used is
unknown to the others, for I have copies of all theirs
and this goes by cable to Vera Cruz."

Milly smiled through her tears as he handed the papers to her, and, drawing a little box from his pocket, placed a magnificent ring upon her slender finger.

"There's hardly room for any more, *alma mia*," he laughed, as he caught her in his arms, "but you will think of me when you see this. Wear it always."

Her heart still thrilling with her lover's last embrace, Mildred Smiley stood with outstretched arms unavailingly reached toward him, for the loud clang of the door told of his departure.

As she turned, an object on the floor attracted her attention. As she stooped and examined it, standing under the golden chandelier, an awful convulsion of passion shook her breast.

Mutely gazing at the picture she held, Mildred Smiley, for the first time in her life, saw a fairer face than her own! A woman whose youth and tenderly passionate loveliness beamed in every line of the exquisite miniature. On its reverse the words were engraven, "Panchita to Ramon."

"Liar! and false, even with my kisses on his lips!" she cried, as she threw herself on a divan in an agony of heartbreak.

In a half-hour she raised her weary head, as the ticking of the clock, in metallic monotone, was interrupted by the gong announcing a visitor.

"If I can not live for love, I will live for a *woman's revenge*," she cried. "I will balk these plans now dearer to him than life. Steele shall be my very slave, my *blind* slave, and when my chains are riveted on him forever, I will ride over this lying traitor, grovelling in the dust. I will wear his ring till I am avenged, and *then* he shall surely know who struck the fatal blow,' she cried, twisting the visitor's card in her nervous hands.

"At home," she nodded to the butler. "I will be Mrs. Senator Steele in six months!" was her resolve as she swept toward the door, fairly startling the late visitor with the unearthly beauty of her passion-lighted face. "This ring shall blaze on my hand as a daily monitor," she cried, as she slipped it on her slender finger.

The chimes of midnight rang out before Ezra Steele unwillingly paced the silent streets to his rooms in the great hotel.

"Milly *is* a wonderful woman; fit to be a queen," he mused; and he was startled as his lips dropped the murmur, "Why not?" Cynic, adventurer, and voluptuary, he had not dared yet, in his shallow self-conceit, to admit Mildred Smiley's mental superiority; but on this fated night, radiant, dazzling, every nerve centre thrilled with all a scorned woman's pride and ambition for revenge, she stood revealed to him, a being with a woman's heart, a man's courage, and all the sensuous beauty of an awakened Galatea!

Swept off his feet by her unusual brilliancy, Steele wandered to his rest, glad to learn, by a brief note, of Maxan's departure.

"I want him well out of the way if—if—I marry her," thought the statesman. "Death may fold both these young fools in his shadowy wings, and I—"

He was asleep before he finished his pleasing ruminations as to the "survival of the fittest"!

Under the same roof, the calm, pure sleep of innocence blessed the girl who thought, each night, as she gazed on her glowing beauty in the mirror, "Am I right to give Jack my heart friendship, to think so much of him?" The fair head rested happily to-night on the maiden's snowy pillow, for rosy Dan Cupid had deceitfully whispered: "For Jimmy's sake," as her eyelids drooped like falling rose leaves.

Mrs. Winifred Marshall sat gazing at the long line of lights along Pennsylvania Avenue, after her three lovely charges were dismissed for the night. The widowed mother was conscious of a vague uneasiness, a haunting apprehension.

"No one is left to advise me,—none to guide or guard," she sighed, as she thought of the useless harvest of her husband's sword and the weary years of her lonely widowhood.

"That handsome Mexican is gone at last," she gratefully commented. "How his eyes blazed as he said 'adieu' to Katie to-night! If I can help it, he shall not be a very welcome visitor at San Miguel Rancho. I must write to Mrs. Leavenworth and warn her."

"This Maxan may have business with Katie's father, who must be friendly to all powerful borderers. But with young James, so fiery, and Mr. Manson, there might be trouble. These young hotheads are so wild in youth." The still fair woman gazed helplessly around her quiet room and thought of her own spirited brother Fairfax, killed in a romantic duel before his college laurels were withered.

"The election will be over in a week. I shall be glad to see the dear girls on their way home. Surely with a brother and young Manson there can be no mishap."

The very trees around Arundel House seemed to be calling her home. The gentle Virginian was out of her element amid the unsubstantial splendors of an American hotel. Even as she sat, the clash of wine glasses and the shouts of excited politicians rose in chorus from the café below.

"I am happy to take Gertrude home again," the mother concluded, as she finished her review of the social situation. "I shall not have her long," she

thought, with a smile, for gallant, impetuous Jimmy
Leavenworth was no laggard lover. And no Marshall
heiress ever lingered on the ancestral tree. They were
all belles by inheritance!

"It is well," was her last thought. "I like Mrs.
Smiley; and yet—and yet there's nothing like our own
Virginia people after all."

Jack Manson's heart. was happy as he sped away the
next evening to New York to receive his final instructions from Mark Manson, as the overwhelming tide of
popular favor ensured General Grant's re-election.

Senator Ezra Steele, returning from the White House
in great good humor, cheered the young man on his
way. Federal prominence and power were now assured
him, and the very name "Rio Grande" seemed to roll
off his tongue in golden accents. He was radiant as
he sped away to a tête-à-tête dinner with the "Empress."

At this very moment the pretty free lance sat in her
boudoir casting up the chances. Steele had showed
her all his confidential telegrams and data as to the great
political struggle.

"It is done," she cried, as she noted the hour for her
robing to meet the senator. "He will surely be in power
four years more. He has wealth. I will risk it! And
now, on to victory! I will keep him to his purpose and
move him up to a formal declaration before it is too
late. And yet, I am not fading. I might "—she saw
her loveliness reflected in the glass. The thought of a
sweet revenge decided all.

"It is done. Mrs. Senator Steele!" she laughed and
nodded to her smiling self as she mounted the staircase
that night!

While the senator was basking in the smiles of the
"Empress" in the dying gleams of evening, Mrs.
Marshall sat in her private rooms with frightened
Katie, the Texan Rose, as a confidant.

"I do not know what to do, dear Auntie," cried the young beauty. "Read this letter! I fear to answer it. I have not told Alice, and I am afraid to let Brother Jimmy even know of its existence."

It was a passionate, burning letter from Ramon Maxan, the formulation of his jealous passion. In terms glowing with tropic fervor, he begged for even a word, one word in answer. His address was given as the "Crescent Club," New Orleans.

I may not go to Mexico till you arrive at New Orleans. I shall pay my respects in person and I beg only for one little word. If I do not see you, I will ride from Hacienda Maxan to your San Miguel.

"Leave the letter with me, my child," the Virginia lady said. "I will return it. I shall see that you do not receive any visits from this ardent stranger at New Orleans. You must decline to receive him after such a rash missive. Once at home, you will be safe, for I will let your mother know all."

There was a grateful relief shining in the maiden's eyes. "I am so glad. I am really afraid of him. He is so passionate. So reckless of everyone else. Not like Jack."

Katie rose with crimsoned cheeks, as she found a sudden occupation at the mirror. She had noted Mrs. Marshall's astonished glances. There was an awkward silence.

"Do you then find 'Mr. Jack' so agreeable?" brightly queried the widow.

"I meant—I meant, he is more reserved; yes, that is what I wish to say," smiled Katie.

"Ah! I see, quite reserved; yes, he seems to be so," dryly remarked Mrs. Marshall. "It is time to dress for dinner, my child."

Katie fled away like a bird, and all unconscious that she only carried half her secret in a fluttering woman heart now.

"It is well! It is right," smiled the good patrician dame, who remembered certain little plans lately made "For Brother Jimmy's sake."

While the rejoicings over the unparalleled majorities returning General Ulysses S. Grant to the White House were convulsing the national capital, the bustle of departure enlivened the friends of a brief life holiday.

Mrs. Marshall pleaded fatigue as the reason of returning early from Madame Mildred Smiley's last ceremonial dinner to the circle now breaking up.

"Perfectly good style, and a delightful hostess, and yet, I have not found out what good Gulf family this lady is related to; I would really like to know!" the departing Virginian dame murmured as she sought the hotel, for she had forgotten to return Ramon Maxan's impulsive letter.

"I must mail it to-night, so it will reach New Orleans at least a day before they arrive," was Mrs. Marshall's resolve.

As the carriage rolled away, the "Empress," gazing after her departing guests, thought bitterly: "She is only a quiet home woman, and yet all my splendor has not imposed on her. She doubts my position; she suspects me. I will make sure. Mrs. Senator Steele needs no past history!"

Turning to Jack Manson, whose devotion to the sweet girl he now madly adored was clearly evident to all, Mildred Smiley murmured:

I must see you alone before you leave to-morrow. It is vital to you; it concerns your very existence."

"To me, madam, I can not understand," whispered Jack, as with a happy inspiration he led the hostess into the spacious picture gallery.

Passing a mirror, wherein was reflected Katie Leavenworth, in all her virginal charms, the "Empress" pressed his arm.

Motioning with her fan, she murmured "You love her madly. She is pursued by a desperate suitor. Ah! you can not deny your love? Come and breakfast with me alone to-morrow. I will put you on your guard."

Manson bowed his handsome head in assent, for his blood leapt to his heart. Every nerve and fibre was thrilling. He whispered:

"Maxan?" The "Empress" bowed as she turned. "I will come," he whispered, for his blood was boiling. No smile shone on the sculptured face of the "Empress," but the first delightful throb of anticipated revenge thrilled her aching woman heart.

While the hours passed gaily at Mildred Smiley's fête, Mrs. Marshall achieved a triumph of epistolary, polite coldness.

Mrs. Marshall begs leave to return a letter received by a young lady, now in her charge, and to suggest to *Mr. Ramon Maxan* the propriety of ceasing such correspondence, and refraining from visiting the person addressed, until he is admitted to the acquaintance of her parents.

"I think that will be effective, especially in view of this letter." The relieved duenna read once more the friendly letter of Mrs. Leavenworth announcing that Colonel Thomas Bayard of the Nueces Valley would meet the party at New Orleans and take charge of the transportation arrangements, as he had also business with her son. "The Colonel is a business associate of my husband, and one of the bravest and best of our soldiers, for he led a Texan regiment at Corinth and Vicksburg." Such were the reassuring words.

"I can *now* see them go in perfect tranquillity,"

thought the widowed lady, as the three beauties came laughing up the stair. " There will be a man of experience to watch over Katie. Alice," said Mrs. Marshall, as she laid the letter away, "what do you know of Colonel Thomas Bayard?"

"He is the best and bravest of men, and a trusted friend of my father's," replied St. Cecilia Alice, with a moss-rose glow on her placid cheek.

"Yes; and he swam the Nueces River and braved death not to miss saying 'good-bye' to you, when we left San Miguel," cried Katie, gathering her drapery and flitting away, leaving Alice in helpless confusion.

"Ah, yes! He must have *very* important business in New Orleans now," sighed the widow, as she dispatched Maxan's letter. "I think I see what it is!"

CHAPTER VI.

ON HIS GUARD—THE CRESCENT CITY—TOM BAYARD SEES A FORGOTTEN FACE—AN AWKWARD RENCONTRE—RAMON MAXAN'S OATH.

THERE was an intense anxiety in Jack Manson's eyes when he offered his beautiful hostess his arm on leaving her table next day. Mildred Smiley, during the hour, had sounded every corner of the young engineer's heart. "No place for me in his honest bosom. I am destined for a higher life, a loftier station, even if my wedding diamonds are only sparkling tears! I must be 'sisterly' and aid him in his wooing. Steele, the Mansons and the Leavenworths must work together, and I will know, *I must know*, when I am a senator's wife, who the mysterious No. 4 is."

She smiled as Jack led her into the little Turkish room. "After I marry Steele I only have to follow up his intimacies and the riddle will solve itself. Can the unknown be a cabinet officer?"

Even the bold adventuress dared not think of all the possibilities of a discovery so dangerous as a State secret!

"Now," said the "Empress," suddenly, in an alert, business-like tone, "I will not detain you. I know that you must leave to-night. I can easily imagine you have many commissions." She smiled archly.

"I have brought you here alone to tell you that Ramon Maxan is your mortal foe. He menaces your lovely Katie with his wild, reckless Creole passion. That man will stop at nothing. He has a plan to worm himself into the confidence of the circle at San Miguel. His schemes bode no good to young Leavenworth and they are also opposed to the interests of your Uncle Mark.

"Be warned by me! Beware of him! He is as sly as the jaguar of the wild Mexican mountains. What you would call bloody crime, he merely sneers at as intrigue."

"I am not likely to be brought in conflict with this half-breed," replied Manson warily.

"Say not so! He is intimate with those high in this great Rio Grande Company, whose roots, trunks, and branches spread farther than you now know," said the woman at his side earnestly. "He is at New Orleans by this time."

"Are *you*, then, so intimate with him? Has he ever crossed your path?" replied Manson.

"He has a hold on one whose interests may soon be my own," Mildred Smiley answered, with a faint blush. "But as to him, I speak of what I *know*. He has not been loth to try and extend that influence through me. The traitor!"

She sprang up and paced the floor, her bosom heaving in disdain.

"I hardly see any direct menace to Miss Leavenworth here, Madam," said Jack coldly. He was averse to opening the golden chalice of his first love to this world-worn society woman.

"Jack," cried the "Empress," seizing his arm. "Are you blind? He has urged me to bring Katie Leavenworth here, to separate you, to aid him to press his suit, as he knew time was precious. He wished to dazzle her young heart with his cosmopolitan graces. He seeks to be the lord of San Miguel Rancho, to be the sole king of the Rio Grande frontier."

"And why?" persisted Manson. "He is young, gay, and rich. He can rove at will over the world. He has a splendid hacienda in the Zona Libre, has he not?"

"True," cried Millie, sinking into a chair, her eyes blazing. "But you are singularly obtuse to-day. It is the future and prospective millions of the Rio Grande Company he aims to control."

"I fail to see how he can do that," sturdily replied Manson. "Steele, my uncle, and Si Leavenworth dominate that. The railroad lands and franchise are in my uncle's name with Leavenworth as associate."

"You are only a boy yet, although a veteran of the plains," answered the "Empress." "Come back to me after you have ridden the Rio Grande a year. You will then know the secret side of the Rio Grande Company's mysteries. If you don't divine them, you are not fit to guard your own life down there."

Manson started as the silver chime of the clock rang out "two." "I thank you. I feel that you have a deeper knowledge of the hidden mystery of the border than I thought. Tell me what I shall do?"

"Listen," said the superb woman, bounding like a velvet-footed tigress to an ebony cabinet, over which a superb ivory crucifix hung, in mockery of its dark secrets.

She turned and held out to him a packet of letters. "I have never yet broken the confidence of one in my power by virtue of these poor charms"—she flashed a triumphant glance at the mirror. "These letters might bring you face to face with Maxan at ten paces. Watch him for your friend Jimmy's sake; for Katie's sake— for your own! I swear he plots evil against you all. Be patient, prudent, bold *at the right time only!* His arm is long; he has spies and agents scattered over the sandy Golgotha of the Rio Grande. You are more than a match for him in manliness. Be as wise and cunning as you will be brave. Now, go! Do not forget my words an instant by day or night. Keep Maxan and young Leavenworth apart."

She turned and replaced the letters. As Manson in astonishment approached her, he saw there were bright tears in her splendid eyes.

"Tell me more," he begged. This strange passionate woman excited him like the wine of Cyprus!

"Not another word! You might guess all!" she said softly, leading him out into the splendid lonely drawing-rooms. "In three months I shall be the wife of another. It is because it is the last time I am free to do so, that I tell you what I do to guard and guide you.

"Now leave me," she cried, her voice failing. Manson faltered, irresolute. In later lonely rides under the stars of the silent deserts of the Rio Bravo, he remembered a royal woman clinging to him, pressing on his lips burning kisses. Her last words were: "Jack, *I* could have loved *you!* Watch over your beloved at New Orleans. God keep you from Ramon Maxan's treachery!"

Before the still bewildered Manson had joined the laughing circle at the Arlington, Mildred Smiley, with

flying fingers, indited a note to Senator Ezra Steele. A
trusty messenger, hastening with it, found the still excited
engineer busied in his adieux with the statesman.

"Will you excuse me a moment?" the senator
begged. Manson bowed, but with quick eye noted the
now familiar hand of Mrs. Mildred Smiley.

"Brief and pointed," mused Manson, as the senator
scrawled a line, hastily sealing it and dispatching the
messenger.

"Some new leaf of an intrigue which seems to reach,
octopus-like, from the Rio Grande to the White
House," thought Jack.

He was right. The words of Milly Smiley were:

Come to me at once! Must see you before they go!

"My dear Manson," said the senator, "I have received
an important summons. I will meet you at the train
and go on a few miles with you. I may be delayed,
and I am to have a few words also with the President.
Some important delegations of Southern republicans
are to be presented. There is strife and trouble at New
Orleans. We can, however, have a few words in
comfort to-night."

The responsibilities of Manson were great in the
impending departure, for, with all a watchful lover's
care, the young Texan cavalier, after tender leave-
takings, was convoying Mrs. Marshall and Miss
Gertrude to Alexandria.

If tears shone in Gertie Marshall's eyes, they were
happy ones, for Alice and Katie easily divined the
shining bow of promise over the happy lovers' heads!

Crafty Ezra Steele was in his flood-tide of happiness as he joined the departing pilgrims to Texas.
Grateful pride beamed in his eyes, and his heart

was overflowing with happiness. The President had entrusted to him a secret political mission to the Gulf States. This very fact would enable him to receive, with due public honor, the merited testimonial of his re-election as Senator of the United States for six years. His own State could not afford to reject the chosen representative of a party flushed with an unexampled victory. In the happy excitement of the moment, he had imparted the news to the woman whose fascinations of the last days had awakened his very inmost being.

Quick to decide, having " burned her ships," Mildred Smiley had promised to become his wife the moment that his new credentials were signed. For in her ear he had whispered, "Another stroke of luck. My friend, No. 4, is safe. He will be kept in the new cabinet!" The blood surged back into her heart with a gasp. " Was the secret friend already so near the counsels of government? This is safety! I will know all when I am his wife! " Dissembling her triumph, the " Empress" begged Senator Steele to keep Maxan employed on the Mexican side of the Rio Bravo.

"You are right; I will do so," replied the statesman, proud of her quick wit. He felt that he had a " helpmate" now!

As he seated himself in a private smoking compartment with Manson, when the train drew out, Steele rejoiced that he had telegraphed to Maxan at the Crescent Club, New Orleans.

Party leave to-night for Texas. Avoid them. Will explain. Meet me in Mobile one week from to-day. Special duty for you.

" He will be useful there. I will go down in a day or so and attend to my election. Then I can keep an eye on this hothead, for I must see Chisholm at New

Orleans about the rival legislatures. By that time they
will have sailed. I must be decidedly friendly with
Maxan until my new senatorial credentials are signed.
He could use a powerful weapon in blackmail and
scandal against me. Dare I warn Manson against him?
Not till I am safely re-elected must I join my fortunes
with Mark Manson and Si Leavenworth."

The young engineer smoked thoughtfully, and
keenly watched Steele. "He is the coming bridegroom," so Jack decided, after the note and its quick
response by Steele. He had an added mystery weigh-
ing on his tired brain, for grave Mrs. Marshall had
seized a propitious moment and begged him to specially
watch over Katie at New Orleans. Milly Smiley's
renewed warning startled him.

"Hover near Katie while you are in New Orleans,"
wrote Mrs. Leavenworth. "I know Alice will have
Colonel Bayard as an escort, but Jimmy may be away,
and I hope you will watch over Katie." Manson's teeth
were set as he thought of the gentle Virginian's warning.
He could not know that the widowed lady refrained, in
womanly delicacy, from disclosing to him (an anxious
lover) the secret of Maxan's impulsive, burning words
of proposal.

With these ominous signs of future trouble, Manson
was not overpatient when the senator, having pompously
hinted of his re-election and "public business" in the
South, ventured to gravely refer to the necessity of
caution in meeting the fiery Mexican, and his future
·value to the "Company's" interests.

"Remember, you are going into a strange land and
among a strange people. This man is able, young, and
fearless. I hope you and Leavenworth will get along
well with him."

Here was a third warning in one day! Jack Manson's mind went back to past days when he had guarded his scalp and defended his life, rifle in hand, gazing steadfastly at the yelling Cheyenne "dog-soldiers" and the wild, shrieking, long-haired Sioux.

"Senator," said Manson, with cold concentrated bit-terness. "I have had some little experience. Even with Ramon Maxan's manifold powers of strategy and per-sonal powers, I shall try and treat him civilly. Should his peculiar unreliability (which I think some seem to fear) and his supposed easy mastery of all comers throw him across my path, I shall try to make him feel that two can play at any game he practices! As for Mr. James Leavenworth, I am not intimate enough to coach him in his conduct. I think the Mexican War taught us the Texans could hold their own with their wily neighbors. Leavenworth, I am told, is a past master of the prairie arts, and the best rider and shot in Western Texas. God knows, these fellows are bold enough! We had to blow them from the mouths of the guns at Battery Robinett. There at Corinth, the Colonel and the Chaplain of the Texan assaulting regiment were killed, side by side, crawling into the flaming embrasures. I will back Leavenworth with fair play against two Maxans," concluded Manson, his good humor returning as he heard Katie's silvery laugh in the near drawing-room compartment.

" Fair play is just the idea. Be patient, prudent, and remember you have much to learn in your new life," oracularly remarked Steele, as the whistle warned him of the good-bye to the ladies.

" I don't doubt it, Senator. I will try and keep my eyes open. Thanks for all your kindness and hos-pitality," said Jack, as they joined the ladies.

In the uneasy rest of a rattling journey over a rough railway toward the Tennessee hills, as they sped on,

Manson's dreams were haunted by all these vague intimations, and more than once the brilliant eyes of Ramon Maxan disturbed the plainsman's dreams.

"An Indian eye; watch it," was Jack's first thought, as he woke in the clear frosty air at Knoxville.

The Tennessee mountains towered above them as Jack, with a growing sense of proprietorship, led the rosy young Aurora, Katie Leavenworth, from the car.

These were happy hours, not a cloud flecking that blue of the present happiness. Her sweet welcome was shyly given—*not* all and all "for Jimmy's sake."

Two of the happiest days of Jack Manson's eventful life drew to a close when the train drew into the Jackson Depot at New Orleans. Brief period of unalloyed bliss! There was no shadow on the fair girl's brow as the glorious mountains of Tennessee flashed by. Her heart beat high as the dense pine woods, fragrant of life-giving balsam, were reached in wild Mississippi. Dark and lonely, these almost primeval forests indicated the home of a warrior people. Every turn of the wheel brought her nearer home!

Here and there, on knoll and ridge, an ugly star fort told of the yet unsettled chaos of the Civil War. Block-houses frowned from hills beetling above them, and long lines of crumbling earthworks brought back that war whose cannons still seemed to echo discord in the scowling, sullen, defeated people.

Crowds of timid negroes gazed blankly at the voyagers, avoiding the harsh, bearded masters of their race, who lounged around the stations, eying all south-bound travellers truculently. The sting of Grant's triumphal re-election embittered these loiterers, whose glances were wicked as they noted here and there a Federal uniform. For no banners here wafted on high the Stars and Bars a generation had died for. A military occupation still held down the yet disorganized people.

The air was redolent of strife at New Orleans, where two would-be governors, two legislatures, and rival city officials and police, struggled for control of the once peerless Crescent City and the fair State of Louisiana.

Jack Manson, in a delicious day-dream, lingered by Katie Leavenworth's side in these happy hours, while Brother Jimmy seriously communed with St. Cecilia Alice, or smoked his cigar, finding congenial friends among the swarthy Southrons of his natural liking. In the unrestricted intercourse of travel, Manson learned many quaint stories of the Rio Grande country from his lovely companion. The land of Austin, Houston, Crockett, and Travis, was a fascinating subject to the Northern engineer.

He knew that Texas had really been enriched and peopled by the war. The wave of Southern veterans, turning away from old homes desolated by war to the vast prairies of a vague empire, was now moving the best blood of the Gulf States away from the " negro belt." Month by month, the rapidly extending railways were bringing to its frontiers new citizens of Texas. From the North, South, and West, as well as the North-west, following the railway wheel, a peaceful army was invading the great empire, bearing palms of peace instead of bayonets!

But from the lips of the winsome girl, Jack Manson learned stories of the wild border life; old tales of the Alamo, of Gonzales, of the glorious San Jacinto, were her cradle memories! In her eager, passionate way, the bright Texan maid painted the vastness of the green prairie-sea, the silent grandeur of the star-lit deserts, the beauty of the wooded openings of the fertile Nueces, and romantic border legends of all the wild races of the Rio Bravo.

Fresh in her youthful enthusiasm, ardent and spirited,

Katie called up word-pictures which fascinated Manson. The bold, generous, bronzed riders of the unpeopled wastes, swarthy Comanche, revengeful Seminole, black-hearted Kickapoo, and all the banditti of the border were pictured in her own glowing words.

"You shall see the brightest skies on earth, and breathe the prairie air in crystalline purity. At night the great stars flash down from clear, blue skies, and the breeze from the Monterey mountains sweeps over the wooded islands of the Rio Grande. They tell me of the old days of Cortez and Montezuma, of the Spanish chase for new empires, of the wanderings of the first Spanish cavalier from the Mississippi. I love the great, silent land! I am proud of my native State."

"You *are* loyal to your Southern home," cried Manson, his eyes resting on the impassioned face of the young beauty.

"Wait till you see it! There is a picturesque life in our freedom, our unpeopled plains! Our riders are the boldest on earth—the last of the wild horsemen!"

So, growing closer every hour in spirit to the woman by his side, Jack sighed as the journey ended. His brow clouded as he thought of the one haunting shadow on his path, Ramon Maxan.

"He shall not disturb her peace of mind while I can watch over her," the lover soliloquized.

In his well-meant enthusiasm, Jack forgot that he was not altogether unprejudiced in his self-imposed burden of watchfulness. For, as yet, even her sweet eyes had not, in their frank glances, yielded to him the right to be her bounden knight.

It was true! Katie Leavenworth's dauntless heart was to be won only by a victor champion. With all her delicacy in mind, the heritage of a gentle and refined mother, the Texan heiress had the high-souled bravery and spirit of her fearless father, the hero of a hundred adventures as ranger and frontier king! For far and near, his tenure of life depended often on the ready pistol, his matchless horses, and the courage of the indomitable Anglo-Saxon aided by the border skill gained in thirty years of danger.

Manson's elaborate courtesy in aiding Miss Katie to leave the train was interrupted by her joyous exclamations as she stretched out both hands to a handsome stranger, whose greetings to her brother and sister were frank and hearty.

"Colonel Tom! I am so glad to see you once more." Clasping both of her hands, the stalwart Texan laughed good-humoredly as he said: "Little lady, you are grown out of my knowledge. I have letters to make you happy. Your father and mother send you love, and your horses must know you are coming home. They are dancing pictures!"

"Let me make you friends!" cried the happy Katie, who had noted already, mischievously, Alice Leavenworth's blushes, "Colonel Thomas Bayard, my friend, Mr. Manson. You must be comrades too, for *my* sake," said the audacious beauty. She was regaining her kingdom.

"Right heartily," cheerily said Bayard. "I am glad to know you, Mr. Manson. You have the 'star' recommendations on the Rio Grande when you are Miss Katie's friend."

Jack Manson grasped Bayard's offered hand. The Texan's bronzed face, broad shoulders, and genial brown eyes, his cavalier mustaches, and free stride, proclaimed him a genial plainsman. For a "confederate fire-eater," his ready smile and the pleasant ring of his voice, were singularly winning.

In an hour, a pleasant circle at the St. Charles was ruled by the audacious little Prairie Queen.

While the ladies rested, Colonel Bayard and Manson smoked the evening cigar on the portico of the famed old hostelry. Its huge pillars had sheltered generations of the princely river planters. The dome of the old rotunda below them had re-echoed the voices of the last generation of patrician slave-owners America will ever know.

"We have three or four days to wait here for our steamer. You must allow me to show you the local lions," the colonel politely said. "Our young ladies have their shopping to arrange. There are also many family friends to call on them, and I can take you down the road and you'll meet some nice men at the Crescent Club."

Jack Manson felt drawn to the frank, manly borderer, and they rambled together over the old city. Past the custom house where the national flag drooped over granite portals guarded by troops, down the streets thronged with the vivacious throng, into the old French quarter, with its foreign air and old mansions closed to the modern American, they strolled.

In the soft starlight the deserted avenues seemed peopled with the shades of quaint old Creole characters and the romance of French noble and knightly adventurer. Alas! The glory of the old time was fled forever! In timid self-defense, behind their lattices, the melting, dark eyes of beauty shone no longer. It was the desolation of silence. That shadow has never been lifted which fell on New Orleans when stern Farragut anchored the old "Hartford" off the levee, and trained its guns on a mob only a shade less frantic than the Commune.

With delicate reserve Manson ignored all war topics. Returning to the hotel, the new friends avoided the great rotunda saloon, where an excited mob discussed the "situation."

"Come up to my rooms, Colonel," remarked Manson, who, in secret, desired to know of Maxan's
whereabouts.

"You are right. There's hardly room enough to ,
get shot here with a fair show. All these people are
crazy on politics," answered the Texan.

Threading the grand old drawing-rooms, where the
fairest women of the South once lingered, enchanting their proud suitors by a perfection of graceful,
indolent charms, they learned that the Leavenworths
were already visiting in that mysterious "inner circle"
"which gently but positively contracts at the touch of
'Northener,'" leaving the stranger without its invisible
barrier.

Proud, patient, silent, unforgiving, and unforgetting,
the best blood of the South is linked, with really touching fidelity, to that "Lost Cause" whose flag went
down in battle and in storm.

The "entente cordiale" was already established
between the two men. Bayard frankly told Manson
that he was fully advised of Si Leavenworth's connections, and handed him a brief letter extending the
hospitalities of San Miguel. It finished with stating:

Colonel Bayard has my full confidence, and with my lawyer,
Nordensklold, will be your associate in many affairs. Please do
not fail to go with him and meet my friend, Chisholm.

Discussing a few points of the enterprise, Jack Manson, already watchful (for he felt the change of social
latitude), carefully interjected the name of Ramon
Maxan.

"He's a queer party; has Mexican blood in his
veins. Where did you meet him?" asked the Colonel
with some surprise.

Manson recounted briefly his acquaintance with the
brilliant Creole at Washington.

Bayard smoked reflectively and dropped into soliloquy. "What can he be scheming after up there? Why, he has a lordly rancho and hacienda on the Mexican side."

"So he's intimate with Senator Steele?" he remarked interrogatively, stifling the natural Southern epithet, "d—d carpet-bagger."

"They are inseparable," replied Manson, tentatively. He hoped that Colonel Tom would unbosom himself.

"I have not met him for years," thoughtfully said Bayard; "since I went to the border after the war. Maxan was very active in the days when the Rio Grande was our only safe cotton outlet and we ran in the guns and munitions we could not get elsewhere."

"There's his picture," said Manson, with affected carelessness, for, in the first days of florid civility, Jack had been favored.

"Ah!" said the Colonel, "Quite a cavalier! Yes, that is the man. He is just a little dangerous. I think I would keep an eye on him if he rode past me on the prairie."

Manson was, as yet, ignorant of the code of the road on the wild Rio Grande.

"Hello! You've dropped a picture." Bayard stooped and good-humoredly handed it to Jack with a smile.

He could not avoid seeing the face. As he glanced at it, he turned eagerly to the wondering Manson as he cried:

"By God! Bob Kenyon's runaway wife. Where did *you* get this?" The honest Texan was wildly glaring first at the royal beauty of Mildred Smiley and then at the engineer.

"Tell me your story first, Colonel, then I'll tell you mine," said Manson, as Bayard sank into a chair, his eyes riveted on the surpassingly lovely face with an expression of stern hatred.

As the Texan laid the picture on the table and essayed to speak, a sharp knock interrupted him. At the door stood a sable attendant with four cards on a silver waiter. His ceremonial manner was a relic of the olden days, "befo' de wah!"

Jack Manson silently handed the visiting cards to the tall Texan.

" Speak of the devil—" muttered Bayard. " Here he is. What is Maxan after? "

Jack Manson coolly gathered up all the cards again from the salver. " Was the visit for me? " he questioned, as the negro servitor gazed at this wholesale appropriation.

" De gentleman's down in de drawin'-room, sah. He sen' de cyards an' his compliments to you an' Mass Leavenworth an' de young ladies," replied Niger Africanus, with a flourish, as he gazed longingly at the half-dollar in Jack's hand.

" Say that the whole party is out for the evening. I will see Mr. Leavenworth when he returns."

"Dat's all?" queried the negro, pocketing his douceur.

" That's all," sternly said Jack as the door closed.

" Now, Colonel Bayard, we must act quickly! " cried Manson, springing to the Texan's side.

The mist of years was clouding Tom Bayard's eyes as he threw down the woman's pictured face.

" Poor old Bob ! " he muttered. " What's up Manson? " he eagerly said.

" I must be brief with you. Do I assume correctly that you have a personal interest in a member of Mr. Leavenworth's family? "

For Jack remembered Mrs. Marshall's gentle hint, and fair Katie's laughing raillery. The three warnings as to Maxan came back in full force.

" Please God, Alice Leavenworth will be my wife,

I have loved her for years," simply answered the manly wooer who had braved the swollen Nueces in its sudden fury to gaze on her beloved face.

"We must then protect her sister Katie—you and I," cried Manson. "You, for the sake of gentle Alice, and I owe it to my old comrade, Jimmy."

"What threatens her?" sternly said the sunburnt Texan, his voice as clear as a sentinel's challenge.

"You will see all the more clearly if you first tell me of this woman. She is a link in the chain closing around the girl we must guard till her parents receive her," replied Jack.

"To be brief," said the impatient Texan veteran, the war times coming back to him, "after I was desperately wounded at Vicksburg, I was paroled and taken to Montgomery, Alabama, for exchange. It was a close fight between death and the Yankees for my poor bones. Well," said he, with flashing eyes, "I pulled through after all, and joined my regiment at Atlanta, under the lion-hearted Hood. Dear old Bob Kenyon, a chum of mine, was Major in command, and they gave me a royal welcome back.

"Some ladies of Atlanta, to inspirit our boys, presented the regiment, through me, with a splendid flag. The boys had done honor to the Stars and Bars at the 'salient' in Vicksburg, on May 25th, the year before, for our flag was literally shot to pieces there, and half the regiment lay dead around it. The new flag and the other half went away in the crater fire at Leggett's Hill, when Hood set a bloody seal on his rash courage, and offered up half of his great army, on a mere point of honor, to fight 'outside of Atlanta.'

"There is such a thing as too dauntless intrepidity in a general. On that lovely evening when I received that flag, so soon to be steeped in our best blood, Bob

Kenyon fondly gazed at the wonderful loveliness of the woman we speak of. His girl wife, whose love he had won by his reckless heroism, smiled proudly at him by my side. She was the shining star of a circle of devoted women whose tears fell later for the dead defenders of their token. Human nature was keyed up then to a pitch of intensity equalled only by the French Revolution or the late Commune! Love and laughter, varied with hate and tears, were daily tidal emotions. The quickstep, serenade, and waltz changed to dirge and funeral march without notice. In the midst of joy and woe, smiles and sighs, Major Kenyon's strange honey-moon was an alternation of battle-lulled hours, stolen visits, occasional leaves, and brief camp visits. The wonderful loveliness of Florence Mortimer carried the ardent man's heart by storm. The dazzling beauty had voyaged from Mobile to Atlanta to search for a wounded brother who died later in her arms. It was in such a mood the spirited Southern girl was wooed and won.

"My bad luck was shifted to Kenyon at Peach Tree Creek. He was hard hit and fell into the hands of the Federals. I was blinded with smoke and flame when I led our shot-torn fragment back in mute despair, after three desperate assaults. Tell me Northern men wont fight!" the ex-rebel cried. "That day they were demons, and their yell, 'Remember McPherson,' was the death-knell of our peerless veterans. Our beloved regimental Stars and Bars fluttered to the ground to be grasped by the stranger and conqueror. Never again did it float to the breeze! There was no longer a semblance of the ten full companies I was so proud of. During the siege of Atlanta, I gave Mrs. Kenyon all the money I had or could get. I sought relief in death. We learned from the pickets that Bob Kenyon, as a wounded prisoner, had been taken

North. When Sherman bounded on us like a tiger, Mrs. Kenyon went South, and I heard later, escaped via Mobile, ran the blockade to Bermuda, and reached Europe. I was told after the war that she queened it with Gwin, Mason, Slidell, Erlanger & Co., at the Confederate quasi embassy at Paris. Since then I have never heard of her till to-night." •

"And Major Kenyon?" questioned Jack Manson, eagerly.

"Wandered away, gave himself up to drink, and is a flitting, homeless shadow. I believe he is still yet living. His mind was affected, at times, by the shell wound he received. Poor Bob! The wreck of a gallant soldier! He has lands of great value yet in Texas. Whisky, sorrow, and the desertion of his wife dragged him down!

"Now tell me of her. Does she think him dead?"

"I believe so," Manson said guardedly, "for I think she will soon marry Senator Steele. I believe she was married in Europe to a rich man named Smiley."

Manson recounted the situation of Mrs. Mildred Smiley and the splendors of her home.

"Bob Kenyon *may* be dead. I, however, doubt it. Now, this Maxan, what connection has he with all this?" Bayard was awakened in his watchful eagerness.

With great caution the engineer unfolded the story of Maxan's growing passion, the Washington scenes, and the three warnings.

Colonel Tom Bayard smoked reflectively. He spoke slowly: •

"I don't like it a bit. I wish the young ladies were at home with their parents. My first fear is that this mad, erratic lover may thrust himself forward. Now Jimmy is fiery and too high-spirited—even for Texas! If the

young ladies have returned, he may have drifted over
to the Crescent Club. Let us walk over. I wish to
register your name. I suppose that the ladies are with
the Chisholms. I have a friend there to escort home
with our party to Indianola. We must keep Maxan
and Jimmy apart. Once at San Miguel, Ramon
Maxan will be powerless to intrude. Old "Si" guards
his home as a tiger its den, and woe to the man who
would venture there uninvited. But these Creole people
are the most hot-headed and impulsive in the world. A
fracas in New Orleans means blood. The whole community is half-crazed with pent-up feelings of the reconstruction quarrels, war enmity, and class hatred.

"Let us remain near the ladies, and, keeping Leavenworth away, be watchful of Maxan." Manson agreed
with the Texan, and they wandered through the
streets to the Crescent Club rooms.

After the formalities of the introduction of Mr. Jack
Manson, as a visiting guest, the two friends strolled
into the splendid interior.

"It will be a temporary home for you, as far as club
life goes, on your visits here, and our associate, Chisholm, is vice-president now. Politics may distract him
to-night, for a collision between General Emory's
regulars and the McEnery malcontents may occur at a
moment. I will call to-morrow at the bank with you.
Chisholm will ask you to his home and I will go over
to-morrow evening with you. I wish you to meet his
family, as well as Mrs. Wayne Barker, an old Southern lady who will travel under my care."

In friendly chat with several hospitable and graceful
clubmen, Jack Manson was soon at home. "I am
glad Jimmy is not here," whispered Colonel Bayard.
"We will quietly keep him busy should he come, and
take him home. The steward says he has not come in,

But Chisholm is upstairs in the card-room, I'm told." The colonel smiled as he said: " Wait here. I will bring him down, if I do not break in on a four-handed game."

Bayard turned, leaving Manson in the midst of a pleasant circle of new acquaintances.

Jack's eyes roved around the rooms. No sign of Maxan or Leavenworth. The coast was clear. The engineer felt relieved. In ignorance of the chilling letter of Mrs. Marshall, Manson decided that Maxan would simply repeat a formal call, satisfied with the message sent him.

" If we sail so soon, there can be no contretemps here." So Jack's brow was unclouded as he entered the wine-room of the Club, at the request of one of Colonel Bayard's friends. Seated in a neat alcove, while sipping a glass of wine, Manson noted the delay of Colonel Bayard in his return.

" Let us have a cigar," said Achille Bienvenue, his entertainer. " They may be a long time deciding the fate of this jack-pot!"

Manson's eyes were fixed on the door in stealthy watchfulness awaiting Colonel Bayard, when suddenly Ramon Maxan appeared at its curtained portal. His face was flushed, and he was followed by a dark, rest-less-looking young Creole, whose studied evening dress bespoke the lounger of distinction. Gliding by with snake-like tread, Ramon Maxan and friend seated themselves in an adjoining alcove. By a chance hazard Jack Manson did not catch the Creole's eyes. Yet, in his heart, he felt that the baffled visitor had observed him. Jack was vaguely uneasy.

" If Bayard were here, I would, at least, have a wit-ness. I can't leave, and that man's face looks ominous."

In a moment his nerves were at the normal.

But with one ear Jack Manson was forced to hear the rising inflections of Maxan's voice. Striving to be polite to his host, the engineer watched the door. The absent colonel still lingered. "I do not care what happens," thought Manson, with a young man's pride, "if he only keeps Katie's name out of his talk." For the raised tones and vicious inuendoes of the excited Creole began to attract attention. Even his host became uneasy. The references made, while sparing Manson's name and Miss Leavenworth's, were too meaning to ignore longer.

Jack's face reddened as he noticed his companion watching him with eyebrows furtively lifted. It was a clear case of "calling him down." Reflecting on his duties, on the possibility of scandal, and outraging club hospitality, Jack Manson smoked steadily, though his face was ashen. It was the pallor of a brave and outraged man, nerving himself to a supreme self-control.

From his angle, Maxan's companion could observe Manson's uneasiness. A telegraphic glance passed to warn Ramon Maxan that his words were heard by others than the quiet Northern visitor. The Creole's voice was raised till it rang out clearly in its venomous scorn.

"Yes, sir! The Yankee coward sheltered himself behind an old lady's letter and insulted me through her. But I will see her, the fair Katie, yet, if I have to ride to San Miguel alone. He lied when he sent me word to-night they were out."

Like a panther, Jack Manson leaped lightly to his feet and stood before Maxan. The "running mate" of the slanderer gazed superciliously at Jack.

Ramon Maxan on his feet glared like a crouching tiger, his hand thrust in the breast of his waistcoat behind a white silk handkerchief. Mr. Achille Bien-

venue stood behind Jack, his finger lifted, for Colonel
Tom Bayard and the impassive Chisholm stood transfixed at the door. The loungers at other tables paused
with suspended glasses, and a hush fell on the room.

" You used my name with disrespect and dragged a
lady in by inference. It is infamous! "

Maxan's dark eyes glittered with deadly light. It
was the supreme moment.

" Ah! You wish to creep into Rancho San Miguel
as the Texas girl's defender. I—."

The rest of Maxan's infamous sneer was unfinished,
for Jack Manson's right arm caught him between the
eyes.

There was a crash. Tables and glasses went down.
A general rush was made as Maxan, springing to his
feet, made a wild rush with a glittering knife in his
hand. The Parisian-bred fencer had half broken the
force of the blow by a slide to the rear. A howl of
anguish escaped his lips, as with a leap Colonel Tom
Bayard twisted the knife out of his uplifted hand.
The wrist was broken.

" You treacherous dog! Insult a stranger and try
assassination. This is my quarrel," sternly said Bayard.

While Maxan's companion and a volunteer peace-
maker restrained the Creole, Jack Manson said:

" Gentlemen, I am responsible for this; I only regret
the place and any such occurrence." Turning to Achille
Bienvenue, who was a " code master in affairs of
honor," Jack Manson handed him his card. " Will you
kindly act as my representative? "

" Pardon! " said Colonel Bayard. "I have been the
unwitting cause of this. May I act with Monsieur
Bienvenue? " Manson bowed with dignity and left
the room with Bayard, who still held the Creole's
knife, banker Chisholm walking on the other side.

In a private room the three awaited the return of Bienvenue, to whom a frightened steward had taken a message as to their whereabouts.

A card from the vice-president of the Club was brought by a steward following Bienvenue, whose eyes now gleamed with the light of battle.

"Monsieur Maxan, he insist on ze double affaire," said the new-comer, in his soft French patois. "I have ze personal regret I have not understand ze enmity. I have state ze St. Charles as ze residence."

Bienvenue stood with punctilious formality. "All right, Achille. We'll both fight, of course, when his wrist gets well," said Bayard fiercely. "But this must be kept quiet. It is infamous! Is he drunk?" continued the colonel.

"I zink he is only crazee," plainly said Bienvenue, tapping his forehead as he returned to the scene of action.

"We must get home before Jimmy Leavenworth hears of this," whispered Bayard to Manson. "Steward, show the gentleman in and call a carriage."

In his stately manner, Chisholm advanced to meet the club official. Manson and Colonel Bayard merely bowed.

"I have called to say that whatever is the outcome of this unfortunate affair, there will be perfect silence, and I am authorized to say on behalf of the club members that the violation of our traditional hospitality is deplored. The person in the wrong is only a non-resident member. As the cause of this quarrel is foreign to us, it is a case of 'noblesse oblige.' Mr. Manson, I offer you the apologies of our members. I shall ask Mr. Chisholm to step in with me and personally receive the same remarks on your behalf."

"Very proper, very considerate," said the banker,

who was now awake to all the serious consequences of
Maxan's mad folly.

"Eustis, will you drive over to the telegraph office
with me when we are done?   I wish to talk with you,"
said Chisholm with a preoccupied air.

"Certainly," replied the gallant Louisianain, whose
face bore the traces of a profound regret.

"Await me here, please," said the banker.   "I will not
be long."

"Thank God we have kept Jimmy safely out of this,"
said Bayard to Manson.

Jack nodded gloomily.   His three warnings and his
careful uncle's caution returned to his mind.   A blood
quarrel on his hands before he had even gained a sight
of Texas!

"Let me handle Leavenworth when we meet him."

"All right," said Jack, rising, as Bienvenue and
Chisholm returned.

"I will see you in the morning, gentlemen," said the
banker.   "I hope to extend the hospitalities of my home
to you now and in the future.   The other party have
gone."

Escorted by Bienvenue, the two friends reached the
St. Charles.   As they sought Colonel Bayard's rooms,
Chisholm, at the main telegraph office, gave the sleepy
operator a double fee as he handed him a dispatch
marked " instant delivery: "

Spare no expense.   Come here instantly. Deadly trouble
between R. M. and the Northern engineer. Imperative. Take a
special engine. Answer.

It was signed A. R. Chisholm, and addressed Senator Ezra Steele, Planter's House, Mobile, Alabama.

"Send the reply instantly to my house.   A man will
be waiting at the door."   Chisholm dropped a bill on
the desk and left.

"Some political fracas, I suppose! There will be bloodshed in this town, I fear," yawned the operator as he made the key fly under his finger, for Chisholm was a haughty autocrat.

Silence brooded over the deserted club-house. The sobered revellers had gone home in deference to the vice-president's wishes, and only the wondering negroes, cleaning away the debris, whispered with trembling lips:

"Dey's shuah to be some blood spilt on his hyere quarrel. De Yankee man was dead game, too! An' Mass Bayard, he's a powerful desperit shootah!"

In his rooms at the "St. Louis," Ramon Maxan, his bruised face smarting, and his broken wrist aching, swore between his clenched teeth a deadly oath. His second had retired to return on the morrow. "You will have to wait, Ramon. The fates are against you till your wrist is well. You can't fight now. It is a puzzling case," said the flaneur, whose enthusiasm was considerably dampened.

"I will stuff that woman's letter into my pistol and drive it through this Yankee cur's heart wrapped round a bullet. Caramba! As for Bayard, I will waylay him and shoot him like a dog." His veins swelled, as he swore in secret that Katie Leavenworth should feel his vengeance. His disgusted friend left him raving.

"By heaven! I have it! I'll reach the whole gang through her." He tossed for hours revolving a plan dark with murder and foulest crime.

Before he slept, Chisholm, still awake, read the simple word:

Coming—special engine. STEELE.

"Good," growled the worried banker. "I'll make him muzzle this half-breed fire-eater. He *must* do it for the R. G. Company."

The slumbers of the banker were disturbed by the haggard senator, who had left a night of "poker" and politics to hasten to the neighboring city.

Before Bayard had completed his careful story to Jimmy Leavenworth over the morning coffee at the St. Charles, while the sweet sisters slumbered in happy ignorance, Senator Ezra Steele was seated by Ramon Maxan's bed.

"Have you done anything this morning?" he asked roughly.

"Not yet. How did you get here?" queried the astonished Creole.

"That's my business! Now, sir! I will not be ruined by your d—d murderous folly! There's a steamer leaves for Tampico at noon. You will go on it."

"And be branded as a coward! Never!" howled Maxan.

"Then you will lose forty thousand dollars a year, and get shot, for Bayard will kill you, if the other fellow does not. Tom Bayard can kill a quail with a pistol!" shouted the infuriated senator. "Chisholm told me you acted like a crazy brute. Look out for that Texas boy, too. He will be as wild as a Comanche."

Chisholm and Steele arrayed against him! Maxan drew a long breath. Revenge *was* dear at forty thousand dollars a year. "I must do the deed secretly," the baffled would-be murderer thought.

"But my character," he urged.

"I will take care of it, such as you have!" snorted Steele, who saw his own future endangered. "Listen; Chisholm will attend to the Club. I will go to the steamer myself with you. You could not fight these men for a month. You shall not have an open quarrel now. You had better let them alone. It would be traced to me. If you do not do as I bid, I will turn old 'Si' and the boy loose on you. They would chase you to Yucatan and ' wipe you out.'"

" When does your friend come here?" he sharply said.

" At nine," snarled Maxan, for his aching wrist bones told of the herculean Texan's wrench.

" I will go over to the St. Charles with him and we will all dine at the Club to-night—the other second and Bayard, as well as Manson. There will be no remark. I will arrange all. Chisholm will be there, but not Jimmy Leavenworth. You will go to your ranch and wait for my telegrams via Brownsville and Mata-moras. Would you ruin the company? Your life would not then be worth a pinhead."

" Go on, fix it up," groaned Maxan, turning his face to the wall. " Let me see my friend alone."

" All right, you can send to the office," said Steele, as he departed in victory. Sending a note to Chisholm by a messenger, Steele sat down to the enjoyment of a giraffe mint julep, and a sheaf of morning journals.

" I've done a rare bit of work," he smiled. I have tied Chisholm, old Manson and the engineer, Jimmy Leavenworth, and Bayard to my future interests by this lucky stroke. But I must watch this young villain! He is a born murderer, and he is lying to me. He means to draw blood by and by in some sneaking way; but they are all warned. Let them fight it out."

At ten o'clock Senator Steele's superb bit of character acting was over. " He deplored, etc.,"; and with the seconds, and after an interview with Bayard and Man-son, he returned to bear away Ramon Maxan to the steamer sailing for Tampico. At one o'clock he dropped in at the bank to notify the busy Chisholm of the departure of the Creole.

It was a happy day for Jack Manson as he rode down the beautiful shell road with Katie's sweet eyes shining on him in the tenderness of gratitude. For Jimmy had easily divined Jack's championship, and the girl's heart went out to the generous man who risked his life for her.

Brother Jimmy, with Mrs. Wayne Barker, drove along in a splendid team at a discreet distance, with Colonel Bayard and Alice, the happiest of St. Cecilias, on the rear seat in quiet converse.

While they lingered at the Lake House, Ramon Maxan was gazing at the pictured shores of the "Lower Coast" as the steamer sped along. He had locked his dark secret in his heart, and every aching throb burned revenge into his brain.

For, to a Creole, an unrequited blow means blood even across the mist of years. The awful seal of a forfeited life can alone atone for the past disgrace.

In stately fashion, Senator Steele presided over the parting dinner at the Crescent Club, to be followed by a reception at the banker's lovely home, bowered in roses and magnolia. It was evident to all the habitues that a formal adjustment had been effected. The tongue of gossip was silent, though several of the younger hot-bloods quietly wagered a champagne dinner that Ramon Maxan would wipe out the insult in blood later.

"Wait," said one. "Do you remember how he killed Francois Vargas about 'La Rosita?' The Cuban thought he was safe. Ah, Ciel! Ramon never forgets!"

For all these gloomy auguries, there was peace and happy laughter, with best wishes following the party, as, two days later, they gathered on the ferryboat stemming the tide to Algiers.

Chisholm and Senator Steele having chivalrously

presented the ladies with floral adieux, found time separately to whisper to Jack Manson a last warning: " Beware of Maxan. He is unforgiving. He knows the frontier. This fracas will keep him away from San Miguel. Yet the border is lonely and he may attempt some foul stroke."

Gazing on the broad bosom of the Father of Waters, Jack Manson's bosom swelled with manly independence as his eye rested on the delicate face of the woman he loved. Her laughing eyes grew strangely tender as she noted Manson's earnest colloquy. He said simply in reply:

" The border is open to all, and Ramon Maxan can ride it unchallenged. I do not seek him, but if he harms that girl, it is his heart's blood or mine! "

The two leading spirits of the mysterious company conferred in the carriage as they drove home.

" Senator, go back to Mobile at once," said Chisholm. " There will be a bloody conflict here between the rival governors and the warring police. You might be involved. Keep away from political circles. Leave here quietly, as we must not lose our influence over the President. You and No. 4 might suffer, and also our business interests later."

" You have done a noble day's work with those quarrelling young men," cried Chisholm, as they parted.

" Ah! I fear the end is not yet in sight!" gravely said Steele, as he descended at the St. Charles.

Before he reached Mobile, the square of New Orleans was alive with an armed mob and the factional police fighting at short range in the streets.

Far away, through gloomy cypress swamps, and moss-laden sycamores, ghostly in this mournfully waving drapery, the pilgrims to Texas journeyed by rail to Brashear City.

There, on the bayou inlet, on its sluggish tide, with watchful alligators sliding along the oozy flood, the light cockle-shell steamer, " Gussie," waited the signal to steam out of the river inlet to the wild, cyclone-swept Gulf of Mexico.

" Ho! For Texas!" cried Jack Manson, gaily, leaving all care behind, for, by his side, stood the gentle and loving girl who was the "one fayre mayde" of all the world to him now.

CHAPTER VII. •

ON THE GULF — THE STORM KING'S WRATH — THE SPIRIT OF LOVE—OUT OF THE JAWS OF DEATH.

"THIS looks like the River of Lethe!" said Jack Manson, as the old lake boat, "Gussie," glided away from the wharf at Brashear City. It was not an inspiring scene. The straggling wooden houses, backed with dense pine woods, rested on the ashes of the old slave barracks burned by General Banks' army in an ignoble skirmish. A few listless darkies angled for the leathery cat-fish, with long fringed mustaches, lazily floating in the heated waters of the turbid inlet. As these dusky fishermen dangled their legs over the rickety wharves, huge round-eyed alligators slid along the tide, displaying formidable jaws, a gray, stony glare fixed on the tempting morsels of negro flesh just out of their reach, the saurians leaving a strong, musky odor on the polluted air. The greasy, leaden waters of the bayou blackened under the heavy pines and cypress of the muddy swamp banks, whose hummocks were crowded with huge copperhead and moccasin snakes.

From the shores of the bayou, a hundred yards wide, the cane-brake led away into the pathless interiors— those weird, silent tangles where ferocious slave hunters once chased the desperate and defiant runaway African with canoe, torches, rifles, and slavering blood-hounds.

From the gray trees, dying in the poisoned waters, hung clouds of the thin, filmy gray-green Southern moss. It was a scene of gloomy silence, broken only by the dash of the two forty-foot paddle wheels of the steamer and the semi-profane caution of the anxious pilot to his subordinates. Clouds of cormorants and flights of buzzards sailed slowly away as the yellow sun sickened and died in the west. There was a broken, coppery look to the sky.

"Our sunny Southern home!" remarked Manson, with an unconscious sneer.

"Wait till you see the emerald sea of a Texas prairie. Wait till you ride alone through a ten-mile grove of cactus in blossom, showing richer dyes than the crimson-hearted rose, the Tyrian purple, or the blue and golden blossoms of the Lotos Land," said Katie Leavenworth. "This is a forgotten River of Silence."

They were sitting alone on the upper deck of the metamorphosed old lake boat.

Sister St. Cecilia, with tact, was watching over that dejected matron, Mrs. Wayne Barker, in the "bridal chambers," so called, as two shabbily decorated double-sized state-rooms usually are named down in Dixie's Land.

Below, in the saloon, Colonel Tom Bayard and Brother Jimmy were engaged in a long and serious conversation. From occasional words overheard through the open ventilators, Jack realized that the veteran was gravely unfolding to the heir of San

Miguel the facts of Ramon Maxan's wild impru-
dence.

Anxious to spare "Miss Bright Eyes" any anxiety
as to the future, Manson paced the long upper deck
with Katie clinging to his arm. The sun was sinking
in fiery-red clouds as the Gussie swept out upon
the green waters of the Gulf, leaving the gloomy windings of the bayou behind them.

The winds were rising and lashing the shallow waters
into yeasty foam, as the flaming disk suddenly dropped
and evening darkness hid the low shores of Louisiana.
On the port quarter a flash-light shone out over the
Gulf at the mouth of the Pass.

"Let us go down! I pray there will be no storm,"
said the gentle girl, shivering slightly. "These Gulf
cyclone storms are terrific."

When the party were seated in the dining saloon,
gorgeously hideous in flashy ornament, the bronzed
captain showered every attention on the party whose
social prominence made them especially worthy of his
care.

A river and gulf sailor of experience, Captain Ludlow
knew every twist of the Father of Waters and every
inlet of the dangerous Texan coast.

"Wind rising, Captain?" said Bayard, cheerily,
noticing the grave air of the sailor.

"Yes, a little too much, Colonel," the mariner replied;
"we have a light cargo."

There was a decided air of preoccupation on Leavenworth's face, for he was pondering over the Colonel's
disclosures. He had caught a few hints of some trouble
at the Club, and now he recognized in Ramon Maxan a
sneaking enemy of unfathomable wiles.

"I'd like to look at him along a Winchester barrel,
the half-breed Mexican cur!" Jimmy grimly soliloquized.

" I must put Jack up to all the border tricks. I'll give him old Don Basilio to watch over him."

A quiet settled over the table soon, as the creaking of timbers, howling of the rising gale, and a sudden change in the vessel's speed, announced the gathering of the storm-furies. With a meaning glance the Chief Engineer excused himself and sought his engine-room.

" I think I will retire," faltered Mrs. Barker, with furtive glances at the younger women.

Assisted by their friends, the three ladies sought their cabins, and there was no joviality around the half-deserted tables as the young men returned. There were but few other passengers, and little was heard save the mournful howling of the rising storm and the dash of the broken waves, throwing volumes of salt spray high over the smoke-stacks.

" Is this sort of thing usual? " queried Jack Manson.

"We often run into these circular storms," replied Bayard. " The 'northers' sweep around the western shores of the Gulf of Mexico, are turned in by the Florida Capes and swing around backward here along the coast. If we cut through it, we may run easily in at Indianola. If we must, we will run around with it. To try and head these tornadoes would blow the works and machinery out of the boat in six hours. These old things are only knocked together with nails and a hammer. It prom·ises to be a nasty night! I have buffeted around here a week trying to run in to Galveston, Indianola, or get back to New Orleans.

" I wish the ladies were safely on shore," the Confederate concluded, as he passed the cigars and gazed at his friends.

Jack and Bayard watched from the cabin windows the black driving clouds with a silver star now and then breaking through. The decks below were noisy

with the hoarse echoes of command and sharp reply, as
the negro roustabout deck hands, urged by the officers,
secured all for the night.

"These old walking-beam engines are by no means
too safe," muttered Bayard, as the frail, top-heavy boat
settled in the swooping waves, with a creaking groan
and shiver of her timbers, or pounded into the irregular
seas, striking her with heavy blows, making everything
on the tables dance in wild confusion.

Above, the straining of sails and trampling of feet
told of the efforts to steady the storm-beaten vessel.

Leavenworth thoughtfully devoted the hours till late
midnight encouraging his now frightened sisters.

"Thank heavens! They are asleep at last!" cried the
young Texan, as he groped his way along the swaying
cabin floors.   Bayard and Manson were ready to seek
the precarious shelter of their cabins.

"There is no danger?" queried the anxious lover.

"Not yet," replied Jimmy Leavenworth cautiously, as
the Captain, enveloped in a "souwester" and stalking in
sea boots, brought a goodly share of the storm in with
him, as he sought his midnight coffee.

"It's as mean a night as I ever saw on the Gulf, and
the storm is rising! I'm afraid for that working party
and the light-keepers at the Pass," growled Ludlow.
"I wish to heavens I had a hundred-ton fishing schooner
under me and was out on the Banks of Newfoundland
to-night. We have no place to run to here! The
nearest harbors are all dangerous. It's like sailing in a
boiling pot," concluded the disgusted skipper.

"What's the matter with the Pass light-house?" said
Bayard to break the pause.

"Your Confederate friends burned down all the Gulf
light-houses during the war, and Uncle Sam is taking
his time to rebuild them. The twenty-five men in that

half-finished iron cage at the Pass may be swept off
to-night. It was suicidal to destroy all those light-
houses and beacons. Now, I can see the beacons and
range flags at Indianola in the day, but I might run her
dead on shore at night. I can't see in the dark!"

The captain was wrathy.

"And if we went ashore?" modestly questioned Jack
Manson, for his heart leaped up at the thought of the
fair, dear head pillowed near him on this wild night,
with only a plank keeping away the angry waves.

"The Gussie would be spread along five miles of
beach in ten minutes," snapped out the captain, as he
grasped his outer coverings and went forth to battle
with the storm-fiend.

Throughout the weary hours till morn, Manson's tired
brain was thronged with pictures born of the excitable
hours of the voyage. The winding bayous, where
Lafitte and his bearded sea banditti once reigned (murderers and sea rovers under the skull and crossbones),
seemed to bear in victory the black flag once more!
Barrataria's dim retreat, pictured in fancy, seemed alive
with lusty pirates, their sashes bristling with pistols.
Around their camp-fires, the freebooters on shore, wild
with rum, crazed by victory, wagered their doubloons
at cards for the choice of some fair captive.

The breeze, sweeping down the great plains and from
the valley of the Mississippi, whispered old legends of
the days when Ponce de Leon and De Soto unfurled
the bloody flag of cruel Spain under the blue Floridan
skies, or bore it to the shores of the mighty stream, at
once bold De Soto's glory and tomb! La Salle, an
inland Columbus, had floated, awe-stricken, down the
great Father of Waters toward the Gulf whose breezes
had blown over the peaceful waters, the gorgeous
Spanish ensign, the Bourbon lilies, the battle-torn

Union Jack, and on which the Stars and Bars had flaunted when the ill-fated Hatteras sank under the guns of that peerless ocean rover, the Alabama.

The romance of four centuries of piracy, slave-trading, and smuggling, the dark mysteries of a hundred maritime atrocities linger around the grassy keys, the winding inlets, and coral reefs of the Gulf whereon Spain, France, England, Mexico, and the United States warred for the final dominion of vast Texas.

Dashing onward toward Padre Island, the uneasy sleeper dreamed of Katie Leavenworth; of a quest for the unfound buried treasures of bold Lafitte, on the Texan Island, his favorite lair. The scattered silver "pieces of eight" of the vanished pirates were leading him to the hidden hoard! In these wild dreams, the sinuous form of Ramon Maxan, his scowling face distorted with passion, appeared, a tiger on the path, his blazing eyes fixed on the lady of his dreams.

There was a loud crash as Jack Manson awoke. The sound of woman's voice, in frantic terror, was heard! Manson sprang up and hurried to the cabin. A wild tempest was blowing off shore, and in the gray light of morning, the low sandy shores of Galveston Bay were visible. The cabin was thronged with half-dressed and excited passengers. Colonel Tom Bayard stood at the main cabin stairs, a haggard look on his face.

"What's up?" called Jack, through the din of the storm.

"We had to go about or go on shore! We came near rolling over! This old flat-bottomed tub may be our coffin!" grimly said Bayard.

He muttered into Jack's ear: "The Captain told me to keep all the passengers in here. Jimmy is with his sisters. The ship is working well now, and we may run outside of it. They blow over in three days, these northers." Bayard motioned him nearer.

"Get yourself well fixed," he said, with a significant glance at his own revolver, strapped on. "We might need them in the boats," he sternly said, "if it comes to that!"

From his window, Jack Manson eyed the rolling green billows, their tops blown keenly off, as if cut with a knife, by the sixty-knot tornado driving the boat back toward the Mississippi Delta. The few rags of sail and the half-speed working of the engines served to guide the Gussie over the rugged quartering seas, lifting one racing wheel high out of the water in the shock of their blows.

It was a wild and awful scene on the Gulf! Gray, ghostly, storm-wrack clouds were blown past, and the wearied crew, with life-lines attached, crawled about the decks whereon no passenger was allowed to venture. In the cabins the frightened negro stewards mechanically pottered among the debris of the table-service, while in the pilot-house, the stern captain watched every plunge of the overstrained boat in the relentless seas.

From hour to hour, after Manson rejoined the Confederate Colonel, Jimmy brought tidings of the woes of Mrs. Wayne Barker, the steady fortitude of Alice, and Katie's bright bravery.

"Take my place," whispered Tom Bayard to the brother, as he sought the room of the women. There were happy tears in Alice Leavenworth's eyes when Bayard's few words made her heart bound.

"I am here, near you; all will be well!" The war-worn soldier's heart beat high at the glances of the loving eyes turned on him in their distress.

The day crawled on, the even scourge of the storm beating the angered waters like a mighty flail.

Before sunset, Captain Ludlow entered the cabin and cheered, with a nod of approbation, Katie Leavenworth,

who was seated, propped up with pillows, in a corner.
Her little hand was nestling in Jack Manson's brown
palm. There were few words spoken as the anxious
hours crawled away. In another corner, steadfast
Alice calmly read the solemn, yet comforting words of
her prayer-book. Beside her Tom Bayard sat when
the captain motioned him to the centre of the cabin.

" Tell the other two men I don't wish you to go to
sleep till you hear from me to-night. The boat is
heavily strained. I may have to throw the cargo over.
It has shifted some. Don't alarm the women unneces-
sarily."

" What did he say? " murmured Alice, as her lover
regained her side.

" Nothing. We are doing well," the stalwart
Texan answered, but there was a look of intense affection in his brown eyes. They could not lie, even to
cheer the woman he loved more than his own life!

Without another word, she closed her hand in his.
"Don't leave me, Tom," she simply said, as her frank,
steady glance rested on his grave face.

The soldier raised the little hand to his lips.

" My own Alice," he whispered, " pray for us all.
Say nothing to Katie. It will do no good!"

Their eyes anxiously turned to where the girl sat, her
eager face fixed on Jack Manson at her side.

" We will do all we can." The lovers were silent,
as the darkness of night threw a greater gloom upon
them all. Mrs. Barker was unconscious in a sleep of
exhaustion, and at the cabin gangway, James Leavenworth, a stern sentinel, watched the doors. Without,
the storm-king raged in even wilder wrath!"

As the evening wore on the sullen plunges of the
steamer became heavier, and the shivering thrill of her
timbers more sickening. By pre-arrangement, Colonel

Tom Bayard, with well-feigned cheerfulness, persuaded the sisters to rest.

"We will lie down," answered Alice, after consultation, "but only to rest. If anything occurs you must call us."

"Very well," answered Bayard. "The captain might find an inlet to run into. I would lie down and sleep if I were you."

It was a pious fiction to impress those who might overhear, as well as to cheer the daughters of Texas.

Left alone, Manson, Bayard, and Leavenworth faced each other silently. It was in sullen despair! Bayard pressed Jack's hand significantly as Jimmy finally burst out: "I do not care; but, my God, the girls! It will kill the dear old mother!" There was a sob in the young plainsman's voice!

"Jimmy, we will stand by to the last," cried Bayard.

"I know it. God bless you both," said the Texan, as he clasped Jack's hand in silence.

Twelve o'clock. A howling midnight! The eight bells, struck in mere habit, sounded ominously like the tolling of the wave-washed bell on a floating wreck, in the wild sea gusts of spray and rain. Captain Ludlow entered the cabin. His face was haggard in the stern intensity of a sailor's last resolve. The three men joined him at a table under the wildly swinging lamp. The few exhausted fellow passengers lay around on benches in ignorance and peevish discomfort.

Ludlow hoarsely whispered: "She has three feet of water in the hold. I shall get her about and run for Indianola. Our patent log is carried away. Dead reck_oning shows us now in the radius of the southwest Pass-light. That is gone, with all on the structure! In an hour we would run ashore on the Delta. I will keep the cargo in her till we get around. Then I shall call the

whole crew, and throw out all I can to trim ship, and
call all hands, passengers and all, to the pumps. It's
our last show. Now, gentlemen, my officers are nearly
done for. When I set all at the pumps, I shall put you
three in charge. I count on you alone. Don't fear to
use every argument, if needed, to enforce obedience and
order. One of you can watch over the ladies and stand
by. Stay here till I send a quartermaster for you. Better see the ladies, one of you."

Leavenworth resolutely sought his sisters and·
informed them of the going about of the vessel.

With a fearful careening, the boat swung into the
teeth of the storm, and when she breasted the quartering waves, digging into the swell at half speed, there
was a floating mass of debris entangling the half-
drowned sleepers in the after cabin. A green walled
wave rolling over had crushed the after-cabin upper-
works like an egg-shell.

In a voice of thunder, Captain Ludlow yelled as he
sprang in: "Stop this hubbub! We're all right now."
The three friends were shaming the men into obedience.

Four hours later, the steam pump working at its
fullest power, with a hundred tons of shifted cargo,
jettisoned, the Gussie drove along toward the Texan
shore once more. The sickly gray of dawn showed
them a wild waste of waters, and in the distance a struggling bark and a full-rigged ship driving close-reefed
before the wind. At the two donkey pumps, with set
teeth, the frightened passengers toiled in two reliefs;
a third squad, under Jack Manson, in readiness, supplied
instant help, when a tired man fell out. In charge,
Bayard and Leavenworth encouraged the laboring
passengers.

Forward, the exhausted crew rested in the fore-
castle, awaiting the abatement of the howling gale, or

gloomily speculating on the ability of the now over strained boat to ride the sharp-fanged surges.

"D—n me!" cried old Liverpool Jimmy, a deep sea tar. "If we were only out of this boiling pot we could run out to sea somewhere. It's my last trip in a flat-bottomed old 'laker.' If we hit the Texas sand-bars, the 'Gussie' will be splinters in no time. Yer Yankee match box!" the irate reefer cried.

Scurrying around the slanting decks, cup and bowl in hand, the negro waiters essayed to distribute soup and coffee. Their eye-balls rolled wildly, and on their dark faces the sickly ashen pallor of fear was plainly visible.

Hour after hour crawled on. The gloom of an ugly silence, portentous in suggestion, unnerved the workers at the pumps. Finally, with an oath, a stalwart passenger left the brakes. His task was only begun.

"What's the matter?" sternly questioned Bayard.

"I'm no d—d fool to work like a horse. I've had enough," cried the stubborn malcontent. Several others followed the leader.

"Jump back to that bar or I'll scatter your brains over the deck!" said Tom Bayard, as he clapped a revolver to the man's head.

"There are women on board!" rang out the Colonel's voice. "Show yourself a man. Here, take *my pistol* and watch *me* work!" The others laid hold and a shout went down the wild wind. It was the awakening spirit of men willing to face fate at the last like heroes!

In an hour, through blinding gust and wild commotion, the captain shouted, his face lightening for the first time in a day: "We gain on the leak! Steady, boys, and I'll see you through yet!"

The Gussie moved more lightly on her long tack

across the Gulf. As the evening shadows began to
fall, cups of stiff grog animated the toilers at the pumps.
A cheer went up as the captain laid off one pump gang
to rest. "She's all right if her seams don't open
further. One pump will keep her down now with our
engine."

And still the storm howled on! The waves, lashed
by the two-days' full play of the elements, rolled in huge
masses over the shallowing bottom. As bell after bell
tapped off the half-hours with hollow, resonant clang,
in the cabin the three women gazed at their protectors,
bent on aid and counsel to the still vigilant captain.
Fortitude, woman's brightest jewel, came to their aid.
Calm-browed St. Cecilia Alice gazed with fond earnestness at her spirited sister. The gray-haired matron,
Mrs. Barker, forgot to moan, and on her face shone the
calm resignation of that devoted sex whose life-long
burden of pain and heart-ache seems to be the unsolved
mystery of the world!

At ten o'clock, Captain Ludlow approached the three
friends, for a volunteer relief was now handling the
one working pump.

"My officers are now rested. I must be all right for
the morning," said he, his steady sailor eye flashing.
"We shall be off Indianola by daylight. I shall take
my sleep now for I will be called at the first light. I
will rouse you instantly then. Rest yourselves. Gentlemen, we can not tell what daylight may bring, but
there will be no doubt when morning comes where we
are. What to do then, is another thing!"

As the sisters, clinging to Bayard and Jack, sought
the safer shelter of their cabins, a world of tenderness
beamed in their glances. No olden knights could, on
bended knee, swear fealty truer than the men who forgot self in this hour of awful uncertainty.

Even in the wild tumult of the night, Jack Manson
felt a spirit of love abroad to be a bright harbinger of
good cheer. The sweet Texan girl's voice thrilled his
very marrow, as she frankly clasped his hand in fond
"Good-night. I know you will be near me. Let me
know the truth, if—if—." Her voice broke, as the
tears filled her eyes.

"God bless and guard you. I shall not sleep. Will
that make you happier? I will watch here, near you."

Jack fought manfully with his bounding heart in the
mad desire to fold her stainless innocence to his loving
breast, and whisper: "Darling, be of good cheer."

The rose-flush on Katie Leavenworth's face paled to
marble, as on her knees the girl knelt to the God above,
in a prayer wafted far beyond the Storm-King's wrath!

Strange fantasy of bright womanhood! A smile
was on the girl's face as her tired eyelids drooped, and
she whispered softly to herself: "He is so brave, so
generous, so tender!"

Her last sigh faded into the name her brother so often
spoke. It was a gentle murmur, lest even her beating
heart might tell a maiden's prisoned secret.

With every simple precaution for sudden action, the
three comrades sought their silent rooms.

"God knows what we *can* do, but let us *do it* like
men," whispered Bayard. "There will be a crisis
to-morrow!"

"Why?" quickly replied Manson, "the boat rides
easier."

"We have not coal enough to run beyond noon to-
morrow," said Bayard, his voice sinking into a half-
groan.

Broken and wearied, Jack Manson lay in a deep sleep
of exhaustion, for he had "turned on" at the pump
brakes. As he sprang up, a friendly hand was shaking him.

"Rouse, old fellow, we are off Indianola Bar!" It was Leavenworth, his voice thrilling in its earnestness. "Come into the main cabin."

In the gleam of early daylight Captain Ludlow and Bayard were gazing through the window and talking eagerly.

"Now, gentlemen," gravely said the sailor, "we have a few minutes. I'll conceal nothing. There is our port, if we *ever make one!* We have all something at stake. I've a wife and two children in New Orleans, you have your sisters, Leavenworth, and there's the others, as well as ourselves." His bosom heaved. "I have fought this storm. I don't know how strong the boat is now. She's had a terrific strain. But the coal is nearly out. I'll move her as easy as I can, till it's fair and full light, then I will get her as trim as I can. I will wait till I get all the bearings I can, and I must try and run her in. It's our last chance! She'll never answer her helm with the few rags of canvas we have. You must take your chances with the ladies and stand by them. There's nothing else to do. I'll give you half an hour's notice. Come forward with me!"

Groping their way along, clinging to life-lines, up to the pilot-house, the four men gazed at the long, low, shelving shore, with here and there fringing wooded groves. To the north it swept away in a sandy curve, where the flash of white spray was just visible as the giant breakers broke. Far to the south, the thin line melted in the gloomy gray of the blowing scud flying athwart the bow, as the Gussie spun the parted waters from her forefoot. Scattered houses could be discerned, and a slender steeple marked the place of prayer.

"That's what I fear," said Ludlow bitterly, as he pointed to a seething mass of churned foam flying high directly ahead.

"What is it?" cried the three landsmen in chorus.

"It's Indianola Bar at its very worst!" answered Ludlow, his voice sounding harsh and changed. "There's no chance that a pilot could brave that bar to-day, no sail-boat could be handled in that channel. I must trust to God and—to my poor memory!"

"Are there no beacons—nothing?" cried Jack Manson in amazement.

"The rebels burned the light-house and destroyed all the channel beacon stands, in the war. They sunk schooners there and the new channel is changed. I used to know it well. It's a forlorn hope! Now, leave me. I've saved the four life-buoys, and I'll send them into your rooms. There are ample supplies of life-preservers. When I am ready, after we have had some warm coffee served to the men, and I see the ship trimmed, I'll cast all loose on deck for floating help, my men will man the boat davits, and I'll run her in at full speed!"

"Why so?" demanded the agitated men.

"If she strikes at full speed, she may carry over any mere scrape; if she rises and falls three or four times, there'll be no boat under us. That's all," said the sailor, fixing his eyes on the storm-beaten shore now looming up. A tear was moistening his cheek. "It's for the women! Sweethearts and wives!" he muttered,

The longest hour of Jack Manson's life was spent watching the nearing line of breaking surf, with here and there a gap made by a winding of the channel. The houses were distinctly visible and at half speed the boat swept along, rocking madly as the wind caught her wide guards. The three helpless women gazed mutely, as their companions addressed themselves to preparation.

The full crew, roused now, and on the alert, took their stations, and the two burly officers approached the cabin door. In the pilot house, where four picked men made the wheel spin under Ludlow's sharp signals, there was silence, and the shrill wailing of the wind sounded a reply to the shrieks of the soaring sea gulls. In the cabin, the stewards and quartermasters were warning the passengers.

"Is it coming?" cried Katie, as she saw the piles of life-preservers hastily thrown out, while the sailors were busied with rope and boat. No one spoke!

"Captain wants you, sir!" sharply cried a messenger to Bayard.

He darted away. The women's eyes followed the tall colonel. They could see him grasp the captain's hands. In a minute he sprang back, with the man dragging four buoys with life-lines.

The captain's bell clanged loudly as he signalled the engine room. "Full speed!" he cried, as he faced the seething eddies of broken foam now half a mile away.

The clank of the machinery resounded and the boat raced along. On either bow a leadsman stood, watching for the captain's uplifted hand.

"Now, Ally, Katie, don't be frightened; it's only a precaution!" cried Jimmy Leavenworth, as the three men threw off their coats and shoes! In a moment the cords of the life-buoys were attached to the waists of the women. A life-preserver quickly adjusted was the last preparation, and the three men donned their own cork jackets.

A tongue of low sand-bank loomed up right on the starboard bow! The breakers dashed twenty feet high on it. Quick shouts arose as the captain yelled to the wheelmen. The passengers poured out, clinging to rail and rope. Near the half-fainting women, the three men, with loving care, formed a cordon around them. The boat rose and topped long rolling waves, sweeping over the channel scourged by an undercurrent. On the port bow, the sand-spits opened their cruel jaws!

"We're in it now!" yelled the second mate, as with a mighty rush the reeling vessel swept on in a staggering, swerving course, driven by the huge wheels.

A chorus of cries rang out as the boat quivered from keel to mast, striking with a shock, throwing nearly all prone on the decks, where a toppling roller swept from stem to stern!

"Hold hard all!" yelled the captain in a voice of thunder, as the boat sank from the crest of a giant wave.

Jack Manson's spray-blinded eyes could not see the face of that dear one whose arms were around his neck as she cried, "My God, save me!"

The settling, sinking swoop of the racing boat carried her far over the breaker line, left a hundred yards astern. While Jimmy Leavenworth and Bayard knelt by Alice, lying senseless on the deck, with frenzied, passionate embrace Jack Manson held the woman he adored to his breast. He never knew how pale the lips were whose kisses sealed the love of a life, as the gentle girl's head rested like a broken lily on his ardent breast.

"My own darling! Mine!" he cried in a happy dream; for her blue eyes had told the old, old story in the face of Death!

BOOK III.

ON THE BORDER.

CHAPTER VIII.

THE TELEGRAPH'S MYSTERIES—ON THE MAIL YACHT
— THE BURNING BARK OFF PADRE ISLAND—AT
CORPUS CHRISTI — A SENATORIAL MARRIAGE
MAKES STRANGE FRIENDS.

"TAKE the ship, Mr. Bowers," cried Captain Ludlow, as he shut his binoculars and crawled down out of
the pilot-house. The sturdy mate touched his cap, with
a smile on his face. It was plain sailing now; for the
Gussie, though torn and dismantled, her decks swept
clean, was gliding up the smooth inlet toward the long
wharf at Indianola. Far beyond them outside the bar,
the dashing spray shone silvery in the rays of a sun
now breaking the gray clouds to the east.

As Ludlow tottered to a seat in the wave-drenched
cabin, he was fairly mobbed by the delighted passengers. They were rapidly abandoning the life-preservers hastily donned with scant ceremony. The joyous
negro stewards were dragging out the luggage.

As Captain Ludlow drained a stiff brandy-and-water,
he gazed at the shattered glories of the tawdry cabin.

"'Old Hutch' will have to give the 'Gussie' a little
shake of his pocket-book. It's all right," the bronzed
sailor thought, as he drained his glass, the faces of wife
and children shining on him from afar. "By Jove,

I'll send them a dispatch at once. Emily will worry till she knows the Gussie is all right!"

The sailor's brow relaxed as sweet Katie Leavenworth, on Jack Manson's arm, approached.

"Oh, Captain Ludlow, you were so grand crossing that awful whirlpool! I shall never forget you fighting that storm!"

"Don't speak of it, Rosebud," the mariner said, as he clasped *both* their hands. "I have carried you safely over from baby times up to the great girl you are. You brought us luck!"

"And someone else too," silently finished the skipper, for the light of a love brightening in storm and tempest, flashing out even in the face of death, was shining in the happy girl's eyes. Jack Manson, bewildered and overcome with the words the wild waves heard, showed in his dancing eyes a joy he could not conceal.

St. Cecilia and the sharp-eyed Bayard, Mrs. Wayne Barker, prayer-book still in hand, and Jimmy Leavenworth, with radiant face, crowded around the hero of the hour. An eager crowd waited to find words for their gratitude.

The grassy banks narrowed before them as the Gussie glided up to the wharf. It was crowded with anxious watchers, and thronged with the wild riders of the prairie land. Before them the white cottages of Indianola nestled under the green oaks, a long street parallel to the shore, and a bridge spanning the lagoon beyond. Clusters of horses and wagons crowded the beach, as scores had gathered to watch the passage of the bar and the seething channel.

The tired engineers straggled up, their anxious faces relaxed to join in the general ovation.

"I will meet you at Frenchy's Hotel for breakfast," said the now happy Captain, for the wheels were now

stilled, and Jimmy Leavenworth was already the
centre of a throng of stalwart friends fairly mobbing
him on the wharf. Broad-brimmed hats, Southern-
frontier overshirt, Mexican riding trousers, and the
ready revolver and bowie-knife marked them as
"cattle men." Jack Manson gazed at these fearless
riders, heavy braided riding whip in hand, as they
held the lariats of their vicious-looking steeds. These
wild-eyed samples of equine "cussedness" were
playfully trying to kick the spikes out of the wharf
planks, or distribute their cumbrous, ornamented Mexican saddles and loose gear over the driveway. With
eyes like maddened stags, limbs like deer, and a distinct
flavor of the unconquerable mustang, they were living
pictures, as their riders pranced away with the good
news for anxious friends. A slight touch of the braided
horse-hair reins, swaying the huge bit with its cruel
jaw ring, controlled the frantic bounds of the chargers
of the plain.

There was general rejoicing over the escape, greater,
a week later, when the sinking of a fruit steamer, the
foundering of several sail vessels, and the loss of the
South Pass light and its thirty occupants were known.

No merciful eye looked through the dark wrack, as
the iron-piled cage was swept away in the blackness of
night! The yells of the drowning were blended with
the remorseless howling of the cyclone!

As the party rode to the hotel at the head of the
wharf, Jack Manson noted a swarthy, Mexican-looking
rider dashing up to the carriage in which the heir of
San Miguel was riding. As he handed over a bundle
of letters, Jack saw a villainous, pock-marked face, a
tigerish mustache, and a countenance exciting the keen-
est aversion.

"Who's that chap, Jimmy?" asked Manson, as his

friend gave him several envelopes at the door of the little inn, where a stranded French sailor-cook, flourished as boniface.

"Oh, he's only Joaquin Ximenes, my father's riding messenger," said Leavenworth carelessly.

"He has a bad face," said Jack, tearing open his dispatches, as the messenger lounged away.

"That visage would hang him in a strange land," laughed Jimmy. "Where he came from no one knows. He has a network of chums from No Man's Land to the City of Mexico, and from New Orleans to El Paso. A splendid rider, the best trailer I ever saw, and a deadly scoundrel. He was Head Devil of a Mexican border gang till a 'pronunciamento' drove him over here. He rides better stock than I do; I fear he steals them."

Jack Manson gazed into the glittering, dancing black eyes of the desperado, whose two ivory-handled revolvers flapped on his hips. They were ornamented with carved spread eagles clasping a snake.

"Look's like a half-Indian. I suppose he stole the pistols from some Mexican officer's dead body," mused Jack, reading his dispatches. They were two in number. One in cipher was from his uncle.

"I must get the key for that. It must wait till the baggage is ashore," thought Manson, his eyes wandering to the upper rooms of the little Hotel de Bordeaux, whence he had just caught a glimpse of as lovely a laughing nymph as Greuze or Watteau ever painted. It was the precious Rose of Texas exulting in her safety. Her dainty foot had touched once more the soil which gave her birth!

"Ah! this is serious," muttered Jack, as he folded away the second telegram. It read:

Beware of R. He has sworn revenge for New Orleans. I know all. Remember our interview.

Though unsigned, Jack saw the warning finger of the " Empress " in its lines.

" I'm tired of this delving mole of a villain. I would like to have it out with him!" muttered the engineer.

A brief letter from Si Leavenworth welcomed him to San Miguel. Its closing sentences were pithy:

Trust no one, speak to no one on our joint business except my son and Lawyer Nordenskiold, whom he will bring to you. This is important.

At the side of the hostelry, perched on a grassy bank, a little rose-trellised garden told of the stranded Frenchman's native taste. Jimmy was intently reading a letter, and by his side stood the erect form of Olaf Nordenskiold.

" There's a man of nerve and brain," thought Jack, gazing at the gray eye and beak-like nose of the stranger.

" One of the born Rapacidæ, a modern Roman," was Jack's verdict, as he slipped through a little gate and gathered a few of the prairie roses. He gazed around him in delight. The winds were falling, and far away to the west and south, the rich, emerald green of the prairies broke through the openings of the oak groves.

" This might be God's own country," thought Jack, the roses in his hand. As he waited, the sweet woman whose head lay on his breast in the supreme moment of the storm, stood beside him. In silence, her tender eyes met his as he offered the tribute of her own land.

" Come with me, Jack," she said shyly, leading him on beneath the trellised vines shading her lovely face. " This is *my* State, *your* State. You are to be a true Texan, now," Katie brightly murmured.

" And you? You do love me! It is no dream of a day, Katie," softly answered Manson.

"I do; and, Jack, you must make my father and mother love you too. Mother, I know, will understand," faltered the blushing girl, "but father is a man of unyielding will. If you gain him as a friend, it is forever. But you must win your way to his stern heart."

"Shall we tell Alice and Jimmy now?" queried the delighted lover.

"Alice knows already," Miss Katie slowly said with downcast eyes, "and Jim is so much in love with Gertie Marshall that he sees nothing else. You can tell him all on the mail yacht, for it is a day and a half to Corpus Christi, through the beautiful lagoons and bayous. We will sail to-morrow. It is delightful.

"Now let us go in. There is old Alphonse!" said the beauty, as the rosy face of the Frenchman beamed at the open door. "Before you go in, my Jack," the girl cried merrily, as she pinned a rose on his coat lapel, "you are a new Texan; my own particular Texan. I wish you to be proud of your new State. It's a gallant State! It was not *stolen from the Indians*, conquered, or bought with yellow gold to enrich a king's coffers. Texas came into the Union with the bright star of its own sovereignty shining on its brow. Its victorious sword was reddened with the victor blood of San Jacinto. We, of all the States, *had-* and *have forever* the right to secede! We were annexed by our unconstrained consent. Yes! It is the most glorious blood of America; the hero blood of San Jacinto! My father fought there. He helped to give this great empire to the Union."

"A hero's daughter!" cried Manson, as he kissed the slender hand nestling in his own. "It will be hand in hand always, Katie," said he, as they walked out from beneath the roses which heard the spirited girl's low reply: "I am yours, but you belong to Texas now!"

Brother Jimmy was so engrossed in presenting the new Mentor to Manson that he noted not the fugitive blushes on the fair face of the proud Texan girl. Jack, now bought for Texas with the treasure of a matchless woman's love, envied not even the heroes of San Jacinto's plain, where the ravens feasted on Santa Anna's fierce followers.

An impromptu levee followed the termination of that never-to-be-forgotten feast of Thanksgiving. The captain tried to blush behind the sea-given bronze of his weather-beaten cheek. His name was on every lip.

"Ludlow," said the Dane, "I will see that permanent beacons are ranged on the channel line before a week is over. Our own vessels often run in here," said he, with a meaning glance at young Leavenworth. It was evident that Manson knew nothing of the mystic private flag of the R. G. Company.

Nordenskiold was so engrossed with his schemes that he overlooked Manson's ecstatic glances fixed on Katie. Brother Jimmy vaguely wondered, while Alice and that jubilant Confederate, Colonel Tom Bayard, were deep in the mysteries of a sub-rosa conference.

Soon a coterie of excited relatives dragged away Mrs. Wayne Barker, who querulously thanked Captain Ludlow, and piously vowed to keep thereafter several thousand acres of Texan prairie between her and the seashore.

"I was never a great hand for ships, Cap'n," remarked the old lady, as she remembered her journey from Missouri, in an ox-wagon, to the strange region where her stalwart frontier husband obtained the broad domain her wild sons now chased their countless cattle over.

With impartially distributed embraces and handshaking, the good matron disappeared in "the am'blance," as she termed a covered spring road-wagon, drawn by four steeds, only a whit less fiery than the wild plain horses still careering over her unmeasured, fenceless prairies. In simple fortitude, the frontier wife and mother had often laid herself down to sleep in peace, surrounded by the yelling Comanches, trusting to the rifles of her sturdy brood, but she vaguely distrusted all ships, sails, and steam gear.

The two sisters were reigning as queens of the local gathered women visitors, while Leavenworth, Manson, and Nordenskiold communed over their cigars on the porch.

Manson slipped away and deciphered his uncle's telegram:

Trust only Leavenworth, his son, and their lawyer. I will take care of Steele. Remember your safety. Be prudent. Important movements on the frontier expected. Report often. Use the cipher by wire freely.

"Dear old boy!" thought Jack, as he wondered how he could explain to cool Mark Manson the unfortunate fracas at the Club. "I'll say nothing unless he finds it out," murmured the new Texan, as he indited and dispatched a brief answer. And, as he turned to rejoin Jimmy and the crowned lady of his love, still the distorted face of Ramon Maxan rose between the new friends. ·

"For life and love! I will try and be as sly as a Cheyenne scout on his first warpath," resolved Manson, as he sat down to talk gravely with the two men.

In ten minutes, Manson had his cues from the

Dane.   They were " Silence, Discretion, Watchfulness," for an envious and rebellious few were ready to
vigorously contest the great grants and valuable privilege of the paper railroad now carried in Si Leavenworth's pocket.

" I wonder how I shall like him," mused Jack, and,
as Katie's laughing voice rippled out under the rose
leaves, Manson added with a deeper concern, " I wonder how *he* will like me."

" We will have time to talk things over on the mail
yacht, Jack," said Leavenworth. " I will let Katie
drive you around Indianola a little, as we leave at
daybreak. Colonel Bayard and Alice are going to see
his sister at ' Las Flores,' a few miles from here. I
have written a letter to father. I will send Ximenes
cross country with it and ask them not to come down
from San Miguel to Corpus Christi to meet us. The
girls have written. Nordenskiold says that it is not prudent for us to appear to gather and swoop down on the
railroad project as a family affair. After you and my
father agree on a plan at San Miguel, on approval by
Senator Steele and your uncle, Nordenskiold will have
a public meeting at Corpus Christi and then a legal
organization can be had. A few figure-head directors,
named to satisfy public sentiment, can quietly resign in
your favor, and bring me in. That, with my father's
vote and Steele's proxy, with Chisholm, will hold the
franchise and land-grant safe.

"And you are, for the present, only a gentleman
looking at your uncle's ranch. Everyone knows he has
one. I will organize your party and escort so you will
be safe. I will go with you on your first trip. If you
write a few lines to father I'll send Joaquin off. He
will ride the eighty miles before sundown to-morrow.
The family carriages and some of our men will come in

for us. I wish you to make a show of dallying at
Corpus Christi like an ordinary traveller. Nordenskiold
will show you the local sights of interest."

The Dane heartily assented. "I will be responsible
for him while with me." The crafty lawyer made no
mention of his trip to Washington or his knowledge of
Ramon Maxan's enmity. "I hold all sides in my
power now!" thought he, for Colonel Tom Bayard, with
a grave brow had sketched to lawyer and client, the
inside history of the New Orleans rencontre.

"We will talk it all over on the mail yacht," said
Nordenskiold to Bayard. "I can't afford to lose either
of these young men. We need them in the country.
Manson seems a remarkably fine fellow."

Gallant Tom Bayard echoed Nordenskiold's views.
He admired Jack's manliness, and Katie's strange and
sudden happiness indicated to him a nearer tie than
mere border comradeship to tie him to the game New
Yorker.

As Jack returned with his letter, Joaquin Ximenes,
lightly poised on his steed, awaited the precious packet
of letters, the first greetings of the three Leavenworths.
His Kentucky blood-horse leaned his clean-cut head
toward the fresh prairies.

"Where did you get him, Joaquin?" Tom Bayard
asked, with a horseman's approving nod.

The plainsman turned his flickering eye toward the
veteran. He dropped his gaze and humbly said:

"There was a Yankee lieutenant killed off him at
that fight at Howard's Wells last year, when the
Comanches cleaned out the negro cavalry. He's a
thoroughbred horse, sir, and 'Antelope Killer' run him
over to Mexico for sale. He can't stand an Injun. I
bought him at a long price. They couldn't manage
him or the chief would never have sold him. I got

him from the head chief of the Kickapoos over the Bravo."

As the desperado buttoned the letter safely in his hunting shirt, and knotted a loose handkerchief around his neck, his roving eye rested on Jack Manson with a cold malignity which made Tom Bayard start. Jack was looking into Katie Leavenworth's eyes as they jointly admired the beautiful racer, quivering in intensity to stretch away toward the grassy meadows of far San Miguel.

"What in thunder can that sneaking devil be concocting?" mused Bayard, as he lit a cigar and strolled away. Still eying Jack, the rider seemed to measure his every inch.

"I have it!" Bayard suddenly grasped the idea. "That devil of a Maxan has posted this scoundrel to spy and dog Jack Manson. He used to hang around Hacienda Maxan till that last rising of old Cortina men swept him over to us. By Jove! Little Mejia would shoot him in a minute without priest or drum-head court."

At Jimmy Leavenworth's nod, Joaquin loosed the rein, and away bounded the graceful thoroughbred, unmindful of the far Blue Grass Country, and forgetting, in the luxury of motion, the gallant boy who fell wounded from his back, only to die under the scalping-knife of a jeering Comanche.

'If you play false, you devil-masked fiend, I'll bore a hole through your carcass with my Winchester."

Tom Bayard registered his vow in silence.

Far afield that afternoon, under spreading cottonwood and green oak, Katie Leavenworth, her slender wrists as firm as steel bars, drove the new Texan behind a pair of half-civilized ponies. Their antics disturbed not the happy lover who drank in every accent falling from the rosy lips of the little autocrat at his side.

"You are to look at Texas only *through my eyes*, sir," she daintily ordered, as she explained some of the salient peculiarities of the landscape of the fringe of the frontier. "After our romantic sail over the old inlets once haunted by the Gulf pirates, you will see one last outpost of civilization at Corpus Christi. After that you will pass wild cattle and horses, gray deer and antelope by thousands, but not a house until you reach San Miguel. I shall laugh at your wonder. It is at once a camp, a plantation, a fortress, and the abode of a patriarch of flocks and herds. But the breeze, sweeping a thousand miles from the silvery-peaked Rockies, the mocking-bird's song, the hush of the silent prairie sea at dawn, the long shadows in the moonlight of the forest groves of San Miguel, and—and— fifty miles to the nearest neighbor," laughed Katie. "There's no land like Texas, no sun as bright, no skies as clear, no glittering stars trembling richer jewels of the night above the lonely rider."

"You are a romantic lovely Bedouin sprite," Jack replied to this flight of fancy.

While the tired ponies trotted briskly backward in the dusk, from a rising knoll the stilled waters of the blue Gulf stretched far before them. The Storm King had swept far on in his wild rage to scourge the diamond islands of the Antilles.

Along the shell-strewn shores, the heaving bosom of the ocean pulsed still in dying throes upon the glittering sands. A white sail here and there flecked the broad expanse. The last dying gleam of day faintly tinged the west. Far in the east the wild gulls still screamed before the gray pall of night-fog crawling landward, and the saucy sixty-ton mail yacht, "Wanderer," swam, swan-like, on the glassy waters of the lagoon.

"There's our beautiful boat! We will run down seventy miles through that net-work of lovely islands —the rarest hiding places. Those boats sail like the wind. Father has all the mail contracts along the coast. There are eight of these boats; some run here, and some to the islands and Havana. They are truly racers! Father had them built especially for speed and safety, and I love to sail on them. He owns them all—that is the Company does, said Katie modestly."

Again that *mysterious company!* It appeared at every turn. Jack Manson forgot for a moment the loving blue eyes at his side to wonder how far its hidden influence reached.

"That is an extensive business, is it not? The company, I mean," said Manson.

"They have all kinds of interests from El Paso to San Antonio, and from Point Isabel to Galveston by land and sea," proudly said the young heiress. "Father is going to put Brother Jimmy in charge of all, by and by, and only direct the ranches himself. We send ten thousand cattle to Kansas every year, and you will see a whole vaquero regiment here, mounted on horses with the San Miguel 'crowfoot' brand."

While the lady and her lover drove down the grassy slopes, in the gloaming by a rocky spring, thirty miles away, Joaquin Ximenes watched his peerless horse nipping the tender prairie grass, under the fifty-foot radius of the picket rope. A little camp-fire under a sheltered knoll lit up the messenger's face. Covered with a matchless Chihuahua serape, impervious to wind and rain, Joaquin smoked, in succession, uncounted papelitos.

A few bits of toasted jerked beef, cut from a bunch of leathery-looking strings behind his saddle, a draught of aguadiente, and a bed of pulled wisps of bunch grass gave him supper and rest for his limbs.

"Diablo! Muerte de Dios!" I can't see what Ramon wants to murder this green 'Gringo' for. It can't be the girl! The stranger certainly hangs around her. Ramon has never met her, if I am right, and yet he tells me to watch him day and night. But if I can make peace with Colonel Mejia by cutting this young fool's throat, it's easy bought."

And Joaquin Ximenes laid his head upon his rolled saddle blankets and dozed like an animal resting after a chase.

"I'm to get orders from Pancho at the Hacienda. I suppose Ramon wants to lay this fool's death to the Comanches. The old game."

The scoundrel chuckled and slept under the sparkling stars of the lonely night.

By the still inlet, with the wind-blown fragrance of roses blown through her open casement, Katie Leavenworth's pretty head rested in happy peace. There was a smile on the fair woman's lips. For, as her tired eyelids closed, she murmured, in maiden confession, "I love him, I love him, as he loves me."

Her fair cheek glowed as fresh as the roses sighing near her, and trembling on their slender stems lest fairies should steal their sister's secret.

Jack Manson's slumbers were haunted by the recurring question of his life. "She is wooed, but is she won?" for the redoubtable king of the frontier was now foremost in his thoughts.

The first twittering bird awoke Colonel Thomas Bayard, whose ears were more attuned to the noisy picket-firing at reveille than the songs of the Texan mocking-bird. No larks of morning sang more gaily than the happy girl children of the land baron who was now anxiously waiting at San Miguel for his returning brood.

Trooping on board with merry laughter, the San Miguel contingent bade a warm adieu to Captain Ludlow. That worthy mariner gazed on the sapphire zone of bluest water, stretching toward the mouth of the Mississippi, a peerless Bride of Silence. To-day the soft murmur of the lazily rolling surf was not as loud as the song-bird's chant. Yet, high on the sands around them, lay great drifts of sea-weed and the wreckage of the deadly storm!

"I'm all right now, I will surely have an extra week at home while they patch up the Gussie. Look at the smooth smiling devil to-day! That placid Gulf! I could paddle home now with a shingle. The Gulf's like a capricious woman, from sunshine to storm, with no sign of change. Lady Bird!" he whispered to Katie, in adieu, "I hope to take you over on your bridal trip. I'll have the cabin filled with roses for you!"

Katie's only reply was a brilliant blush and one glance of her eyes, which grew strangely dreamy.

"Oh, I can keep a secret! A pretty girl can always trust a sailor!" Ludlow whispered, as the party filed down to the Wanderer's snow-white deck.

The rattling sails drew tight under a cloud of fleecy canvas, and the graceful yacht sped away, her lines mirrored in the unruffled lagoon.

Ludlow watched the last fluttering handkerchief and turned to the chief officer. The smoke was now pouring forth from the salt-crusted funnels of the Gussie.

"All ready, Mr. Bowers?"

"Yes! sir," answered the mate, with his hand at his cap visor.

"Take the ship out, sir," ordered Ludlow, as he gazed at the fast receding yacht. "There goes the sweetest girl in Texas, and she's got the fastest thing on the ocean under her pretty feet. Talk about the

old 'Wanderer.' She wasn't a patchin' to this flyer."
The stout sailor recalled tales of his youth. Stories of
sixteen-knot rushes, as the famous pirate slave-yacht
used to stagger under a ship's canvas from Havana to
Mobile or Savannah with two hundred Congo negroes
chained below, and her rail buried in foam, came back
to him.

"The old pride of the Gulf was a terror, but this one
has tricked Uncle Sam out of gold enough to sink her.
I reckon some of the old frigate captains opened their
eyes to see the slaver leave them, hull down, in a day's
run. This chaser can dodge the swiftest steamer the
United States navy can boast. Old Si knew his business
when he had these skimmers built. I really wonder if
the Custom House fellows do not know that boat after
boat of these innocent 'mail yachts' run in here from
Havana untouched with a hundred thousand dollars'
worth of cigars, silks, and brandy for a home cargo. Old
Leavenworth must have an awful nerve and a strong
friend at court. I suppose they keep old Wilson Dayton
here in free brandy and cigars to shut his eyes. That and
a little poker money will blind him as long as he is Collector! Well, it's none of *my* business," ruminated Ludlow. "But I will bet my life savings that Mr. Jack
Manson learns more of life on the border in six months,
than he would in six years among the painted Cheyennes.
Good luck to him. He has a first mortgage on that
girl. I'd laugh to see the old man when he asks for
the daughter."

Ludlow chuckled and went below to inspect his
square-case bottle, for the Gussie had slid over the
bar as if sailing on a mill-pond.

While Ludlow attended to his " spiritual " refreshment, the fast-receding Wanderer turned in among the
bewitching islands, dotted bayous, and inner lagoons

fringing the Texan coast from Galveston to the mouth of the Rio Grande. On the decks, lulled by the ripple of the splashing waves, Jack Manson was "squire of dames" to the sisters, whose spirits were bounding in ecstasy. At the prow, seated under the sail's shadow, Jimmy Leavenworth discussed with Bayard the fullest detail of Ramon Maxan's madness.

In grave discourse, the Danish lawyer, alert, noiseless, and active, listened to the captain of the Wanderer, in eager discourse. There were no other passengers for Corpus Christi, and the dainty yacht swept on alone over the silent waters of the Laguna del Madre. The crew were idling in the cock-pit, and with its snowy racing-sails set, the boat rushed on to the far point shutting off Aransas Inlet. The blue sea showed between the two outer keys off Aransas Point, and to the west the fringing shores, a half-mile distant, hid behind their graceful trees, stretches of emerald-green billows rolling gently toward the delightful valley of the Nueces, with its circular oak openings, the scene of the theatric old-time duels between the wild Comanches and the dauntless Rangers.

Manson caught the words, as the two men paced up and down: "Bark Hesper"—"valuable cargo"— "missing"—"long overdue"—"company's flag"— from the earnest captain, while the lawyer's deeper tones replied. The words "Aransas"—"telegraph" —"report for orders," reached him as he listened to Katie's stories of her beloved natal land of future empire. With smiling faces, obsequious negroes anticipated the slightest wish of the heiresses. The crew knew these girls were princesses by right of the "almighty dollar," and their heritage of vast tracts peopled with countless flocks and herds.

From time to time Manson saw Jimmy Leavenworth

and Bayard gravely regarding him. He knew that over the sunshine of their hearts to-day but one black and menacing shadow lingered, the shade of the brilliant and reckless Creole. The balmy breeze, the sparkling waters, alive with leaping fish, and the weird old stories of buccaneer and adventurer, of slavery days and Indian wars, beguiled him. For Katie Leavenworth had caught from veteran and world-wanderer the stories told around the winter fireside in her Texan home, where Silas Leavenworth sat dispensing the patriarchal hospitality of the Southwest.

Road there was none but the open prairie, inn and hotel, save in the towns, were yet unheard of, and either in strong parties of horsemen, or teams of guarded wagons, the anxious wayfarers were forced to voyage, braving storm, privation, the circling Indians yelling in hideous emulation to secure the first scalp, and the attacks of horse thieves, Mexican marauders, and the fugitive desperadoes from the Indian Territory, or the No Man's Land of the three jutting territories of New Mexico, Texas, and Arizona.

Katie had seen many a wandering stranded scholar, refugee, world waif, government agent, mail carrier, and straggling soldier go forth from the armed camp of San Miguel to die at water-hole, in lonely ravine, or under the overpowering attack of numbers. To Jack Manson these early stories had a weird interest. It had been so far off. It seemed now so real, for the rosy lips of the daughter of the Border King were now painting these old days in truthful colors.

The breeze freshened and the beautiful Wanderer leaped over the rippling waves, her glancing copper shining like burnished gold. The varied shore seemed to glide by, an endless and diversified panorama.

Already, a table spread in the after cabin tempted

the select voyagers to an inviting meal. The two-days'
trip required the after cabin for ladies, while the forward hold was reserved for the men. Racing up to
Aransas Head, the yacht sped away toward the distant
village of Aransas Pass.

In merriest mood, Katie sallied forth to summon the
two Texans, still in conclave, to the repast.

"See!" she cried, "Mr. Manson, there's a steamer
making for Aransas Pass. It may have letters for us.
I warrant Brother Jimmy will now be happy. He may
hear from Gertie at Aransas, if we stop for the mails."

"It must be a stray boat, not the regular steamer,"
said the captain of the yacht, touching his cap. "She's
way off the regular course, Miss. But the storm may
have driven her far south," the sailor muttered, as he
went below for his field-glasses. ·

In a half-hour, the noonday meal was finished in
jovial style, for the still freshening breeze gave the
nimble sailors a reefing drill, and the service of the
little yacht table took frantic leaps hither and thither.

Nordenskiold presided with old-fashioned courtesy.
He had not yet forgotten the courtly politeness of the
days when he wore a sword

Many another scion of good family, driven on by the
storms of life, had found a new name, strange occupation, and a romantic career in the shifting scenes of
frontier life.

Bayard and Brother Jimmy were silent and moody.
Their long conference seemed to have brought them
face to face again with the realities awaiting them on
shore. For eye and brain, heart, hand, and foot, were
at the beck of the strangest summons, the moment the
men would leave the very outskirts of the two last
towns. Danger and intrigue hovered in the very air
blown from the debatable shores where stout old Zachary

Taylor opened the war which gave to our country the treasure-houses of the West. In anger and ill-concealed aversion, the prowling Mexicans crouched under the jeers of a superior race—filibusters, slave-holders, and desperate adventurers.

"Colonel Bayard! Mr. Leavenworth! come up on deck. I fear this is no steamer, but a ship on fire," sharply called the captain.

There was a scramble for the deck. Every bound of the staunch schooner brought the burning vessel nearer. Clouds of thick, black smoke rolled skyward, and she was driving straight on shore, with all sail set.

"Can she make the inlet?" anxiously queried the lawyer, with a strange look in his eyes.

"I fear not," answered the captain. "Hold! There goes up a signal to us for assistance." The sailor gazed intently for a few moments and then handed his binoculars to Nordenskiold.

"What shall we do? Her flag is Union down and she flies the private signal of the R. G. Company!"

While the lawyer gazed, the driving vessel, a large bark, showed blacker volumes of smoke pouring skyward.

"Ah! the poor sailors! Captain, can we not save them?" cried Katie Leavenworth, with tears in her eyes. The fair woman had clasped Jack's arm impulsively.

"I don't know what to do," cried the captain. "I have the United States mails on board. See here, Mr. Nordenskiold, you and Colonel Bayard must advise me. There goes her signal for assistance and a pilot; the people are on board yet," he shouted, as a large ensign, Union down, was run into the main shrouds.

"How far out is the vessel now?" said Nordenskiold, as the village of Aransas hove in sight, ten
miles up the inlet.

"About three miles. But I dare not take the risk
of going out without you authorize me. It might for-
feit the mail contract for Mr. Leavenworth," the
captain said doubtfully.

"Don't wait a minute for that! I'll answer to my
father for this. I will not see brave sailors lose their
lives under our very eyes," cried Jimmy Leavenworth.

His sweet sister Alice softly added: "And our own
lives were saved by a gallant sailor almost in sight of
these sufferers. Let us help them!"

It did not need Katie's impassioned appeal in second-
ing her gentle sister, for, at a nod from Nordenskiold,
all hands sprung to the sheets.

The captain took the tiller, and in five minutes the
dainty Wanderer was dashing out through Aransas
Pass toward the bark which was driving straight on
shore. All eyes were glued on the vessel now shrouded
in smoke; with glasses in hand the lawyer stood by
the captain, his old nautical skill aiding in this crisis.

"By Heavens, it's the 'Hesper,' one of the Company's
boats!" sharply said Nordenskiold. "I know her rig.
See! there the crew go in their boats, towing astern.
I suppose they have lashed the tiller in hopes she will
drive in shore and save the hull."

"It's a queer manœuvre, Squire," hoarsely whispered
the captain. "I wonder what she has on board. She's
been missing some time."

Nordenskiold shot a savage glare at the skipper from
under his bushy gray eyebrows.

"You are here to save life, not to fight for the
Marine Insurance Companies," said the lawyer, with a
meaning gesture of silence.

Eagle-eyed Tom Bayard, who could see an Indian further than any ranger in Texas, shouted from an excited group:

"They've cut the tow lines! The ship is deserted!"

It was true. In ten minutes the bark drove by, near them, flames pouring from her hatchway.

"What are they signalling for?" cried the soldier to Nordenskiold, who was sternly silent, as the captain bore down toward the three boats, now keeping together, waiting to be picked up.

"There may be explosives on board," said the captain with a grin, as he called out: "Clear away the lines there. We'll tow them in to Aransas."

The quick-witted castaways had already joined their boats with strong lines as the Wanderer swept up.

Motioning the mate to take the tiller, the captain yelled: "Stand by for a line! All hands now! Look sharp!"

At his signal the Wanderer went about, two strong lines were caught by the inmates of the first boat, and the mail yacht sped away, on the other tack, to the smoother waters of the Laguna.

A third of a mile in advance, the doomed Hesper was rushing onward to the certain destruction of the tossing breakers.

The mail yacht raced after the abandoned vessel now wreathed in flame.

A hoarse hail from the leading boat warned them: "Look out! not too near; she's full of powder!"

The Wanderer bore well away. The flames now leaped up shroud and mast, and while all gazed in eagerness, the bark heaved up, a bright flash of blue and red flame lit up the skies, and far and near the water was covered with wreckage. The fragments of her hull settled and sank as the masts fell sideways, dragging along the shallowing water.

"It's all over! Thank God! There's no loss of life at any rate," cried the excited Jimmy.

In an hour the swift Wanderer drew alongside the wharf at Aransas, and the three boats pulled in, with twenty wearied sailors on board. While they related the story of their disaster to a gaping crowd, the fragments of the ill-fated Hesper were grinding to pieces on the sharp sand of the lower key outside the Laguna. Apart, on the deck of the Wanderer, a bearded sailor conversed in low tones with Nordenskiold.

"We will only wait here long enough for the mails," said the lawyer. "Take all your men up to the hotel and treat them well. I will send the mail boat back for you at once. You had better come down to Corpus Christi, then. I have no doubt the Company will send your people to New Orleans and give you another vessel."

Such was the lawyer's outspoken disposition of the rescued. Jack Manson wondered at the roving commission of the speaker. The *mysterious Company* again. He would have been astonished if he had known that the Hesper had discharged a hundred thousand gallons of smuggled brandy during her mysterious absence. The Collector of Customs at Corpus Christi, convinced easily, cancelled the export bond, on the facts, and two dollars in gold, on each gallon, was thus easily earned for the annual "secret fund" of the octopus combination.

"I hope you saved all of your papers, Captain," remarked Nordenskiold.

"Every one," briefly answered the mariner, who pointed to two flat tin cases, strapped and cork buoyed. "I made them ready when the fire gained on us. My last hope was to batten the hatches."

"On second thoughts let the chief officer take charge of the men. You may as well go down to Corpus Christi with me. You'll get your new ship the sooner. Were you insured?"

"Yes, sir," said the captain. "They put twenty thousand dollars fresh on the old Hesper after we refitted this spring. That made eighty thousand dollars, all told."

"All right, then. You've made no loss for the Company. I know that the cargo was insured. So come along with us, and bring your papers. Here; your men may want money. There's an order on Lovett, Fox & Co. for what your officer may need. Take this for yourself."

A peculiar smile played on the lawyer's face as he extended a hundred-dollar bill. "I'll give you half an hour on shore. Don't be late."

The mariner hastened away to bestow his men, and Olaf Nordenskiold walked to the stern to conceal a glow of satisfaction.

"The cargo was well insured. That was Chisholm's smartness. But this scheme to destroy her when empty, in the theatrical way it was done, was worthy of a modern dramatist. I suppose Chisholm will claim a champagne supper for that. Of course, the captain fired a couple of bundles of oakum, well soaked in coal oil, himself, before he closed the hatches. Well, it's money easily made. I'm glad Chisholm plants the insurance on foreign companies. There will be no sneaking investigation. The duty stolen from Uncle Sam is a righteous reward for smashing the late Confederacy. It's a good beginning for next season. A very neat turn."

Olaf Nordenskiold rubbed his hands in glee, as he lit an especially fine cigar and nodded good humoredly,

as the Wanderer's captain gave the order to cast off
and make sail.

"Rather full of incident, this voyaging along Texan
shores," muttered Jack Manson, as he sought a cosy
nook near Katie. "What will the interior be if this is
only the introduction?" His brow darkened as he
thought of Ramon Maxan.

"That's an unsuspecting chap, young Manson," mused
the sly old legal fox. "Somebody will cut his throat
here in Texas and he wont know it. He's not smart
enough for Texas. But little Katie may open his eyes.
That sweet witch is bright enough to be 'queen of the
Texan Rangers.' And yet," he mused, "gentle and
refined. I suppose it is her Northern education and the
good family stock of her mother. Blood will tell! Old
Si Leavenworth is rough as a file, God knows,"
thought the old lawyer, who preferred his own "suaviter
in modo" to the cattle baron's "fortiter in re."

Nordenskiold indulged his last remaining human
passion, "good old gentlemanly avarice," in a smooth
and secret way, letting violent natures like old Si run
into all the desperate environments.

"Why force? Slyness is better," thought he, with a
vague regret at the two human lives sacrificed to his
now regretted personal ebullitions of passion. "Decidedly, excitement is always wrong," he concluded, as he
paced the deck. "Not always," he quickly added, as he
caught a glance of Katie Leavenworth's sweet face
crimsoning under Jack Manson's whispered words. "So
the breeze sits in that quarter! It will ruffle a little
under old Si's cyclone when he asks for that child. I
would sooner face a wild panther with a paper-cutter
than brave the old devil's anger. A genial old father-
in-law to be!" The man of deeds and parchments
fairly chuckled in controlled mirth.

But, as the boat sped along the lagoon, threading the beautiful straits and wooded reaches of the islands, passing here and there a square redoubt, relic of the late unpleasantness, built to protect light blockade runners, another sequestered couple enjoyed the romantic hours.

Colonel Thomas Bayard (late C. S. A.) was earnestly painting to sweet sister Alice the superior advantages of his rancho as a permanent residence. It was a conversation which had been interrupted by the terrific gulf storm. Bayard, who had marched up unflinchingly to the flaming embraces of Battery Robbinett, was now holding a council of war with St. Cecilia, as to the best method of " regular approach " to capture the granite fortress of her father's heart.

" You shall have everything you want in the world, my dear one!" said the frank soldier. "I have waited long enough for you, too long," the laconic veteran said with a sigh. "Marry me before the year closes. I don't care for your father's money, I have plenty of my own."

" You must gain my father's consent first, Tom," said Alice, her eyes sparkling. " Mother I am sure of already."

" Can't you tell your father that you are tired of San Miguel, and like my place on the Nueces better?" simply remarked the colonel. He was dodging the issue!

Alice's ringing laughter startled even Katie and Jack Manson. They were soon wandering away in cloudland again, building castles in Spain. Neither suspected the depth of eager love in the soldier's naive proposals.

" I'm afraid that father would be unapproachable for a week," Alice answered, smiling gaily. " But, Tom, you must ask him in some other way. You are the only man in Western Texas not afraid of him."

"I'll pay old Nordenskiold a good fee and get *him* to talk the Chief over to see the thing in a reasonable light," mused the Confederate.

"If you wish to have me preside over that famous rancho, you must ask for me *yourself!* No substitute, sir. Am I not worth asking for?" said the gentle girl, as she fled away to the cabin for her favorite book.

Tom Bayard's honest eyes followed her.

"You are worth every broad acre of Western Texas," he proudly soliloquized.

"I shall cost you a good deal in repairs, extension, and some comforts for that bachelor den of yours," whispered Alice, when she returned. His eager eyes were a promise.

"I think that you will be successful," the lady continued, "for with mother I can always gain my little battles, but I wish you to put father under some new obligation to you. Then he *could* not refuse." Alice bent her dark eyes tenderly on her lover.

"I'd lay down all I have for him, save my life," began Bayard.

"That belongs to me, sir, now and always. I have a plan. Be guided by me. I will tell you when to act."

Colonel Bayard was fain to yield to the quiet beauty. As the sun sought the western heavens, by the osier-shaded banks, wild-eyed cattle gazed at the gliding vision of beauty, for the Wanderer was a snowy cloud of canvas. Wild duck and plover whirred away, and on the little islands flocks of stately wild turkeys ran in sudden alarm. Herds of graceful deer gazed fearlessly from knoll and grassy mound and trotted a few steps with tossing antlers, as the boat glided noiselessly on.

Manson, as the prospect varied, listened to Katie's

legends and stories of the early time. The old mail-
clad wanderers lived again under her word-pictures.
The story of De Soto's lost cavalier, who wandered
alone from the Mississippi in 1541 to the Mexican
silver-buttressed mountains, and joined the men of Her-
nando Cortes four years later, after living (an object of
wonder) with the great Indians of the Arkansas, seemed
almost incredible.

"I've read his book, found in an old deserted Mexican monastery," said Katie, who lisped Spanish in her
infancy as well as her own tongue. "They thought he
was a strange god. His armor and trappings mystified them. Those fiery old Spaniards! Their memory
lingers in our herds of wild horses, bred from their
abandoned steeds."

Jack recalled, under this fairest of Scheherazades,
the little fort built by LaSalle at Matagorda Bay in
1679—long after Ponce de Leon and DeSoto had
joined the innumerable caravan. The bloody wars
between Spain and France for the coveted shores were
sketched as well as the legendary story of mysterious
San Saba Mission, far in the interior where cowled
priest and fiery horsemen fell under the fierce rush of
the proud Comanche horsemen, undaunted after three
hundred years of battle. The wild coast warfare, butch-
ered settlements of even the English, and the lawless
rule of the pirates of the Gulf were pictured. Katie
proudly wreathed with romance the early days of the
century which gave Texas its gallant "Lone Star."
Mendoza, daring Spanish prototype of Aaron Burr, a
self-elected military despot, dying before the muskets
in 1813, after the slaughter of two thousand wandering
Mexicans and predatory Americans, even then water-
ing the debatable soil with blood, was not forgotten.

The spirited girl spoke of grim Lafitte holding the

coast by the pirate's sword, from 1815 to 1821, with his great lair at Galveston—a prophetic suggestion of the future.

"There is Padre Island," cried the glowing girl. "Even to-day its sands, after a storm, are rich with the wave cast-up dollars and doubloons of treasure vessels secreted here by him, in these secret bayous."

"And where does your inheritance of title come from, my princess?" questioned Jack Manson.

"Ah! we real Texans succeed to all the rights of Moses Austin. He crossed the Sabine Boundary in 1820, and bought a huge grant from Mexico. That great Northern schemer began to fill Texas with useful emigrants to aid the wandering Americans. Mexican duplicity in 1830 forbade the further influx of our race. Yet, in 1833, the twenty thousand anti-Mexican dwellers here decided to raise the 'Lone Star,' and conquer or die under it. In 1835, Sam Houston, the greatest frontiersman since Daniel Boone, a worthy peer of Kit Carson, drew his sword and drove the Mexican invaders out. The world knows the undimmed heroism of the Alamo. As long as the breeze waves the long grass over them, the names of Travis, Crockett, Bowie, and Evans, will be deathless. I am proud that my father joined in that wild war-cry 'Remember the Alamo,' when the Mexican flag went down forever at San Jacinto. What matchless men! Sydney Johnston was a simple soldier, in our ranks; afterwards the South's costly offering on the field of Shiloh. And the deeds of our little navy! Splendid men, from under every flag, joined the heroes on shore. Yes, we have indeed a heritage of glory. It belongs to the whole Union, for Moses Austin was from Connecticut, and in the great days of the Mexican War, Zachary Taylor, a Southerner, marched to the front of the army which fought Palo Alto and Resaca de la Palma. You shall see the plains which he camped on, to-morrow, for on January 13, 1846, brave old 'Rough and Ready' moved out from Corpus Christi to plant our flag in victory at Fort Brown, where it waves to-day. It has its deathless romance, dear old Texas," said Katie, as her dreaming eyes met her lover's. "Every lonely grave of our early settlers should be an altar for their children's children. There should be nothing mean or base in the heirs of such dauntless pioneers."

The sun sank far beyond the hills, and under the soft starlight the lovers, hand in hand, dreamed of a future brighter than the sunset skies of even. Morning's fresh breezes came with the golden sun leaping up from the blue sea outside the bar. The day-god climbed toward the zenith, as Katie pointed to a distant town crowning rolling bluffs and backed with the swell of the unmeasured prairie.

"There, far beyond the eye's reach, fifty miles away, lies San Miguel. You are going to my home— to the green prairie land where freedom breathes in every waft of the far winds from the Rockies."

"What fate lies before me here?" mused Jack Manson. His nerves tingled, his heart beat high, for a gentle hand lay softly nestling in his own—the hand of the lovely woman who would be the prairie star of the newer day.

A convocation of polyglot characters welcomed Nordenskiold at the landing, as the Wanderer's sails fluttered down. That handsome young Texan, Mr. James Leavenworth, was hailed by a circle of sternly chivalric-looking country leaders, and, with characteristic Southern courtesy, the ladies reached their carriage through a lane of lifted head-gear. At the door of the St. James, the lawyer tore open several dispatches.

"See here, Manson! Wonders will never cease. Read that. Do you know the lady?" It was signed "Ezra Steele," and said:

Married to-day to Mrs. Mildred Smiley. Shall pay Chisholm a visit in New Orleans. Can you meet me there in two weeks? Would like to confer before Congress meets.

Jack Manson stifled an exclamation of surprise. "She is a charming woman; one of the loveliest I ever met." He handed the dispatch to Colonel Bayard, whose soldierly face grew stern.

"Poor Bob Kenyon!" he muttered, "It seals his forgotten tomb, and closes his sad story!" He passed it back without further comment.

Jimmy Leavenworth's eyes opened widely as he read the lines. "She will be a great aid to Steele in his public career," said the Texan.

"Yes, and a tower of strength to our Company," mused Nordenskiold quietly. "Now, what is his game?" he silently reflected, for he knew not that Steele had been deftly snared by the ambitious woman who stood under the Stars and Bars at Atlanta as Major Bob Kenyon's peerless girl wife.

After reading a few more words, the lawyer drew Jack Manson aside. "I know Miss Katie's impatience. There are four wild demons being harnessed that will take them up to San Miguel in five hours without a break. I must see Leavenworth about this wreck. It's a serious loss," he sighed. "It demands instant action. He will wish his children gathered quietly around him for a few days. Now, do you make your temporary adieux to the young ladies. I will put you in the hands of chosen men here who will 'naturalize' you in a few days. You can trust them with your life. But, silence as to your own business and my intended organization here to secure the benefits of the franchise to our inner circle. Say not a word as to your affairs or past history." He finished with a smile: " It's a way we have in Texas."

The angel of silence guards yet the passionate good-bye of Jack Manson to the beauty whose bright eyes gleamed through tears as she whispered: " Good-bye! my heart is yours. My home lies *there*. My heart is with you *here*. When you meet me, remember that our future is in your hands." There was a mist in Jack's eyes as the wild racers stretched their lean heads to the smooth prairie paths. Katie, his beloved, was gone!

CHAPTER IX.

A NIGHT AT "JOE GARCIA'S"—"OUR FIRST CITIZENS"—OLD MARK'S LETTERS—MRS. SENATOR STEELE — MAXAN IN AMBUSH — A FRONTIER KING.

" So THIS is to be my future headquarters!" mused Jack Manson, as he gloomily watched Jimmy Leavenworth dashing away with his wild escort toward San Miguel. "I'll send you in a couple of good men as escort, and a driver. Nordenskiold comes out to-morrow. You can trust every man he makes known to you, just as he tickets them. Sly old fox!" were the Texan prince's last words.

Pacing the long porch of the St. James Hotel, Jack gazed on the splendid Laguna, with Padre Island's sand-dunes swept gulfward by the silver surf. The blue waters of the Laguna teeming with turtle, sea trout, mullet, pompono, oysters, and rare fish worthy of a modern Vitellius, was unflecked by a sail. Far to

the south, a bluff a hundred feet high indicated the
depth of the virgin prairie soil, with a lean strip of sand-
beach at its foot. The plateau of the lonely beach
widened where Corpus Christi nestled half below the
bluff. Its " upper ten" dwelt on the splendid head-
lands, whence a grassy prairie, smooth as a tennis-court,
stretched hundreds of miles to the Nueces, Pecos, and
San Antonio rivers. Out in the far southwest, the
prairie joined the arid sands, cactus groves, gray hills,
and bare knolls of the great " arid zone." It is a natural
boundary from the mouth of the winding Rio Grande
del Norte ("El Rio Bravo") across two great States
and twin Territories from Point Isabel, Texas, to San
Diego, California. Not a lonely mile of this horrid,
burning desert silence which has not had its unwritten
tragedy since the " Conquistadores" first crossed it!
The unceasing war of the Apaches devastates the western half, the operations of thief, renegade, raider, and
wandering criminal make the eastern strip a land where
blood flows freer than water. The considerable town,
well built, in Southwest frontier style, seemed handi-
capped only by the shallow water of the inlet.

" Some day," mused Jack, pocket-map in hand,
"great ocean steamers will discharge foreign cargoes
here. The channel must be deepened."

While Nordenskiold left Manson to the hospitalities
of the host of the St. James, he called a secret meeting
of his "notables" at the great local "tienda de Joe
Garcia," the substitute for a club-house.

As Jack reflected that General Zachary Taylor had
chosen this as the base of his Mexican operations, he
noted the situation of the town like the hub of a wheel.
A radius of a hundred and fifty miles swept from
Point Isabel to Fort Brown, Ringgold Barracks, Fort
McIntosh, Fort Duncan, San Antonio, and near to
Austin and Galveston.

" With a virgin soil, immense cattle herds, countless bands of sheep, undeveloped iron and coal, and the water of the rivers," Manson murmured, "here should be great settlements, thousands of farmers, and thriving trade. Through this circle, the friendly advance on Mexico must be made. Will my paper railroad ever cross these rich plains?"

Gazing up and down the few streets, Manson noted the lethargy of the easy-going nomadic Western Texans. The only sounds in the blazing sun were the click of billiard balls, or the shouts of idlers in the drinking " saloons." Along the sandy unpaved streets, knots of wild-looking steeds were tied before the flimsy " stores" ! The usual "plaza" was the market place. It had served as the convenient theatre of many impromptu duels. Huge storehouses and " corrals " contained mountains of hides and pelts; pens filled with wild horses and cattle, and by bands of sheep, represented the only exchange medium of value—animals alive, or their proceeds when dead.

Jack Manson gazed on the motley passing crowd. They were Southern borderers, Mexicans, stray negroes, half-bred Indians, stranded sailors, Italian "dagos," and a few suspicious, broken-down-looking Americans of the baser sort!

He ventured to express some surprise to his companion at this singular panorama.

" It's a d—d poor country to come to, this yere Rio Grande," said the hotel-keeper, cutting a lump of plug tobacco with a bowie-knife deftly produced. " An' a mighty ·sensible man what gets out of hyar, while he kin pay for a ticket to New Orleans, an' before he gets his throat cut. Come, let's have a drink."

Jack followed his host. The drink was a brevet of social recognition. The tawdry pictures of Lee and

Jackson over the long bar were out of place hanging over the fly-infested, poison-filled bottles. A stuffed jaguar and a dilapidated-looking gray wolf ornamented the rear of the bar under a pithy notice:

GENTLEMEN WILL PLEASE DEPOSIT

THEIR WEAPONS WITH THE CLERK.

"This country does not seem to please you," said Manson, as he broke the ice of local custom with his first drink.

"The people hyar, suh, are a mixed lot of loafers an' man-killers. I wisht I was well out of the hole. Thar's some rich cattle men in back. They've gobbled up the whole country like old Leavenworth. But the average lot are lazy cusses. I wish the war had swept 'em all off. They was too big cowards to fight, an' got rich on swappin' cotton over the Rio Grande."

"Would not a railroad help you here?" cautiously said Manson.

"Yas," replied the disgusted boniface. "Ef old Grant would only grab the three border States of Mexico an' turn all these wanderin' Confederit' veterans in to whippin' the 'Greasers,' it would start us up."

"What are 'Greasers'?" innocently queried Jack.

"Oh! Mexicans! That's what we call 'em. They're like Injins—only good to kill! Now, ef this yere Rio Grande Company," the host began, as he motioned for a duplication of the fiery cocktails—Jack's eager attention was here cut short by a warning glance from Nordenskiold, who filed in at the head of a crowd of friends. They were, indeed, a strange assembly!

"Our leading citizens," Nordenskiold whispered, as he drew Jack away from the loquacious landlord.

" Don't speak of the Company to a living soul," he muttered. " That landlord is dangerous. He trains with the opposition crowd." Manson was puzzled. He advanced to meet the " leading citizens " in a strange frame of mind. Did the too communicative host run a mysterious " company " of his own? Was he a specialist in occult operations from smuggling to fancy throatcutting? Queer people—these " leading citizens"! He saw before him in the almost shabby daily undress of the ambitionless Southron several middle-aged men.

Nordenskiold said gravely: " Gentlemen, I hope to meet you all this evening at a little supper at ' Joe Garcia's.' I wish you to know Mr. Jack Manson, my friend. He has been on the plains in Dakota. Now, I have to go and look after my shipwrecked sailors. I have a telegram telling me they will be in before night. Colonel Hodges, you will kindly take charge of our young friend."

Jack grasped the offered hand of the new cicerone. He was a stunted, grizzled man of fifty-five. His head was fastened forward by a seeming injury, but two coal-black eyes blazed over his grizzled beard, and his step was as light as the velvet-footed panther. Every one knew cut-faced Hodges—a cattle millionaire, a veteran of the Mexican War, a ranger, and the father of some desperate children, born of a Spanish mother whose dower in lands was that of a duchess! All Texans hailed him as the hero of countless encounters, and his historic wound was a slashing machete cut, severing the neck muscles. Yet, simple and quiet in manner as a school-boy, two bull-dog pistols were always carried in the pocket of his loose sack-coat. From El Paso to the sea, his quickness in planting their deadly balls into the falling antagonist was known.

He said simply: " Glad to know you, Gentlemen. Let's have something."

Jack soon knew Judge Ketcham, hulking, vulgar, greasy, shabbily-genteel, with a Bardolphian nose.

"Our Federal District Judge, sir." So he was, and a better judge of whisky than law. "I'm told that you know my friend Senator Ezra Steele," he lazily remarked, for he too was a " carpet-bagger," floated up in the time of the disqualification of the competent rebel jurists. Manson gazed and briefly acknowledged the honor.

" Queer running mate for Steele. Three grades lower in vulgarity," he thought. " Probably a portable human whisky-tank. Yet, he sways here the balances of Justice, blind indeed, in these days of the unsettled war upheaval," Jack decided.

" My friend, Colonel 'Rip' Ford, said Hodges warmly. Jack's eye brightened. Here was a real man; tall, fair, silver-haired, he bore his sixty years with a slight stoop. An honest blue eye, a kindly smile and a simple, frank, soldierly manner were a passport to respect and confidence.

"I'm right glad to know you," said the old veteran. He extended a crippled right hand, and Jack Manson, gazing in his honest eyes, knew he had met the typical Texan. He could still ride eighty miles a day, sleep under the stars, and face death as calmly as when he followed Sam Houston as a boy at the Texan field of honor, San Jacinto. As a Ranger, he had chased the wild Comanches through the glades of the Nueces and Pecos. The whole frontier knew of how Captain Ford twisted round when his right hand was nailed to his saddle by a Comanche lance, and slew Gray Eagle, a giant chief, with his Texas Colt revolver held in the left hand, as their mad steeds raced side by side. Major

Ford had followed General Taylor to Buena Vista to see his old foe Santa Anna, the greatest of Mexican generals, flee before the Stars and Stripes! And, simple minded, when Texas "went out," Colonel Ford, C. S. A., followed the waning Stars and Bars and rode in the last fight of the war, on Palo Alto's sacred field, where, strange to say, the last battle of the war, fought after Lee's surrender, was a final gleam of victory before the night of defeat blotted out the Southern Cross for ever. Simple, frank, abstemious, generous, a devout Christian, only gently partaking of the habits of "old-time gentry," dear old "Rip" Ford's word was his bond and his heart was true to the great growing State he had fought for in its dark hours—its throes of crystallization into the gallant "Lone Star."

"I suppose you surely know Mr. Leavenworth?" hazarded Jack, as his heart warmed to the quaint old Ranger.

"We've rid thousands of miles together an' fought the Comanches an' Mexicans, side by side, fifty times! Many's the time one blanket has covered us two in a freezing 'norther,' when the mustang horses whimpered from cold. I'm at home at San Miguel—that is, when I'm not ridin' the perara," he concluded.

Major von Blucher and old Henry Miller were the next notables. The major, a bullet-headed, square-jawed old Prussian, with gleaming spectacles, was the pride of the frontier. A self-exiled German noble, he spoke all languages. Short and sturdy, a grim philosopher, he dropped the student's cap at the University of Berlin to plunge into a wild Texan career. Surveyor, engineer, lawyer, translator, scientist, and adviser, his trenchant tongue was a flail to the unlearned. In his quaint bungalow, at the head of the cañon, a gentle German lady presided over his home. Her graceful daughter portrayed the mother's refinement, his two stalwart boys were Texan copies of the sturdy von Blucher. Instruments, books, classic works, curious specimens, and uncanny gear lumbered up his house. He mingled all languages, from the fragments of Horace, never altogether forgotten, with the dialects of Kickapoo, Seminole, and Comanche. Fearless, sturdy, and fate-defying, he smoked, drank, philosophized, and fraternized with every border passer-by from Caballo Blanco, the great Mexican bandit, to the round-faced Catholic priest at the little town, with whom he fought, over the dinner table, the battles of orthodoxy and of agnosticism.

At this moment, the old Prussian was watching his favorite drink being compounded under the eyes of jovial Henry Miller, who, in feudal times, would have been the rosy cellar-master of some jolly set of monastery roisterers. At Brownsville, in face of Matamoras, by the rushing river, across which the shells from Fort Brown silenced the Mexican guns, Henry Miller was the landlord par excellence. Poor and rich had of his best. The "stranger within his gates" was even cared for like a brother, and easy-going old Henry calmly nursed friend and stranger, in the awful days of yellow fever scourges, with a heroism worthy of placing a halo around his kindly old face. Dear old Henry sleeps to-day by the murmuring river he loved, but his memory is green!

Mr. Beriah Mott, the ferret-eyed banker who plotted around Milly Smiley's table, was also added to Jack Manson's gallery of friends, his partner Bainbridge, and the Collector of Customs, a faded and inert politician who lived only by official blackmail, skillful poker, much internal suction, and sported a snappy-looking, over-

dressed, black-eyed "wife," vaguely suspected of belong-
ing to some other forgotten Menelaus.

"If I am not to be a three-bottle man, I must try some
strategy," finally Tack decided, as the grave ceremonies
ended.

"I hope to meet you this evening," said Jack to the
gentlemen. "I think I will take a little drive."

"Let . me show you around," said Hodges, and to
Jack's relief a pair of bounding half-tamed horses soon
whirled him away to where, from the tops of the rolling
green prairie swells, he could follow, by Hodges' whip-
stock, the air line of fifty miles dividing him from the
blue-eyed woman he loved.

Deft questioning brought out a fund of anecdote as
to Si Leavenworth's romantic life. Manson groaned
inwardly as he thought of the redoubtable old "Giant
Despair" he must face before Katie Leavenworth's
slender hand would wear his wedding ring. The state
of the border was painted briefly by the old ranchero.

"Yes, sir," said Colonel Hodges, as the foaming
steeds trotted back exhausted, for his thin wrists were
firm as steel bars, "it's a queer country, this Western
Texas. You see, many men come here with new-
fangled notions about Northern ideas and a whole lot of
nonsense. If a man comes in with us, and lets politics
alone, and makes himself neighborly, he can do well
here, if he's civil and a leetle careful." His voice took a
fatherly and prudential tone: "No, our people won't
stand any meddling."

"And if he *should* meddle?" said Jack good-
humoredly.

"Then most likely he'd get shot right off by somebody," said Colonel Hodges very simply, as if effective
shooting was a sort of natural "clearing-house" process for the removal of human busy-bodies.

"Don't they ever hang anyone down here?" said Jack, quite amazed, as they drew up before Joe Garcia's, for the supper hour was nigh.

"Oh, yes. The 'Regulators' hang a good many fellows prowling around the cattle ranches, and there's been a good many 'niggers' hung, but it's too much trouble for our young fellows. They mostly shoot them! There were some few Northern men hung here about war time. I'm sorry to say they were mixed up in politics."

Plain old Colonel Hodges' voice sank in a pensive regret. It was with a vain effort to prevent a smile, that Manson said seriously, as he dismounted: "I meant regular trial and hanging by law. Legal executions, you know. Criminals."

Colonel Hodges looked in wonder at Jack, who actually burst into laughter, as he said:

"Certainly *not!* Those fellows mostly light out for Mexico if they raise a rumpus. Nobody bothers with them. It costs too much. Somebody fills them full of lead if they are fools enough to hang around after hoss-stealing or killin' a good man."

The word "Mexico" recalled Maxan.

"Do you know a rich young fellow over there—Ramon Maxan?" said Jack, as Colonel Hodges finished tying his horses.

The old man wheeled with a sharp glance of astonishment. He said slowly: "He's the biggest liar and sneak among those fine gentry of the Zona Libre. He's got a poor girl, Panchita Lopez, walled up there in his hacienda. He run her off from the convent up at Laredo. Poor Panchita! If I was ten years younger, I'd take a gang of the boys and run over there and hang him in his own 'paseo' and burn the robber nest. He's not so safe on this side of the 'Bravo,'" said

Hodges. "I knew Panchita's mother," and a look of the old times drifted over the old borderer's eyes—the shadow of a lost and perished love. A memory of his old times of "storm and stress." Poor girl! Poor dead mother!

"I think I see now why Mrs. Milly Smiley married Senator Steele, and follows up this reckless young devil," mused Jack, as Hodges led him into the resort of the cattle princes, where lively Joe Garcia served the smuggled champagne, his white teeth flashing under smiling lips.

"But how the dickens did the Washington beauty ever find out about 'Panchita'?" Jack thought, as he answered Nordenskiold's bow of welcome.

He began to see the tangled threads of the web of life, stained in wine and blood, broidered in fool's gold, twisted by the hands of the Fates, with fair women's jeweled fingers playing in the meshes, stretching from Texan camp to Cabinet on the Potomac, from Hacienda Maxan to royal San Miguel, and from Havana and Liverpool to New York!

Here in the presence of these queerly-assorted lay figures, he mused as he sat at a rich feast, wondering how deeply these sly, secretive adventurers were in the secrets of a company which swayed the Texan legislature, owned Federal judges, dominated banks and telegraphs, and reached up to New York's millions and smooth pharisaical merchants, and farther on into the United States Senate, through the bewitching "Empress."

Why had Senator Steele married this waif of the Stars and Bars? Who was the hidden No. 4? A secret powerful protector who could reach even the secrets of the White House portfolio? Was he in the Cabinet? Did the railroad franchise, the princely grant, the mur-

murs of "a movement on the frontier" mean a dash on
Mexico as cowardly as when President Polk loosed
Scott and Taylor in the march to the Halls of the
Montezumas?

The young engineer's head swam. How far had he
his uncle's confidence? Did Katie Leavenworth's tender eyes lead him on to fortune, or a forgotten grave in
the cactus-bearing sands trodden only by bandit or
relentless Comanche? As he listened to wit and
wassail, old stories, war reminiscences, and freer allu-
sion, as the wine flowed and loosened tongues on all
sides, he saw ever the sphinx-like face of Olaf Nordenskiold, calm, stony, self-possessed, rising out of the
smoke wreaths. The gulf oysters, dainty fishes, wild
turkey, filets of grass-fed beef, and saddle of venison
were discussed, and every liquor and wine which the
daring "contrabandistas" could smuggle in, were spread
in profusion before the polyglot circle. And this was
the Rio Grande country—the open gate beyond which
bold riders took their lives in their hands. In a
moment of observation he noticed that Nordenskiold's
eyes never left him long.

"I have it!" he realized, in his heart of hearts.
"Milly Smiley and this man know all the dark secrets
of this strange Inner Circle. Leavenworth and Uncle
Mark are pillars at the east and west, but Senator Steele
is the 'open sesame' to the mystery of No. 4; and it
was to solve that enigma the beauty gave herself to that
senatorial Silenus. Ramon Maxan would dominate all
through her passionate love! He failed her and now
she hates him!" Jack's blood chilled as the sweet face
of Katie rose between him and his unseen foe. He
would strike all through her. "It is his life or mine,
now!" Jack swore in his heart. "I am glad I will
have letters from Uncle Mark and Mrs. Steele before I

go to San Miguel," was Manson's inward comment. "I think I will adopt the manner of William the Silent. I think that I will not let a soul know I can speak Spanish here. I may catch some local scoundrels off their guard. I am sure of Bayard, Jimmy, and old Colonel Ford here. Hodges and Blucher are wise and wary. I will meet them half-way. Every other man here I will hold *guilty* till he proves himself *innocent!* As for prairie craft, we'll see if I have forgotten the tricks taught me by the buffalo-killers of the Black Hills."

" I am glad to see that you do not drink to excess," said Olaf Nordenskiold, as they walked under the silent stars toward the St. James.

" Many a good fellow has told his story in his cups here, and has been followed, or artfully ' removed ' at the right time," said the old lawyer.

The sound of revelry followed them from the supper·room. Von Blucher and Henry Miller were singing the " Wacht am Rhein," and the sound of wild bacchanalian laughter drifted out on the night. The lawyer bent his steps toward the wharf, and handed Jack one of his private cigars.

" Let's take a turn around," he said, "we are alone." There was no sound but the soft swish of the phosphorescent waves on the shingly beach. A silver moon painted the waves of the Laguna with its broken reflections.

"What do you think of them,—our 'leading citizens'?" said Nordenskiold. His sharp-cut features wore a sneer like Mephisto in his scorn of the louts carousing in the cellar.

" I can't make them out. Are those the real Texans?" said Manson.

" No," sharply said the lawyer. " The nearness of

the Zona Libre attracts all sorts of human flotsam and jetsam. Here intrigue is always rife! I brought you here alone to tell you that Ford, Blucher, Hodges, old Henry Miller, and Tom Bayard are men to 'tie to.' Distrust and watch every man else whom you meet for a year, and above all be guarded with Si Leavenworth. He's a man who is staunch and true. He would die for you if he fancied you, but his temper is fiendish when aroused! No man but Tom Bayard ever bearded him in anger. Bayard is the only man alive who ever took a bottle away from him! Never speak *to* him on business unless you are alone. Never speak *of* him at all. He's as grim as the 'Black Douglas,' and as watchful as the tyrant of Syracuse. He never pardons an indiscretion, never forgives an injury, and reigns as unchallenged a king of the border as if he wore a trumpery crown in Europe. His heart is open only to Jim (who is as frank as the day) and his tiger-nature softens to but one thing, the voice of Katie. It is 'Una and the Lion.' The little maid alone can twist him around her finger. She is a sly little puss."

Jack Manson's brain was at its highest tension. He knew well that the searchlight of Nordenskiold's intellect was turned on him now. A sudden inspiration caused him to murmur: "Silent above all to *you*, my legal friend!—Major Blucher has asked me to drive with him to-morrow. Shall I go?" he said, changing the subject.

"Certainly. You are safe with the men I named. You asked me for the real Texans. They abide between the Sabine and the Nueces and as far north as the Staked Plains. Simple, hardy, and hospitable, they try to live no nearer each other than a hard day's ride. Averse to manual labor, they are unrivalled horsemen, guarding their flocks and herds. Great

land-getters, they live by the increase of their stock.
Their homes are quiet, their women loyal and unpretentious, they disdain the written details of small traffic
and correspondence, and seldom trouble the civil law.
Equally at home camping alone or riding in armed
bands, their word is their bond! An entire devotion to
the South, a plenitude of useless profanity, and an
Arabian hospitality are the natural result of their surroundings. Jealous of their personal honor, a blow,
an insult to the aged, or a stain upon a woman's name
is atoned by blood alone! With those primitive people,
plain in dress, taciturn and hearty, a man of prudence
can live his life with neither open quarrel nor secret
enmity. But, here on the banks of the Rio Grande,
the five senses are not enough. Eternal vigilance is
hardly sufficient. Each bush may have its concealed
assassin, any day bring some tumult, Indian raid, or
Mexican inroad. Unpunished marauders lurk everywhere, and the eye of distrust, the hand of violence,
the snares of malignant devils are around you every
day. I would not dare to be seen talking habitually
even with you alone! This silent night is our safeguard.

"As for a typical Texan, in the best form as to himself and his home, Colonel Tom Bayard is an exemplar.
At his ranch on the Nueces, his quiet, sweet-faced
old mother is the household deity. For a great frontier
establishment, San Miguel is a model. Neither it nor
Bayard's ranch can be approached without scores of
wary stock-men, riding the range, spying even a single
intruder.

"To realize what a Texan wife and mother can
be, you must observe Si Leavenworth's noble help-
meet. Her plain home-made gown covers a heart as
pure and true as a crystal. For fortitude, kindness,

long-suffering, and a patient, self-supporting struggle against uncouth surroundings, she is a star of her sex. Quiet, watchful, self-controlled, she has the modest dignity of nature's nobility. Withal, her immediate surroundings are dainty. Though poor, her father, a model Southern clergyman, was of gentle breeding. Her education, a little antique, is yet sound, and she would, in her unobtrusive merit, grace any station. To do old Silas justice, her slightest wish is his law in her own province. Alas! He has had an unending fight —a wild battle with fortune. I have all his affairs in my hands, as legal adviser. I expect to see him some day brought to my door, dead in his travelling wagon. It is a steel-clad, portable fortfication, and his personal arsenal is a wonder. His life has been attempted twenty times. So far he has foiled all attacks. I think one reason that he wishes to encourage the railway is to bring in a little army of reliable citizens around his baronial grant. But like all frontier kings, he can not see the benefits of sub-division, and assisting small farmers. The error of the South has ever been to look down on independent, honest labor. There's no medium here yet between the 'ranchero,' or great planter, and the poor white trash. Wherever the railway touches, worthy people come in. Here on the border," said Nordenskiold, with a sigh, "only Leavenworth can afford to keep a private army of retainers to fight Comanches, horse-thieves, and the lawless mongrel wanderers."

The two men paced up the wharf, and Jack Manson, watching the silver moon swinging west to San Miguel, thought fondly of the little Texas princess safe within the guarded lines fifty miles away. "A queer, strange land of every future promise. To-day, it is under the ban," he muttered, as the wild stories of

the night's revelry led him far out into the dim future.
It was a devious path, by unknown ways, yet along it
shone the loving eyes of Katie Leavenworth, brighter
than the argent moon far above him in the blue ether!

There was a grim smile on Major Blucher's face
as Mr. Jack Manson surveyed the stout buckboard
and two gaunt, vicious mules, which formed the exiled
noble's equipage, when he drove up next day. Manson
was amused. It was a queer outfit.

"Donnerwetter! They're not so handsome, but they
can smell an Indian a mile away, and need no whip.
Jump in," cried the jovial Teuton, as he reflected he
had a bottle of "cocktails" to sustain him. "I wished
to bring along Henry. Miller, but, between you and I,
he's been playing poker ever since you left us, over
at Joe Garcia's. Ah! he's a wonder! He takes all our
loose money away. I wish we had him here, not
thrown away on Brownsville. He's too good to live
at that smuggling hole."

With much Teutonic interpolation, and occasional
Spanish objurgations directed to his mules, Blucher
piloted his guest. He was a fiery character, and
remarked, in explanation of his cursing, in recondite
Castalian: "They seem to go better when I swear in
Spanish. I've tried *all* languages. Spanish suits these
stubborn fellows best!"

"It is a little strange, Major, that Mr. Leavenworth
did not come down and meet his children on their
arrival," said Manson, who wished to reap the benefit
of Blucher's sagacity.

"You think so!" laughed the German. "The last
time he came down, he got here safe, for he had a good
guard. But going home they waited for him. A dozen
fellows hid in the big Arroyo, and fired into his ambulance. They killed a young German who was going

out to survey the new ranch lines. The horses ran away and there was a bad time. That's why he keeps quiet a little."

" Was he hurt?" said Manson, with a show of interest.

" Oh, no, he just lay down and fired out of the rear of the wagon. He emptied a Winchester into them."

" What was it done for?" Manson queried.

The Major smartly cut his rebellious mule, and slowly said, with an air of indecision: " Old Si had been mixed up in hanging a lot of men found skinning cattle on his ranch. I suppose they were these fellows' friends."

Blucher's voice was very unconcerned. Manson was amazed. " For skinning cattle?" he said.

" Yes, the old man has a ' matanza' of his own and kills ten or twenty thousand cattle now and then to thin out the herds. The hides, horns, tails, and tallow are all he saves. The meat is fed to swine which the poorer Mexicans buy and drive away."

" What became of the young German?" Manson was interested in the poor stranger.

" We buried him by the road!" Blucher replied, and added, with pardonable pride. " I wrote a nice letter to his mother in Nuremberg!"

" It was not on account of the Rio Grande Company?" said Jack, after pondering a moment.

" Himmel! my lad," roared Blucher, " If you want to keep out of trouble, don't talk freely here about the Company. Best drop the subject! It has its friends and enemies," the Prussian sharply said. " I tell you this for your own safety."

Manson reflected: " An agreeable field for a rising young engineer! Where is the nefarious side of this Company? Has Mark Manson sent me here on a fool's errand, or is he hoodwinked?" He was puzzled.

The old German resumed more kindly: "I will tell you, my boy, all is under the rose here! Things are not what they seem. It has been so since 1846. Every gambler in New Orleans flocked here after Taylor's army. The United States was betrayed through the War of the Rebellion. There was no real blockade here. I was Major of Artillery; we had only one old thirty-two pounder at Corpus Christi to defend the town. We did not dare to fire it. We had a blockade of an old Yankee sailing bark, the 'Sachem.' You may judge of the fierceness of the war here! We captured the commander on shore down at Flower Point trying to buy some buttermilk." Blucher roared, "We gave him buttermilk! We put him in the log slave pen at Corpus, with a sign, 'A Yankee Pirate,' and sent him up to Libby Prison to get buttermilk nearer home. Now," the Prussian's keen gray eyes flashed, "a hundred mile from there, I saw on the Mexican side of the Rio Grande, at Bagdad, a pile of commissary stores a mile long, marked 'A. C. S. U. S. Army, New Orleans.' The same vessels which slipped through the paper blockade with them went back, loaded in exchange with Confederate cotton." The jolly old ex-rebel roared: "It was an opera-bouffe war here. We got arms, medicines, ammunition, and all we wanted the same way. Many cases were marked 'New York' and 'Boston.' Somewhere there was a great leak in the Union lines! The war made the border rich. Look at old Leavenworth. He and his partners were the biggest rebels here. They took the oath at the surrender! They bought a dozen river steamers from the Yankee quartermasters for the price of the ropes and cabin dishes alone, and went at once to hauling freight up the river for Uncle Sam."

"Was it possible!" Manson said in astonishment.

"Certainly," said Blucher, lighting a fresh cigar.

"The quartermaster and commissaries, I suppose retired with fortunes when the cruel war was over."

Blucher laughed heartily.

"Old Si bought seven thousand mules and horses at an army sale here. They were pastured on his ranch. The boys lamed them with horse-hair cords tied around their fetlocks. In lots of a hundred they were condemned and sold at a dollar apiece. The 'disease' was soon cured, and Si made the Government pay for their pasture 'during treatment.' That was a joke on Uncle Sam."

"What did he do with them?" Jack merely asked; "start an army of his own?"

"Nein," said Blucher, "he took contracts to haul the army freight at enormous rates to all the new posts with these steamers and animals. He got the wagons, too. They bought a railroad twenty-three miles long, for the price of the spikes, from Point Isabel to Brownsville. Ah, yes, Texas is full of simple people like my old friend, Si Leavenworth, and his partners."

Jack Manson thought of No. 4. "Was he also a mysterious war veteran?" His head was swimming.

"Can these stories be really true?" he said half-aloud.

The old major roared at his simplicity.

"I'll tell you the best yarn. Two blockade runners were chased ashore in Padre Island at the close of the war. They were really consigned by Fraser, Trenholm & Co., of Liverpool, to Si Leavenworth, Foley of Monterey, Park, and Jimmy Mulvain. Old Silas was 'loyal' after taking the oath. He bought them at auction. One of the boats was hauled off, the other was dismantled. The cargoes were all saved.

The old iron in one week paid for all, and the boys divided seven hundred thousand dollars. I got a few thousand dollars for the engineering, and twenty boxes of the best champagne I ever drank. Ah, yes, it pays *to be loyal now!* Old Si is loyal. He furnishes the beef, carries the mails, hauls the freight, sells the mules and horses to the army, and contracts all the hay and forage west of San Antonio."

"I should think that his accounts would betray him," said Jack, as No. 4 loomed up in his mind.

"Dey keep no accounts," remarked Blucher. "Old Rudolf Harbeck burns his books once a year, and Chisholm, at New Orleans, keeps the hard cash—all get a dividend! Every army purchasing agent down here drives better horses than old Si himself. As for money, bah! It is nothing. They roll in it."

"It's a nice country!" said Manson, with some sarcasm.

"Yes! to get out of," rejoined the saturnine Blucher. "This railroad charter was rushed through the same way. Olaf Nordenskiold has got the Texan legislature in his pocket. He *will organize* the road. Si Leavenworth and a few friends up North will grab the lands for the mere price of the survey. I suppose they will square him with the Government men and divide these pickings."

Mr. Jack Manson felt the scales falling from his eyes.

"There's the mail boat," joyously said Blucher, as they drove down the main street. His "cocktail" bottle was empty. "I could tell you some real strange things if I had time," the major concluded as the team drew up at the "St. James."

"I don't doubt it a moment," replied the neophyte, with some dryness of tone. "It *is* a very interesting country, I am sure."

"Oh! Decidedly! You will find it so, my young friend," remarked the old surveyor cheerfully, as he led the way to the bar for a solemn libation.

Before Manson escaped from the clutches of the hilarious German, who often neglected to visit "Castle Blucher" on the hills for days, while he contemplated the adornments of the St. James bar-room, Nordenskiold entered.

"Come up in the upper verandah. I have letters for you," he whispered, as he chose a cigar.

Jack's hand trembled, as he opened a letter sealed with a crest. He allowed even Mark Manson's cipher letter to lie unheeded as the perfumed sheet he held was eagerly scanned. It was unsigned.

I am now a wife. My telegram will have told you *whom* to fear. From this day, my interests are only those of the man whose name I bear. Steele has told me all, and one I will not name, wrote from New Orleans. I know that human tiger. He has imprudently exposed his plans. He vows vengeance on you, on Leavenworth, on the girl you love! Find out if he knows your side of the river. Search his past history. Watch for his friends and spies. Distrust anything happening, not clearly explained. He will be behind it all. You do not know yet a Creole's revenge. Pray God you may never! The Senator has told me all, for Chisholm held nothing back. Watch even the shadow by your side. There is danger in the very air you breathe. I know the rage and resentment of your foe when he will learn of my marriage. Write me under my old name at my residence. S. trusts me in all; I have his every secret now. Whatever I may be to *others*, you will always find me the same. Send me a safe address for your letters. Had I not better confide in your uncle and let him advise me? He can telegraph you in cipher. I will go to New York and see him alone. Ladies have always "metropolitan shopping" to do. If you wish me to, telegraph only the word "Yes" to the address I send. Do you not think I am at heart true? I will know if you answer by telegraph. A woman's friendship is not to be lightly thrown away.

"Would she tell me the secret of 'No. 4'?" Jack questioned, as he folded the letter. "Mark Manson will divine it, if he knows it not already! A strange guardian angel!" There was a shadow on his brow as he opened his uncle's brief lines.

Steele's marriage astounds me. I learn of it by the telegraph announcement in the journals. I shall try and fathom the mystery by seeing her. He is a waxen mask. She has married him for reasons of her own. What they are I know not *now*, but I will, *soon*. The air is full of border rumors. Some great movement is-imminent. Urge on the organization. Do not vary my instructions. If Leavenworth and his lawyer act openly and deal with you as I wish, all is well. Send news by the wire of the completed formalities. Money and materials ready. When the details warrant, go out and thoroughly examine the line. Then, lose no time. Use every dollar and man needed. Watch over your own safety for your own future and the sake of your

UNCLE MARK.

"I'll burn my ships," said Jack, as he rose to saunter away to the telegraph office.

"One moment," whispered Nordenskiold. "I leave at once for San Miguel. No one here knows I am going. I apparently take a walk. My team awaits me hidden on the hill. We will send in for you. Distrust anything but Jimmy's hand or a letter from Bayard or myself. Be prudent. Don't say good-bye."

"So even this Machiavelli sneaks away unknown to his friends. Nice country!" ejaculated Jack, as he ran against Major Blucher at the foot of the staircase.

"See here, do you know a man named Ramon Maxan?" The Prussian drew him into a dark corner. He hoarsely whispered: "A dangerous, slippery devil! A human jaguar! He sneaked around the Mexican border and helped in those dark deeds of the war I told you of. That combination had to use him, and he knows *too much*. He keeps away from here. His knowledge of languages and graceful appearance helped him. He played off as a rich young Cuban, and he slid in and out of New Orleans, Matamoras, Havana, Paris, and Liverpool during the whole war. He was *paid* a good deal and *stole* more! If you should ever have a word with him, shoot him first and explain afterward," said the wily philosopher. "They don't care to murder him openly over the Bravo, for he has lodged papers abroad implicating high Mexican officials. His ' hacienda ' is a tiger's den. Its walls hide many secrets! He is hand and glove with every scoundrel here from No Man's Land to ' Las Cuevas,' the robber - crossing. He will not live to be a patriarch!" oracularly remarked the major, as he remembered his hungry mules, now lifting their voices in protest.

Manson, with bowed head, clutched the slip of paper with the pencilled address. He sent a dispatch as indicated:

Yes, see him at once!

" I will write to her and Mark and then trust to love and luck!"

CHAPTER X.

AT SAN MIGUEL—" FOR MY SAKE "—WITH THE WILD RIDERS—A FIGHTING TRINITY—THE TIGER BALKED OF HIS PREY.

IT WAS midnight when Manson threw down his pen. "There, I can do no more," he cried. " Every bower anchor is out now. I must ride out the storm of Texan life."

Roused at eight o'clock, he sauntered over to the post-office. He had taken the precaution to cover both his letters to his uncle's banker at Washington. Nordenskiold had warned him of the local mysteries of mail transit. "I have brought them both en train now. My route is clear. San Miguel, the survey, and my report! Then, the construction of the road! Or do they only wish to do enough to secure the land? I must drift along with the tide which bears me nearer to Katie."

He returned to the hotel, his letters safely mailed.

When Jack left the breakfast room, the clerk said: "I have a box of cigars sent to you." Passing into the office, Manson carried it to his room. The card bore "compliments O. N." "Ah! some sign to me. I'll look therein." Opening it, a folded slip bore the words:

Not one imprudent word. You are now alone. When we send for you leave quietly as directed by the messenger. He will bring your luggage. Say not when you go. Your hotel accounts have been provided for. You will meet friends outside the town. Wait in patience. It may be a week.

The signature was the lawyer's.

"More mystery," growled Jack, tossing the box on the bed. "Is there nothing straight-forward and above-board here? I must find some means to kill time, to avoid that beastly drinking-room, with its blinking caricatures of the heroes of the Lost Cause, its noisy cowboys, drunken loungers, and dust-begrimed wayfarers. There are weapons enough carried around the old billiard table to fit out a pirate ship." An inspiration came to him. Several of the sailors awaiting orders were lounging around. Selecting two of the most intelligent, he cruised far and near in a stout sail-boat, sketching the harbor, studying maps furnished by the mystified Blucher, and thus gained a local insight into

the port's features.   At night, alone, he smoked his
cigar on the verandah and waited for his summons.
While thus seated, a week after Nordenskiold's departure, he started in surprise as two men near him carelessly began to canvass the name of Ramon Maxan.
" I'll play listener. All's fair—in Texas," he decided.

Several visits to the " bar " had made the strangers
loquacious. " Where did you see him? I thought he
was in Europe," began a cavalier in local riding costume.

" At his ranch. I came over with the buck-board
from Brownsville. He's just up from Tampico," the
other replied.

"What were you looking up?" said the first carelessly.

" I wanted twenty or thirty good cattle horses. I'm
sending a drive up to Kansas soon. Maxan always has
lots of good horses over there," the traveller continued.

"Yes; if you don't look into the brands," chuckled
the speaker. " Did you get bargains? "

" I made out pretty fair. I'd 'a done better if the
d—d yellow Jaguar himself hadn't 'a come home on
the sly. I'm solid with his major domo, old Antonio.
He's a rare scoundrel; so's his master."

" Right you are. Is that pretty gal from Laredo,
over yonder yet. You know; the one he run off," the
drawling borderer continued.

" Yaas; an' ole Antonio keeps her precious close! I
couldn't get a sight of her. That department is kept
like a fort. I wouldn't give much for a man's life who
fooled around there. But the 'Jaguar,' as them
' greasers ' call him, has some big scheme on foot. He's
gettin' a band of about twenty or thirty of the worst
scoundrels together I ever laid eyes on."

" What's up? " was the brief query, as the speaker bit
off a huge piece of tobacco.

"He's strikin' out for Eagle Pass, an' I suspicion he's goin' to run over some silver, or make a big contraband crossing. He's doing the dirty work for all that crowd of Mexican generals. They're thicker than flies on the border. I suppose he'll meet some of them outcast devils from No Man's Land, up on the Pecos, with a lot of fine stolen horses from the Indian Territory or New Mexico, and when he works back he'll run off a good band of our fat cattle."

"That's about his game. I heard he was operatin' with that hatchet-faced thief, Caballo Blanco. Some of the boys back from the river told me so," said the second.

"Now that's strange," the first replied with an air of decided interest. "This Mexican 'blood' is rich and puts on lots of airs. I suppose he's dodging old man Leavenworth and Nordenskiold."

"Old Si would hang any fellow from the other side, with a band of cattle, even if they had bills of sale painted on their sides. As for that lawyer devil, he's afraid of nothin' livin'. He's got it in for him about Panchita. The old fox used to be very sweet on her mother."

"You're right, Bill. I fancy Maxan's crowd would take in most anything that comes along, and yet he's been playin' a sly game. He likes to put up his jobs mostly by other fellows in his train. If he's a comin' to this side, there's blood on the face of the moon somewhere."

"You bet there is, an' it's something special. He told me if I wanted any more horses to send a note to him to ole man Castro, up at San Diegita, any time in a month or so. That's just off Leavenworth's ranch, you know, the fandango house," said the speaker. "Let's get a drink."

As they unsteadily toiled down-stairs, the other said:
"He is a cunning devil for cards an' women an' throatcutting. I've known him since Confederate war times,
an' never knowed the first square thing in him! I wish
to God some fellow would take his sign in."

"Amen!" silently added Manson, as the prairie lords
vanished. "I must make a note of this. Leavenworth
should hear this at once. It looks ominous. Maxan
is hovering around already!"

Jack stepped to his room. The clerk stood at the
door. "There's a man in there with a message for you.
It's all right; he's Mr. Jim's private ridin' messenger."

Manson entered his room and by the single flickering
candle saw a tall, raw-boned scout of fifty standing, hat
in hand. He silently gave the engineer a scrawl in
Jimmy Leavenworth's well-known hand:

This is Basilio, my own man. He will give you a sealed
letter.

The curtains were drawn and Jack motioned the old
man to a seat. He was a sun-bronzed Mexican half-
breed, with the lank, straight hair of the Indian. Two
pistols and a knife ornamented his belt. Drawing a
pouch from his goatskin riding jacket, he gravely made
a cornhusk cigarette, ceremoniously depositing his broad
sombrero and heavy silver-mounted rawhide quirt at his
feet.

Jack ran over the letter. "Good!" he cried. "I will
be there."

In very fair English, Basilio announced that he would
await Manson at the head of the bluff at daylight. He
then noiselessly disappeared.

"Ah! moccasins! I suppose he's a half Cherokee or
Kickapoo. Now for San Miguel, for Katie, and to outwit 'el Jaguar,'" cried Jack, as he sat down to study
the letter. "Even if we are not bandits, Bayard,

Jimmy, and I will try the old Three Guardsmen's motto, 'One for all and all for one.' It's for Katie's sake," he mused, as her fair young face beamed on him in fancy again, as delicately lovely as when she trembled in his arms when the white-veiled spirit of Death sought her in the Gulf cyclone.

Manson sprang to his feet at dawn, for a light tap at his door roused him.

"Your man has been here already!" said the sleepy clerk. "Pack your little things. I will send your breakfast up. As for your trunks, Don Basilio will get them from the tienda on the hill. I'll send them up in the ox-cart, when my lazy niggers wake up. Then slip out quietly; they are ready. Here's an eye-opener." The roughly amiable Texan deposited a mixture on the table, calculated to unsettle the good resolutions of a saint.

The Texan frontier cocktail, like the border pistol, is heavily loaded, and of utmost potency. Civilized drinks are to it in the ratio of an ant-hill to a budding pyramid.

Slipping out in the gray of the dawn, Manson turned his back on the misty Laguna, and reached the head of the gorge unobserved.

Don Basilio, a spectral-looking Don Quixote, sat his rebellious charger with the air of Cervantes' great hero. His gentle sadness was not disturbed by the frantic bucking of his wall-eyed, raw-boned mustang. The deep lines of his face never changed. With a graceful flourish of his whip, he motioned Jack into a side alley of the Mexican adjunct of Corpus Chris.i, vulgarly called "Greaserville."

"It's the white men they wish to hoodwink, not the Mexicans," thought Manson. "The great Company's enemies are of their own envious neighbors."

In a strong spring wagon, double-seated, with four superb wiry mules as motive power, Colonel Tom Bayard at the reins, Manson recognized in the other muffled passenger, the indomitable Hodges.

"Jump in, Jack," cried Bayard gaily. "Here's your chariot. You will have your coffee poured by Miss Katie, at San Miguel to-night. Basilio will send on your trunks in another team." With a bound, the Spanish-bred mules briskly trotted away. As they drew out over the broad prairie, through which the spring grass was peeping, Manson noted the armament of his companions. Huge revolvers and knives were swung from their cartridge-filled belts. A Winchester carbine lay beside each seat, save Hodges' nook, where his old reliable "army gun," a cut-off Springfield breechloader, was in readiness.

"You prefer the old service gun, Colonel," said Jack, as he smilingly waved away a flask of three-star Hennessey.

"I can kill a Mexican with it a half-mile off, if I can sight him fair," quietly said the grim old borderer.

Manson understood his peculiar smile when Bayard told him later that Hodges' life had been one long pot-hunt after that fated class since a band of guerrillas had murdered his parents at the outbreak of the Mexican War. "They have paid dearly for failing to cut his own throat scientifically. He is insane in his unsatisfied revenge," said the soldier. "He has already killed a couple of dozen of his enemies. They call him 'El Terror.'"

The mists of morning rose from the far-rolling prairies. Before them not a tree was in sight. Hundreds of hares fled affrighted, and stray deer and antelope bounded across the road, leaping out of the low shrub bushes.

Colonel Tom Bayard whispered: " I will not repeat all the hospitable messages I bring. You will soon hear them. We will travel along easily." A light spring wagon soon overtook them. Beside the boy; driving the baggage, rode Joaquin Ximenes on his beautiful steed. Jack caught a vicious glance from his furtive eyes.

" What is that unhung wretch doing here with us? " Manson demanded of Bayard.

" I suppose," said Colonel Tom, " he rode in for Rudolf Harbeck. .He carries all the confidential business dispatches. He is very thick with the old book-keeper, and I suppose they both pick up crumbs from the Company's table. Harbeck knows too much to be set adrift. This fellow is under his special protection. He rode down yesterday with Basilio for company. Now, there's a man as true as steel. He can throw a bullock as well as our best. He is a perfect rider. I've known him to take a canteen, his ' papelitos', and a couple of pounds of ' pinole' and do a hundred and ten miles in a day in the Indian country. He can spot a moving form on the desert, and tell you what it is, further than you can see it with a glass. Utterly ignorant of books, he is a walking map of Texas. Hardly a corner of its two hundred and seventy-five thousand square miles he does not know. He has seen Texas grow from thirty thousand to nine hundred thousand in population. In twenty years more, Jack, we will have peace, railroads, and two million people. But one thing can stop it. That would be a cowardly war on Mexico! Why do we need to attack a weaker republic? The North will frown down a needless Mexican war. General Grant's immortal phrase, ' Let us have peace,' is the new gospel. I believe him as wise in the days of calm as he was brave in war and generous in victory. I only hope he can rule himself! "

" What do you mean?" said Manson astonished.

" There are fools already plotting, in view of Grant's triumphal re-election, to tempt him to a third term, a military regency over the United States and conquered Mexico. The unemployed Northern floating veterans, and the yet unreconciled Southern soldiery would tender him the crown of Mexico on their bloody bayonets. But not till the last armed Mexican went down. They have learned modern warfare thoroughly in whipping the French."

" You dream, Colonel Bayard," said Jack indignantly. "Grant's pure citizen-bred greatness is above any such crime! And the spotless integrity of William Tecumseh Sherman would lead the great General of the Army to hurl anyone from a dictator's seat."

" You think that I dream," Bayard gravely said. " Manson, the Knights of the Golden Circle are neither all dead nor supine. There is even Northern money and railroad kings behind the treasonable plan."

Jack Manson thought of No. 4, veiled in mystery! Was the great conqueror of Lee to be fed with the fulsome flattery of a Cæsar?

While they parleyed, Hodges, cigar in mouth, blurted out: " There goes your greaser spy, Tom." Like an arrow shot from a bow, Ximenes' lithe racer stretched away over the firm red wagon track till he was a mere blur on the rolling prairie.

" You or I will have to kill that fellow some day in Leavenworth's interest," the old planter growled.

" I resign in your favor, Colonel," said Bayard politely. " I have other thoughts!" So he had. Alice Leavenworth's brown eyes were daily tempting him to a quiet home by the shady banks of the beautiful

Nueces. Far before them rolled the great swelling prairies. In its hollows the grass was already rich. The fringe of trees behind them dwindled to a dark line. A fresh breeze moved the pure prairie air. Distant bands of deer raced away in elastic strides, yellow antelope danced away, flickering patches of light against the green, and the stray horses and cattle increased in number. It was the glorious prairie ocean of America!

"What a land!" Bayard proudly said. "Spaniard, Englishman, Frenchman, Mexican, the Indians, German colonists, and all have given way to us. The 'New Phillippines,' Spain called it—LaSalle's old rusty guns still lie honeycombed at Matagorda. But the Bourbons lost it. This shall be the home of the planter, the farmer, the miner. Manson, I have ridden over Texas from border to border. It is an empire. The east will give us cotton and sugar; the middle and north ship-timber, general farm products, iron ores, and coal; the west, cattle, sheep, and horses, in millions. Across these plains the entire Mexican trade will roll on steel rails not yet made."

"You paint a rosy future," said Manson, whose eyes followed the spy. Why had he ridden on in front? Jimmy's letter said:

Watch Ximenes; keep him well out of ear-shot. We must trap that scoundrel. I wish to get rid of him.

"Will timber grow here?" said Manson, his eye roving over the plains.

"There is unfailing water twenty-five feet below the plains. Small settlers will raise an abundance of trees," Bayard said. "We have scattered forests of oak, cypress, pecan, cedar, ash, walnut, hickory, and pine, with the alluvial trees. We have coal, silver, lead,

iron, marble, and other minerals. No man yet has
even skinned over the unused treasures of the State.
We need good people only."

" Your border unrest must cease first," replied Jack.

" Then give us peace and railroads, with American
shipping, then Texas can feed the world!"

The young engineer smiled as Bayard broke his team
into a changing run. He little dreamed that twenty
years would more than verify the boasts of the ranchero.
But time has worked all these wonders! The out-
lines of a heavy wooded arroyo loomed up by noon.

" There's a nice spring in this cañon. We'll lunch
nown there," said Bayard, as he drove down into a
dense wood, sunk two hundred feet below the plain.
"Here's where they attacked old Si." He started as he
spoke, for the shrill neigh of a horse broke the silence.

Hodges threw up his heavy rifle; his eyes were lit up
with eagerness. ·

" Pshaw, only a stray mustang!" said Bayard, driving
merrily along.

There would have been a rain of bullets poured on
the unsuspecting travellers, if Ximenes, hidden in the
bushes, had not restrained " Caballo Blanco." For
twenty murderers awaited the chief's signal near them
in hiding!

" He said: ' Don't kill him unless alone.' You see
Bayard and Hodges' death would bring out every
Texan," the hidden spy whispered, as the team dashed
out of hearing. " I only want you and your men to
mark that face. The big Gringo—the young fellow.
After this, kill him whenever you get him alone!
Five thousand dollars is ' El Jaguar's ' price to the man
who does it. He will come back in a week or so.
He's going out with the old man's boy to see the
border. After he leaves San Miguel kill him, but

not before. If at night, make sure of every one with him. Now scatter! I will ride up the arroyo and get in to San Miguel first. You can cross lower down and get over to the South."

"I hardly like this place. Too much cover. Many a man has been killed here," said Hodges, as he lay at rest on a serape, after the noon halt in the deep cañon. The mules, with a good roll while unharnessed, freshened up in the shade.

"Pooh, not a bit of danger now," said the fearless Bayard, and, even as he spoke, the black rascals in hiding were begging "Caballo Blanco" to let them wipe out the party of five.

"Madre de Dios! Fools! It's easy enough to kill them. I want the money," said the bandit leader, a coarse-looking young Mexican of thirty. "But, Maxan must be obeyed. You see it might get him in trouble."

So the human bloodhounds slunk away in the coppice.

It was four o'clock when Jack Manson said, looking at the sinking sun, as the team trotted briskly along, "When do we reach the Rancho San Miguel line?"

"You've been on old Si's land for an hour," answered Bayard. "A few thousand acres near the 'home place' are lightly fenced, but the tract is not closed in."

"How large is it?" said Jack in wonder.

"Three hundred and forty thousand acres in four counties, with seventeen lakes and ponds, one river, and about two hundred thousand more acres of pasture which no one will ever take up for twenty years," simply said Bayard.

"Why not?" questioned Jack.

"Old Si has located and fenced and paid for every pond, spring, and water-hole, so the land is under his control," Bayard replied, beaming in admiration of the frontier king's slyness.

"How could he do that?" Jack eagerly said.

"There are *no* United States land surveys in Texas. Don't forget we were annexed as a sovereignty. None of your factory-made States," laughed Bayard. "Major Blucher. made the surveys, and Nordenskiold got the land patents."

"So money does wonders, even in Texas," remarked Manson, quite enlightened.

"Yes; just as wit and hard cash do everywhere," Bayard replied, with a resigned smile, as the glories of the three children's heritage were revealed.

"Leavenworth has nearly three hundred thousand cattle, sheep, horses, and mules on this range, and there are two hundred men riding it always. It's a great, a princely estate," Bayard said.

"Do they live well?" measuredly queried Jack.

"With the easy simplicity of wealthy Southern families," his friend answered. "And now, Mr. Jack Manson, I can give you a sight of the house."

Manson's heart beat high as he discerned toward the west a rich fringe of varied trees. On a raised plateau, fifty feet above the plain, was a huge masonry square keep, three stories high. And, at some little distance, a great, roomy Southern planter's home rose from bowered gardens, and in the rear an extensive series of offices, with immense stacks of prairie hay, rising unhoused toward the blue skies. Down into a rich valley, Bayard lashed the team, for several riders were cantering along the slope below to meet them. Manson schooled himself to the conventional, as a beautiful chestnut Kentucky thoroughbred raced up, bearing proudly the little queen of San Miguel.

"That's *two* dozen gloves, Brother Jimmy," remarked the glowing Amazon, as Leavenworth's sorrel blood-horse bounded up, a few lengths behind.

With a silent greeting of her dancing eyes, Katie leaned over her saddle as Jack Manson touched the tips of her fingers. The little hands were gauntleted, but Manson could have pressed them to his lips in secret joy.

"Welcome to San Miguel! You are now my prisoner, sir!" laughed the fair one with the golden locks.

Colonel Bayard's deep voice was murmuring to brown-eyed Alice, whose dignity of bearing in the saddle was regal. Under this fairy escort, the party swept up to the twelve-foot porch, where the redoubtable master of San Miguel waited to greet his guest.

"I am glad to see you," said Silas Leavenworth, scanning Mr. Jack Manson's handsome proportions. "How is your uncle? You must make this your home and feel it such. I leave the details to Jim. My wife, sir," said the old borderer.

"Mother, here's our young friend Mr. Manson. I shall hold you and the girls responsible if he does not like San Miguel."

Jack's heart went out at once to the quiet, thoughtful-faced woman, whose gentle greeting charmed him. Her modest dress, smooth brown hair, with its few silver threads, and slightly apprehensive eyes, denoted the unobtrusive and beloved Southern woman of position.

Eager blacks swooped down upon the wagons, and, while Hodges and Silas Leavenworth fell into a chat, Jack Manson's eyes drank in the beauties of the lovely scene. From grove and copse the song of birds rose, and far and near, in countless number, great flocks and herds dotted the plain. The flowers of my lady's garden were a token of home's graceful employments; corn-fields and gardens stretched far beyond. With surprise Manson noted the absence of orchards and many other usual farming features.

"We Texans only raise wild cattle, sheep, and horses," laughed old Silas. "We're not 'gentlemen farmers'! We even get our general supplies from New Orleans. Our people are so lazy, but farm produce should grow here like in the Garden of Eden. You will see many things to astonish you, my young friend. Sometimes we have hardly any milk or cream." Even the placid mother joined in the general laugh.

"But you always have *horses to ride*," replied Manson.

"Yes, if one can *stay on them*, or the Mexicans and Comanches don't steal them," answered the ranchero, with a grim touch of humor.

Manson gazed in surprise at the quiet-mannered, compact, medium-sized man in plain dress who ruled this domain. A steel-gray eye, a slow, deliberate speech, a furtive, repressed activity of movement, and a mouth as stern as a Cæsar, marked the hero of a hundred desperate adventures. His eyes were seldom lightened, and his smile was as wintry as the gleam of the blue pole-star on the lonely Arctic seas, where eternal silence is king.

"To-night you and I and Nordenskiold can have a chat. He's working up our papers. It will take him a few days. In the mean time Jim can show you the ranch and you can look into our quiet ways of killing time out here."

Old Silas never hurried, but his eagle eye, retentive brain, and lynx-like ear never missed in their secret activity. Already, in his stern presence, Manson felt a steel spring bearing down on him with steady pressure. He eagerly embraced Katie's invitation to join her mother and inspect the "Castle Dangerous," as she laughingly termed her home on the outskirts of the wild border. Colonel Bayard and Alice were walking in the rose alleys, and Jack failed not to notice Silas Leavenworth's eye following the stalwart Confederate.

"His future is safe. Mine is in my own hands now," he thought, as he walked over the threshold of the great low Southern house.

It was a tender flash from heaven's own sunlight, the glance of Katie's eyes as she turned and silently bade him welcome. The gentle dissembler had not yet dared to breathe her momentous secret to the dear mother by her side, but a dangerous loving glance made her eyes tell-tale blue jewels of the soft evening. Jack started in surprise as he gazed around the ranchero's home. For, not even Mark Manson's palace was more superbly adorned. Unpretentious in its exterior, the great low plantation house was a very dream of refined luxury.

"It is evident that the ladies rule within these walls," was the stranger's comment, as he passed up the great hall, through a forest of the trophies of the chase. Strange robes and skins covered the polished floor, and heads of unfamiliar beasts grinned from the walls. The "Big Horn," superb elk and deer antlers, antelope, spikes, great bison heads, and the open-jawed trophies of bear, panther, jaguar, wolf, and cat surrounded him.

"Products of the country?" said Manson, smiling, as his chum led him up the stairs to his rooms, where one of eight guest chambers was allotted to him.

"Yes," cried Jim gaily. "You can shoot a buck in our cornfield any day. Wild turkeys, by the drove, wander in our home woods, and bird and beast without end. I will give you object lessons in our woodcraft, but first I must get you up a real Texan outfit. This is your boy while you are here. I picked him out. He was my own boy before Abraham Lincoln finished slavery with an immortal pen-stroke. Strange that both the President and Czar Alexander II. of Russia

met a violent death at the hands of the assassin. The
world's thanks for freeing serf and slave! Bob is a
good plainsman; he knows every inch of the border.
I can't *give* him to you, *I could have done so once!*
but I will lend him till further orders," said the hospitable Texan. "Give him all your keys, Jack; he
will fix you up. This is your headquarters now."

The smart colored lad grinned at his master's com-
mendation. Maxan nervously hastened his simple toilet.

" Let me show you our own special corners," Katie
said as Manson descended the stairway. Under her
guidance the glories of the home place were explored.
On all sides, every adjunct of wealth and taste—
books, rare pictures, and the thousand-and-one evi-
dences of woman's sway. A foreign air marked the
general decoration and furnishing.

"We had everything brought in by the blockade
runners in war time," Katie merrily said. "Our.
French and English agents sent out commissioners to
Bagdad, and from the Rio Grande our own teams
brought the goods in. I am told that the old Mexican families have their haciendas royally adorned.
You can get anything in Matamoras, through the
Zona Libre. But I must show you my curios some
day. See! we are quite antiquarians." In cases, in the
great rooms, were countless treasures picked up in
the Rio Grande Valley—Mexican silverware, ornaments, and pottery; superb embroidery, and knightly
saddle-gear; minerals, Aztec relics, rare carvings;
Indian spoils in endless profusion, and an extensive
collection of weapons, personal ornaments, and masses
of old books, religious ornaments, and costly vessels.

Manson's frankly expressed surprise was great at
beholding such treasures!

"You don't know how many friends I have. All

our people bring me queer things, from the city of
Mexico to Mazatlan, and from the Zuni Villages to
the Staked Plains. Dear old Major Blucher saved all
the rare books and goods you see when the furious
Mexicans dismantled the churches, monasteries, and
convents. He gives me all that he can find. Mr.
Nordenskiold knows everything—he is so learned—
and he helps me arrange them, and so do Alice and
mother. This is my 'curiosity shop'. I have a real
Watteau fan, given by the Empress Carlotta to Prince
Salm-Salm's wife. There is one of the ten gold
pieces which brave Maximilian gave to each of the
firing party; a Mexican general gave it to me. But I
wont tire you further to-day. There is the dinner-
bell."

Preceded by the master of San Miguel, the family,
through a covered corridor, walked out to a long dining-
hall (a separate house), similarly connected with a
long servants' department. At the patriarchal table
the grave lawyer was already seated, with a ferret-eyed
man of years, whom Manson knew as Mr. Rudolf
Harbeck, the silent accountant. By his side a bronzed,
fearless-looking man sat. Hiram Elam was the right
hand of the chief, and ranch foreman. Devoid of
ostentation, the table was yet worthy of a noble. The
wines and service were faultless. Mrs. Leavenworth
silently directed, as old Silas never appeared personally
in matters large or small. But his slightest wish was
instantly executed!

Jack ventured to compliment the ranchero upon the
cuisine.

"Old Ned is the best cook in Texas. He directed
the establishment of the Bishop of St. Louis until he
became too haughty. I bought him before the war,
and thus saved him from flourishing a hoe on the

Red River. He was too saucy for the good Bishop!
I have to touch him up a little myself now and then.
He samples my best cigars and wines, and he is a rare
old scoundrel.   I put up with him, for, smart as he is,
he can not believe yet that he is free, and he fills the
place admirably.   My wife and the girls are a little
too kind to him, that's all," said the autocrat, as he
glanced with almost a loving look at the poor clergyman's daughter who had been the blessing of his
life.   Rude, and wholly wrapped up in his schemes,
Silas Leavenworth still was truly devoted to the modest
woman who had given to him the children of his heart.

Generals, diplomats, foreigners, army officers, rich
traders, explorers, judges, and governors thronged his
board, and none failed to admire the simple elegance
of the Lady of San Miguel.   The nearest neighbor
was forty miles away, and rich and poor, with beast
and burden, were sheltered within the open gates of
San Miguel.   Repayment was sternly refused, and a
bachelor's den of a dozen rooms adjoined the great
masonry fortress and store-house, where Leavenworth
kept a year's supply of outfitting for two hundred men.
Over this, Harbeck and the ranch superintendent presided, with a corral master to watch the coming and
going of wayfarers.   No one ever crossed the invisible
line drawn around the " home place," as it was simply
called, unless bidden, and twenty messengers, Cowboys,
and Vaqueros lounged within the great door-yard of the
" Ranch House," as the depot building was termed.
From its roof, fifty miles of prairie could be swept by
telescope, and behind its barricaded doors, with the
arsenal within, Silas Leavenworth could withstand any
attack unsupported by field-pieces.   The alarm-bell at
any moment would bring a hundred men, Winchesters
in hand, to the bidding of the grim chief of San

Miguel. Not a man, save the house servants, but carried his Colt's frontier and belt of copper cartridges on his person. Under the long sheds, fleet prairie steeds stood saddled day and night in uneasy squads.

"To-morrow, Jimmy will show you over the ranch a little. The girls can drive you around, but I don't fancy them going too far away. There's a dozen rattlesnakes to every acre and the woods are too near. Some bad men might be loafing around us. We've got a few panthers also who drop in and pick up lambs and calves now and then. They are ugly devils and extremely fond of my blood colts. They pick out the very best."

When Mrs. Leavenworth rose, after a quiet glance at the rooms, Silas led the way, followed only by Nordenskiold and Manson, to a small brick building detached from the main house. As the sisters sought the broad portico of the mansion, Katie cast one wistful glance at her father.

"Remember that we are to have some music, padre! Don't be too late." The border chief smiled as he opened the door with a private key. The visitor looked around in surprise. The room was but twenty feet square. Its thick walls were each broken by but a single window; the sills were laid breast high from a high knoll, wherefrom the whole surrounding country was visible. Heavy iron shutters and a folding iron inside door matched the ponderous safe against the farther wall. A large square table, built with drawers on all sides, gave seating-room for eight. Besides a strong couch and several easy chairs, the only other decorations were racks of a dozen Winchesters, Spencers, and heavy Springfield rifles; with several rows of revolvers. The whole appearance justified its title, "The Den," for spite of the cheerful lamps, the room looked like an incipient fortress or a prison guard-room.

"Sit down; I'll get some cigars," curtly said Silas, as he disappeared toward the mansion. Decorations there were none, save in a glass case on the wall a tattered Confederate flag, shot-torn and ragged. Its faded silk, its blended stars and bars bore the gilded legend,

"FOURTH TEXAS INFANTRY."

"Ah!" said Nordenskiold, as Jack regarded it gravely, "Colonel Tom Bayard gave that to Miss Alice. His heart went with it. It's all that he brought back from the war."

"What are these?" said Jack, noticing three well-polished bell-pulls on the wall. The lawyer laughed.

"They are 'House,' 'Depot,' 'Corral'; old Silas can summon fifty armed men in an instant by touching these. He has wires buried in pipes for these simple alarms. The house is similarly furnished, with special bell-cords in the rooms. The old wolf needs every safeguard here. He could defy anything in this retreat until his retainers would swarm in." As they spoke the ranchero returned.

"Now, gentlemen, we'll have a few words," he said, his manner as alert as a general at the moment of sending away his reserve on the last charge. He unrolled his maps and plans.

'Mr. Manson, I will leave it to you to discuss the purely engineering features of the road with Nordenskiold. I am not competent to judge such matters. But as to what we wish to do practically with this frontier, it is only the matter of a few moments. Nordenskiold has all the plan of organization and will explain all. You can look it over with him. I would like you to ride over the whole line of the road with Colonel Bayard and my son. That can be done in ten days. Then, when you have approved the papers and

plans, you can make your suggestions and we will
jointly endorse them and send them on to your uncle.
He has already generally joined in my plan of organization, as well as Senator Steele. There are their
letters.

"Now, while you and my son look over the ranch
a little, I'll get your party ready, and you will learn
more in a trip to Laredo and Eagle Pass than in six
months' study alone. When you return, I can give
you a good assistant and draftsman. He's a nice fellow,
an Austrian engineer who came out here for his health.
Poor fellow! he got a cross of honor and a bullet
through his lungs at Solferino. Harbeck also has a
good working office and a set of instruments here. We
have Brother Blucher up often to trim out our lines
and lay off what our land business calls for here.
Strange to say, the old man is as accurate as the coast
survey, and his maps and drawings are the best I ever
saw. Even if he does take his 'toddy,' his mathemat-
ical brain seems unaffected by 'three-star Hennessey.'
I tried to get some 'four-star' for him, but that is
'above proof' and the edition is exhausted!"

Silas laughed and showed a set of teeth as fine and
white as a prairie wolf's.

"We can look all these things over in a day or so.
When can you start?"

"Whenever we are done. I've been on the frontier
for years," Manson replied.

"Good! That's the talk! Look over these two letters and we will join the ladies."

When old Silas swung the doors of his great safe and
replaced the letters, he murmured as he turned out the
lights, "I like that young fellow's looks. There is
some snap and life in him."

Jack Manson, entering the parlors, would have been

glad to know that his few answers and comments had satisfied Silas.

"A practical and experienced young fellow. He will be decent company for Jim," thought the millionaire ranchero, as he glanced around his lordly possessions in the mellow moonlight.

"I'm late! Must be late!" said Manson next morning, when he was awakened by a babel of cries. He laughed as he threw open his windows, for the morning sun was but peeping over the prairie. Already pacing the lawn, Silas Leavenworth was in conference with his superintendent. His morning coffee and cigar were already dispatched.

"If we were bound for the prairie we would be already miles away," Jim gaily said, as he joined him. "We will take only a social breakfast to-day and ride over the home place. To-morrow I will show you our outlying camps. We can ride far enough to get a good view of our topographical surroundings. There's one bluff which gives a great prospect. A bit of hunting may fall in our way. I want to show you some rough riding, roping horses and cattle, the 'matanza,' and have had a hundred horses got up to pick out a couple for you. I have six or eight kept up, but I wish to suit you."

"How many 'broken' animals do you keep up?" said Jack, amused.

"About five hundred. We use up two or three hundred every year, and the boys are always picking out the best."

"And what do you do with the worst?" said Jack, in a bit of raillery.

"Oh, sell them to Uncle Sam for the army! Anything *goes* for a trooper. We use all our home-bred mules for teaming," Jimmy carelessly answered.

"And for plowing?" Jack seriously queried. Leaven-worth laughed loudly.

" Texans don't plow, my boy! A dozen horses can do all the plowing we need. We live on hoofs and horns here. We actually buy nearly all our grain."

In the fresh, magnetic morning air, Jack Manson fairly started at the beauty Miss Katie's appearance lent to the growing day. The subtle telegraph of love told her that all was well. For the sweet witch had gained Alice's steady support in her plans to lead her father up "to see things rightly." Colonel Bayard kindly lent himself to a scheme to engross Silas the evening before, as the music of the fair sisters closed the intro-duction. Manson adroitly laid gentle siege to the affectionate regard of Mrs. Leavenworth. Therein, Brother Jim had made the way smooth. He had love schemes of his own!

Miss Katie, en Amazone, was ready for the ride.

"I only go with you," she said imperiously, "because I am responsible for my prisoner." Her pretty feet peeped out from her habit, and she was a moving picture of grace as she led the way to the early repast.

"Now, sir, let Jimmy provide your accoutrements only. I have ordered my 'Lexington' saddled. Brother always said he was too tall and strong for me."

Every drop of Jack's blood tingled as he sprang on the splendid dark-brown Kentucky horse, who nibbled a bit of sugar daintily from his mistress' hand. The white star in the forehead, keen eye, and delicate nostrils, told of the Blue-Grass land.

" You are at last a Texan," merrily cried Katie, critic-ally regarding Manson's dress, as he appeared fully supplied from Jimmy's trappings. Both were armed, and behind the party of three, Don Basilio, grave, and smoking a precarious-looking papelito, ambled along,

his lariat, pistol-belt, and Winchester, in its Comanche
sheath, under his leg, giving a modern air to the sad
countenance of the typical Don Quixote.

With the easy elastic bounds of equine perfection
the three swept along. Jack was not averse to displaying before the dainty queen of San Miguel his superb
horsemanship gained in the wild buffalo runs on the
Platte.

"You will do, sir; you need not remain in the *primary
class*," said Miss Leavenworth. "You need only pass
the thirty-third degree of Texan 'bronco' riding; you
are then quite au fait."

With the woman he loved by his side, in the glorious
morning, Manson's exulting spirits rose to the zenith.

"Ramon Maxan may meet me now with as stern a
welcome as he cares to give!" Gazing on Katie's fair
face, he vowed himself to a ceaseless vigilance.

Crowds of lithe, alert young borderers, with a dark
back-ground of half-breeds, were moving in all directions. Teams going afield, wagon teams drawing out,
ringing smith hammers, and all the bustle of a fixed
camp interested Manson, when he could not use the
intervals of Jimmy's side excursions to exchange a few
low, passionate words.

"Patience, for my sake," the spirited girl enjoined.
"Remember my father's eagle eye, his unbending
character."

The little cavalcade passed wild herds of spreading-
horned cattle, their eyes glowing fiery red in the
harassing charges of men "rounding them up." In
great enclosures, the duels of the centaur-like "lasso"
hands were living, changing tableaux of fight between
man and beast! Shouts and yells arose on the silence
of the morning. Bands of sleek mules, lazily dusting
themselves with whip-like tails, wandered in the

sunlight. As far as the eye could reach, horses and
cattle in piebald confusion of color covered hill and
knoll. Far away as they rode on, great bands of sheep
hobbled along, the gaunt Mexican "pastores" following
them with long wands. The horse corrals, where a
score of swarthy fellows were roping, blinding, hob-
bling, or chasing fifty frantic "broncos," rivalled the
very maddest rush of a Spanish bull-fight.

"Those horses seem to have mingled quicksilver and
fire in their veins," cried Jack, as he watched one or two
exemplars, who had been lassoed, thrown, their legs
tied, until with bandaged eyes, they staggered under
the heavy saddle, and screamed under the first cruel
tearing of the "ring bit." When the riders, vaulting
fearlessly on these equine demons, signalled for the
bandage to be slipped, every variety of rearing, plung-
ing, rolling, and tremendous panther-like bounding and
"bucking" proved the "original sin" embodied in
these wall-eyed, thin-chested, vicious brutes.

With an amused smile they rode on to the "matanza." A two-mile run brought the rich blood to
Katie's cheeks as, her lover by her side, she led the
way on "Starlight."

"I could ride on *forever!* Now I feel at home again,
on my own plains." She was peerless in her graces,
this Flower of the Border!

Great V-shaped picket-fence walls led out of a huge
corral toward a long building, half-buried in a glen
where a flowing brook furnished water for tanks and a
steam engine. As Jack rode up, he noted the easy
grace, the splendid attitudes of the dozen riders, who,
at a signal, cut out bullock after bullock from the
bellowing herd, as, game as prairie deer, they scented
the blood of their fellows gone before. Dashing forward and whipped on by footmen, a wild plunge

under an overhanging plank platform, led them within reach of two naked-chested, half-breed matadores.

A razor-sharp broad knife, set in a long pole, with unerring aim, severed the spinal cord behind the horns, as the animal passed beneath the "killers." Prone, with a crash the steers fell, rolling down an incline, within reach of the hooked rope of a steam wind-lass. In an hour, hides, horns, and tail were added to the piles, and the tallow vats received the carcasses for rendering. The thoughtless waste of the rude process struck Manson.

"Oh, we only kill those we can't drive North," said Leavenworth, carelessly. "A few thousand culled out never diminish our herd. There is a rough system in it all."

Away, through dell and opening, threading mes-quite groves, where buck and doe bounded away in jerky gallop, past copses, where rushing flocks of wild turkey scattered in noisy confusion, on beyond a chain of dimpled lakes, priceless here, the merry trio sought the highest knoll in sight.

"It *is* a royal domain," Jack Manson said, as from his panting steed, his eye swept far away to the beautiful oak openings of the Nueces, and far down below them the glories of San Miguel lay unrolled. To the west, wooded ravines and arroyos cut up the prairies, flecked with thousands of grazing animals. Far away south-ward, a yellow strip of gray, spotted with cactus groves, swept toward a far-winding dark band. It stretched, an emerald snake in endless twists, beneath the distant beautifully pencilled profile of the Monterey Mountains.

"They are a hundred and fifty miles away," cried Jimmy, as he regarded his horse, "and over there, within those willow and cottonwood groves, cut up with islands and fertile bends, the Rio Grande runs. Between

us and it lie the 'bad lands', and there man and beast alike
lie in wait for the lonely traveller."

"There's *no* such fair land, *no* place like Texas!"
Katie positively decreed, her eyes sparkling as she
flourished her riding whip. Manson's glasses, pocket
map, compass, and sketch-book were soon in requisition. Seated, with the fair face of the woman he
loved bending over him, Jack dashed in a panoramic
outline.

In an hour, with the sagacious counsel of his chum and
reference to the skeleton maps, the two comrades had
fixed their route of exploration and laid out the young
engineer's first ride on the border.

"There's a wounded deer below us there! Look!"
said Katie, as a buck limped painfully along the
side-hill, a hundred and fifty yards away.

"Yes, and a gray wolf after him!" added Manson, as
he picked up Leavenworth's carbine, and, quick as a
flash, fired, rolling the gray marauder over neatly, with
a ball through his shoulders.

"Well done!" cried Jimmy. "Where did you get up
that snap-shot practice?"

"Out shooting for antelope and black-tailed deer in the
Black Hills," laughed Jack.

"Let me see! You ride *pretty* well," Miss Katie
began. "You can shoot a *little!* I think you will do
for the Rio Grande, but I must examine your revolver
shooting. I am hard to please."

Miss Katie gracefully accepted, on their return, a
five-spot of spades, which Manson neatly punctured
with five shots of his revolver, knocking out the pips,
when Brother Jim took them out to his range to try
a half-dozen rifles and carbines for the flying visit.

"You are *now* accepted as a candidate for the crowning honor of being declared, in due form, a Texan.

But that is only bestowed when you have ridden the Rio Grande. You must do it for my sake!" the heiress cried, happy in her lover's unsuspected prowess.

"I'll ride it, Miss Katie," Jack replied, his eyes meeting hers meaningly. "I will cling to my old Sioux trophy also 'for your sake,' " he thought, as he replaced the weapon he had won from a gallant Indian warrior in fair fight. "I *may* not be a Texan yet, but I think I can *learn*," he resolutely exclaimed.

Three days of conference enabled Silas Leavenworth and Nordenskiold to lay out the general line of the projected road, with the aid of Jack Manson's practical talents. Jack was astonished at the old ranchero's sagacity and depth of mind. Boundary survey maps, coast survey charts, State maps, sketches, reports, projects, and a mass of invaluable data were ready at hand.

"How could you get all these together?" said Manson, in wonder.

"I know but *little*, but I know *enough* to have competent men around me," said old Silas. "Senator Steele, Chisholm, Nordenskiold, Blucher, and the army headquarters' people at San Antonio, give me all the points. All our State surveys here are run and tied on to my own lines."

"You should have been an engineer, Mr. Leavenworth!" cried Manson in admiration, as their final discussions ended.

"I began life *practically:* shovelling coal for the steam engineer of a quartermaster department steamer in Florida, when I was a workman attached to the army. I never got into the 'Topographical Corps,' " said Silas, with a grim smile. The arch-millionaire was certainly no snob! "If Jimmy is ready, you can run over the line now and sketch it out. Then we will organize. We will all slip down to Corpus Christi. We need there all our votes."

As Silas finished speaking, an express rider galloped up to the door of the den. His horse, flecked with foam, staggered as he dismounted, handing the millionaire a letter. "From Major Blucher!" he said, as he waited Silas' orders.

Old Silas tore open the envelope. Leavenworth's eye was flashing when he pulled the depot bell-handle. The superintendent dashed across the court-yard on the run. "Hitch up your best double buckboard and swiftest team. Have Harbeck over here in five minutes. He must go to Corpus Christi as fast as the animals can be urged. Send 'Texas Pete' and 'Prairie Joe' to escort him. Let Bill Haley drive. I may need a few good men down there. You must take good care of this messenger. I will have letters to send down by him to-morrow."

The rider thanked Silas, as the cattle king thrust a Mexican doubloon in his hand.

Turning to his friend, Silas sharply said: "We will put off the preliminary examination of the line for a week. The Corpus Christi *Gazette* has a whole page stirring up a wild opposition and attacking the Company. I wish you, Olaf, and Jim to take the big ambulance and half a dozen good men, and leave in an hour for the bay. I will keep Mr. Manson with me, and we will get there somehow," he said, with a peculiar smile. Go all to your own house; don't go near the hotel, or show up. Nordenskiold! get hold of Blucher; keep him steady, and send out for Colonel Rip Ford and your best men." Touching the house-bell, a negro briskly trotted over. "Send Mr. James to me at once!" he cried.

No handsomer son ever stood before a proud father than the hero of San Miguel as he dashed in. "What's up, padre?"

In two minutes Jimmy had his orders: "Take six picked men, Jimmy, and be careful. By the way, let Ximenes and a half-dozen of his fellows ride on ahead and clear the road. Keep them all in sight. I'll take Basilio. Of course, Tom Bayard goes with you. Get away as quick as you can, Nordenskiold," Silas concluded. "We must act at once. We will organize and have a special election at once, and get a half-million county bonds also to improve the harbor. These opposition fellows have only waked me up!"

In half an hour, the ambulance dashed away over the prairie, and Silas Leavenworth, smiling, handed Jack the glass. "Pretty good gait," he said.

It was a good gait! But Joaquin Ximenes, riding a mile ahead, grinned as he knew the half-naked Mexican boy he had sent ahead, racing along under cover of the straggling mesquite groves, would reach Caballo Blanco's camp *first!*

"The old man is going to sneak down to town after dark. I will wager that the big Gringo comes with him. If the boys only shoot straight, I'll earn Maxan's five thousand to-night, and pay off old Silas too for many an insult—the old dog! If I make sure of this Jack, I will then cut away and join Caballo Blanco and Maxan."

When dusk drew down, and the prairies were darkened, Joaquin Ximenes, at the further outlet of the arroyo, sat composedly smoking, his double revolvers and charged Winchester ready. His noble horse nipped the grass, tossing at the restraint of a twenty-foot picket rope.

"I know Silas! the old fox! He will dash along in a few hours. He always travels secretly. As Mr. Jim left me *here* to warn them of this wash-out across the road, I can't be blamed if they are attacked on the *other* side of the cañon. It's a full quarter of a mile across. How lucky that last rain cut out this hole. If any one comes this way I will warn them. They will have to drag the wagons over by hand if they cross. Caramba! I'll surely see these two dogs dead to-night. Caballo Blanco's party is in position now. The Gringos *can not escape!*"

While the gloating traitor lay in wait, and the concealed robbers at the head of the glen on the west side awaited in ambush, with their animals at a safe distance, the nimble lad who had borne Ximenes' message lay waiting in the road leading to San Miguel to warn the murderers, of the approach of Silas Leavenworth's flying double team.

. There was solicitude in Mrs. Leavenworth's kindly eyes as she pressed her husband's hands on his departure.

"*Do be careful,* Silas! I will have no rest till I know you safe at Corpus Christi."

"Don't fret, mother. I'll show them a Texan trick."

"Yes; but there is that awful cañon! It is so dangerous."

As husband and wife parted, Jack Manson stole a dozen kisses from Katie's rosy lips, in a friendly shadow.

"Do be watchful every instant! Stand by father for my sake," she whispered. "The robbers have vowed to take his life."

"I'll die with him, Katie, beloved, for your own dear sake."

With a last embrace Katie slipped away, a sweet, white-faced apparition.

"All ready!" rang out Silas' voice, as two splendid steeds dashed up. A strong road-wagon, with a servant's place behind, was provided with Winchesters and revolvers under every seat.

Three heavy-hearted women watched them dash out of the gate. There were no lights to guide. Behind the men, "Colorado Bill," a gray-eyed, lithe plainsman, sat ready, his revolvers lying across his knees, his rifle at his side.

Katie's eyes were full of blinding tears as she threw herself fondly on her mother's breast.

"If anything should happen to dear father—and—Jack," the little heiress murmured.

Her gentle mother easily divined the maiden's secret. She knew, at last, what glowing inner heart-love had tinged the roses on Katie's cheeks with deeper royal richness. And in her faithful arms the darling of her heart told the sweet story of a first love!

Jack started as a dozen dark forms swept by the travellers, a gaunt rider before. Even in the gloom he recognized that angular Castilian, mediæval-looking relic, "Don Basilio."

"That's only a little Texan Joke. I'll have Basilio go on and prospect the cañon a little," said Silas dryly, as he noted Jack's movement. "Some of *my friends* might fancy I was really coming alone."

There was no sound but the sighing of the night-wind across the lonely prairie! Excited by his parting promise, Jack saw goblins of the night in every clump of bushes. His revolvers well to the front, his Winchester ready, he watched Silas guide the flying steeds. Half-way to the arroyo, he spoke: "I wonder how you can lead such a life here with your family."

Silas said simply: "I like the South. I like Texas. I have a large property here. I wish my children to be secure in their future. I shed no tears over the fallen Confederacy. But if your Northern friends think that our country will hold together always, you are mistaken. The natural interests of the sections are opposed to permanency! Look at it! You have the Middle and East given up to capital and manufacturing; the Mississippi Valley to agriculture; the great Northwest to timber, stock, and wheat; the Pacific Coast and Rocky-Mountain States to mining. The great money, iron, coal, and transportation banded interests prey on the people. For convenience of those who have snapped up all the valuable franchises and are rich employers, the ruling element throws open the doors of America, and its too-easily won citizenship, to the ruff and scruff of Europe. I wish my children to live in a strong community, governed by *white*, *native* Americans. We know how to treat the negro *practically*. You do not. Northern sentimentalists always fail to understand or handle the black. In the day, my boy, which you may live to see, of natural disintegration, the great West, Northwest, and Pacific States will break away and the East and Middle States will stick together. Our Southern States, led by pure American statesmen, will stand by the Union, in a spirit of real devotion to the Constitution; the Southwest, from natural sympathy, will go with them, and the *future battles* against communism, anarchy, socialism, and imported pollution will be fought by our representative Southern men, who will work up into the national councils again!

"There is no real devotion to the Union or our home institutions in a section where *the Dollar alone is God!* You are daily drained of your heart's blood by the enormous influx of undesirable foreigners. In fifty years the American character will only exist in the *South* and *Southwest*. I wish my son to be a representative man, true to the real Union, even *if his father was a 'rebel'*. No, sir! The war did *not* decide the fate of the Union. The great battle is *yet* to be fought. It is against hostile Europe; its influences, its pauper classes, its rotten social schemes, and its bitter hatred of us! Your Northern people can not fight it *alone!*"

Jack Manson was astounded at the depth of feeling shown by the old Texan.

"Here I will stay! Here I will leave my bones!" he cried, as he halted his steeds a quarter of a mile from the cañon. "Texas is the future Empire of the Gulf."

In a moment Basilio reined up beside the wagon.

"Here, Bill, look out for the horses. I'll change seats with you," Silas directed.

Receiving a few whispered injunctions in Spanish, old Basilio disappeared. The ranchero briefly gave "Colorado Bill" a last word of advice.

"If there's any hornet's nest in there to-night we'll run over it," sternly cried Silas. "*All ready now!* Go ahead. Should there be an alarm, we will keep on at full speed. If there's firing, jump out and join me behind the team," he said to Jack in a low tone.

In the darkness of the night Manson's relaxed nerves thrilled as the winding road to the head of the cañon was reached. All was silent. In the dense woods of the arroyo a pair of lonely owls boomed out their mournful call. Suddenly Jack noted four of their escort close in at the head of their team. He gripped his loaded Winchester tightly. Its seventeen cartridges could be flashed out in a fusillade of less than a minute.

On the brow of the hill at the cut, Basilio and his raw-boned charger were revealed clear-cut for an instant against the starlit sky, backed by two followers. At a wave of Silas Leavenworth's hand they briskly dashed down the slope. A wild figure darted away from under their very feet. It was the boy spy!

"*Shoot quick!*" Silas yelled, firing as he spoke.

BOOK IV.

THE JAGUAR'S DESPERATE STRUGGLE.

CHAPTER XI.

MANSON'S MATCHLESS STEED—A HARMONIOUS DIREC-
TORY—AN HOUR IN A WASHINGTON BOUDOIR—A
STRANGE WARNING.

THE TWO guns roared out together, followed by a
snap shot from Bill's revolver. Before a yell of pain
subsided, the thicket on the south blazed with the discharge of twenty rifles. A wild cry was borne back
as the advance guard dashed through the ambush. The
four men on the crest opened a rapid fire on the low
bushes.

"Empty your guns! Fire low! Shoot by their
flashes!" called Silas, whose voice never changed tone.
The old man was "game!"

In a few moments the rattling fire from the ambushed
bandits ceased.

"That will do," said the ranchero, shortly, as Jack
dropped his heated gun from his shoulder. "Cease firing!" he called in Spanish to his faithful escort, who,
with Sharp's rifle, musket, and revolver, were, from the
crest, sweeping the now silent wooded belt to the south.
"It's always safest after a storm," Silas chuckled, as he
blew the smoke out of his repeating rifle and reloaded
it. Manson had refilled the chamber of his rifle.
"Keep your revolver ready! Let's pick up this chap;

I want him for *subsequent investigation*," Silas coolly
said. "Drive as near as you can, Bill." The groaning
fifty yards off continued. "I think that *you* winged this
fellow, Manson! You are the right sort!" said Silas,
revolver in hand, gazing at a prostrate form. "Quien
es?" sternly challenged Silas, poking his revolver near
the face of the wounded spy. "Strike a match, Jack!
Devil take it! It's that peon boy Josè! By God,
what's that?"

Three or four sharp shots rang over the cañon from
the other side; then the echoes died away; all was
ominously still.

"Jack, watch these horses!" cried Silas. "Bill, hold the
head of the road with these four men! Let them dismount and lie down. It may be that the thieves have
formed up again over there. What will we do with this
fellow? I see it. There's some treachery at the
Ranch! He sneaked away from us and put up this job.
Stand by on guard, Jack!" Manson with joy noted
these familiar words.

Jack's ready rifle covered the road. A horseman
loomed up in the darkness, leading an animal.
It was the unmoved Don Basilio, who, in a few words,
reported to Silas Leavenworth, who stood at bay,
revolver in hand.

"Well, I will be d—d if I don't hang every loose
'greaser' between here and the Rio Bravo! Fetch
the horse here. Jack," he called, "come here." Basilio
took the impatient steeds in hand.

"I will now give you the best horse in Texas, my
boy," said Silas, as he handed him the bridle rein.
"You will do me a favor to shoot Ximenes on sight if
you ever see him again. The mean sneak put up this
whole job. He fired on Basilio's advance party himself! But they dropped him from the saddle. I sup-

pose the felons ne posted here lugged him off safely!
He betrayed us. But why?"

Jack Manson's heart beat wildly. Then Silas
Leavenworth did not know yet of Ramon Maxan's vow!
Even in the robber's cañon Katie's fair face beamed
on him. Her gentle lips seemed to murmur: "Stand
by my father for my sake."

"This helps us," said the ready ranchero. In five
minutes the wounded boy was lashed on the rear seat,
Jack was mounted on his royal charger, and the
unflinching Basilio led the way through the cañon. A
trusty rider was already racing back to San Miguel to
bring twenty men to hold the arroyo till after the millionaire's return.

"Search the ground and lug all the dead robbers
back to the ranch. I will get the truth out of this poor
fool if I have to hang him."

At the farther brow of the hill Silas left Basilio on
guard with three men.

"You will patrol the cañon steadily! Twenty men
will join you here in four hours. Then come on to
Corpus and report to me, leaving them on guard."

"Bueno!" answered the spectral Don, as he pocketed
a handfu. of Silas' best cigars. He was not astonished!
Nothing broke his habitual calm!

"*Now*, Bill, turn her loose!" Led on by Jack Manson
on his matchless racer, with two riders as rear guard,
the undaunted cattle-king swept along in safety
through the hushed night, to draw rein only at Nordenskiold's door on the hill at Corpus Christi.

"Not a word of the attack!" cried Silas, as the astonished trio saw the wounded man. "Another jump at
the old place! Don't let a man go into the town."

In a quarter of an hour the old ranchero was sleeping like a child. " Texas Pete," and "Bronco Bill " were

merrily laughing as they rode away to trail the robbers
and locate their headquarters. They were light-hearted,
for Silas growled: " I'll give you a ranch and stock it,
boys, if you will run down this gang and bring me
' Caballo Blanco's ' head. Go where you want to. You'll
find old Rip Ford and the rangers somewhere between
Eagle Pass and Ringgold. Take some of the men
from the cañon, and get what supplies you want any-
where. I'll square the bill. Don't spare money or
horseflesh!"

"All right, squire," the happy scouts answered, as if
they were bidden to a picnic.

By the dying fire, in Nordenskiold's snuggery, Tom
Bayard, Jimmy, and the new Texan communed
briefly. Nordenskiold listened in silence.

"We must have this Ramon Maxan and Ximenes
shovelled under, before you and I can ride the border
safely. A Creole always keeps his oath of blood
revenge," said the sturdy son of a dauntless sire, as
Jack Manson sought his couch. "You have won the
best horse in Texas, anyway. Good-night, old boy.
The ' padre ' tells me you fitted the situation to a hair!
It's a good deal for him to say."

There were lovely eyes beaming on the sleeper from
misty dreamland, and Jack saw the sunlight of the
future from behind these clouds!

Silas Leavenworth was quietly comparing notes with
the stony-faced lawyer when Manson was awakened by
the sun peeping over Padre Island. He rubbed his eyes.

"Well! a night on the prairie may be followed up
by a wild day at Corpus Christi. It is a lively country."

His first care was to go to the stable and look at his
beautiful trophy of the fight at the arroyo. Jimmy,
in low tones, at the breakfast-table run over the details
of the abortive attempt at murder.

" They must have 'laid' for you and father! Now, Jack, you know why we have not fully warned my father before. We *must* do so now, but he would have found out, anyway, the reason of Maxan's enmity."

The "we" was evidently Katie and her brother. The two lovers clasped hands in silence. Jimmy was thinking of that beloved one far away in her ancient Virginia home.

"When we get back, you and I, with mother and my sisters, will have a private understanding. I see clearly that we must hunt these fellows down and not let them 'pot' us, like a couple of prairie chickens. But I do not wish to arouse my father's ferocity. He will hang every suspected wanderer for six months. He is no man to fool with."

" I should say not," said Jack, dryly, as he thought of old Silas pumping out his Winchester cartridges as deliberately as if firing at ground-squirrels.

" Don't show off your new 'caballo, yet, young man," said Silas, good-humoredly, as he shook hands; " I am keeping this whole thing quiet. My men are on the trail now, and I never admit these attempts on my life here; it might encourage others. Besides, they may have Mexican chums here to warn them. Now, be at hand all day; I will need your professional advice. I have sent for the editor of the *Gazette*. I will have a special edition of the paper printed to-night. To-morrow it will go fifty miles around. We will organize to-morrow morning, and to-morrow night a grand public meeting will make them all wake up. I will make these three counties too hot to hold any one who fights the road or the Company."

" We will have a full through mail to-day, Jack," remarked Jimmy, glass in hand. " There is the Wanderer sweeping down with a cloud of canvas."

" By the way, what have you done with your ship-wrecked crew?" Manson asked Nordenskiold, as he took the glass.

" Put them on the 'Ariel,' a new bark Chisholm had bought for the Company," said the lawyer, with a side glance at old Silas, who was calmly studying his cigar. " I had a telegram that they sailed yesterday from the Spanish Main and Tampico."

" Well, I wish them better luck this time," said the engineer simply.

" Oh, a *new* ship seldom gets lost!" the advocate carelessly rejoined.

By the evening a wonderful revolution in public sentiment had been wrought. The press was throwing off a triple edition of the special issue, and four hours of close conference, and the deft fingers of Norden-skiold had closed up the legal organization of the railroad company.

" You see, I will detain the mail boat until we send the whole set of papers away, registered. One set to Houston, our State capital, the other certified set to your uncle, for himself and Senator Steele, a third to Chisholm," said Silas.

" It is nearer to Houston by land, is it not?" asked Jack.

" True. But our Dogtown and Uvalde boys occasionally nab our mail-riders on the way and rip open the mails. 'The longest way round is the safest way home,'" smiled old Silas, who was now in good humor.

" What do you suppose those funny devils once did? Last year a special Treasury Agent went overland from the Rio Grande to San Antonio. He had got up a lot of spy information and papers, and proposed to realize 'Civil Service Reform' here. He found out later that the boys had quietly examined his valises at

Brownsville. On the way over to San Antonio the buckboard was stopped, his team and property taken, and he made the last forty miles on foot to San Antonio, and left for Washington cursing Texas! He was a pompous fat man, and he has asked 'for another sphere of duty.'"

" Who did that?" laughed Jack.

"Oh, I suppose it was 'Mexican marauders,'" Silas murmured as simply as a child. He did not know that Father Blucher had bragged of this very trick to Jack! "In vino veritas," is applicable even in the land of cactus and wild horses!

Before the swift Wanderer swept away to Indianola with her precious freight, Jack Manson's cipher telegram announced to Mark the good news of the completed legal organization.

In four hours an answer dated Washington, D. C., contained private directions closing: "Address me Arlington Hotel."

"See here, Manson, *now that we are partners*, I wish to give you the private tip to be kept a secret between your uncle, you and I. I see you have sketched out your road about one hundred and thirty-five miles. I wish you to survey it up to measure two hundred and eighty!" The ranchero was driving Jack dinnerward.

Manson stared in amazement.

" Why it's unprofessional and wasteful " the economic student hotly said.

" *Yes*," Silas slowly answered. " My boy, you are not yet up to our simple frontier ideas. I had Nordenskiold fix up that bill. It is now a law, and my property, our property! We get twenty miles square of alternated land on either side, for merely 'perfecting the survey and visibly locating and mapping the line.' This extra one hundred and forty-five miles, which

by running *hither and thither* you can gain, gives us
an extra slip of land amounting to two thousand nine
hundred square miles, or a million eight hundred thousand acres. That will build the road in itself! But
it is an extra profit for you and I—*our private interest!*
We are no fools!"

Manson began to grasp at Silas' sagacious trickery.

" But you can not secure it unless you *build the line*,"
Manson affirmed.

"See here, my boy!" Silas handed him a printed
copy of the law. " There is a clause enacting that
where lands have been taken up along the line as
built, we can locate in lieu all we are entitled to in
other places. Now, we earn it by simply surveying
and locating. There is also a clause permitting us to
shorten and alter (in the public interest) later. Now,
I have located all the land along our real line myself."

Jack's eyes were widely staring.

" I have the tracts we wish to cover all mapped out!
Our lieu selections take precedence of all other Texan
grants in the interest of the public." There was a
comfortable grin on Silas' face.

" Did Nordenskiold do this? " he asked.

" No; he only *put the law through* as I *wanted it;*
but Blucher mapped my lands, and these we want.
I had the old chap six months at it, and everything is
now locked up in my safe. I have to pay these two
old files heavily, and I keep them always blind to each
other's work."

" It's a wonderful law," said Jack, rapt in admiration.

" It *is* a pretty good law. I paid three thousand dollars a man for 'niggers' and 'carpet-baggers' enough to
vote it through. You see," said Silas modestly, " it
was when we were *under the heel* of the Federal
Government, just after war time, I devised this! "

"You should have been a chief justice," Jack vent-ured to say in compliment.

"Yes, probably it would have been easier to be at a law college than shovelling coal on the old 'Planter' as a quartermaster laborer. But here we are at dinner."

Jack Manson began to realize the mental calibre of the cool, self-made frontier king.

"You must inform your uncle only by word of mouth or cipher of this. I am frank with you, my boy. He must provide the iron, cars, and funds. He can do it. I can not. I am land rich and money poor. I am sending a drive of ten thousand cattle to Kansas and the market in a month. I will not get that money till next spring; but I will have a million dollars loose then. If I did not wish to build the road at once, I would do it then *alone!* But I want your uncle with me. These fellows may kill me any day, and Jim needs more experience than he has. Old Steele is only good to keep me 'square' with the administration. I'm not popular up there. *Too big a rebel*," said Silas, leading on the way to the table.

"Do you not think Southern sentiment will change in time?" said Jack, with curiosity.

"Never!" sternly said Silas. "Whatever anyone may say to you, we are as big rebels as when we poured over Hancock's stone walls at Gettysburg! The growing children drink secession with their mother's milk. Our women are implacable, fiery, unyielding, and untiring. They sneered the men 'to the front' when they could not wheedle them into danger, and they're now whipping the 'lost cause' into their children. Wait, my boy! You will see our Southern statesmen crawl slowly on top. They will work twenty years to weaken the North, and cut the

West off.   Then we will regain the balance of
power!"

"Do you believe it?" Jack doubtfully said.

"I know it! It is written in the stars!" said the
ranchero, as he compounded a mysterious beverage
which sealed the secret intimacy between the young
man and himself. Jack drank to Katie in silence!

While Silas Leavenworth was closeted with a rider,
who dashed up after dinner with reports from the
cañon, and Nordenskiold and himself were later inter-
rogating sternly the wounded Mexican boy, who had a
severe thigh flesh wound, Jack Manson read, with
intense delight, a few words from Katie:

You have won the way to father's heart now. You hold
mine forever! Be careful—for my sake!

Below the bluff, where Nordenskiold's residence
dominated the town, the one great hall over the market-
house was ablaze with light.   Crowds of excited frontiersmen were assembling to listen to addresses suggested by the lawyer, and trimmed up by the crafty
ranchero.

The collector, the judge, the editor, Colonel Bayard,
Major Blucher, and other prominent citizens, in due
sequence, demolished every iota of suspicion and objection.   The throng of six hundred swarthy, bearded,
pistol-carrying plainsmen shouted themselves wild under
the glare of swinging oil-lamps in assent, and unani-
mously howled their approval of the half-million-dollar
bonded harbor subsidy.   A set of resolutions, skillfully
prepared, were rushed through "nem. con.," and the
Corpus Christi *Gazette* was also requested to blazon
the sentiments of the meeting forth at once, to awake
the attention of the interior and reassure the Northern
capitalists.

The presence of the local schoolmaster, priest, the Baptist preacher, some progressive German-Jewish merchants, the only banker, the freight-handlers, the coasting sailors, and the few working mechanics united all Corpus Christi in a golden circle of unity.

Alas! the uninitiated could not see the foxy hand of Silas and his lawyer in this great "outburst" of enthusiasm, but the whole town *did* appreciate the "Pansaje" or general "blow out" which followed.

The hand of Rudolf Harbeck, the astute financier, was deftly employed in opening, gratis (on account of his master) the St. James, the Magnolia Saloon, the "Planters' Hotel," "Joe Garcia's," and every place for the distribution of the "wassail bowl" to all comers. The flaring light of tar barrels, the music of the polyglot "band," and the shouts of the joyous revellers, reached Silas Leavenworth, as he left the "Star Chamber."

"I hope that the boys will not *overdo* this spontaneous demonstration," remarked the ranchero, as Jimmy, Manson, the lawyer, and himself sat at their ease.

"Those low-bred fellows in Indianola, Brownsville, and the interior, might gibe at us a little. They are up to these tricks, but only in a poor way. They have no 'style' about them!" Silas was in a flood-tide of complacency. He had already extracted from the terrified boy spy all he knew, and chewed in anticipation the sweet cud of revenge!

Within six months many a lurking prowler around San Miguel met short shrift; the nearest mesquit, a handy lariat, and a volley of bullets, to make sure, easily settled their prejudged cases.

"Young men, you may look around town a little to-morrow. I want to talk things over with my banker and the editor. Then we will go home in daylight, openly, as I have men enough here. The cañon is now clear. They found three fellows dead in the 'chapparal'. So, Mr. Caballo Blanco did not 'make the trip' this time!" Silas rose, and going on the porch, dropped into the earnest hum of business conversation with his lawyer. Nordenskiold knew, that much as Silas trusted and feared him, he could never thoroughly fathom the depths of the inscrutable ranchero. Manson watched the two cold schemers at work.

"You can't tell where a man will finally turn up, my boy," Silas had remarked. "Keep the whip-hand on everybody. It's all right; if they wish to be your enemies, you are ready. As for friends, any man's your friend—as long as it *pays him to be*." Jack Manson did not wonder at this pearl of frontier wisdom, for Silas had grown up in the hard school of adversity.

While the railroad triumphed over the cabals of its envious enemies on this memorable night, at Washington, old Mark Manson was seated in the room where Mildred Smiley had once opened her passionate heart to Jack Manson.

The luxury of the residence was unchanged, but during the dinner and at the tête-à-tête following, Mrs. Senator Steele was the ideal senatorial consort. Ezra Steele rode calmly on the tide of political success, and seconded by his argus-eyed wife, was now a leading feature of the incoming administration. A certain stately, dignified silence became him well. He was now more honored for the things he did *not do* than those he *did* achieve. And, daily, Mildred Steele was building a wall about the past of Mildred Kenyon Smiley. No keen eye had traced, as yet, the particular 'prominent Southern family' to which she owed the blue blood coursing in the delicate veins under her dazzling, tinted flesh. "I only feared Mrs. Marshall's eye," the beauty owned to her mirror, as she gazed at her own loveliness. "She had a quiet, searching look which always shook my nerves. Never mind; I have 'arrived!' as the French say. And Mrs. Marshall has no real cause to hunt me down."

There was a gleam of satisfaction in her eye as the senator gravely departed for a special "conference committee caucus."

"The public business," he mournfully said, with an old-time wave of his hand, forgetting that he could not impose upon the old financier, and that his able wife had already honeycombed his conceited nature in a resolute search for every secret. She possessed them all. Even the whole intrigue, the fatal knowledge of No. 4—a dangerous discovery!

Mark Manson's ashes of life warmed a little in a flickering old-time glow when the "Empress" said: "Now we can have a cosy evening in my den." His nerves thrilled a little at the nearness of the beautiful social "carpet-bagger."

"By heavens! She's too good for that oaf," murmured Mark, with the easy egotism of man's submission to throbbing, sentient physical beauty with its adjuncts of royal dress, burning passion, and gentle, half-suggested dalliance. "She is thrown away on him. What a woman! As calm now as the lovely Caribbean. I would like to see her in a tornado of feeling!"

Mark was destined to note only her sunny hours, like an antique sun-dial.

"I will have you in my power. I will not be led by you, pleasant as you are!" thought Milly Steele, waving her filmy fan over a matchless bosom.

" If I can get the secret of No. 4 from this successful 'lost pleiad,' it is worth as handsome a necklace as Tiffany can furnish. By Jove! I could clasp it on myself." Mark was now within the " danger line!"

Mrs. Steele was happy at last! Her table was thronged with the cards of even the great " unapproachable." She had passed beyond the penumbra of social uncertainty into the clear glow of the "inner circle." "Old family " representatives *might sneer*, but the senator's wife was planted in the ring surrounding the White House. In duty bound the administration ladies must fight her battles, and no one dared to touch her golden shield with the sharp point of the lance. But one man she feared! It was Ramon Maxan. For, hidden in her bosom, she carried the words of Maxan's latest scrawl:

Your finesse leads you to betray me through marriage. Remember, when I strike you it will be to the heart. I will slake my burning revenge in Manson's blood. His promised bride may sit in shadow many a day and recall my name in her bitter tears. It is now war to the knife!

" He would never dare to attempt violence toward me. I am safe. His deeds have shut the door on him. He will never return!" The superb woman, in her royal loveliness, could not hear the noiseless spinning of the thread. The Fates, unswerving, unrelenting, give no sign!

" Mr. Manson," the beauty murmured, as she toyed with her jewelled coffee-cup, " I hope that you will realize how devoted I am to the Senator. His every interest is dear to me, and I wish the benefit of your powerful friendship and your frank advice. I can do much to cement the union between you as well as the Leavenworths. Our interests are naturally the same."

Perfectly understanding the key of this little social prelude, Mark Manson decorously played second violin. Gravely on his guard, the financier, in an hour's gentle fencing, became assured that No. 4 would not be disclosed in his obscurity, unless some pact were made with the beautiful sphinx. After exhausting his special knowledge of the Company—the secret projects and the future—Mark felt that his fair antagonist was much better armed, at all points, than himself. Her knowledge was far beyond his as to the mystery of Texas. The clock struck ten. Its silvery chime reminded Mark that Senator Steele's imposing form might bear the invisible " toga " homeward any moment. Manson knew that the lovelorn Samson had yielded his locks warily under the charmer's graceful manipulation of the shears.

" I am so sorry you must go," Milly's flute-like voice intoned, as she gave him a delicious cordial. " I have written your nephew many things to guard him. I am deeply interested in him. In these graver matters, I might have things of moment to confide to you. I am now tied to new duties. If your nephew confided in you in cipher, you might confer with me. But it must be secretly. He will have the inner confidence of old Silas, soon. You can guess why," she said, with a rare smile. " But Senator Steele is sometimes uncertain! He is venturesome in politics. I look to his permanent future interests, and my own. And yet, he must not know how deeply I confide in your sagacity. Although I have *no secrets to conceal*, it would be dangerous for us to correspond. A messenger could not be trusted. I am trying to look keenly into the future of this growing Mexican scheme. If I knew the way—" she faltered.

" You could come to New York!" cried Mark Manson, now eager, as he grasped her hands. " You know

what I wish to know. Who is No. 4? I must have
an independent hold upon him. I will see that your
visits are made safe in every way."

Milly's smile fascinated the financier. " I know only
that there is power, place, millions to be divided. I
wish to plant myself on a rock above the storms of politics. Senator Steele does not see what I observe. I
know that the negro foundation of Southern republicanism will melt away under the men now in power.
The astute, dominating men of Dixie will regain control! Steele may be left without influence, a stranded
man. He has been very kind to me. I love luxury;
it is the breath of life in my nostrils. I fear his heavy
party contributions, and the public burdens attached to
his place. The laurels of the war are already fading.
A practical *home government* alone will settle the
Southern question. Shall we work together?"

" Will you tell me what I must know?" Manson
cried, his grasp on her jewelled hands tightening. " It
will ensure your future."

" I may tell you—*in New York*," she answered,
flashing back the promise of her brilliant eyes, as she
sought her cabinet and handed him a card. It was a
simple address. " If *you* need me write or telegraph,"
she said, in a whisper. "And you, how shall *I* com-
municate?"

The ebony escritoire was soon locked on another
secret.

" We are comrades, are we not?" Milly said archly.

Mark Manson stooped and kissed her jewelled hands
with unnecessary fervor for a mere business association.

"*For life!*" he said. "We understand each other.
I think my lady will have that necklace," Mark soliloquized, as he greeted the returning senator at the door
on his exit. Milly Steele sweetly smiled an adieu to

one, and a welcome to the other, as she stood under the arched frescos.

"I am secure now. I can defy poverty and chance. I am safe forever!" thought the siren.

"She will not be caught with mere gew-gaws. I must make her half a million!" ruminated the retreating Midas.

"A good evening's work!" proudly cried Steele to his wife. For a great measure was in the "becalmed" region of his committee, and an all-powerful lawyer had whispered over a bottle at the Arlington: "If you can only *see this thing rightly*, you will be one of us, Senator."

The brooding peace of work well done, and the happy consciousness of judicious and well-placed effort blessed the slumbers of the worthy trio just parted.

So the subtle influence of magic " gold," the dazzling, dreamy fascination of easily made money, spread its trail, a bright comet from New York's buttressed mansions to the distant borders of the Rio Grande.

For gold and the lust of gold the soldier has bled, the mariner dared the pathless sea, friend betrayed friend, blood conspired against its kindred, youth struggled, and age schemed since the world began! Hardly won and lightly held! It has bought the smiles of blushing beauty since Jupiter blinded Danäe with the golden cloud!

" There's not a horse in Texas like him," said Jimmy Leavenworth, patting Manson's new acquisition, as the heart brothers strolled out under the moonlight to the stable to see their animals well bestowed. " What a scoundrel Ximenes turned out! I am sorry; for he knows our whole system and inner lines. You see, Jack, the devil was such a peerless courier, that we kept him against good judgment. My fear is he may keep up disaffection among our men and betray either of us. If you ever clap eyes on him, kill him like a dog! He is merciless, and a really dangerous fellow."

As Jimmy spoke, a tired rider entered the stables. "Well, Bill!" The young Texan had a pleasant word for the scout who had been away on a secret mission for Silas.

"I have a letter for you, Mr. James. Don't ask me when or where I got it. It was up Dogtown-way though. The gentleman said you knew him in old times."

Bronco Bill placed his pet horse in comfort and watched Leavenworth read the letter by the stable lantern.

"Poor old Wes Hardin!" he said, with evident concern. "Come in, Jack, I wish to talk to you." As the gallant fellow walked he murmured: "Out alone! On the prairie! A price on his head! It's pretty hard! But he's game to the last!"

In their room, Jimmy handed Jack a brief scrawl. It was in pencil, on the backs of old envelopes, their addresses torn off, and it was fastened with a buckskin string:

DEAR JIM:
I've been hanging around to see some one of your people. I know Bill is square, and wont put anybody on me. Take care of yourself, Jim. You were always good to me. Maxan, el Jaguar, offers five thousand for your head, and same for your friend. Caballo Blanco got cut up in the fight, and swears he'll do the business himself. Ximenes was shot in the shoulder, and I struck them at the Fandango House, above Los Angeles. They've taken him away. He swears to kill that stranger to get his horse back. Look out! If anything happens, strike red-hot for Las Cuevas. They always cross the Bravo there. If you have to follow, run them clear to his ranch. Take a good gang. He has

a hard crowd. Don't be off your guard a minute. This is dead
square for old days. Good-bye, Jim. I slipped away to warn
you.

JOHN WESLEY HARDIN.

"There's a man with a good mother, and a fine old
Baptist preacher for a father. He was shoved in the
Confederate Army, a mere boy. When he came back,
father gave him a show, as my old schoolmate. He had
to kill a quarrelsome rancher. The man had a lot of
enraged relatives. Poor old Wes! He took to the plains,
and that lean-faced boy (he's only twenty-four) has
killed a dozen men. Hunted like a dog, there's a big
price on his head. Every one is gunning for him—
Rangers, deputies, and troops. I ran on him once.
We had a talk! I begged him to leave the country.
He has too much pride. And he sends me now this
warning. Jack, I am sorry for you. This hangs over
us both! I've got to be used to it, but it is a doom
you did not seek. It's really no quarrel of yours.
Poor old Wesley! He is kindly at heart. If those fellows knew what he did, they would broil him on a
cactus fire."

Jack Manson read the simple words. His eyes
flashed.

"Jimmy, I'll stay through this thing with you," and
two voices joined in the heartfelt words, "For Katie's
Sake."

Two days later, in leisurely style, Silas Leavenworth
departed under the knightly escort of his son, Bayard,
and Jack Manson. A strong squad of his retainers
enabled them to laugh at attack.

"I'll see you safely over the cañon and then go off to
my ranch," said Bayard, who had a pair of lank Texan
lads of wolf-like appearance in his train.

Riding in advance, the three friends discussed the

cañon affair, Ximenes' treason, and the warning. "I would tell your father the whole situation at once," said Bayard.

Father and son communed an hour as they leisurely travelled along, for Silas was conveying the crippled prisoner to his ranch. As the train approached the arroyo, the son, with glowing face, joined his friends.

" The padre will leave half a dozen men here, now. Next week he will send a band of sheep down here. The pastores, with two or three good men, can build a permanent guard cabin here, and the grazing will war-rant it. It will break up any chance of an ambush here. On the prairie any of us alone can stand off a half-dozen of these sneaking thieves. It is a good idea."

An hour's rest for luncheon at the spring brought Col-onel Tom's companionship to an end. " I'll be over every two or three weeks to see you," he said, as he shook hands with Silas. "I have got to look over my cattle a little now. If you want me, send an express rider. I'll show up as quick as old 'Baldy' will bring me." With a few last words the chivalric soldier rode away. Jack Manson well knew the sweet, dark-eyed St. Cecilia was the magnet drawing him "every two or three weeks" toward the stately domain of San Miguel. But Alice herself knew that the beautiful oak-shaded knoll of the Nueces was being beautified for the home-coming of his promised bride.

" There goes as gallant a man as ever sat a horse!" said Silas, as the party moved on toward home.

On the porch at San Miguel, a happy circle waited for the returning travellers. Silas Leavenworth's grave, gentle wife kept up her usual composure, until alone she threw herself on his neck in fond emotion.

Manson's heart beat with all a lover's pride as Katie whispered, in the tumult, "You are now my *own* Texan, sir. You have won my father's heart. To-night, you can walk under my roses with me. For five minutes only! Remember—no longer."

"Katie," said Jack, "have you forgotten the roses at Indianola?" With one fleeting glance of tender love, the conquered maiden disappeared.

After dinner, Silas addressed his son: "Jimmy! you can now organize your party. I am going to give you twenty good, picked men, to take Jack here over the line, and I wish you to go out one way, and take your time. · On your return, push hard, and come back on a different trail, at least twenty miles away. I may have a telegram to go to New Orleans and sign the railroad bonds. I will take Nordenskiold with me. Of course, I would sooner have you at the ranch when I'm gone; but we will start the big drive, and then you can go. I will send a rider out to meet you when I start—if you are on the prairie."

Jack Manson blessed the happy chance of Silas' withdrawal to his den. Under the starlight, the roses heard Katie Leavenworth's sweet lips frame again the words which thrilled her lover's heart.

"The roses are our friends," she whispered, as their graceful vines shaded the two lovers, for the little queen's heart was beating close to the breast of the man she loved. "Good-night! Good-night again!" was the soft refrain of the two whose eyes met in the pledge of the love of a life!

Three days later, Manson had verified every preparation for the border ride. As he rode out to see the "big drive" start away, the mail-bag arrived. He thrust his letters in his breast, save one which bore the handwriting of his self-elected guardian, the senator's fair wife.

The bitter letter of Ramon Maxan was enclosed. Milly Steele's pithy words touched him.

You are fighting for *me* now; I am for *you*. Your uncle and I are agreed as to joint action. I see, now, that Maxan wished to control the Company by governing my husband through me, or by marriage with your promised bride. His quarrel has made the *one* impossible. My union with the senator broke the *other* chain! Now, his revenge embraces the Leavenworths and you; and his plan also includes my disgrace. I again warn you. He will strike like the blind rattlesnake in summer—at what is nearest and dearest. For my sake, beware! Continue your private correspondence with me. Be warned in time!

"Jimmy, that scoundrel is entirely too near us at present! Why, Los Angeles is only thirty miles from your home in a direct line," said Manson.

"That's true, Jack, but we can not break up that village. There are some decent people there, as Mexicans go; but every one of them will shield a malefactor of their race. Time alone will sweep them over the Rio Grande. We must strike the gang on their raids, or catch them crossing the river. It is hard. They scatter like quails when surprised: I will have one of our four companies of State Rangers ordered down here, to cover the zone between here and Brownsville, Ringgold Barracks, Laredo, and Eagle Pass. The regular troops are good enough, but the raiders avoid them. It is like chasing will-o'-the-wisps. Our cavalry along the river has been diverted by false raids, and enormous trains of the most valuable goods are often smuggled over while they are away. The customs inspectors riding the Rio Grande, two and two, from its mouth to El Paso, have lost twenty-three men by ambush and murder in the last two years! A telegraph might help us, but it would be cut everywhere. Your road will bring in settlers, and only then will we be freed of these scoundrels."

" I see your great difficulties," said Jack reflectively.

" Yes. At home, in the comfortable North, people can not see why we are forced to take the law in our own hands. An alert and indignant people do make mistakes in their fury; but what can we do? Our homes can not be pillaged. And look at the whole Texan situation! Sweeping emancipation has thrown the improvident negro on his own resources. The worst of them were formerly carted to the Red River, or fled over here. A few bad negroes cause our sullen, impoverished youth to attack the respectable blacks right and left. The disorganization of the war has torn the South to pieces. In time, it will settle down. No sane people wish to brutalize their patient, subordinate laborers. We do not. But the South resents negro-suffrage. By fair means or foul, the whites will *make the negro-vote ineffective.* When the generation which knew slavery and fought the war has disappeared, *to the last man,* then the negro will assume his secondary place in quiet. You had slave markets once in New York City; and now you wish negro equality *elsewhere.* Look at the hub-bub over one colored cadet at West Point! How would you like to live in a Louisiana parish with five hundred whites and two thousand blacks? The Northern man is the *first to howl* when he is forced to put up with it. We know how to treat the black. Your ideal philanthropy fails. God alone knows where the black will stand in fifty years! We have the unsettled frontier, the negro problem, and the Indian raids to meet. It is like sleeping on one's arms. We will wipe out the marauders, drive back the Indians, who raid in now from the open Northwest and the big bend of the Rio Grande, and the negro will finally gravitate into his quiescence. Twenty years from to-day smiling homes will reach from Brownsville to Eagle Pass, and over to San Antonio. Your railroad is the harbinger of peace and prosperity. But here's the drive!"

From a rising knoll, as far as the eye could reach, ten great bands of cattle, each under control of thirty or forty riders, with tossing horns, wild, hoarse bellowing, and thundering hoofs, made more noise than an army taking position for battle. Separated by a halfmile, each band had its captain and its little wagontrain. Armed to the teeth, their kits lashed behind them, the lithe riders, with easy sway, glided among the maddened beasts.

"You have here our wild country life! There's a sight worth coming from Paris to see. Discipline, experience, foresight, every resource of self-reliance are here. These men march, guard, drive, repair, and move along like the main train of a field army. Over the great trail across the northeast part of the State, over the Indian Territory to Kansas and the fattening pasture, this great animal crop *carries itself*, and in good condition, next spring, will be a month's subsistence for Chicago or New York. Ten miles a day for four months is their route."

" Do you lose many?" Jack questioned

"We allow five per cent for food, wastage, and accident. Let us go back; they are under way."

A distant rumbling thunder, the shouts of three hundred men, and the firing of signal shots announced that a half-million dollars moved slowly along in the tossing horns, sleek hides, and wild charges of the doomed spoils of the Texan prairies.

"To-morrow, Jack," said the heir of San Miguel, " we will draw out at noon, and make a start! I'll have a few out-riders skirmish over our whole home place. I will keep pickets riding around us incessantly.

In daylight we can whip a hundred marauders. At night, I'll have a ring of sentinels to prevent anyone sneaking up on us. Now, Jack, I will occupy the 'padre' to-night," said his friend, a little maliciously. "I fancy that mother and Alice will have some of their usual occupations to engross them. If you wish to say anything to Katie, I would suggest a sort of private 'musicale' in the great parlor. I believe that my father is *not* devoted to music. I will entice him to the ' Den'!"

"Thanks, old fellow," said Jack, blushing under the fast deepening prairie bronze of his handsome face. " Do you work similar tactics at Arundel House?"

"Oh, Gertie and I have a 'safe conduct' already. Our Rubicon is passed, as far as her mother is concerned! But you and I are still in the same uneasy predicament as to our brides, Jack. *I* have to creep gently on the 'padre's' outworks. *You* will be all right. He will surrender to Katie. She rules his heart. But he does not know my Gertrude."

CHAPTER XII.

FOR LIFE AND LOVE—ON THE WILD PRAIRIE—MRS. MARSHALL'S LETTER—SILAS' VOYAGE—AT HACIENDA MAXAN—PANCHITA—THE JAGUAR ON THE TRAIL— A THUNDERBOLT—LOST KATIE — FIRST BLOOD FOR JACK—A CAPTURED MESSAGE.

"WELL, young man, are you all ready for the road?" calmly remarked Silas Leavenworth, as the official circle began to drop away at the close of the dinner. ·

"Right as right can be," merrily answered Jimmy, but the lines of his face hardened as he caught a glance from Katie's eyes, shadowed with anxiety. "We ride out at daybreak, sir," concluded the young man, while he finished his coffee.

"Bring Harbeck and the foreman out to my office, James. I wish to have them understand my instructions to you, if I am away, so that we can all work together. Mother, you and the girls can entertain Mr. Manson. I know it's dull enough for him here."

Katie's mother nodded her head demurely, while St. Cecilia gazed steadily at Miss Katie, who was strangely indifferent in her manner.

"Then it's all settled now," said the ranchero, rising. "I will inspect your outfit before you go. Take the best stock and no poor break-down rig." A grave anxiety marked Silas Leavenworth, for, since the cañon attack, he felt that his enemies were ever prowling near.

"Don't wait for me, Jack, but turn in when you wish. I will be some hours at the 'Den' to-night, I know. I'll wake you myself in the morning!" whispered the heir of San Miguel.

Jack Manson flashed one grateful look at "Katie's brother," who evidently was determined to make this night session a memorable one.

Manson strolled over to the house with the ladies. The broad portico invited the usual half-hour's general gathering. The witching moonlight began to silver the knolls around the home place. A gentle silence was accentuated by the tinkle of the distant herd-bell. Miss Katie was distraught, while Jack Manson, with unwearied politeness, sustained the most unmeaning conversation of his life with Sister Alice and her mother. Grave, gentle Alice's thoughts were far away on the Nueces. She was deeply interested in certain extensive "improvements" of Colonel Tom Bayard's home.

"I will let him have his way. I can change all *very*

easily," thought the gentle girl, whose steadfast heart was fixed on the amelioration of the social surroundings of the gallant veteran. " I *will* write him, though, not to give 'carte blanche' orders to strangers North for things I do not need. He is so generous, so anxious to please me." It was even so! But Colonel Tom's ideas of luxurious decoration were derived from certain gorgeous Mississippi River steamboats he had voyaged on during the late Confederacy, and some fantastic stage-settings at New Orleans!

" I have letters to write," calmly remarked Alice, as she rose to leave.

" I suppose I know *to whom*," said Katie, with fatal audacity, as her queenly sister moved out of the circle.

" You are fortunate, Katie, that you have *none to write at present*," quietly said Alice, pausing at the door.

For once the madcap heiress was silent. Jack Manson heaved a sigh of ecstatic relief as Mrs. Leavenworth said: " I find it a little chilly; I think that I will go in."

" Of all nights, the night for a walk in the garden!" cried Katie, with sudden decision, for she had felt in her heart of hearts the graceful riposte of Alice.

" Do not linger too late, my child," said Mrs. Leavenworth, with a meaning inclination of her head toward the " Den," where the " council of war " was already convened.

Jack Manson felt assured that the grave, dark-eyed woman was already his friend. But the variable, imperious Silas!

Down the rose alleys, side by side, the lovers walked in silence. The parting hour was coming! When Katie's bower was reached, the little household tease threw herself into the open arms of her lover.

"My God! How can I see you go out upon this ride! I have the strangest forebodings. Jack, my Jack! Have I led you into this wild land?" The girl's sobs thrilled Manson's inmost soul.

"Dearest! my Katie! Why? What risk can there be with Jimmy and twenty picked men? We could 'stand off' the whole Mexican border till we could get help." Manson was astonished at her depth of feeling.

"It is so cruel! I can hardly speak to you," the passionate girl cried. "And I have had such dreams! That fiend who seeks father's life will follow you and Jimmy. My God! Be careful. I know this fearful land." Katie was clinging to him in loving emphasis!

Manson folded her to his breast. "Sweet one! It is now a struggle *for Life and Love!* Your brother is resolute. I am no child. If that lurking assassin hounds us, he will meet the sternest reception. Jimmy has not wished to alarm you. We can not attack him in Mexico, but if he falls into our net, it is war to the knife! I know Creole revenge. He will meet the penalty of his mad folly. Let me think of you only as bright and happy, my own heart's darling. Till we meet again, I will bear your smiling face in my heart. You are a *Texan girl*, remember."

Katie's tears lingered on the lashes shading her eyes until the impetuous flow of her lover's tenderness chased away the haunting phantoms of Ramon Maxan!

It was an hour, a brief, happy hour, too short for the hearts beating each to each, when Katie cried, with her arms around the man to whom she had shown the whole intensity of her ardent soul: "*We must go in!* I shall see you, my heart's darling, in the morning. Do not look at me when I look at you; I should break down. But I will ride out with you, and say good-bye. My life goes with my love. By all you hold dear,—be not one moment off your guard."

The roses alone saw the lovers' parting. There was the supreme moment, as when the warrior falls into the waiting line. But there was not a tremor in brave Katie's voice as ten minutes later she said "Good-night" in the parlors.

Jack Manson was glad to escape the keen, gray eye of old Silas, and his hasty reference to "an early reveille" was the signal of departure.

While they slept, the wounded boy spy was steal-ing furtively through the mesquit bushes beyond the men's camp, with a brief scrawl hidden in his rags. It read:

The two young Gringos leave for Eagle Pass to-morrow, early. Make sure of them.

Away toward the hamlet of Los Angeles, the boy dashed in mad fear, for a stolen bridle, thrown on the first half-tamed "cow-horse" he met, gave him the means of reaching Ximenes' hiding-place before day! For the wounded and baffled traitor only waited his coming to send his waiting riders to warn Maxan in his safe eyrie across the Rio Bravo.

The gray of morning lingered over the fair slopes of San Miguel, as Jimmy laid his friendly hand on Jack Manson's shoulder. With a bound the engineer was on his feet.

"Our men are already breakfasting. The wagon is ready, and our horses wait at the door." Such were the brief words of the Texan.

As Jack Manson entered the breakfast-room, there was a general movement of surprise. Clad in his fringed suit of Indian Valley tan buckskin, the supple form and manly beauty of the young lover were dis-played to striking advantage. His soft, gray frontier hat, and belt with his hunting-knife and the tried pistols, were the finishing touches of a becoming attire. His noble face, serious and calm, was shadowed with mingled expectancy and resolve.

A nod from Silas, a gentle smile from the mother, was the greeting received by Jack, who felt his heart bound, as Katie Leavenworth, in riding costume, entered with her frank-faced brother, whose sun-burned countenance was eager and bright. Sister Alice was the last to join the circle.

"Well, Lady Bird! are you, too, going to Eagle Pass?" said Silas, in genuine astonishment.

"I will give my horse a morning gallop," said the wilful heiress of San Miguel, as she tossed her whip and gloves on a side table. Her thrilling beauty was heightened by the high courage shining in her stead-fast eyes. One flashing glance told Jack that the woman he loved had, in her night vigils, followed his dangerous pathway! The roses were faint tints this morn on the dauntless Texan girl's face. The courage of her race and time shone through a complexion as pale as alabaster, tinged only with the repressed current of her heart's blood.

Grave-faced Mrs. Leavenworth shyly glanced at the darling child of her heart. A fond mother's love told her that her beautiful girl now knew the lot of the frontier woman—in riches or poverty, to wring blood-less hands and wait till every lurking peril would be passed! When Manson forced himself to speak, he started at the unfamiliar sound of his own voice. And yet, the two lovers, with hearts surcharged with burning, unspoken tenderness, ran the gauntlet of crafty Silas Leavenworth's keen gray eyes.

Half an hour later, Jack Manson, as he put Katie on her splendid horse, heard joyously her brief whisper: "We will have ten minutes to say good-bye at the edge

of the mésa!" She glanced gratefully at Brother Jim.
Katie's diplomacy!

The tall Texan youth's head towered above the dark-
robed matron whose head rested on his bosom.

"Dear mother, you must not worry. Why, I've
made this same trip dozens of times! Besides, a rider is
in with news that McNally's Rangers will patrol for a
month from Ringgold to Eagle Pass. I have taken
our best men, and I am ordering in some extra boys to
scout around our march. We will be just as safe as you
at home here!"

For all these cheering words, Silas Leavenworth's
face was troubled as he said: "Now, my son!" and,
with a silent grip of his boy's hands, led the wife and
mother weeping to her room. Though it was a
shadowed parting, the old ranchero gave no special
admonition to his lion-hearted son when he galloped
away! The cavalcade was already a half-mile away,
winding along the edge of the mesquit thicket, stretching to the groves of the sweet lakes "Los Olmos." In
the early freshness of the day the slim gray deer
bounded easily across the path. Hundreds of long-
eared hares were saluting the morning sun. The wild
turkeys rushed noisily across little openings, and at the
point of the timber Jimmy Leavenworth turned back
and gaily swung his broad sombrero! The anxious
parents walked into the great house.

"Did Katie take any one to bring her back?" said
Mrs. Leavenworth to Silas.

The old ranchero paused and briefly said: "Yes, I
sent on a couple of the stockmen to watch the edge
of the timber for any prowlers." His heart was full of
the last ringing "good-bye" of his gallant son. But
he paused once more. His eagle eye swept the kingly
domain which called him "Master!" He divined his

patient wife's uneasiness. " I wish we really could get
farther from the timber here, but the water is our only
salvation for stock. That long patch of elms and
mesquit from lake to lake gives too much cover for
these cowards." Silas was not wise in his generation.
He eyed the dry, sweeping knolls a few miles out, now
covered with his cattle and horses. Twenty years later
they were blooming gardens with wind-mills pouring
the never-failing underlying water out freely. Yet he
said: " Now, out *there*, mother, if we had water, no
one could approach us for miles without discovery. But
nothing will grow there!" He checked his forebodings, for his pale-faced wife was gazing steadily down to
where their brave young rider had waved his knightly
adieu!

" There's Katie coming!" joyously cried the reassured
matron. For, with far-flowing mane and wild leaps the
little lady's blood horse was bearing her homeward.
Her henchmen followed fast behind, their broncos vainly
coping with the elastic stride of the gallant Kentucky
blood steed she guided with her dainty hand.

"She rides like the wind," the gentle mother said.
But Mary Leavenworth did not know her spirited
child was murmuring, as she urged her horse forward:

" I hope the breeze will dry these tell-tale tears. No
one must know."

It was bashful maiden art! For, as the generous
brother Jimmy, after folding her to his breast, spurred
away to the head of the column, whispering, " Ten
minutes only, dear Katie, happier days will come
to us both soon!" Jack Manson had sprung to his feet
when they were alone, and covered her dainty hands
with kisses as he lifted her from the saddle. In his
strong arms, her head nestling upon his throbbing breast,
the brave girl smiled through her tears as her lover

stole a wayward curl from the wind-blown tresses of the frontier princess. The dull forebodings of her heart were hidden as she dropped in his hand her one school-girl ring!

"You shall have mine in return. I'll take *yours*, now, Katie, for love! But you shall wear *mine* for life."

"For Life and Love," she whispered. "Now!" after one last embrace, she grasped her steed's reins, as Jack swung her to the saddle. Her blue-veined hands were bare, for he had thrust her dainty gauntlets in his bosom, and the brave girl never turned her head, as she swept homeward, for she knew that Jack Manson would linger on that hallowed spot as long as she was near. Setting his teeth, as he gave his captured steed a cut, Jack Manson dashed away on the wild prairie, to rein up beside Katie's brother. A mist, not of the dreary morning, lingered in Jack's honest eyes. His heart was beating wildly, for the dearest voice on earth had whispered: "Come back to me! Be watchful over my brother! Come back and claim me for Life and Love!"

In varied rides with his associate, Manson had sketched and mapped in the environs of the ranch. The old Prussian engineer's careful and exact maps connected San Miguel with the exquisite work of the coast survey at Corpus Christi and the Gulf.

So, following the general course dictated by the sagacious Silas, from his private reports and the gleanings of years of expectancy, Manson, sketch-book, compass, and aneroid at hand, was busied till the setting sun saw them nearing an elm-shaded spring in the centre of a mesquit opening, two hundred yards in diameter. Before the chill of evening settled over the prairie, the camp was in order. The twenty lithe, quiet, active riders, dividing the duties of guard, picket, stock-herding, and wood and water finding, were now resting by the blazing camp-fire. Two active Mexican lads, and a cook of the blackness of the tartarean shades, with the dexterity of practice, offered a substantial meal. Jack Manson appreciated the delicacy with which Jimmy Leavenworth simply said: " I know this is a new country to you. I will inspect the guard! You turn in and have your rest." While Jack Manson, worn out with repressed feelings, with a pain of parting which was a revelation, muttered a prayer for the sweet girl grown now so strangely dear, as his tired head fell on his blanket pillow: stern Jimmy Leavenworth, his Lone Star revolver at his feet, gazed into the watch-fire, and saw in the flickering blaze the patrician face of sweet Gertrude Marshall, far away, where the old oaks of Arundel shaded her ancestral home.

And neither brave Jimmy Leavenworth, alert and soldierly: watchful Silas Leavenworth, in his guarded stronghold: nor sleeping Jack Manson, could dream that across the harsh gray sands, tearing through cactus bramble and sneaking through mesquit groves, the waiting riders were now speeding away to tell Ramon Maxan that his prey was out on the lonely wastes. For the wounded lad had safely reached Ximenes, and, dog-like in submission, delivered his note, and slunk in with the aimless crowd hanging around the frontier fandango house at the squalid village of Los Angeles.

Day after day passed, the cavalcade pricking along with care over the tortuous line marked out by Silas Leavenworth's greed of land-grabbing. While Jack Manson, with growing map and busy pencil, filled his note-books with data, and stored his mind with the photographic impressions of a skilled road-builder, Jimmy Leavenworth, hawk-eyed, guarded and directed the line of march. Twenty-five miles a day, over varied scenes—now cañons, mésas, flinty hillsides, and dry plains, breaking into broad, rich prairies—they drew on toward Eagle Pass.

A straggling clump of jacales (Mexican dog-like huts), an abandoned cattle-camp, here and there a ranch house of adobe, were the only variations of the scene. It was in varied wind and storm, in blinding storm and chilling norther, they pressed on to their goal. One day, the flashing of trappings betrayed the approach of a military express of a corporal and three men.

" This is rare good luck! Jack!" cried Leavenworth, who was now as brown as a Comanche, "I have a note here from the commander at Fort Duncan. Two of the best companies of the Fourth Cavalry are ordered to patrol the river between Eagle Pass and Ringgold Barracks. Lieutenant Buller commands one. He's the ideal of a frontier soldier. He knows more about the Comanches, Lipans, and Kickapoos than the whole war department, and he can nose a desperado, a horse thief, or a smuggler a mile away. This will be a great protection for our road-building and the ranch and stock. Buller is the only regular officer I ever knew who was a good frontiersman. He's as game as a knife and a right good fellow. We'll ride into Ringgold on our way down and see him."

The corporal and his alert troopers trotted away briskly, not without refilled canteens and handfuls of the best cigars of San Miguel.

Two days later, as Jack Manson dreamed, in the sunset, of the graceful girl who fled like a Scythian princess from his arms, a dusty rider dashed into the camp. It was Bronco Bill. In silence he handed Leavenworth a packet of letters. While friendly hands cared for his horse, Bill joined the mess around the generous

board. For the prairie deer and turkey, fat beef and
sheep from the countless herds passed through, gave a
larder to be envied. The unerring marksmen stalked
the game as they rode. With ready lasso and revolver
a beef fell before them at need. The hide stretched
on the nearest tree or rock was left as a tribute to
frontier hospitality. Countless " mavericks " or strayed
cattle were roaming at the disposition of the travellers,
and the stock was almost as wild as the gray wolves
howling at night around the lonely camp.

"Anything for me?" queried Jack, in despondency.

"Nothing yet," his voice grave and troubled, as he
pored over several documents. "I want to talk to you
by and by," said the Texan. "Several suspicious
things have occurred near the ranch, and my father is
away at New Orleans. I'll send old Basilio in as soon
as I can write. Bill has ridden up in three days."
Jack Manson turned away, his heart full. Was he
then so soon forgotten! He wandered away to the
edge of the camp. A touch on his elbow made him
start.

Bronco Bill stood beside him. He held a packet in his
outstretched hand.

" Beg pardon, captain. I was to give you this *in
private.* I hadn't no show till now. Miss Katie's
orders, you know, sir. Must obey the ladies!"

With rough courtesy the plainsman was gone. And
Jack Manson knew that the proud and shy woman who
had given him her impetuous love, sought to shield its
avowal from all but the eyes of the chosen lover of her
heart! "Katie!" The very name thrilled his heart.
And fingering the pages, he sought the one shelter-
tent to read the precious lines and await the Texan's
confidence. ·

It was half an hour before Jack raised his head.

Every word of his darling's womanly confidence was
clearly fixed in his mind. Each girlish phrase of love
and endearment thrilled his lover heart. The perfume
of the flower of love, the growth of one happy day of
magic power, intoxicated the youth who had fed " on
the honey-dews of Paradise." Yet his brow was clouded,
for the clear-headed Texas maiden had written:

For my sake, for Life and Love, dearest, be ever on your guard!
Father and Nordensklold are gone to New Orleans to perfect
the railroad bonds. He had telegrams from your uncle; also,
from Senator Steele. Jimmy will tell you all. But the boy who
was wounded at the cañon has disappeared. I fear treachery.
Some lurking parties have been chased away by our stockmen.
I do not wish to alarm mother or Alice. The ranch, *of course*, is
safe. We have fifty armed men here always. But I fear they
may cut in behind you. I dread your return journey. For my
sake, beware! I can not bear to walk here in safety and think of
your dangers. I am sleepless for your sake! Never forget these
words! Colonel Tom Bayard can not take charge of the ranch
for these two weeks, as he is closing his business at Brownsville,
at the District Court, and will come home by Ringgold Barracks.
You may meet him. Alice is in ecstasy, dear old solemn angel,
for Colonel Tom has arranged with father that their marriage
will occur as soon as possible. The Colonel is State Senator, and
will look after all father's interests at Houston this winter. His
pay is "*nothing*," for Alice is all he wants. She will be a star at
our Texas capital, and, so timid as she is, will be happier there.
I am glad at heart that Bayard's ranch is so much farther from the
Rio Grande than ours. Alice needs a safe home and a protector.

Jack's eyes fell on Leavenworth, whose face was
stern as a Roman sentinel.

"Come here, Jack," he said, and the friends paced
by the dying fire in soul communion. Around them
lay their fearless guards, and now and then a wary
rider, swathed in his Navajo blanket, circled the camp,
for the night was chill and the rising wind began to
howl over the prairie.

Manson was soon a partner of all Jimmy Leavenworth's news and feelings; he was sad and depressed as he finished.

"What's the matter, Jimmy?" said Jack tentatively. "No bad news—from Virginia?" He laid his friendly hand on the Texan's shoulder.

Jimmy turned, his voice softened with emotion. "It's about Gertrude, you know. I may never get Mrs. Marshall's consent to bring her here to the Rio Grande. I have letters from both of them. She's a strange girl. Her brother's and father's deaths have shadowed her womanhood. Her loving heart is centered on those she cherishes as dear. She is almost clairvoyant now. She writes me of an awful vision! It is all born of her anxiety over this trip and this project. How can such a woman ever be happy here, even with the luxury of San Miguel? I cannot avoid these dangerous trips. Half my time must be spent on the border. I can not shirk the risks and duties of my position; I must stand by my father. As for flinching from the duties of Texan life I will not. I would be sneered at as a coward. Jack," he said, with impulsive energy, "if I lose that girl, I will *blow my brains out!*"

Manson grasped his hands. "And if she loses you, it will kill *her!* Think of that! Now, my dear Jimmy, it is this rising norther, and the news of the second-sight business unsettles your nerves! Take a good pull of coffee and you will be all right at daybreak." The cowboy coffee-pot was ever in requisition, and Manson signed to the colored boy, who never slept while his young master was on foot.

Rolled in his blankets, as the wind rose, and the keen, icy blast cut like a knife, Leavenworth told Manson of the loving Virginia girl's vision: "Strange forebodings! Woman's mysterious double nature is life's riddle! She sees me, you, and strangers, in a far-away hostile haunt. *Katie, too, is there!* And soldiers and fighting." His voice was sad.

"And the outcome?" broke in Manson, who wished to energetically dispel this cloud.

"Always the same! I am lying in the arms of a strangly beautiful woman, and—and dying!" Leavenworth was silent a moment. "And her mother," he resumed, "writes me privately that this vision always haunts Gertie, whose dear face is transparent as alabaster. Her singular mind recurs to this, and struggles through the clouds to see the rest of this devil-painted picture! She wears her vital force out. But all is dark beyond that! Mrs. Marshall begs me to break this morbid spell cast on her by coming North. She says Arundel House shall be my future home. I have wealth, you know, Jack. It is not that. I can not abandon my father in this great project. I know his credit and your uncle's is involved. As for living North—impossible! I could make San Miguel safe, but will her mother give her to me? Could she live among such daily scenes as you have had glimpses of?" His voice died away, and only the sound of the sobbing blast was heard.

"Leavenworth, you must rouse yourself. This is mere delusion," said Jack with vigor. "Why, look at the *other side of the picture!* In three months Alice will be Tom Bayard's wife. He will guard the west and north. Our road, if pushed, closes up, with its telegraph, the south and east. The opening toward the frontier will be guarded by the road itself. You have told me McNally's Rangers and your cavalry friends will be scouring the desert strip here for months. It will be a general 'round up.' I will have strong working parties out at once, if the road is pushed, and you shall ride the Rio Grande no more." Jack Manson paused, and said, with softened tone: " When I win Katie, you shall be made to *obey our wishes!* Take your station then at San Miguel, and run the whole thing. Your father is getting old."

" That's all true!" moodily replied Jimmy, " but he has a dozen private schemes and connections I know little of. They are legacies of the war. He will not give them up till some great disaster occurs. I have always feared it."

" I see that you really could not settle in Virginia," said Jack, wishing to divert his friend's mind from the haunting vision.

" You and Tom Bayard could easily manage the estate, but I would not live under Northern influence. Virginia is only a lonely graveyard. The fact is, Jack, the North must have us as a counterpoise to foreign influence, for socialism and anarchy will follow your throwing open your ports to the men who shot down native-born Americans to gain your ' bounty'! I'm not bitter, but I will give you a few plain truths. No commercial, trading, and manufacturing nation ever kept pure blood. I'm no aristocrat! But the woman I love is patrician born. Now *here*, our family take rank in the higher classes. We are farmers, planters, drovers, herdsmen, and horsemen! We do not look to the slow returns of manual labor, to the petty tricks of trade, the shifts of capitalistic and skilled-labor struggles. We have a patient, docile, secondary race, the negro. He serves us. He shall. *He must!* All your reconstruction and carpet-bag governments will fall of their own weight. Once in the higher classes, lauded and socially recognized, a man is *held up here.* At the North, changing turns of fortune's wheel make the servants of one generation the mistresses of another!

Your alien classes, robust, hard-working, and clannish, eat into your political circles. They *breed and save!* You *waste*, and in Yankee egoism, dread large families. Your great centres of population thrust all real American feeling out of your circles, your marts, your journals, and your homes.

"Deny it as you may, you worship the dollar! You truckle to it, you flatter it, you marry it! Your German, Irish, Hebrews, and other foreigners are toadied to in business, flattered in your elections, and we native born must yet overthrow your temporary control of the heritage we were all born to. In twenty years these swarming people will fill the cheap lands of the West. We don't want them South. We will not have them. We will work together in opposition! Strange as it may seem, the sons of the rebels of Appomattox will be truer friends, wiser sons of loyalty and liberty than your ' truly loyal ' freedom shriekers.

"Wounded and bleeding, we need no help. We scorn your pity. States' rights we bled for. We hold sternly to State pride. You give your daintily-bred daughters to the man of the dollar. We marry in our own race and blood. Decade by decade the South will quietly gain. Backed by our prolific and docile negroes, we will control the land from Richmond, Louisville, and St. Louis to Denver and El Paso.

"The Southern Cross will be firmly fastened in our country's flag, when the East, North, and West, torn by your quarrels of capital and labor, millionaires and anarchists, may fall away from the Union! The North will be the home of every ' ism ' that greed, craft, fraud, and socialism can invent. You are pledged to it by your political adherence to the ' social equality of man.' It filled your Northern armies, but it will ruin the Union yet ——" A fusillade waked the echoes!

"My God!" yelled Leavenworth, as a volley of bullets tore through the tent. Louder than the howling of the storm the crack of Winchester rifles roused the indomitable Texans.

"Don't get up! I'll give the word," sharply cried Jimmy, pushing Manson a rifle. "They are shooting high."

Rolling over behind the blankets, the two comrades opened fire on the copses whence the volley had come. A chorus of defiant yells rang out as Leavenworth's men, from behind the wagon, or with bended knee, rained a platoon fire into the bushes right and left.

"Now, Jack!" cried Jimmy, springing out. A knot of brave riders was already formed behind the wagon. The firing was over. The camp was a hornet's nest! The attack had failed!

"No danger now. These scoundrels never run in," laughed the young Texan. "Here, Walton, a half-dozen of you, scatter this fire," and the Cowboys energetically kicked the smouldering brands over the prairie.

"No pursuit!" sharply said Leavenworth, as his two leading scouts sat ready to lead the riders into the chaparral. "The *dead* will be there in the morning. The *living* are a half-mile away now. Double the guard. Let all lie on their arms. Any one hurt?"

In five minutes the damage was found to consist of several wounded animals, one or two slight flesh wounds to a couple of the videttes, and the well-riddled tent-fly covering the comrades.

As Leavenworth lay resting, his head pillowed on his saddle, behind the wagon, Manson was near him. The wind rose to an icy gale, yet no fire was lit. Its tell-tale gleam had betrayed their location.

"Indians or Mexicans?" queried the young commander, of the head herdsman.

" Mexicans, d—n them! " sententiously said the disgruntled Cowboy; " I'll——." He did not finish his imprecation, as he walked away in disgust at the sneaking wolves of night.

The heir of San Miguel never concluded the political harangue, to which Jack Manson had listened in patience. His charmed life was safe from loyal Jack's outraged Republicanism. He was Katie's brother.

"Hello! what's this? It was a close call!" Jimmy's hands were warmed by a trickling stream from his temple. "Just grazed me! I'm glad my head's all right."

" Well, your *heart* is, anyway," said Manson, cheerfully. " That's in Virginia!"

"Jack," replied Leavenworth seriously, " we are followed on your account alone! That volley was aimed at our tent. Some devil knew we two would be there; that's why I yelled not to rise. You can always see better and shoot safer from the ground. If we had jumped up, one of us might have got his billet, or both! You saw that my men fought ' coyote fashion '; I will fool these devils. I will light a *half-dozen* camp-fires after this. I will put two or three men in ambush near them; we will pitch no tent, and I will cover our main body in some hollow or little arroyo. Besides, I will send old Basilio down to Laredo. He can telegraph from there to Mrs. Marshall that we are, so far, safe. The ladies can laugh at the vision. I will send a dispatch to Buller and McNally to look out for these fellows. Besides, if Basilio meets Tom Bayard on his way back, I will ask the Colonel to join me abreast of Las Cuevas, and we will scout the country back together. Old Basilio can rest, and ride back to tell us of Tom's march; he has a dozen picked men with him." The wearied speaker slept heavily after the exciting episode.

As soon as the gray dawn made it light, Leavenworth was astir. Dividing his party into four strong
bands, the circling bushes were searched. Shouts and
yells announced the finding of two saddled horses tangled in the bushes by the trailing gear, and, staring up
from the sward by the now blazing fire, where the
servants hastened the morning meal, the stiffened corpses
of two villainous-looking Mexicans lay, wide-eyed and
cold.

"Just as I told you, Jack! From the other side; no
one knows them. Now, I'll get the dispatches ready
while the men break camp." Leavenworth's stiffened
fingers could hardly hold the pencil, for the roughened
coats of the horses, the whimpering of the negro servants, and the sullen movements of the blanketed riders,
proved how bitter was the norther, now at its height.
A cold line of ice seemed to mark every bone of the
exposed plainsmen. From their concealment, whisky
canteens were suddenly produced, and gallons of steaming coffee followed these "morning nips."

"The needle is dancing so I can't do anything till
the wind calms down," said the engineer.

"All right, Jack! I'll move camp to the best place,
post some sitting guards, and we will wait till this blows
over. I'm sorry, for we are short of rations, and these
terrible northers are often followed by floods."

Jimmy Leavenworth selected a choice horse for Don
Basilio, who received, in Spanish jargon, his orders.
Carefully secreting his letters in a buckskin band he
wore in lieu of 'undergarment, with a couple of
fresh rounds of cartridges, a flask of whisky, a box of
matches, a few yards of dried beef in strings, and his
Navajo blanket tied behind his saddle, the old servitor
lightly touched the rowels to his bounding steed and
was soon lost on the prairie. His mournful eyes never

moved, as with a corn-husk cigarette defying even the wild norther, Basilio struck forth, in Indian style, travelling so he could not be seen from a distance.

"There he goes! Wherever a weasel, fox, or a tiger can go, old Basilio is safe. He is the best plainsman in Texas next to Rip Ford! Now we'll move camp."

Manson sprang on his captured steed and the command moved out to a spot selected by Leavenworth.

"What has become of the bodies?" said Jack, as a half-hour later they lay at ease in one of a half-dozen quickly made "wick-i-up" brush shelters.

"The wolves and coyotes are the guardians of that valuable property," said Leavenworth grimly. "The strangers came to my camp uninvited. I left it to them."

From the knolls near them four men watched, rifle in hand, the approaches to the new camp. A careful ride around the new position had enabled the now doubly watchful friends to prevent a recurrence of either surprise or covert attack.

Toward noon the fierce, chilling wind, which had driven the stray cattle for miles into huddled bands crouching in dell and arroyo, suddenly flickered, fell, and finally ceased. From the northwest a growing patch of dark clouds drove down rapidly. An unearthly hush replaced the hissing wailing of the dry, icy norther!

"I am afraid we are in for it," gravely remarked Leavenworth, as he ordered the spare rations, ammunition, and heavier arms to be stored in the one wagon with its heavy cover. Before "slickers" and rubber "ponchos" were adjusted, a perfect cloud-burst broke around them. The far summits of the Monterey Mountains folded themselves in gray mantles of thick, wet, gray fog, and the winding course of the island-dotted Rio Grande, with its cottonwood groves, its elm, and maple-shaded banks, was veiled from them by torrents of blinding rain.   One straggling fire alone was kept up under a jutting rock where busy hands had piled a huge mound of dry mesquit and fallen scrub oak.

"Only *two days* from Eagle Pass, and in these times when I should be at the ranch! This is dreadful!" chafed the Texan, as he folded his rubber cloak closer under the shot-riddled tent-fly. " If you had tied your line on to the Boundary Commission's monuments at Eagle Pass, we might scout quickly down in a circle, and swing back toward the ranch. I could show you the route, even in a storm."

"That's true!" replied Jack, though the rain was pouring from his frontier head-gear. "But I must keep up the chaining, sketching, and road-measuring, with our odometer. I can easily lay down a railroad where anyone can drive a wagon without locking wheel or using brakes. The first hundred miles is as level as a parlor floor, and, even here, a few turns will pass any obstacle so far. But I must be able to make a handsome, completed map, and secure the general advantages, as well as length of route your father has dictated."

" We may be here a week," ruefully replied Leavenworth. "If we had a schooner, we could sail almost to Eagle Pass in the waters of these rolling pockets."

Five days later, chilled, stiffened, and benumbed, the party were still beleaguered by flood, swollen streams, and impassable arroyos. The violence of the tempest was beyond memory, and scanty rations of coffee without sugar, dough cakes baked in the ashes, and the half-cooked flesh of the strayed cattle, were the only means of subsistence. Manson and Leavenworth had relapsed into a gloomy silence. Each harbored anxieties and cares which wrapped him as a mantle. It was,

indeed, a cheerless camp. The drenched cattle, hovering near, became too weak and chilled to fly from the
men groping through rain and knee-deep water-pools
to put a ball through the unresisting bovines. On the
morning of the sixth day, the sun at last broke through
its veiling clouds. Far and dim, the exquisite profile of
the Monterey range hovered in the dim blue air.

"It will take us a day to dry out our camp, and I
shall now send eight men, with pack animals, over
to San Pedro Springs. We must have flour, coffee,
sugar, and bacon. It's only eighteen miles north!"
So joyously spoke Leavenworth, his good humor
returning. As the men briskly trotted away, Jimmy
turned to Manson: "Now, Mr. Engineer, run your
work into Eagle Pass as soon as you wish. I will lead
you a dance down the valley, on our return, that you
will never forget. I feel that I am needed at the
ranch."

By dusk, the return of the messengers gladdened all
hearts. By the blazing fires, the good cheer and fragrant coffee enlivened all. Tobacco, man's best friend
on the march, reappeared, and the replenished canteens
circulated gaily, as the men drank "adieu to Camp
Calamity."

"There is no use to deny that we are under some
shadow of bad luck!" growled Leavenworth, as he closed
the first decent repast of the weary days. "Walton tells
me that the military express rider, passing San Pedro
Springs for the Pass, warned everyone the whole lower
border is swarming with horse thieves, desperadoes, and
roving Mexicans, gathering up stock and horses strayed
south, driven before the great storm. They have killed
several well-known citizens. We must break camp at
peep of day, and only rest and refit a single day at the
Pass."

"You will find me sharp for work," cheerfully answered Manson. "Then, my boy, we'll see if any Texan can do better than an old plainsman of the North in a forced march home."

The friends sought their brotherly bivouac-couch, and while the moon sailed high above the tranquil scene, only the boom of the prairie owl, or the hoarse yell of a snarling gray wolf, broke the stillness of the night. Through the softened night a single swarthy horseman rode along toward Las Cuevas at full gallop over the sandy sward from which the waters had disappeared as if by magic.

"I wonder what the Jaguar's game is?" the half-breed spy murmured, as he drove the rowels in with Mexican ferocity. For he had sighted the distant hut, whence a fresh messenger would bear on the tidings that the "Gringos" had broken camp to push into Eagle Pass at last. "Well! I'll soon know if he crosses with fifty men. Carajo! There is always fandango and aguadiente, monte, and pretty women after El Jaguar works a scheme. He treats us like a royal 'contrabandista.' But he is risky. So risky, that some day these 'diablos, los Tejanos' will wipe us all out!"

While the dark-browed villain rode, pistol in hand, and the heart brothers waited in their distant camp for the dawn, Ramon Maxan sat in a vaulted room in the great old rumbling stone hacienda which called him its lord. In the midst of splendid groves and bowers, in the rich foot-hills of the Monterey hills, it overlooked the little town of Zacate. No fairer bower nestled in rich Nueva Leon than this splendid old two-story mansion. Around it spicy groves and orchards breathed their budding richness. The heart of the Zona Libre is a paradise of natural beauty.

The moonlight streamed in from an open window,

heavily grated, and the sound of a woman's voice, ringing high above the tinkle of a guitar, floated in, borne by the night breeze.

"It is a royal spot," mused Maxan, as he pushed back a map and strode to the window. "Old Juarez was right to kick the Churchmen out of these splendid places! They surely found snug nests for their retirement. I wonder if my predecessor, the Bishop, ever enjoyed secular music here! Who knows! Very likely some fair one queened it here before Panchita. Ah, yes! I must tell her some convincing pack of lies. Why does the report not come? If I had it, I would leave at daybreak. It's hard to keep fifty cut-throats quiet, even in luxury. Let me see."

El Jaguar turned to his maps again. Seated at the table, the high intelligence of his nature shone in his delicately chiselled face. His dark eyes beamed with earnestness and he was the ideal of supple elegance, as he gracefully tossed off a "petit verre" and lit a regalia. His green jacket, buttoned with golden half-ounces, rich leggings, and crimson silken sash, marked the man of highest local rank. A pair of richly chased silver spurs, a revolver belt, and the bullion-decorated gray sombrero lay on a table near, with a heavy loaded riding-whip. On the tiled floor lay a saddle, bridle, and housings, fit for a knight at the Field of the Cloth of Gold. With a score of armed retainers, a troop of servants, and a village nestling under his heavy-walled castle, Ramon Maxan, in a stolen hacienda, lorded it over a horde of devil-may-care bandits, watching great flocks and herds of the choicest animals, stolen from even the Indian Territory, and passed on by criminal and smuggler.

"Now," he soliloquized, "eighty miles to Fort Duncan, forty to Laredo, twenty to Las Cuevas and the

Rio Grande, and only ninety miles from the border
to San Miguel. Those two curs are at Eagle Pass,
two hundred and fifty miles away. I can easily hide
my party in the cactus groves on the edge of the bad
lands. If I sneak in with ten men, I can keep covered
in the lake woods near the ranch. The old man is still
at New Orleans, with no sign of return. Thank God
for the telegraph! If I can grab the girl, I can have
her run over here; she's safe then as in the grave.
Then, with my whole party, push up the valley, take
the band of Caballo Blanco from Los Angeles, and
waylay those two fellows. Madre de Dios! It will
do! They have four miles to travel to my one. I
will have five men to their one. They will be off their
guard. I'll bring these fellows' heads over here. That
proud devil shall say 'Good-morning' to her lover's
head! And I'll make Panchita tame her down if I can
excite her jealousy. By God! if the messenger—" he
paused and smiled, for the clatter of a horse's hoofs
waked the echoes of the paseo.

"Send him up, Antonio," Maxan called out, as the
major-domo entered. In five minutes Ramon el
Jaguar had read his dispatches, dismissed the tired rider,
and sharply said: "I leave at daybreak, Antonio!
Have every man ready! I'll tie up any man who is
not ready for the road!"

"Bueno, Señor," said a shaven man of middle age,
whose eyes burned steadily with restrained intelligence.

"By the way, Antonio, send word in to Senorita Panchita that I am coming to see her."

The major-domo bowed in silence.

"A cool devil! They spoiled a first-class bandit
when he became a hanger-on of the priests. I can trust
him to hold this place, at any rate. Now, for Miss
Panchita, then for my revenge!" He shook his fists

in rage. "I'll make you feel the tiger's claws, proud Katie!" His cheek still burned where Manson's blow had marred its beauty! "And I'll have his heart's blood!"

Striding through a long corridor, he pushed aside the curtains from the door of a richly furnished room. A woman leapt to her feet. The exquisite form of the young beauty was accentuated by the clinging white robe she wore. Deep, rich, dark, burning Spanish eyes, a cheek crimsoned with the glow of excitement tinting its faintly shaded olive, and silken hair flowing in jetty waves to her shoulders, gave her the air of a queen, as her slender hand, flashing with jewels, clasped a heavy golden cross, rising and falling on her panting bosom.

"I am going away, Panchita! I leave at daybreak. I shall be away two weeks. Antonio will tell you the rest. I have much to do. I came to say adios!" His voice had the callous ring of indifference, for his blood burned within him to be on the road! Revenge was near at last! He slowly moved toward the door, as the startled woman spoke in a dull, hopeless voice:

"And our marriage—your promise?" She leaned forward in eagerness.

"Later, when I come back! There's always time for that," Maxan sneered, as he noted her defiant mien. She dropped into a chair without a word. The handsome Creole's face darkened. "Another fit of heroics." He threw aside the curtain and sought his room. At early dawn, armed to the teeth, he led his waiting cut-throats, by an easy defile, to the Rio Grande. As he rode down the gorge he never turned his head to where Panchita lay in the slumber into which she had fallen in sobs and tears.

The Jaguar was on the trail at last. His resolute

mind was fixed on the blood-red star of Creole honor—
Revenge! As brave as cruel, he recked not of the stalwart foes in front. As cruel as brave, he cared not for
Panchita, the white blossom languishing in his harem
prison!

As he dashed along at the head of his plunder-thirsty
fellows, an ingenious thought came to his mind. "I'll
hoodwink that cross-grained devil, Panchita. When I
come back I'll make Antonio marry us. I will swear
that he is a priest. He knows enough of their jargon to
outwit her. She is capable of anything if aroused.
She might try her hand at some of the Aztec poison on
me. These romantic girls always have some old
beldame crooning their deviltry slyly into love-sick
minds."

With the skill of an old captain of free lances
Maxan led his lean followers on like sleuth-hounds, to
sneak across the Rio Grande before dark. The first
cactus grove, the nearest mesquit thicket, would cover
his movements, until in the darkness, under guidance
of his well-trained desperadoes, he could push forward
to gain a lodgment near San Miguel.

"There's a dozen here who have worked at the
ranch as refugees from our revolutionary troubles or
while dodging across to save punishment. I am not
strong enough to storm the house! I do not care to
destroy it and leave a trail. If the devil serves me
now, I'll carry the girl off, if she leaves her garden
walks alone."

Ramon Maxan exulted in the possession of a map
of the grounds, and a sketch with directions made by
Ximenes in his hours of slow convalescence at Los
Angeles.

Four days later, Leavenworth and Manson rode out
of the parade at Fort Duncan, Eagle Pass, in the fresh

morning, with all the haunting shadows lifted from their brows. The magic telegraph had spoken to the Texan from the white walls of Arundel House. Gertrude was now aware of her lover's safety. From New Orleans the anxious son learned that his father had sailed for Indianola on his way home. Jack Manson, by dint of night labors, had sent a duplicated tracing of his map, one copy to San Miguel and one to be forwarded to New Orleans for New York, via the mouth of the river, for a relay military express rider was to dash on with important dispatches in four days. Mark Manson's cipher enabled Manson to commune with his uncle at New York, through the courtesy of the military telegraph.

"Now, Jimmy," said Manson, "you do not need me professionally any longer. If I should be knocked over, your father could secure his grants by simply pegging off this line. Uncle Mark could, after a day's examination of my papers, safely contract the road by divisions and not waste five thousand dollars. It is a marvelously easy and practicable route. So double up our marches, my Texan friend. All I will do is jot down an itinerary and run off a reconnoissance sketch-line in my pocket-book as we hurry along homeward. You are now the leader. The sooner you take *me* back to Katie the nearer *you* will be to the waiting beauty of Arundel. Thank God, Gertrude Marshall's prophetic vision was only a fevered dream of womanly anxiety!"

Dashing steadily, yet warily, along, swinging and curving down the sandy bad lands, the little troop pressed on homeward. Their way led through stony wastes of sterile sandy bluffs, tenanted by coyote and huge rattlesnakes. They threaded great cactus groves scores of miles in extent, where in dawn and eve, a thousand richest colors of purple, cream, and azure hid the cruel thorns of the serrated leaves. Daintily the timid steeds picked their way past Spanish bayonet lines almost impregnable. The light, powdery red soil rose in choking clouds from under the low, brittle boughs of the mesquit groves, and deer and antelope fled before them. A simple bivouac at night sufficed them. Lightly their clatter enlivened the passing hours. A weird silence wrapped the desert wastes and whitened skeletons of cattle, and here and there only a lonely grave, marked with stones, indicated the presence of man or his belongings. ·A deserted shepherd's hut or mud-walled adobe indicated the uttermost frontier fringe of nomadic life as, a week later, they neared Ringgold Barracks, having swept past Laredo in a great inward curve.

Camped on the border of a seventy-mile stretch, without water, Leavenworth communed with his stalwart companion.

"To cross this 'jornada de los muertes,' we must pull out four hours before dawn. This is the last good water-hole. There is one unreliable one in a stunted grove of trees in the middle of this baking plain. If cattle have been driven by, it may be choked and dry for weeks. We can rest the animals there a couple of hours, and, by making a push, reach the outer side to-morrow night. I'll have water for the team mules taken. It is my custom to inspect canteens, and watch my men, for the sun's reflection is so hot here. I've known men to be found dead, black, and swollen, in seven hours, from over-exertion, in trying to hasten over it. I wish to get across, for old Basilio is getting too stiff in the joints to cross it safely. We ought to run into Tom Bayard's party beyond it, from his dispatch to me at Eagle Pass, from Brownsville."

The stars were shining as the camp was roused from their early nine o'clock evening rest, at the hour of two,

In thirty minutes the cavalcade moved out steadily over the gray waste. When the fiery red sun leaped up, in half an hour, the frontiersmen were riding with bared breasts. In silence the column plodded on loosely, the horses lowering their necks, and a flickering mirage tantalizing the riders. Hour after hour wore on. With parched throats the train pushed toward a scrubby patch of stunted trees in a hollow before them. As the tired animals drew near the oasis, a band of wild, thirst-maddened cattle charged down on them at a furious run. Their tossing horns and hoarse bellowing alarmed the jaded steeds. In an instant the quick-witted young leader was ready!

"Form line!" he cried. "Every other man dismount and open fire!" His voice rang out not a moment too quickly. The thirst-crazed beasts were thundering on. As the fusillade of carbines opened, the reserve men, with yells and cries, aided the stampede of the now divided herd.

Leavenworth laughed as the wild steers tore by at a frenzied run. "Cease firing!" he called out. "That band will be lying panting in death on the sands in an hour. They will run till they throw themselves and never rise again! Jack, ride down and see if there is any water at the hole. I fear they have trodden it down; we must make a dry camp and push on later."

Slipping his Winchester in its sheath under his leg, Manson dashed by several prostrate animals, his racer bounding in fright. As he approached the grove, by mere instinct his hand dropped on his heavy belt pistol. It was the salvation of his life, for, as he pushed up to the cover, a wild figure rose and quickly opened fire at point blank on man and horse. The frightened thoroughbred bounded sideways, as Manson, snatching his revolver, fired three quick shots. The would-be assassin, pitching heavily, fell forward on his face!

In a moment, Leavenworth and half the column
pulled up beside the still amazed engineer. "Here,
Walton, search the whole grove! Send four men to
ride around it. This fellow must have had a horse; he
has spurs on!"

Flinging himself from the saddle, the Texan, aided
by a scout, searched the wounded man's clothing.

"Ah, what's this?" almost screamed Leavenworth.
He was gazing blankly at a piece of paper, torn from
a blood-stained envelope. Manson's ball had pierced
the Mexican's lungs.

Jack was at his side in a moment.

Meet me at *Los Olmos*. I've got the Gringo girl. I'm going
up now to catch the two young fools. If you can't get there by
to-n'ght before daybreak, push on to Las Cuevas, and hide and
wait for me.

It was addressed "A mi amigo, Caballo Blanco," and
signed "Ramon Maxan."

Leavenworth shrieked "Am I going mad?" as he
gazed from side to side. Walton came galloping up.
The men had spread under cover and the wagon was
drawn under the scanty shade.

"Come, for God's sake! Old Basilio lies out there
wounded, dying, perhaps. Bring water, whisky."

Jack Manson pointed to the already retreating man,
sprang on his horse, and Leavenworth, the fatal note
in his hand, rode beside him.

"My God! Katie or Alice, which?" he groaned.

But Jack Manson set his teeth and hissed: "All depends
on your coolness now. We must revive old Basilio.
He knows. There has been a fight here!"

A little group was already gathered around the old
scout. A ball through his shoulder had crippled him,
and it was a ten minutes of agony before his glazed eyes
opened. Carried in under the shade, his face freshened

with the precious water, a swallow of whisky forced in his mouth, he feebly moaned, in Spanish, to Jimmy Leavenworth, kneeling by him. It was an eternity to Manson's bursting heart, when Leavenworth rose, cool and collected. His voice sounded as if echoing in a tomb.

"Walton, keep the wagon, the five heaviest men, and all the articles, save our canteens, ammunition, and weapons. Let each man fill his saddle-pouch with food. Take double ammunition belts. Leave everything else cached behind here. Equalize the water. Strike for Ringgold Barracks with the wagon. Leave Basilio there with the army surgeon. Refit and push for Las Cuevas for your life then. Send a company of cavalry down there. Tell Lieutenant Buller that Maxan carried my sister Katie away into Mexico!"

A hoarse yell from the men rose. Leavenworth cried: "For God's sake, Jack!" But Manson was a hundred yards away.

"Where are you going?" screamed Jimmy, racing up to him.

Manson hoarsely cried: "There! Over there! to find her, Katie. My God! My own darling!"

Leavenworth caught his bridle rein. "See here, Jack! I know how you love my sister. For her sake, wait a half-hour! We'll breathe the horses, wash their mouths out, pick our men, and I will lead you over this waste. It must be! Otherwise we would break down! And Katie!"

Jack Manson glared sternly at him as they rode back.

Lying on the sand in the shade, while the men, with nimble fingers, prepared for a life and death quest, Jimmy told the story, as the tears ran down his bronzed face.

"Basilio camped alone abreast of Las Cuevas. When he got to Laredo he sent my dispatches. The back country was filled with thieves and raiders, and the commanding officer sent him down to meet Tom Bayard's party under escort. At Ringgold he left the escort. Waiting for Bayard, who had started, moving slowly up from Brownsville, the old man hid his horse in a cañon, and was going to the spring for water, when this fellow and another rode up. He listened in hiding to their talk. Maxan had sneaked over the river, and lying around San Miguel, captured Katie walking near the house below the gardens. A light ambulance was hidden below the hills, furnished by some of his Mexican-border friends. Striking for Las Cuevas, on his way to his place, he sent these fellows for help to attack us. In trying to get away, they saw Basilio. He opened fire on foot; killed one, and the other fled. The old man was delayed saddling his horse, and only caught up with the fleeing scoundrel here. The fool would not leave his horse to hide, but he ambushed Basilio. In the exchange of shots, Basilio killed this fellow's horse, and was himself brought down with a ball in his shoulder. The spy then tried to catch Basilio's horse, which ran away and may be dead on the desert. I suppose that he was driven to cover by the wild cattle. When you came up, the robber thought you were alone, and tried to murder you to get your horse. *Now, you know all!*"

"All ready, sir," reported Walton, as he held out a canteen to the young leader. "We have enough water left." The two friends rose, and their men filed by, each face alive for vengeance.

"We'll follow you to the death, Captain Jim," cried one. A yell followed.

"Come on now, Jack!" cried Leavenworth, with a wild stare in his eyes. "It's for Life and Love now to the last drop of our hearts' blood! Seven o'clock, we will strike the well at El Jicaro. There we take three hours' rest, and I'll start our lightest man to Ringgold Barracks and two to meet Tom Bayard. When we start, we'll strike that robber-crossing, Las Cuevas, on a run without drawing rein. I'll not leave a man alive I find in it!"

Jack bowed his head and set his eager eyes toward the distant Rio Grande.

Leavenworth lingered a moment. "Walton, can that wounded Mexican travel?" The scout shook his head. Leavenworth rode on, with a significant gesture. Walton nodded, and muttered: "Count on me joining at Las Cuevas before you leave." He strode through the bushes past the trampled water-hole.

A heavy report rang out as Leavenworth reined up beside Manson at the head of the plodding column of avengers.

"What's that?" said Jack, in a dazed voice.

"They are only killing a dog," coldly said the young Texan, as he motioned to the front.

And the rescue party, grim and silent, nursing every movement of their steeds, drew out toward the grassy slopes and cool, running stream at El Jicaro.

CHAPTER XIII.

THE AVENGERS—DAYBREAK AT LAS CUEVAS—JIMMY
LEAVENWORTH'S FANCY SHOT—OVER THE BOR-
DER—THE RANGERS—STORMING THE WOLF'S
DEN—COLONEL MEJIA'S WAY—PADRE ANTONIO
—A DANGEROUS NURSE.

THE pitiless sun beat down on the mute rescue party.
Hot and blinding the powdery, gray dust rose under
the horses' feet. It was the same unvarying alternation, nopales, cactus, Spanish bayonet, and here and
there a carcass torn by coyotes, or a grossly swollen
rattlesnake blind in the desert sun.

Leavenworth, the gray dust clinging to his eyelids,
glared forward as sharp-eyed as a mountain condor.
He was silent, yet now and then his shoulders twitched.
As a tear stole down Jimmy's bronzed cheek, Bronco
Bill touched Jack Manson's elbow.

"Don't notice him. You'll break his trance! I've
seen men go mad on the desert. He's just wild about
Miss Katie. By God!" he hissed, "there's a reckoning
coming! I never saw the boys roused this way.
They're took awful hard with this!"

Jack Manson turned his eyes kindly toward the plainsman.

"We are in this to the death," said Bill. "You'll
come out all right."

Manson's eyes alone spoke his gratitude, for he knew
now that the rough riders had divined his secret.

As the oasis sank behind them, the two leaders, bearing south, descried Walton's party, moving in a bee-line
for Ringgold. Not a sign of life was visible, and the
blue vault of heaven showed only here and there a
fleecy white puff.

The admiring cattlemen noted the two youths at their head with pride. Jimmy Leavenworth, lean, light, sitting his horse with the easy grace of Forrest's invincible riders, and responsive in the graceful sway of every muscle to the dainty steps of his mount. Jack Manson, his eyes to the front, calm and manly, guarded his matchless racer with the skill of a Pawnee, and his set, clean-cut face was as full of grit as beloved Charly Lowell on that sad day of victory when he rode down the Virginian troopers at Cedar Creek. Manson was benumbed at heart. His steady eye was fixed on the dark-green line, growing nearer every half-hour, where El Jicaro's waters freely ran.

The men chewed lead bullets when the last drops of water were gone. As the sun neared the horizon a waft of breeze drew out of the woods two miles away!

"Thank God!" burst out a chorus, as the flaming disk dropped below the western sands. Two or three of the strongest horses sniffed the air and began an uneasy, restless trot. The deer-like animals scented the water.

"Steady, men," was Leavenworth's only word, and with an infinite patience, they moved on at the fast plodding walk which had taken them safely over the "jornada de los muertos."

As his horse struck solid ground at the edge of the grass, Leavenworth threw up his hand and dashed on! Ten minutes later man and beast were under the grassy shades of El Jicaro Creek. A half-dozen videttes scoured the timber, and, on their report, the unsaddled horses were rubbed down after their freshening roll on the turf. Drinking sparingly and bathing their heads and breasts, the riders waited the welcome coffee bubbling at the camp-fire.

"How long?" was Bill's brief query, as he looked at Leavenworth prone on the turf.

"Two hours, Bill," quietly replied the leader. "I'll lead you down as quick as we can get to Las Cuevas."

"Will you go in before daybreak?" said Bill, his voice shaking a little.

"No, we can not see to shoot before then! I don't want a thief to get away. Besides, the cavalry may get down. I will leave a couple of men on the road to stop them and lead them in. When I give the signal to fall in, Bill, you can inspect every man's arms, and not a word on the march after we leave. We'll hide till dawn. Those fellows come back from the Rio Grande side at daybreak. Tell all the men this. I want you to take five men across and stop the fugitives on the other side."

After Manson and Leavenworth had broken their fast, and drained their cups of steaming coffee, Leavenworth said, "Jack, come out here a minute."

They stood alone under the evening stars.

The Texan spoke, in a hollow voice: "I wish you to know what to do. Gertie's vision may come true. I do not care, for even then I shall see Katie." His voice broke in sobs. "But you will lead them out! I will save a couple of boys, or a woman, and cross the river and push on to that devil's den. We can not wait a minute. If he is there, it may be too late if we delay. Troops or no troops, I can hold his ranch if he is not back. I think he went up on our trail. I do not know if Buller would dare to take his men over. But we will follow on the trail, and if we get her, then, come what will, take her back at once over the Rio Grande. Take her to Ringgold Barracks. There are ladies there. With an escort and an ambulance, push home at once;

for mother and Alice will be frantic. I know but one man who could take us into this place beside old Basilio. That's Rip Ford, but he, I think, is at Houston. Too late to wait for any one. Depend on Bronco Bill. He is as game as steel."

"Jimmy, you speak—." Jack's voice faltered.

"As if I were doomed? Yes, I do," said Leavenworth, wringing Jack's hands. "Tell Gertie — no, not a word. By heaven That girl knows my last drop of heart's blood beats for her alone. *She will know!* She never could doubt me if an angel plead."

There was a sad pride in Leavenworth's voice, as he resolutely strode back to the little fire. An hour and a half had elapsed. The men were even now ready.

"Put out that fire," said Jimmy quietly. "Scatter it. There—not a light or match struck till daybreak. Boys," he cried, his voice ringing clearly in the hushed night, "I will not talk to you. You are all Texans but my brother Jack here. Follow me now. Don't be too eager. Pick your men. If I'm hit, follow him!" He pointed to Jack.

There was a murmur of suppressed voices, as the men swung lightly into their saddles. Twenty-five miles of grassy turf before them was nothing now to the freshened animals. The two young men, pistol in hand, rode in advance, and Bronco Bill, at five paces, minutely directed the cavalcade by his pistol arm.

The spectral line of horsemen moved briskly and at a safe distance from the main road, which stretched across the bends of the Rio Grande, distant from two to five miles. Every half-hour Leavenworth sprang off and listened, his face to the ground. It was two o'clock when he led his men down toward a little valley fringed with thick, flourishing trees. Halting and throwing up his hand, Jimmy called Bronco Bill in an undertone.

" I'll hold your horse. Worm down and take a look around! "

Bill disappeared in the long grass, sneaking forward like a panther.

" These Las Cuevas fellows never come here," he whispered to Jack. " They hide along the river-bank so they can swim across to either side at will. All are smugglers along the Bravo, many horse thieves, but not all murderers. With the Las Cuevas gang there's no mistake."

" How far is the crossing? " queried Manson, glad to break the unearthly stillness, and to divert Leavenworth's brooding mind.

"About three miles due south. The re-entrant of the bend is toward Mexico. All the boys know the crossing."

" Is it fordable? " continued Jack.

" No! The river is about two hundred yards wide. It's fairly high water now. It is fifteen feet deep, with a good current. But there are always dug-outs there. If we can't find a flat, we will unsaddle and swim the horses over. They can all do it."

As he spoke Bronco Bill came racing back, breathless and with no attempt at disguise.

" Tom Bayard and Rip Ford, with fifteen men, down in the hollow!" he almost shouted.

The San Miguel party dashed down into the pocket valley. Five minutes later the gray-haired ranger chieftain, Tom Bayard, his sturdy frame quivering with rage, and the two lovers had closed a brief council of war.

" See here, Bill! " said Colonel Bayard, in an impressive voice. " I had a dispatch that McNally's rangers are at Carrizo, before I left Brownsville. Now, you ride up there as quick as your horse will take you,

and tell him from me to circle round by Aiguilares and
swing in here as quick as he can. Stay! I'll give you
my horse. He is fresh. You can make it in four hours."

There was a dead silence.

" Do you hear me? " said Bayard, with a little sharp-
ness in his tone.

"Colonel Tom," said the cowboy quietly, " I'd die
for you if you told me to, but I'm d—d if I stir an
inch till I've seen Las Cuevas burned down! I'll follow Miss Katie, *if I go alone*, and I'll get her if I go
to the City of Mexico."

Tom Bayard grasped the rough fellow's hand.

" You are a dead-game fellow. Bill, I'll never forget you! Now, I'll make it fair. I'll send the lightest
man."

"Thank you, Colonel. There's Pony Tom. He
never missed a fight before, and he knows McNally;
he was one of his men."

" Will you go, Tom?" said Bayard, as Bill made
way for a delicate-looking stripling.

" Well, sir, if I can't *fight* for the lady, I'll *ride a
good race* for her."

" That's the style! You can call my place your home,
if you find me the rangers," said the Confederate,
handing him his flask. "Here, Tom, it's a cold night!
Bring up that horse."

Tossing aside his rifle and loosening the heavy saddle,
the light plainsman bounded on Tom Bayard's horse.
A single pistol in a belt, a well-muffled canteen, with
the heavy frontier knife, were the messenger's equip-
ments. Throwing up his hand, the light rider pressed
the brave steed with his sinewy knees. Away, like an
arrow from a bow, the willing beast bounded!

" There's five thousand dollars' worth of horseflesh to
be ruined. Well, if we don't save her, I have no use

for *horses* or a *ranch, either*," philosophized Bayard.
"I will never show my face on the Nueces, if we fail.
Now, young men, you know what is before us! Both
of you have had a hard day. Ford and myself will
stir you up in time. Sleep a couple of hours; you have
two colonels in command."

Jack Manson courted sleep to quiet Leavenworth.
In half an hour they slept under the stars, while the
silver-haired Ford glided among his watchful pickets,
or murmured in low tones to Bayard. Tom sat on his
saddle, his eyes glued on the lightening east.

"When it's light enough to travel, it will be good
enough light to shoot by when we get there. Ford, you
had better pick a man to take a squad over below the
ranch and meet Bill's men crossing above. Pick out a
cool fellow—one who wont be eager enough to drown
his men crossing, or excitable enough to shoot into our
own men. You give him his orders; don't let him
turn aside for anything, but *get across!* Let him pick
his own men. I'll warn Bill; we will give them ten
minutes' start of us. They must hide on the other
side and not close in till they hear our firing. Then, let
them hold the farther bank."

"All right. That's a good plan," said the sententious
old ranger, and in half an hour the warned squads were
ready for the word. The night breezes died away into
the hush of dawn. From the rich, low woods the
chirping twitter of birds began to sound. As the first
faint red streak tinged the east, Tom Bayard rose from
his couch.

"Rouse your men, Bill. Saddle up. Let the boys
make coffee and take a bite."

Colonel Ford's good gray head lay elevated on his
saddle, and a gentle droning sound indicated the peaceful sleep of the veteran taking forty winks.

Leavenworth and Manson were awake at a touch. In a few minutes the camp was in motion. The sentinels had kept the coffee-pots in trim at a covered fire. The men stood to horse. In a group the four leaders stood, while on right and left the first detachments were ready, in the saddle.

"Who is to direct this morning's business?" said Bayard, as simply as if it were a peaceful call.

All eyes turned to Ford, as he stood modestly in their midst.

"Well, I suppose it's the old thing," he said placidly. With a few words to Bill and the other squad leader, he dismissed them at a trot. Watch in hand, he gave the vanished pickets the full ten minutes. A faint streak of morning-light lit up the old man's serious face.

"Now, gentlemen, it's for Las Cuevas! Pass the word," he said. "Take in everything that can handle a gun or machête. Look out for the women and children."

The command moved in two squads of fours, Colonel Ford and Leavenworth on the right, Tom Bayard and Manson leading the left. Not a word was exchanged as ten minutes' brisk trot covered half the distance to where the swarthy river-vermin lay in the robber lair of Las Cuevas. Many a wild fandango there had celebrated the murder of a picket party, the cutting off of a pair of the doomed Customs Inspectors, or the slaying of some incautious merchant or ranchero. Haunting the lonely roads, these merciless bandits used ambush and cruel stratagem to effect a victory when they feared the desperate bravery of the hardy American traveller. Watch and trinket, chain and gewgaw, bedizened their sullen-eyed, brown-skinned paramours. A floating population of thirty to a hundred filled the

duplicated dens on the two banks of the bloody Rio
Bravo. For there, in the elastic, invisible, middle
thread of the turbid stream, was the dividing line,
across which Taylor fired the first cannon of the Mexican War.

Without discovery, the stealthy riders reached a point
within half a mile from which the smoke rose in thin
blue wreaths from the thatched huts.

"Just a nice shooting light," said Bayard, turning
his head toward Jack, whose stern gaze was riveted
on the distant huts now visible. "Ha! we're off!"
shouted Bayard, as Ford waved his hand, and the right
column sprang forward on a dead run! The men leaning lightly forward, their heavy revolvers at a poise,
bounded over the turf, their horses straining every
sinew.

"Easy; don't blow your horses. Spread out," called
Bayard. As he turned his eyes to the front, from
a glance at his men, he saw that Jack Manson was
fifty yards in advance of the charging line. Driving
the spurs in his own horse, Bayard rode into the ranch
as a straggling fire began from behind its hedges and
corrals. The ringing crack of the Colt's revolvers
woke the morning echoes as the maddened Texans ride
on their foes. Yells and howls of pain sounded high,
and the plaintive wail of women and frightened children swelled the din.

"Watch the bank, Jack!" shouted Bayard, as the
firing slackened and a few half-dressed wretches threw
themselves over the steep banks into the muddy
stream.

Already the ranch houses were blazing, and, with
execrations, the dismounted searchers dragged out of
hiding-places a half-dozen wretches. Two of the
rangers lay dead, their friends crowding around, while

several staggered away out of the fight with ball or machête wound.

"Secure every living thing! Separate the women and children," shouted Bayard, as the helpless crowded in terror into every possible hiding-place.

A line of excited men were shooting rapidly at the swimmers in the river. One or two had seized logs of wood and were swimming on their backs. From the other side a fusillade was now opened on the desperate wretches struggling for their lives! The revolver balls of the plainsmen tore up the water around the fugitives. The farther bank was covered with fringing bushes, gullies, and holes, into which the fugitives might crawl and baffle pursuit, unless at once picked off by the men under Bronco Bill.

"This will never do," cried Jimmy Leavenworth, dashing up and springing from his horse. "Get your rifles." A dozen rushed for the Winchesters, hanging on their saddles. The horse-holders tossed them down in haste.

"Here!" cried Leavenworth, snatching the nearest rifle. The ping of the rifle-balls sounded shrill as the daylight brightened. Of four men in the river three sank, throwing up their arms.

One powerful swimmer, clutching a log of wood which he held between his head and the rain of rifle-balls, floated down the stream. He was over two hundred yards away. He seemed to bear a charmed life. In a minute more he would be around a bend.

"Who's that swimming?" demanded Leavenworth, as a ranger, pistol in hand, dragged up a villainous-looking youth, a prisoner. He was sulky. Leavenworth raised his hand. The merciless captor clapped a revolver to the fellow's ear.

"Allà esta el Caballo Blanco," he whimpered. Jimmy

Leavenworth set his teeth and dropped on one knee. He followed the swimming bandit with the long rifle-barrel, keeping the sight trained on the floating head. A dozen anxious men held their breath. The word "fire" was trembling on their lips. Leavenworth crouched as if carved in stone. A current bore the swimmer on a shallow. With one wild spring he darted toward the bushes not five yards away. As his arms rose, the Texan deliberately fired, and the fugitive sprang in the air, crashing down prone on the pebbly beach! Leavenworth dropped his smoking rifle without a word. He turned, as a wild yell of triumph rose from a trio of rangers opposite, who reached the shelving point where the body lay.

It was indeed "White-Horse" Caballo Blanco, a fiend on whose head a price was set.

"That was a fancy shot, Jim," cried Bayard.

"Gather in our men; we'll get over," said Leavenworth, in a cold tone. "We have no time to lose. Stop that shooting now, for God's sake!" for the volleying crack of a dozen pistols had told of some recognized marauder's doom, while the force on the bank was clearing the river.

"Stand to your arms!" he yelled quickly, as a body of horse bore down from the mesquit grove above them. The startled Texans sprang to their defense, but a shout reassured them. With a cheer thirty cavalrymen dashed up, stout Lieutenant Buller at their head.

"Ha, Jimmy, the work is over! What can I do? We came down on the run." He grasped Leavenworth's hands as he swung from the saddle.

"Buller, let a sergeant and ten men hold these prisoners. We will cross at once. You know all." His voice was trembling with excitement.

Bayard strode up. "I've got a flat here and the first party are crossing now. There's two dug-outs also."

"Have you searched the whole ranch?" said Buller coolly.

"There's nothing in the burning huts," quietly answered Colonel Ford. "Ten killed, three prisoners, besides those shot in the river. Some women and youngsters here. Three of our men too badly hurt to ride. Anderson and Ellis are *gone*. No help!" The old ranger looked grave.

"See here," said the quick-witted cavalry officer; "leave your wounded with my sergeant's guard.— Let us take all the male prisoners over. We will keep every one of the others till you're back. I'll see they don't starve. I've got a wagon coming. We'll force the truth out of these fellows and take one along as a guide, or two if needs be."

In half an hour the whole Texan party was on the Mexican side of the river. The united force had, in all, seven prisoners. A rough ordeal of questioning forced the truth out of the frightened bandits.

"Pick out your two men as guides," said Buller, as he rapidly made his plans. "I'll send three men back to the fort. It seems Maxan divided his party. He evidently went to his lair with your sister. The other gang are making a diversion to throw any rescue party off their guard. He did not know you were so far down the valley. Now, we will start out a company to cut off their retreat, and send two or three express riders to post McNally. They will be between two fires. Sergeant! Take these fellows over, tie them up, shoot them if they try to escape! Come back for the note to the Commander. Be quick, for we will be off soon!"

Tom Bayard had already rallied the Texans, and their animals were resting, while the men searched the huts on the Mexican side for food, and the women were pouring coffee for the tired rangers.

"Get Bayard and Ford and bring Manson here; we will have a talk alone."

Jack's heart warmed to the keen-eyed young trooper. As they sat in a deserted hut, Buller passed around his flask and cigars. "It's now ten o'clock; nothing has got away from here to carry the news. But this fellow Ramon is no fool. He will be on the lookout till it's dark. If we moved right on his place, we would arrive tired and wearied. About ten or eleven o'clock to-night is the time to storm his place; I know it well."

"You!" cried all the listeners in amazement.

"Yes, I do!" said Buller. "Two years ago, I went over on a secret mission to watch the Kickapoo and Lipan camps, about fifty miles above here. We really drove those fellows over on the Mexicans. Colonel Mejia and myself took a look at their surroundings. *He* had secret orders, through Minister Romero, and General Ord detailed *me.* Now, we went incognito. Maxan was in Europe and I rested a week at the old Bishop's palace. You see, I had a three-hundred-mile ride to San Antonio before me to report to General Ord. Colonel Mejia was in command at Matamoras and had to report there. I staid there, and I slipped over the river quietly near Ringgold Barracks. There was a decent fellow named Antonio there, who, I really think, was a priest left to watch over the place when the clergy were driven out. There is property probably buried there, which they could not remove. It's an old trick of the Padres."

He paused and took a draught of the flask. "I've got an army commission to lose. I can not bring troops over here, so if you don't recognize my men when they cross, do not laugh. We will picket this bank. I'll put a herd-guard over the horses. At five o'clock we will start. I will lead you up into the cañon I came down,

and about ten o'clock we will drop in on the 'Jaguar', as
they call him. I will show you the way. Now Colonel
Ford and I will do the fighting. You three pick three
more men and make a dash straight for your sister!
Maxan is brave. He'll defend the 'paseo,' and you
may have your sister in your arms before the gate is
forced, if you do as I say. What do you think?"

"Buller, do you mean to say you will really do this?"
Jimmy Leavenworth bowed his head, and the tears
rained down his cheeks.

"Nonsense, man! don't you remember I danced the
Virginia Reel with your sister when she was 'little
Katie' and wore a school-girl braid. Why, I've broken
your bread! She's Miss Katie now! God bless her!"

"Amen," said his listeners. The gay young soldier ·
rose. There was a lump in his throat. He tried a
diversion. He could not hear the agony of the two
friends.

"See my ragamuffins," he merrily cried. In fact
that crack troop of the Fourth Regulars looked like
the advance guard of Fra Diavolo's bandits. Clad in
caught-up raiment of the Mexicans, in borrowed jackets
of the rangers, or in their gray shirts, with every class
of head gear, save the army cap, they were gaily com-
menting on each other's appearance as they crowded
the flat-boat.

"I have given them *individually* a day's furlough, and
the sergeant and bugler are at my military headquarters.
The only risk I do take is their desertion, but no man
has ever left K troop's ranks on such a mission!"

With fatherly persuasion, Colonel Ford persuaded
the anxious youths to try a siesta, as hammocks
swung in the lonely huts. The long afternoon droned
away, the only sound being the tinkle of the herd-
bell and the distant wailing of the women and children

on the farther bank.   The command was ready at last
to move.

"Buller," said Leavenworth, who was now cool and
hopeful, "send word over to your sergeant to give these
poor women a half-wagon-load of rations, and I will
see they have some money, if I live," he said gloomily,
for the vision of Gertie Marshall hovered before him
always.

Thanks to the bad character of the Las Cuevas crossing, all respectable Mexican travellers up the Rio Grande
gave it a wide berth.   The sixty men in three squads
moved steadily out, bearing southwest toward Hacienda
Maxan; at the head of each flanking column a prisoner
rode beside a man bearing a cocked revolver.   The
stern orders were, "Death in return for treachery!"
Buller led the central squad, the flankers guiding upon
his movements.   Ten miles from the river they entered
a thick forest, where the afternoon sun was veiled by
the spreading branches.   Nothing but a stray steer was
met, or a wild peccary, perchance a deer bounding
from the covert, and, rising from the plain of Nueva
Leon, the rescue party climbed a gentle slope of nearly
two thousand feet.   It was nine o'clock when Buller,
enjoining silence, turned abruptly to the left and led the
command carefully through a little notch in the hills.
The word "Halt!" was passed.   Enjoining every care
as to horses and arms, the hawk-eyed lieutenant walked
forward to a shelving rock with the Texan leaders.
Below them, in a turn of the valley, the white walls of
Hacienda Maxan were plainly visible!   A mile below,
on the hillsides, a few lights indicated the tributary village of Zacate.

"The Padres never liked the vulgar to live too near
them," said Buller musingly.   "Let me see.   I never
knew a Mexican establishment to keep late hours.   It's

after nine now! If Maxan is there, his march and the cares of his prisoner, as well as his dispositions for guard, have tired him. He will naturally guard the Zacate road. Now Bayard, Manson, and Jim, you can see that long front looking down the exquisite valley of Zacate. The state apartments are the second floor facing the river. I have no doubt the main gate of the paseo is well guarded by sentinels, perhaps even barricaded. The heavy garden sweeps up to the broad platform, along the river-front. The great windows open to the terrace. There is a rear doorway to the corrals and pastures wherein four men can enter abreast. My plan is to ride down in the rear, and leave our animals with fifteen horse-holders. You will take ten men (removing your spurs and canteens). Keep only your pistols and knives. I'll send two trusty fellows with you. I've made some rag fire-balls with kerosene and some tatters I picked up. There are two feed-lags full of them. Gain position near the terrace. When you hear our first firing, burst in the terrace windows and rush upstairs. I leave the rest to you. Maxan has no one whom he can trust! He will dash out at the first alarm and rally his men from the front gate-way to meet us. We will give them a cool volley as they rush out. Our first fire will be only an alarm as we take post in the paseo. Don't fret about us. We will finish them up. Never you mind Maxan. He may escape! I will run him down later! As for the Zacate villagers, they are a poor-spirited set of unarmed peons. We will push back at once to the Rio Grande if your sister is there. If she is not, we will twist the truth out of these devil's necks, and race along like devils on the trail."

"Let us go on!" hoarsely cried Jack Manson.

"Remember, not a move, not a shot, till I send you on your way!"

In single file the riders descended the easy hill, and before ten o'clock, were formed in a dismounted line five hundred yards behind the corral wall.

"Dismount!" was passed from man to man, and, led by the light-footed Buller, the avengers stole on, in shadow and under cover, to the junction of the corral wall, the building, and the low hedge of Spanish bayonet around the deserted garden where the sleek priests were wont to pace.

"Thank God, the wind favors us! If our horses should neigh, they would think it their own stock," thought Buller, as he pointed out the way to the Texans, whose pulses were now throbbing in repressed excitement.

The heavy white walls gleamed ghostly in the starlight, and not a sound escaped from the Wolf's Den!

While the storming party for the front filed silently by, led by Bronco Bill, and Buller exchanged a few last whispered words with Manson, Bayard, and Leavenworth, Colonel Ford's silver head was bared as he warmly pressed the young men's hands and then stole away to hold the eager men quiet in their line behind the paseo entrance.

Pacing up and down like a caged tiger in the great hall of the hacienda, not fifty yards away, Ramon, "el Jaguar" watchfully gazed down the winding road to Zacate. The light from his open windows streamed out over the terrace and lit up the broad road, paved with irregular stones, leading to the river entrance to the paseo. On the table near him his Winchester lay ready, and on his person two heavy revolvers and a bowie-knife hung from his riding-belt. His jacket was tossed aside, and he showed every grace of his splendid torso as he smoked uneasily. His furtive glances ever sought the silent roadway.

"I was a fool, a blind fool!" he mused, "to let those two women meet. I do not care for Panchita's tantrums; she will be cured of that by and by," he sneered, with a sinister smile of dark prophecy. "But her mother, old Nordenskiold's friend of years ago! Her convent life at Laredo! D—n her jealousy! I should have sent her away. But where! Can I trust any one? I should have let Antonio take her away to Monterey, and kept Caballo Blanco here to hold this place! *Then* I could have tamed this young hawk at my leisure! Over in Monclova or Chihuahua I could have hidden her with his friends. I could demand my terms or a ransom. But that beast Mejia at Matamoras would have beaten up this camp if he dreamed that Caballo Blanco lingered here. He never forgets a feud! That comes of my killing his brother Andrès for mere spite!

"Now, my scouts will give me instant warning of any more up the road from Matamoras, or the river. I am tolerably safe for a week. Caballo Blanco's united band, when the up-country fellows come back to Las Cuevas, will make fifty good fellows there. The lazy Gringo troops will not mix up in this. They would have to have *official permission* to cross! The natural jealousy of our river people will cause them to notify Mejia if the Texans should be mad enough to come once in a body. But, spies, assassins, treachery! They have money. This fool of a Panchita! Would she smuggle any news over to the other side? Not after the *ceremony of last night!* She thinks that I have run the girl off for a ransom. I will send the Texan girl up into the mountains when Caballo Blanco comes back."

Maxan shivered. "The air is chilly," he muttered, as he closed one window. Draining a glass of brandy, he gazed on his map. "Yes! The fellows leading the pursuers a dance ought to be back at Las Cuevas now. By to-morrow night Caballo Blanco will be here. I will send the Texan girl away. I can then slip away with 'Señora Maxan' if the enemy approach. Reverend Antonio can tell the story: I am at Tampico on business. Thank God I came over here, instead of chasing those fellows up country. There are no witnesses to this girl's kidnapping. No blood was shed. No traces left. She will never live to tell this story! That mock marriage has quieted Panchita. But, *am I safe in leaving those women together?* It seems to me that the sex has a capacity for sudden love, or hatred, which is astounding.

"Panchita, the love-sick fool, wanted to knife her *at first. Now*, they are doing the sisterly comedy!" He threw away his cigar. "There never was a woman to be trusted! *As varying as the sea and clouds!* Sleek devils!

"But *I trust* gold, and a good knife!" He wheeled quickly. "I must reward Antonio for this mock marriage. He has just enough priestcraft in him to have a greedy palm! *Gold* for the man, *flattery* for the woman! I'll set him to watch them both. I'll call him and give him a sack of yellow ounces. He shall have more if he fools the woman and tells a smooth lie to Mejia if a row is kicked up about this. They will find only an empty house." He laughed as he lifted a red floor-tile behind the first window recess and drew out a heavy sack. "The bishop, I suppose, kept his love letters and his scheming letters to Rome hidden here! Now for Father Antonio. I'll tickle his greed and promise him a golden harvest. He is the man! I'll send off the Texan girl; then, Señora Panchita, I'll put you where you will not bother me, as I go to Monclova. That's a little bit of fine art in the Rigoletto style of my own!

Jesus Maria!" he cried, dropping the gold, as a ringing volley and a chorus of yells rose on the still night air. He grasped his rifle and rushed down the broad stair to the court-yard.

"The Indians! The Kickapoos have attacked the corrals! Alerto! Alerto! Todos!" he yelled, as he dashed into the broad court-yard.

Smooth-faced Antonio rushed into the upper corridor, as the yells alarmed him, only to hear two women's voices in wild shrieks add to the clamor. For the crash of glass and wild cries below proved that the *main hacienda* had been forced!

A chorus of yells "Los Tejanos! Los Tejanos!" recalled Maxan to his senses. Throwing down his rifle, which he was firing at the crowd swarming into the back entrance, he leapt back like a panther. "Out-witted, by God! Follow! Follow me!" he cried, as the guard of the front postern swarmed toward the stairway. By the light of a blazing fire-ball, he saw through powder-smoke the face of his deadly foe! The man who struck him down at the Club was firing into the advancing retainers!

Half the gate-guard were now struggling in a wild melee with the troops led by Buller, and up the stair and in the upper corridor, the invaders and the Mexicans reeled in deathly struggle! "Go on! Go on!" rose the clarion voice of Buller, as he swept into the lower hall with his men loudly cheering!

Springing along the hallway, Jack Manson followed the sound of the voice which he had heard raised to God in appeal in the crisis of the storm! Dashing through the curtained archway, Manson clasped Katie in his arms, as she fell fainting on his bosom!

Tom Bayard wheeled at the door, as he faced the last of the Mexicans now hemmed in, for Buller had

cleared the hall.   Bayard threw down his empty pistol
and drew his knife, dashing at Maxan, who stood at
bay near an open window!   As Leavenworth wheeled
to raise his reserve pistol, Maxan's revolver rang out
sharply.   Jimmy staggered, and fell in Tom Bayard's
arms, as Maxan, leaping lightly through the open casement to the paseo roof, disappeared in the darkness!

"After him! After him!" yelled Bayard, as he knelt
by the wounded man.   A dozen soldiers, with Buller
leading, then rushed down the stair.

There was a pause, broken only by the groans of the
dying and the cheers of the victors.   The Hacienda
Maxan was won! Colonel Ford's clear voice was heard
ringing out below: "Search the house! Put out the
fires! Bring all the prisoners into the court-yard!"

The light streamed out of the room where Katie
Leavenworth was clinging to Jack Manson's bosom
and wildly crying!   Beside her stood the dark-eyed,
gentle Panchita, her raven hair flowing over a gown
not as white as her own ghastly face!

Bayard, his bosom heaving in sorrow, aided by
willing hands, Bronco Bill at their head, bore the
wounded brother into the only lighted room.   And as
they laid him on a couch, Jimmy Leavenworth's sister
threw herself on her knees beside him.

"Speak to me, darling! For God's sake, only speak,
Jimmy!"   Over him bent the beautiful stranger, her
hands crossed on her exquisite bosom.

Jack Manson, smoke-grimed, and with staring eyes,
faltered: "The vision! The vision!" and threw himself down at the feet of Katie's brother.

"My God! A doctor! A doctor!" cried Bayard, as
he loosened Leavenworth's hunting-vest.   The pallor
of death was on the Texan's brow, and from his right
side the warm life-blood was oozing.

"Antonio! Antonio is a doctor!" cried the Spanish girl, awaking from her trance. "Call el major-domo!"

"Bring him, Ford. Is he here?" said Bayard.

In a moment the grave-faced intendant entered the room, followed by Buller

"I know this man; it's all right," he hastily said, as he laid his hand on Leavenworth's pallid brow.

Quiet now reigned, and lights were lit over the hacienda. Colonel Ford had posted his sentinels, and the main body of the besiegers was rallied in the paseo. Buller, returning from his vain quest for the vanished scoundrel Maxan, had thrown out pickets and set guards on the gates.

"Quiet, all!" said Antonio, with dignity. "I must have free hands and my own people to help."

Bayard drew Panchita away for a moment.

"Buller, single out the house-servants from the prisoners and let them pass one by one through the lower hall with a guard. Tell me the ones you want," he said, as Panchita moved away with him.

Bayard, pistol in hand, watched the simple peasants, as the lady of the hacienda indicated them. Their docile faces told the story of innocence.

"Go to your places and obey Antonio only," said Bayard kindly.

The room where Leavenworth lay in collapse was quiet as the two re-entered. Antonio, in brief Spanish words, directed Panchita, who glided like a beauteous wraith in and out on his behest. A draught of brandy and the strongest restoratives were administered by the quiet man of the crisis. No one dreamed now of doubting Antonio's skill. His self-possession proved a long experience!

The wounded man groaned as Antonio cut away the blood-soaked clothing around the wound. With a grave air, the examiner followed the course of the ball, and noted the color faintly returning to the Texan's face.

Ford had examined the second story of the hacienda, and his headquarters were established in Maxan's great hall. One by one the spectators withdrew to their duties. The old mansion was wrapped in silence. In a deep chair, with Panchita at her side, Katie Leavenworth silently awaited the verdict! Her little hand clutched Jack Manson's bronzed fingers as he exchanged a whispered word with Buller.

"Got clean away. Maxan knew every turn! We were nearly all strangers to the place. I could have headed him off, but I was clearing out that robber riff-raff. He dropped off into the garden and is now in the hills. But we'll have him yet. See, Tom," the cool soldier whispered, "the blood *only oozes*. No jetting. Now, if he does not bleed internally."

Antonio, with uplifted fingers, hushed the friendly murmur. Passing his hand around the sufferer's chest, Antonio smiled as Leavenworth half-opened his eyes and cried: "Look out! You torture me."

The major-domo turned to the waiting circle. "In the back muscles! Much pain! A great shock! The ball is heavy and was fired at short range. Little danger if he does not catch cold. *I will answer for his life.*"

"You shall have his weight in gold if he lives!" cried Tom Bayard, as he threw his arms around Katie, whose eyes shone with an ecstasy of thankfulness.

"No more tears, Katie. Our boy will live. Now, Lady Bird, we will guard your sleep, and to-morrow— to-morrow, homeward!"

"I'll not leave Jimmy, never!" faltered the white lady, as she smiled through her tears at Jack Manson.

"Well, you'll have to give him up to *Gertie* by and by. You may as well *learn to live without him*," whispered Bayard, smiling, as Panchita led the way to the chamber hastily arranged for the ladies.

"One moment. This is a father's duty!" gravely said the gray-haired Colonel Ford. "I've daughters of my own. I'll just reconnoitre your room. Good! No one can reach it from without. I have three men already posted under the windows. I'll spread my robe and sleep before your door, and there'll be a sentinel in the hall. I'll kiss ye good-night, for I held you on my knee when you were a babe. Your father and mother must see you again as quick as wheels will travel!"

"And Jimmy?" the reluctant girl murmured, as she paused at the threshold.

Panchita, standing with a light shining on her delicate loveliness, shading with one transparent hand her liquid eyes, softly said: "*I will nurse him!*"

Colonel Ford rubbed his silver locks uneasily. "Ah, yes! I see! Very good. *A dangerous nurse*," he grumbled, as the young beauties dropped the heavy leather curtain of their room. "*A very dangerous nurse!* Too good-looking for safety," grumbled the old man, as he laid his replenished pistols within reach.

With friendly officiousness, Bayard, Manson, and Buller had agreed to watch the hacienda for the rest of the eventful night. They were mindful of the old veteran's stiffened joints. It was nearly midnight. Escorted by four soldiers each, their arms at a ready, the three friends made the rounds. A huge fire blazed in the middle of the paseo, and, guarded by four men with cocked revolvers, a score of villainous-looking rascals crouched on the stony floor of the court. They were tied together, back to back, and by no gentle hands.

"How far out are your pickets on the road, Buller?" said Bayard, as the three heroes of the night strolled up to look at the howling prisoners.

"About a half-mile. I have five men and a good corporal there. There is an ambushed reserve, too, of five of your men. I gave orders for them to seize and disarm any one passing in either direction. There are four mounted men patrolling from our main post here to that picket. There will be no rescue. I have looked these fellows over," he said in a low voice. "I know that a half-dozen of them merit instant death! But, I have no official power here. The killing of prisoners might be inquired into. I might turn them over to Mejia at Matamoras. Then, by Jove! I'd have to tell him *how* I got them, and *where* I nabbed them!"

Bronco Bill strode up and, in an agitated voice, demanded of Bayard: "Will he live?" Bill's face was convulsed with rage. There were murmurs from the mixed crowd of plainsmen and soldiers now glowering at the bandits. Three soldiers and two cowboys lay dead, and a half-dozen severely wounded waited the care of Antonio, whose fame had been noised around. "A doctor priest, a real scholar!" so the tale was bandied.

"It's a bad wound and will be a sore one, Bill," said Colonel Bayard, "but the ball ran round on the ribs and is in the back muscles. This chap says he'll take it out, as soon as daylight comes. There'll be a couple of weeks of stiffness and soreness, but the boy will live to dance the Virginia Reel at San Miguel when he brings that pretty girl down from the Potomac!"

"All right, Colonel. I'll take your word for it. The boys allowed they would *kill all these prisoners if Leavenworth died!*"

"Bill, for heaven's sake, no noise to-night! The racket might finish Jimmy! He's very weak from loss of blood, and the women are frantic! I suppose we'll have to take that pretty Mexican girl over the river with us!"

"We can't leave her here in this lonely roost! Ah! they're at it again below!" quickly cried Bayard, his quick ear catching the report of a couple of dropping shots.

"Don't move, Colonel! My pickets will have a report here in five minutes," quietly said Buller. "They have probably caught a straggler or one of this vanished scoundrel's messengers."

"Buller, you are a wizard!" said Manson, as ten minutes later two of the Texan reserve led in a stunted-looking scoundrel on a pony. His hands were tied and he cowered under the pistol of one guard, while the other held his horse's halter.

"Oh, the frontier is about the same from Guaymas to Tampico. The same deviltry, only at different times and places. What's his story?" said the cavalryman carelessly.

"This fellow clattered up the road in a panic and ran slap into us!" said a hard-faced Texan. "We had to kill his horse to get him. He claims to be a soldier! He says Colonel Mejia is coming up the road with a battalion of the Lancers!"

"Glorious! Great God! I am *now all right!*" shouted Buller, dancing around in glee. "It clears me of all responsibility."

"What do you mean?" cried Bayard and Jack Manson in a breath.

"First, Mejia's a thorough soldier," gleefully said the snappy officer; "second, he'll relieve me of all these prisoners. I will ask him to send a dispatch over the Mexican military telegraph everywhere proclaiming Maxan as an outlaw! They will soon chase that scoundrel to Yucatan or over the big bend of the Rio Grande into No Man's Land! If he goes *there*, sooner or later we'll get him! I can say that I crossed at Mejia's request. I will have him send a military courier and telegraph to Matamoras and Corpus Christi the news of Miss Katie's safety."

" That's thoughtful! By to-morrow night the San Miguel people will know the good news! Say, too, I'm bringing her home," cried Bayard.

" Then Mejia and I will plant some of his men in quiet ambush on this side of the river. We will leave a company hidden here. I will dash across and stir up those bandits on the other side, and we will break up that half the gang. Colonel Mejia will send a company to escort you and Miss Katie to Ringgold. It's your easiest way home. As soon as I've *arranged our stories* I'll start two men to report to my commander and get carriages ready for you. Get Miss Katie across the river. I wish to know from her how she was ever carried off from such a place!"

" Well, the morning will tell us all. It's two o'clock now. See here, Bill! You and the sergeant take charge here. We three will ride down and meet Mejia's column," said Tom Bayard. " There might be stray firing or a squabble."

" Right you are," said his listeners in chorus. " Our men might be taken for a raiding party of ranchers."

Ten minutes later, a little thin-lipped horseman, with a huge dangling sabre, and a princely equestrian skill, rode in at the open gateway. Chatting with the three Americans, he threw away his cigarette, as he rode straight to the camp-fire. A dozen of his escort and two guides were with him. He sprang from his horse and sent an orderly officer to camp his battalion in four lines around the hacienda.

"Turn half the horses out on the potrero under guard, Juan. Let the other horses be fed in the corral."

As the young officer saluted, Mejia's eagle eye fell on the prisoners. "Ladrones!" he hissed, "*how many*, mi amigo," he said, with a cruel smile to Buller who was the negotiator. "Let me deal with him," the lieutenant whispered to the Texans, "then it's all official. You are blameless for what will happen!"

"Señor Colonel, I count twenty-three," said Buller, as the guards stirred up the shivering wretches.

"Send me the *adjutant!*" sharply remarked Tomas Mejia. The line of frightened wretches huddled together.

"What's up?" said Manson and Jack in an undertone to Buller, who gazed at the adjutant hurrying up.

"He's a man of queer ways—is Commandante Tomas Mejia. Don't interfere. They are his own people!" said Buller. The bedizened adjutant, brilliant in lace, gazed respectfully at his stony-faced chief. The two Mexican guides approached the little Aztec warrior, for Tomas Mejia was of the mystic "sangre azule" of that weird race which has a storied past but no future! They whispered a report and retired.

"Give el Señor Teniente Buller a written receipt for twenty-three ladrones, adjudged malefactors, *taken in arms!*" said the Mexican commander. The adjutant saluted.

"And the men, the prisoners, sir?" said the young officer, his voice shaking slightly. There was a solemn silence! The night wind howled wildly over the open court and scattered the blazing brands.

Mejia signed to the two guides, who sprang forward. "Todas malos?" he coldly queried. The uncovered scouts bowed in silence. "Take them out and *hang them!* No noise. Take them down the road! Report

the execution instantly! You will find me in the dining-
hall. Use the machête if you need. No pistols!"

The adjutant was shaking like a leaf. "What command shall I take, sir?"

"First company. Throw these fellows into the cañon
when you are finished!" The adjutant fled away into
the night.

"Shall we go in, Señores?" said the Mexican colonel. "I want a cup of coffee and a few hours' sleep."
He motioned with Castilian grace toward the hacienda.

" *That's Mejia's way!* " whispered Buller, as he followed the pitiless Aztec soldier.

Bayard and Manson followed in dumb amazement.
Before the quartette had finished their coffee, a trampling of feet and shuffling announced the departure
of the doomed captives.

" There they go!" said Mejia carelessly. "*And a bad
lot they are!*" He spoke simply, and with no passion.
With punctilious ceremony, he escorted his guests to the
door, for the three friends were bent on sleeping on the
floor beside good old Ford. "I have to be up at daybreak. You will pardon me." Mejia smiled and waved
his papelito in adieu.

Jack Manson rubbed his eyes as the singing bugles of
the Lancers woke the morning echoes. Was it a dream?
A vision born of a disordered mind? No! The life-
blood bounding to his heart told him that the fair girl
he worshipped was now circled with a band of invincible
defenders. He moved his stiffened limbs. His eyes
rested on Tom Bayard who had been watching his
slumbers. Buller and Ford were gone!

"The old man is an early riser. Let us go down."
The friends sought the paseo. In the early gray of dawn,
the overjoyed soldiers and Texans were recalling the
events of the night. Under a horse-shed, a line of stiffened

bodies, loosely covered with saddle blankets, was proof of the deadliness of the night attack. The trim Mexican adjutant, heavy-eyed, was inspecting and gathering the details for a conscientious official report.

"It's all up! Mejia will see you well fixed. I leave as soon as my men take breakfast," said Buller as he grasped their hands. "Ford has got your men all in comfortable ease. Mejia gives me an escort of his men! Now join me at coffee, and then good-bye till we meet at Ringgold Barracks. I will get right over the river. After that, I do not care what happens! My shoulder-straps are safe. I do not want to lose my captaincy in the Fourth Cavalry. I think that I'll have two bars on each shoulder at the double wedding."

"You will have to have *devilish quick promotion !* " said Tom Bayard, with a meaning smile, as he glanced at Jack Manson, who seemed to find no words. They strolled over to the dining-hall where a green-jacketed sentinel stood guard. The mocking birds were singing from the dense groves whose friendly shade covered the abysmal cañon where the dead robbers lay. Seated at the table, Colonel Mejia pleasantly beamed as he motioned to his visitors.

"Join me, my friends. Señor Padre Antonio, you know these gentlemen already ! "

Buller grasped the hands of the grave intendant, who was seated in confidential intercourse with the thin-faced Draco of the night.

"I knew that you were a good doctor, but, *a priest*, you astonish me!" said Colonel Bayard in the fluent Spanish which, as well as English, is the duplex dialect of the Rio Grande.

"Gentlemen, Padre Antonio has made some disclosures which are of vital benefit to my government—so important that I will not trust them even to dispatches.

A special messenger, *my adjutant,* will leave at once for
the headquarters of General Trevino, and proceed to
the City of Mexico to see President Lerdo. In the
mean time Padre Antonio, as Señor Antonio, will
remain in charge here.   I shall leave a captain and a
company here.   I will be responsible for the safety and
transport of Se or Leavenworth. I know his father
well. A great, a wonderful man! "

"I wouldn't care to be Mejia's adjutant," briskly
interjected Buller, sotto-voce, as he applied himself to
the breakfast.   He signed to his friends to follow his
example.

"It is a strange story. This old bishop's palace,"
Mejia continued.   "I should properly tell you, as you
leave your friend's life in his hands, that Padre Antonio
has voluntarily assumed the civilian status to hold a
legal occupancy of the old domain. He is an honorably
ordained priest. Now, gentlemen, the rest of the story
is the property of my Government alone!"

"And the beautiful lady, Panchita?" said Colonel
Ford, as he seated himself at table, for Mejia and
the Texan Nestor were " compadres," to use the friendly
social term.

" Ah! mi amigo! Exactly! That is also a part of my
adjutant's mission. He leaves at once. This scoundrel
Maxan ' el Jaguar' has been carrying on many schemes
from here.   Caballo Blanco, who fell under your
friend's rifle, lurked safely here at need. Now, to
deceive the poor girl upstairs, Maxan pretended to
have *Antonio marry them! Unknown to him,* it was
legal, for, though the church property is secularized
and sequestered, Padre Antonio has his certificate from
the Bishop of Monterey. It rests with the President
to determine her rights. If she is a Texan, it may be
for Señor Romero and your minister to adjust. If she

is a Mexican born, the President will decide. She will be rich, for she is Maxan's lawful wife!"

Mejia rose, for the bugles were sounding.

"I must see Nordenskiold about this," mused old Colonel Ford, with memories of a sweet-faced woman once at Laredo. Panchita's mother's sad story returned to his mind. The old ranger walked slowly away.

"I'll try and make that sleeping beauty upstairs a lawful *widow*," thought gallant Buller, as he lit a cigar. "She is handsome enough for that interesting station, and I don't care to have her practice long as a Florence Nightingale over my young friend Jim! A man would have to be *pretty dead to stand those eyes !*"

"A nice place for a young soldier to acquire the habit of military coolness and gain experience. Mejia's adjutant, a midnight hangman!" mused Jack. "A morning ride to the City of Mexico—a hundred leagues! It beats the Sioux warpath. I am afraid I would not like Mejia's way!"

BOOK V.

THE LAST THROW OF THE DICE—LOVE WINS!

CHAPTER XIV.

KATIE'S STORY—MAXAN'S REVENGE—BOB KENYON
SEES THE LIGHT AT LAST—AN UPHEAVAL—THE
COMPANY'S DOWNFALL—NO. 4 DRAWS OUT—THE
RAILROAD BUILDERS—BLACK CLOUDS OF TROUBLE
—THE JAGUAR IN HIDING.

"GENTLEMEN, one word," said Buller, as his orderly
reported the command ready. Manson and Bayard
walked aside with the hardy lieutenant. Colonel Mejia
was curiously watching Buller's men, already filing
down the road.

" I have helped you in your quest for Life and Love!
Now, I shall not say good-bye to that simply stunning
widow ' *in posse*,' and I dare not rouse Leavenworth!
I will leave it to *you*, Manson, to make my adieu to
Miss Katie. I shall recross the river and meet Mejia
officially as soon as I can get my fellows in Uncle Sam's
dingy blue once more. So, farewell! Good luck, and
don't forget the Fourth Cavalry if a hungry trooper
ever passes your home!"

" By God! I'll give the whole regiment the freedom
of my ranch," began the ex-rebel, but laughing Buller
waved his hand as his nervous roan dashed through the
portal.

" These fellows look like your regular soldiers,"
said Colonel Mejia, approaching.

" They are a lot of *ex-army men* picked up by us all," said Bayard. His white lie was pardonable.

" I am glad to hear it," said the Commandante, with a queer smile. " I should not *otherwise* have been able to report officially that you came and asked my aid as *citizens merely*. The lieutenant tells me that he left his command at Las Cuevas."

" So he did, Colonel," said Manson, with a low bow. " *Their clothes, I mean*," he mentally added.

The official fiction was understood tacitly by the three.

"I would suggest an immediate move now to Ringgold Barracks," cautiously said Mejia. " Miss Leavenworth would only excite her brother. I wish her out of the reach of this mad outlaw. I will send a troop down with you at noon. Colonel Ford will draw off all your men. As for the lady, my adjutant has arranged the team and a good ambulance here. I will have Señora Panchita send a couple of the least idiotic of these women along. They will fall into a new existence at some of our river camps. In other words, gentlemen, if I must say it politely, I do not *wish to see you here after noon*, for my official report will be dated then. I will take leave of the lady. In fact, ride a mile with you. Ah! Excuse me, my adjutant is ready to depart! I shall have to name a new orderly officer."

The little Aztec spit-fire vanished.

" Jack," said Bayard, "you are not a military man! You may be! Let me give you a piece of advice. That poor devil of an adjutant has had no sleep, but has been playing wheelwright and wagonmaster, and now starts off for the City of Mexico! I'll bet that he has had no breakfast. *Never be an adjutant!*"

" Certainly not Commandante Mejia's!" laughed Manson. "I think that poor chap lives on gold lace and cigarettes, and sleeps in the saddle."

"Let's go up and prepare Miss Katie for departure," said Bayard. "I know these sly Mexican devils! Mejia has unearthed something! He wants us all away. I will wager he and Padre Antonio will dig up a cord of the Bishop's Mexican dollars and divide it 'on the quiet!' Antonio may know where Maxan has buried his loot!"

Preceded by Ford, whose rôle of Brevet Father well became his silvering crown and venerable appearance, the two young men exchanged a few words with the Beauty of San Miguel. Fair Katie had evidently already had a favorable report from the volunteer surgeon, for her eyes sparkled as her pretty head peeped out from the leather curtains, with just a glimpse of a silver shoulder.

"I will be ready. God bless you all for your bravery!"

"We will all meet to say 'good-morning' to our wounded captain, then off for home! The doctor will notify you when he wakes."

Three hours later Colonel Mejia stood by Leavenworth's bed, the centre of an affectionate circle. "I will see your friends through my lines. One troop is already gone to Las Cuevas. Another escorts your sister and her friends. I shall leave one here in garrison with Captain Cristobal in charge, for to-morrow I go to Matamoras with the Fourth. I shall see you to-night. You may listen to your sister ten minutes, speak to her but twenty words, then 'Vamonos!' Homeward bound!"

Jimmy smiled faintly. Señora Panchita, a picture of dark loveliness, brought Katie forth, as the cortege waited. The weeping girl pressed the Mexican beauty to her heaving bosom and cried, "*My home is yours!* Remember your promise!"

Colonel Ford, in stately dignity, occupied the ambu-

lance with the rescued Katie, and Bayard, Jack Manson,
and the lynx-eyed Mejia were a knightly escort.

Passing through Zacate, the Texans riding at ease,
the fluttering banderas of the Mexican Lancers gave
Katie's flitting the air of a mediæval princess' journey.

When the last gaping villagers were left behind,
Colonel Mejia, with florid courtesy, took leave of the
heiress of San Miguel. " Rest at home in peace,
Señorita," he said reassuringly. " Our military telegraph announces Ramon Maxan as a declared felon and
outlaw! If your people use ordinary prudence at the
ranch, there will be no further danger. This fellow
will either clear out to Europe or join the renegades
and hostile Indians. I will see that he never sets foot
in his old haunt again. I will answer for your brother's
return with my life!

" Gentlemen, you are brave cavaliers. I salute you.
You are all my brothers."

With a flourish of his gold-banded cap, little Mejia
was gone. He was followed by a fortunate neophyte,
who had drawn the temporary prize of adjutant. As
Jack Manson admired the exquisite horsemanship of the
wily officer, he turned to Bayard. " Tom, I believe
you are right! Mejia and Padre Antonio wish to secure
the robber's hoard. This slyboots dashes back to see
that Antonio does not secrete it all. I wonder if he has
set the handsome Mexicana on to watch in his absence?"

Jack was partly right and partly wrong. For as
Katie Leavenworth, at the halt for luncheon and refreshment, told her story under the shade of a great oak, by
a bubbling spring, Mejia and Antonio were gloating
over the treasure under the tiles; but Panchita, seated
by the sleeping Texan's coach, kissed his brow lightly
and whispered: " You have broken the chain of my
bondage!" For the true character of Maxan's followers

was now revealed and his bandit schemes exposed   "I
will go back, back to Laredo, where I heard the Angelus
with the pure heart of a girl, and where my mother lies
within the old convent garden!"

The wayside luncheon was a joyous one. But Katie
Leavenworth's eyes were wistful.   In the presence of
Colonel Ford and her sister's lover, the sorrow-shaded
girl avoided Jack Manson's eager eyes.

Frank and open among her bowers at home, fearless
and trusting on the ocean wave, Katie felt now, in the
ardent gaze of her adoring lover, a sense of *asserted
proprietorship*! As her sapphire eyes dropped before
his burning gaze, the blood surged back to her heart!

"I can not tell him all yet! Not until the friendly
roses alone listen."

The maiden's first heart-confidence was for the
mother who bore her, for St. Cecilia, and for the father
hastening home in ignorance of Maxan's fell swoop!
It was only after this, on Jack Manson's breast alone,
she could reveal all the dark menace of her captive
hours.

But it was necessary to recount her movements. Tom
Bayard frankly asked her if she could bear the strain of
a recital.

"We may wish to make some dispositions at once for
the devil's punishment for your future protection. We
will call Colonel Ford and you can then briefly tell us
what you can remember now. If we wish details we
will question you, for we will act as soon as we reach
Ringgold. There we will have our own telegraph, the
troops, and news of McNally's Rangers. It is vital to
run this beast to bay at once!"

With great delicacy the old ranger had withdrawn to
leave the young people alone

"I am of another day. The heart will bind them all

closely together. My life's battle is nearly over. But the Zona Libre! Shall I ever see it under the Stars and Stripes?"

The scarred veteran watched the rings of blue smoke rise from his Tepic cigar and vanish in the clearest air on earth. A stone's throw away the streamlet flashed in the rocky cañon, the narrow, winding gorge behind them opening fan-like in its descent to the varied, rolling plains below. The hills, rising two thousand feet in air behind, through their open notches showed the dim summits of the blue Monterey peaks. Behind, tinkling herd-bell echoes and the song of birds swept down from the dreaming village of Zacate, where in low, one-story stone huts or thatched jacales, the frightened peons cowered out of sight of " los soldados," as well as the fierce Texans. Their own green-coated " defenders" were ruthless foragers and laid heavy hand on man and maid.

In delightful varying beauty of woodland, " mesa," " alameda," and " potrero " below them, lay the rich fields of Nueva Leon, stretching far to the dark-green winding line, marking the Rio Grande. Beyond it the shimmering mirage rose from the sweltering, dry sands of that arid zone, really the border.

" Great Scott! " said Ford, " our people should have left that strip from El Paso to Point Isabel for a coyote pasture to amuse these ' greasers,' or else, grabbed Coahiula, Nueva Leon, and Tamaulipas. We will have it yet, but I will be in my silent grave before the Stars and Stripes wave here." His aged eye noted the beautiful hacienda enclosures below, the fertile fields, the delightful forests, and scattered villages. It was a tranquil landscape of exquisite beauty. Turning his eye to the distant mountains, their silver caverns buttressing the fabulously rich " Bolson de Mapimi," Colonel Ford rejoined his friends. " It's a clear shame," he said, as he answered Tom Bayard's hail, " old General Taylor only did *half his work*. He should have fortified a line and kept the border as far as Buena Vista. I remember that day well." The old veteran's wounds of the glorious victory twitched, as he recalled the lance-thrusts received on his first great battle-field.

" Tell us exactly what happened, Katie," said Bayard, with a brother-in-law-like fondness. " Not your feelings, but we want Ford to judge of the scheme. There may be traitors still at the ranch."

With a glance at Manson, Katie began: " It is really very simple. I never was timid in walking or riding around the ranch, though mother always begged me to take escort. I wanted to be alone " (here a little peep at Jack). " I walked out of our garden, by a break in the hedge, toward the point where Jimmy waited for you, you know," she said, flashing a glance at Jack. It was the parting spot where the lovers had sealed their tryst *for life and love!* "I was absent-minded— father's voyage, your journey, Alice's preparations for her leaving" (here Tom Bayard blushed as all eyes were turned on him), " and, as mother and Alice were busied conferring about some matters, I wandered along alone. It was about ten in the morning. I forgot that I was mounted when I went out to say good-bye to you and Jimmy " (here Jack Manson's cheeks flamed guiltily), " and I was really tired before I was half-way to the point of timber.

"I sat down on a log to rest for a few moments, thinking and wondering where you were on your way! Suddenly a Navajo blanket was thrown over my head. My wrists were seized. I was borne bodily by four men to a little opening in rear of the edge of the trees. I could not scream. I was almost stifled, and when I struggled to my feet two stout Mexican women pushed me into an ambulance. The men aided in no easy way. Four wild horses were in the team, and the driver started away at a mad run! The curtains of canvas were dropped, and while the rough women tied my hands and arms with their head handkerchiefs, they simply laughed at my stupid screaming. It was all we could do to keep from being thrown out of the team. We were flying over hillocks and the rough holes they call 'hog wallows' down here. I could only get a glimpse of a half-dozen fearful-looking armed Mexicans on horseback. Worn out with exhaustion and struggling, for they had to bind my knees and ankles with a horse-hair lariat, I fainted away!"

Jack Manson ground his teeth at this recital and his hand clasped his revolver. The Recording Angel made a quick entry in his book!

" The cool of evening was around when I recovered my senses. I was drenched with water over my shoulders, and I was half-choked with fiery brandy which filled my mouth. I opened my eyes and Ramon Maxan stood before me. I was still on the Texan side of the Rio Grande. There were houses."

" Describe them," said Colonel Ford, his eyes glistening with rage. The girl began her pictured recital.

" That's enough! Las Cuevas! we *fixed that ranch forever*. Go on!" he said kindly, as the girl gave a few further sketches of the place!

"'I will now take you over where you will be more comfortable,' Maxan said," continued Katie, her eyes flashing. " Spite of my protest and appeals, he forced me in a boat. The ambulance was crossed over in a flat; about thirty to fifty men helped."

" They are nearly all now in their graves, or lying dead in the cañon!" cried Bayard sternly.

Katie shuddered and continued: " In the dark, I was driven along by fresh horses. Maxan and the two women were in the wagon. When we arrived where you found me, I was speechless with fatigue and railing at that devil, who simply leered and grinned at my appeals and threats. I was carried up into the room, and the two stout mestizo women laid me on a couch and offered refreshments as I lay helpless, but unbound. I simply motioned in disgust. The hags sat down, cross-legged, on the floor at my side. They paid no attention to my raving when I could talk. I knew that present escape was out of the question. I looked for something to kill myself with! The cowardly kidnapper did not come near me. I heard loud voices in quarrel in the next room—a man's oaths. 'Twas Maxan! A woman's sobs and pleadings, I know not whose! I knew I was in some robber-den, *where I knew not*, for I was rapidly driven in the dark, and counted not the hours. But alone in Mexico, in the power of that snake, I thought of my home, of my absent father, of mother and Alice, of Jimmy's heart-sorrow, and—and, I broke down."

Jack Manson's steadfast eyes read a tender, unspoken message from the rescued girl.

" I finally sobbed myself to sleep. I was awakened by a hand clutching my throat. I could not speak. But my eyes fell on the handsomest woman I have ever seen— Panchita! A dim lamp burned on a distant table. In her long white robe, she looked ghostly. Her left hand grasped my throat, her right held a fearful knife! 'You shall not live!' she hissed. 'I will have no Gringo mistress here!' The maddened woman pressed the blade of the knife against my bosom. I screamed then in affright, and I saw, as I lost consciousness, only the two drowsy women grappling the midnight visitor, and Maxan, followed by Antonio, rush into the room, then all was dark!"

The three listeners held their breath in excitement.

"When I awoke the next day, I was so weak I could not move. I opened my eyes as a pair of soft, white arms caressed me. It was the wild woman of the night before. She was weeping and her fond kisses warmed my hands. Of course you all know I can even *think* in Spanish. When I had taken some of the varied nourishments forced on me by the passionate would-be assassin of night, now the very gentlest nurse, I learned that Maxan was busied with his followers. Grown *doubtful of the whole world*, I listened to the strange woman's story. For while I lay in unconsciousness, Ramon Maxan, to still Panchita's rage, had been married to this woman by the old man, who seems to be a priest in hiding from the popular Mexican clamor against the clericals."

"What is the cause of this rage against the church?" said Jack Manson, as Katie paused. Her memories were exciting and exhausting!

"The Catholic padres aided Maximilian, as a rule," said Ford.

"Now you know nearly all, gentlemen," said Katie, with a faint blush. "I learned much of the Mexican girl's history, and I can only tell it to my mother; but I will tell you that she had been two years at the hacienda. Maxan has explained all peculiar occurrences on the ground of revolution and troublous times. Her frantic jealousy was awakened by my arrival. In his need of freedom to fortify his place, watch the river, and organize his men, he had no time to approach me. He hit on the temporary expedient of this marriage to reassure her, *and to blind her*, he told her I was carried off for a ransom by his friend,

Caballo Blanco, and that he wished to guard me secretly, and, dividing the ransom with pretended robbers, make friends with my father by pretending to return me. I kept my own counsel, for I dared not trust her varying moods. She never left me until three days later your attack ended all. I think his design was simply vengeance and his mad passion!

"His arrangements made, I think he intended to carry me away into the interior. Perhaps to get rid of that poor woman by secret murder. The great ranch is his own, she tells me, and I think it is too near Matamoras for him to play the open bandit. That is all I can say now. If you wish to ask me I will try and tell," she said. "It is a horrid dream! All that fighting, the noise, the blood!"

The frightened girl covered her eyes with her hand, the tears streamed through her nerveless fingers.

"Lady Bird," said Colonel Ford, "don't worry all our hearts! Be as cool as you have been brave!"

The team was waiting, and at a nod from Bayard, the tired heiress re-entered her carriage. With pillows and cushions piled around her, she rested in uneasy slumber, the roses faded from her pale cheeks.

Jack Manson gazed like a wolf-hound on the chase, at the distant Rio Grande banks, as the train pushed smartly on. He swore a silent oath which convulsed his very being. Falling back a few moments with Bayard, he listened to Ford's cautious comments.

"There would have been fearful work if we had not reached the place before he was fortified and had thrown out pickets all round his place. That devil would have killed *both these women* to cover his tracks, cut old Antonio's throat, and, burying his heaviest treasure, or starting it on in teams, would have got away to Tampico and Cuba! We never would have solved the

mystery. But, who aided him at San Miguel? The neat-
est jobs of this kind are the simplest. I have always
noted the common-sense plainness of the most successful Indian strategy! Educated whites put too much
machinery in their plans of crime. They always try to
stop off a thousand possible clues. But in this plot, there
was information conveyed. Ximenes, of course, made
Maxan acquainted with the whole surroundings of the
place; but the time, the knowledge of her *father's absence, the dogging her steps!* Who are the traitors
at the ranch?" Ford mused.

"Whenever you have a Mexican or a half-breed
around, you are in constant danger," finally remarked
Bayard. "I don't care where the men came from around
my ranch, or what drove them to Texas, as long as
they are *white men.* No fancy dark strains for me!"

"Why, look here, gentlemen!" said Jack Manson.
"Katie told me that wounded boy had cleared out when
we did."

"Ah! There was the weak spot! News was sent
to this devil that we were all away. So he sneaked
over on general principles," cried Ford, "and took a
quick advantage of the peculiar situation. We two at
Brownsville, you up the river, Silas at New Orleans,
and the ranch people following their daily work, it was
the devil looking out for his chicken! That's all. This
fellow had both education and social experience enough
to know that the employes would be unusually delicate
in intruding on the family while the men were away.
All these unexplained happenings, when responsible
people are away, come from a quick advantage taken of
happy or unhappy chances. I would not care to be
around Si Leavenworth when he gives the ranch superintendent his opinion of him. By heavens! he is capable
of flaying a man alive. Well, thank God, he knows,

they all know, she is safe now! If the wires are not
down, the courier Mejia sent last night had the dispatch
at Corpus before four this morning. An express rider
could do the trip to the ranch in three hours. But we
must sweep every one off the border now. Clean it up
for once and all!"

Ford was wolfish.

"I never was particular about 'drawing' on a doubtful
Mexican, but I will lose what scruples I ever had,"
dryly remarked Bayard—"that is if Si Leavenworth's
hangings leave anybody to practice shooting on! He
will be like a madman in his suspense. Why, he rounded
up seventeen men skinning his cattle two years ago!
The Grand Jury found that the 'Regulators' hung
them, but I happen to know the 'riatas' used were San
Miguel raw-hide lasso ropes. Ah, yes, he is a terrible
man!" Tom Bayard sighed.

"Do you not think, Colonel, it would help to pacify
this region, if Silas were to turn over the ranch now to
his son's handling?" queried Manson, as they rode down
on the level plain. Ford was at the head of the
column, soldier-like in caution.

"Jack, we will take these sweet girls away from him,"
said the ex-rebel confidentially. "When our marriages
give us a right to talk, I shall ask you to help me show
to old Silas that his chance of dying in his bed
depends on *abdication!* He does not care for money; it
is only the pride and habit of control. It is the very wine
of life to him. But that darling girl in the ambulance
can talk him into tenderness. Jimmy will be all right
in a month, and I shall force my wedding day on rapidly!
I leave you to direct your own action! I will tell you that
you had better break the news of your demand for Katie,
while he feels he owes her life to you! We waive our
glory in your favor. Let's push on. D—n the Rio

Grande! I wish I could cut it out of the map and dry up the valley. A river-line is a fatal boundary. Here, take a drop of Maxan's best to an early double wedding!"

Jack, even preoccupied as he was, laughed heartily as he grasped Bayard's old war flask.

"We can keep each other's secrets. Colonel, here's to the new home on the Nueces!"

"Where can that renegade be?" thought Tom Bayard. "There will be a sharp hunt for his life. Well, thank God, we will be at Ringgold Barracks in two hours. The 'regulars' are not the greatest warriors in the world, but people do not steal ladies from their parade ground. It is a keen cut to the pride of the wariest old ranchero in Texas to lose his pet lamb out of the fold in open day!"

Bayard urged the column on, while Katie, in the delicious self-surrender of security, slept till the ambulance halted at the muddy international ditch, across which the pleasant mansion - quarters of Ringgold clustered around a tall mast, bearing the colors of sturdy old Uncle Sam. The reclaimed Confederate hailed the once unwelcome sight with tears of joy! What thrills an American like the flag of his country floating in God's free air!

Colonel Mejia, as night fell, furthering his secret ends in comfort, free from prying stranger eyes, pondered at Hacienda Maxan over the whereabouts of the vanished "Jaguar," now veritably a hunted beast. From his previous knowledge of the quasi - criminal, Mejia thought the upper Rio Grande around the Great Bend would be his lurking-place. From there Maxan could reach No Man's Land on the Texan border, Sonora, and the Pacific Coast, or, disguising himself, get down to Tampico or Vera Cruz and reach any one of a hundred islands of the Caribbean, or make his way to the Mecca of cosmopolitan rascals, Central America.

The doughty little Aztec would have bounded in rage had he known that his energetic adjutant, the bearer of every sudden extra military burden, had ridden in ignorance, past the very camp where Ramon Maxan lay, perdu, nursing now a demoniac thirst for vengeance!

It was true. Sixty miles from where Ramon Maxan's captured stronghold lay, a straggling camp of Confederate self-exiles were vainly trying to, at once, raise coffee and solve the hopeless problem of Communism! Broken and embittered soldiers, haughty planters ruined by the war, ex-officials of the civil service, and a few Quixotic adherents of the "last ditch" frenzy, were aimlessly talking, planning, and toiling in a foreign land to gain a living free from the overshadowing of their native country's victorious banner. A few clear-headed men among them already began to see that self-expatriation is not profitable, "per se;" that the former planters, unused to personal exertion, were powerless without the unpaid labor of their docile negro slaves, now freed by a sweep of dead Abraham Lincoln's pen! Tender women, high-souled, but saddened, men of good character, and sullen wearied youths growing up without education, were "hostages of fortune" in this disastrous enterprise. Sadly as the Brazilian confederate emigration plans failed, this fruitless scheme, almost in sight of home, was heart-sickening. Each day was a round of vain regrets, of wasted hours. Dividing into little knots, they clung but feebly to each other. In the remote cabins of their straggling settlement were darkened lives—men given over to sodden dissipation, or those fearing punishment for military misdeeds or yet unforgotten crimes of violence. Each man was a *law to himself*, and while tacitly avoiding the bad element, the better Southern colonists suffered their presence, for the dull-eyed, zealous, suspicious Mexican natives cordially hated the whole colony!

In any attack, even these black sheep might fight vigorously. Ramon "el Jaguar" had always kept up a possible line of retreat in coming trouble. Several shady characters in the camp had been known to him in his youthful exploits in the bayous of Louisiana during the war. Smugglers, spies, cotton agents, go-betweens, and criminals, cast out by both armies, these fellows lived in a remote corner of the Confederate village spoken of, under the breath, as Murderer's Row.

When Maxan, in his escape, crawled in the darkness from the low roof he sprang on, dropping on all-fours into his garden, he slipped along to a little paddock, where three or four blood-horses were separated from the vulgar herd on the potrero. A mozo, always sleeping in a hut near, was cowering in fear in his thatched shelter. Indicating a huge tree in the near forest, Maxan bade the man throw a saddle on the nearest horse and bring him there. Grasping the man's machête and serape, he picked up the peon's sombrero and darted into the forest shade. His pistol and cartridge-belt were with him, and he wore a money-belt beneath his jacket. Bidding the frightened servant steal back, and, with a halter, follow him bare-back on another horse, the fearless horseman raced along in the shadow of the great mountain-trees, till out of range, he waited his man.

"It's a good idea to take him. He can not betray me. I leave no trail, and if he demurs, I'll put a pistol-ball into him and leave him to the coyotes. Now for Santander! I can hide there a week."

There were no questions asked him next morning as Maxan rode up to the door where "Alligator Charley," an old companion, lay in a hammock, under the shade, in the Southern camp, a mescal bottle near, and a low-browed mestizo woman ready always to hand him a coal for his cigar.

"Hello, Ramon! You here! What's up? Trouble?" cried Charley, with lazy interest. "Light down! Is your man to be trusted?"

"Yes," said Ramon, as he sprang off and grasped Charley's hand. "I've had a devil of a race."

"Ah, I see! Had to get out quick!" said Charley. "Are you bringing any one down on the camp?"

"Oh, no!" said Maxan, accepting a cup of mescal. "No one knows the road I travelled." He lay down in the hammock.

"That's right," said Charley, as he slouched over and directed the woman to get some meat and coffee for the visitor. Maxan signed to his man to take care of the horses.

"I am not *in favor*, Ramon, with the judges and colonels in 'Quality Row,'" sneered Charley, as Maxan told him he had been driven away temporarily, from his stronghold, but prudently omitting mention of Katie Leavenworth.

"Well! I have a good place to hide you here, and I know you always have money and a nest-egg somewhere. You are a devilish sly dog, old boy! Now, you want to get square with the whole world, you say. I will show you a cabin here where I laid out a little den for myself. You can be made comfortable there. Your man can get one of these Indian women to cook for you. There's a sort of a harmless chap, an old friend of mine, there. He's a little peculiar, is Bob Kenyon. He got a clip on the head from a shell in the war, but he's good company when his spell isn't on him. I'll attend to all your confidential things. I've got the time. I could go to Tampico or Mexico for you, back to the Rio Grande, or even to New Orleans. I'll stick to you."

"You're the very man, Charley; I want to *deal a blow* to some dirty sneaks up North, and I'll tell you later where I have a few Bank of England notes stored away."

"That's the talk," heartily answered the disreputable Figaro. "I fancy you don't wish these grandees of the 'Lost Cause' here to know much about you. Will you ride over to the cabin with me?'

"I had better not be seen around here generally," said Maxan, with some caution. "I have had a bit of trouble with the Mexican authorities over some smuggling and cattle-raiding of friends whom I've given shelter to! But I must lay quiet for a few weeks. Don't mention me at all, Charley."

"Oh, if it's a little bit of the 'contrabandista,' that can be easily squared," laughed Charley. "You can buy the whole gang of Mexican customs officials for five hundred cart-wheel dollars."

"It's *that and more*, Charley! I must get even with a few dirty villains North and South who have tried to throw me overboard in money matters."

"I will bet you will square the account," lazily grinned Charley, who had ordered up the horses, swallowed a can of coffee, refilled his flask, and, buckling on a loaded army revolver, grasped a handful of plantation cigars, which his poor Mexican drudge was twisting up deftly.

"You used to be a dandy! I am afraid you left home rather suddenly," leered Charley, as he gazed at Maxan's uncouth garb!

The Creole's face flushed! The vulgar familiarity galled him. "I *did!* I went out through a window

with a half-dozen six-shooters cracking away at me!"
His face blackened. "But, by God, I'll have the
heart's blood of the two curs who hounded me!" He
checked himself, as Charley, who scented the loose
change of the Bank of England notes, drifting his
way, said good-humoredly:

"Well, you can act from here and think things all
over! I can get you any rig you want from a
Comanche Indian's to the uniform of a Major-General
in the Confederate States Army.

"D—n the Confederate States and their army!" said
Maxan decisively, as he sprang on his horse.

"Easy," said Alligator Charley, "you must curb that
temper of yours a little down here. These chaps are as
proud as they are poor. Bob Kenyon, who will be your
messmate, is a crank on that subject and about his beautiful wife who vanished or was swept away in the war.
It's the only thing he raves about! He's a thorough
gentleman outside of that. Now, keep cool. Study his
little peculiarities. He's as brave as a lion, watchful
and true, and will be a guard for you, as he sleeps little.
No one approaches him for he often gets excited about
the missing beauty he lost. So it's a godsend to a retired
gentleman like you. You can tell me what you want.
I'll get it. I have arms enough for a dozen. I am only
short of ready money."

They rode in silence along the shores of a lagoon to
a cabin, sheltered by three great mahogany trees. A
lazy Mexican boy was fishing from a log, and a few
ponies grazed around. Whooping loudly, Charley dismounted, as a finely-built man of thirty-five appeared in
the door. His clean-cut face showed thought and
refinement, though a furtive wandering of his gray eye
indicated mental suffering. His semi-military garb
conformed to the mixture of Confederate and Mexican
riding-attire, generally worn by the political emigrants.

"Major, I've brought you here my friend Mr. Preston, who is looking around for a coffee and sugar plantation place." Maxan greeted the lonely man who was courtesy itself in his welcome.

"It's a poor place, sir, but I'm glad to see you," said Kenyon in a gentle, abstracted way. Alligator Charley was anxious to settle Maxan's status. Having rebaptized the Creole, he remarked: "Mr. Preston and I are old Louisiana friends. He does not wish to be talked to death by schemers, and I am going to post him, in the two or three weeks he will be here."

"I am glad of your company, sir," said Kenyon, with true Southern hospitality, calling the boy.

In a half-hour, around a table spread with a tropical breakfast of fish and fruits, with good coffee, and Charley's flask, the three were soon in thorough accord.

"I will now leave you, Preston," said Charley, with a wink. "Ill send your things up from Santander, in an ox-cart to-morrow, and let me know what else I can do for you."

"Thank you!" said the newly-baptized Preston. He admired Charley's ready wit. "I did have a rough ride up from Tampico, and I lost my way once or twice. I should have brought a guide instead of trusting to my own man. He's a fool, but honest!"

Before a week had elapsed, Maxan, in the silence of his hammock, dreaming and plotting, had evolved the scheme of a comprehensive revenge. His companion was exactly suited to his mood. Kenyon was reserved and silent. Riding alone in the forest, reading over old letters and papers, smoking and idling in his hammock, he was one of the wrecks of the "Lost Cause!" When the Stars and Bars went down in battle and storm, the chapter of life was closed for him. Reticent and watchful, he never alluded to his private sorrows. Maxan and he got on famously, and Alligator Charley had already provided the hiding Jaguar with writing materials, and enlightened him as to the telegraph, mail, and public facilities of Santander. At night, while the fire-flies lit up the Mexican forest, the two lonely men talked idly of old times and scenes. They were contrasts in nature. Maxan's busy mind distilled only the poison of venomous intrigue. Robert Kenyon, bearing a life's disappointment, and nursing his private sorrows, dreamed along—"the world forgetting, by the world forgot."

Subsistence was to be had almost gratis, and Maxan was a generous provider, for of his Bank of England notes, a few crisp examples were sewed in his belt—one of them marked £100—sufficed to make him a local capitalist. Magic power of money! Its concrete force opens *almost every door* in life.

Ramon "el Jaguar" chuckled; "Let them now ransack the old Casa Maxan! My deposit at the Bank of Havana and Credit Lyonnais of the last year's dividends on the Rio Grande Company are a start for life! I could even take the chances for a couple of years on the diamonds and notes I have sewed in my waist-band."

He mused under the great mahogany trees, and resolved on action. "It is folly for me to risk braving these fellows openly on the Rio Grande. I can not hope ever to face Mejia and these border officials. I can blackmail old Steele and Milly out of any money I want later. He is re-elected for six years. President Grant must sustain him as a party leader, and he has lands and a big share of this railroad. Shall I clear out and go to Cuba? I dare not show up again in Texas or on the Rio Grande. I could crush the Leavenworths by inform-ing on them. The Rio Grande Company! Ah! what a blow I could deal. To inform the Secretary of the Treasury of the smuggling, to give away the whole chain of customs officials, to throw a bomb-shell into Chisholm's camp. Yes! It would be a crushing revenge! I can not face them. That girl's baby face has spoiled my chances. Should I pull down Steele and Milly with that crowd? No! The old fox is too crafty. By Jove! I will send José over to Matamoras and see if Milly has any heart left. She may have written me, and he can also spy out the situation at the ranch. Alligator Charley can go, too! He is free, and I will play one spy off against the other. It's a good scheme."

In the cool of the next evening, Charley rode away, followed by Maxan's men.

" I will cultivate Kenyon in the week they are gone," mused Maxan. Young, energetic, and with surging passions, he dreamed of a new life in the smaller Latin republics where he would be a man of mark. "I could work the State Department through old Steele; Milly will control him blindly. But to leave that hound *who struck me*, yet alive! To let go the revenge of seeing Katie's only brother fall under my rifle! To know her heart-broken. Panchita, the mad fool, has surely told her all. There I was feeble! I should have killed her before I brought that baby-faced Texan to the haci-enda." The thought of Manson's triumphal return, of the almost inevitable wedding maddened him. He clenched his fists and raved in his wanderings. "I have to fly like a coward and leave these lovers the inherit-ance, the girls, the railroad, and the Rio Grande Com-pany! When Manson is married he will fall into the old man's secrets."

Ramon Maxan groaned in helplessness. His bitter heart hesitated between revenge and safety. "Did the brother get a mortal wound?" he pondered. "I'll know that when they come back." In these vain musings he awaited the return of Charley. The seventh day dragged along to a close. Maxan had exhausted every bit of small talk, and Kenyon, growing daily more moody, relapsed into silence. The 'Jaguar' did not dare to approach the main settlement, and, warned by the boy, always retired to a mahogany-cutter's hut, at the head of the lake, when any stranger approached.

"I must get out of this death in life. I must decide soon, for Alligator Charley will be here before midnight. I should go mad here like poor Kenyon." Maxan was seated at a table, his eyes really watching the bends of the road, but trifling with a note-book he always carried in an inner pocket of his vest. Several memoranda and notes, unintelligible to the stranger, spoke to him of the now precious deposits. Manson gazed at Kenyon, lying in his hammock, his eyes fixed on the surface of the lake where the ferocious cayman hid in the reeds and the flamingos waded for the sluggish fish. All was as dull as the banks of Lethe's stream! His romantic and artistic nature revolted at the inane silence, the vulgar surroundings, his mean and supine flight! His active brain ran over the world's map. "A foreign service! Bah! To be the lackey food for powder of a prince! *Never!* Central America! Death, defeat, assassination follows temporary success! South America! Distant and over-run with adventurers! The Northern States! To live under Yankee rule. No! And yet, and yet, if Milly had a heart I might rule, I might rise with her help." He opened a flap of his pocket-book. Her picture glowed before his eyes. A gaze of love in the days of his Washington social career. "Wonderful woman! Can she afford to ignore me? Is she, too, a cold egoist?" As he gazed, a clatter of hoofs aroused him. Alligator Charley, his unkempt hair streaming in the wind, drew upon a foaming horse. But he was alone!

"Quick! Not a minute to lose! Here's my pistol and belt! Gallop to the wood-cutter's hut! Conceal your horse! Soldiers are on your trail! That d—d adjutant of Mejia's regiment captured José and tortured the truth out of him. I gave them a hot race, but they have trailed me. I'll come to you! Lay low! I'll bring all you need! I'll whistle three times the old swamp call. Go!"

A cloud of dust rose around the bend of the road. Maxan dashed away, pistol in hand. The forest tangles had hardly closed over him before the pursuers appeared.

"Help me hide these things, quick!" Charley called to Bob Kenyon, who had left his hammock. The recluse swept the articles on the table into his hammock and lay down. Charley dropped lazily on a raw-hide couch.

"Silence for our lives! You know nothing!" whispered Charley, as the eager adjutant dashed up at the head of a dozen wolfish-looking troopers.

"Where is he? Give him up!" cried that ubiquitous officer, his pistol cocked, his keen eye glittering.

"What is wanted?" said Charley, in lazy indifference.

"Ramon el Jaguar, the outlaw! Five hundred pesos on his head, dead or alive! Search the place!" cried the officer.

Alligator Charley wondered if Maxan had ridden on the trail. "He's a gone coon if he did. This chap means business!"

Ah, no! The Creole, with lightning reasoning, had urged the tired steed into the forest, and ridden far out in a circle toward the head of the lake. There were no tell-tale hoof-prints on the trail!

"Where is your own horse?" demanded the adjutant.

"Boy out hunting meat," rejoined Charley stolidly.
Every moment was precious. Kenyon gazed blankly
at the soldiers. Questioning him was in vain. Charley
tapped his own forehead and murmured: "Enfermo!
Calentura!"

The officer recoiled from a possible fever patient.
After ten minutes of fruitless search, the angry soldier
sternly said:

"Why did you fly from us?"

"I took you for 'ladrones,' road thieves, and I rode
in here to give the alarm." Charley was a past-master
in the art of lying!

"I will flay you alive if I find you lying," said the
officer.

He could not break Alligator Charley's calm.

"I shall see the Jefe Politico about this outrage. I am
a registered emigrant," the stubborn rebel said stub-
bornly.

"But the man whom you had with you?" the
doubtful soldier persisted.

"I met him on the road from Matamoras. He was
afraid—we travelled for company. Do *I* look like a
peon?"

"I shall summon you before the Governor. You
will be shot if you are deceiving me! Give him up!"

Alligator Charley said calmly: "I know the Governor, and you will only make a fool of yourself. I
never even saw your man. I have not left here for
two years, save on this trip to order some goods."

"I will get back and start out the rural guards,"
thought the adjutant. "I must go on with my report
to Mejia." With curses and bravado the patrol rode
away.

"A close call!" said Charley, as he took a fresher.

" See here, Major, those devils might come back. If
I were away they might drag you off to prison. You
had better go up, as soon as it is dark, to the old cabin.
Sound the call three times, thus." Kenyon nodded.
" I will make a pack for my friend and send the boy up
at midnight with his horse and an outfit. He had
better strike out for the upper Rio Grande. They will
catch him sure if he stays here. I know they will
return. I'll write him a scrawl, and there's two letters
to give him that I got from the post-office at Matamoras."

A groan startled Alligator Charley as Bob Kenyon
dashed to the flickering light of the candle, gazing
eagerly at an object clutched in his thin fingers.

" What's up? " cried Charley.

" Nothing! " said Kenyon. " I will go! Let the
woman catch my horse." He folded his arms and
gazed out silently on the darkened lake.

" Off his head again! I can't do better though," mused
Charley, as he selected a bundle of articles useful in
Maxan's flight. " He must have got deeply into dirty
work. Well, he can lay low, escaping over the National
Road, and work out by El Paso or Presidio del Norte.
Ramon had better strike for Arizona and the Pacific
Coast. The jig is up here."

As Kenyon rode away, Charley noticed that he held
a drawn pistol in his hand. " He's a queer fellow; a
fearless soldier, and yet timid in the evening shadows.
He has one of his turns on! Well, I'll thank God to
be rid of Maxan. He's a very lively visitor."

By the darkened shores of the lake, Kenyon halted
his horse at the lonely hut. All was silence. The
erratic messenger paused. " Shall I *do it when he
comes?* No," he thought, with cunning. " I'll make
him talk first, then, I'll kill him. He stole her from

me! Fate brought him into my power." Sounding
the call three times, it was softly answered, and Maxan
appeared, pistol in hand.

"Not now! not now!" muttered Kenyon. He
spoke earnestly to the fugitive and gave him the letters.

Maxan raged like a wild beast at bay, while Kenyon
moodily watched him. He seemed to have no words
beyond his message. "I must send word back to Charley. It may be my last chance to use a trusty friend.
I'll have to strike for No Man's Land. There, rifle in
hand, and a horse under me, I am any man's equal!
There's no cursed law, rank, or character there.
Major Kenyon," he said slowly, "I am in trouble.
I have but little time. Follow me. I've found a little
arroyo here with cover. I can light a fire there, read
these letters, and send word back to Charley. You
can mark the place to tell the boy where to come. If
any one should follow us, you can stay by the fire. I
will escape by the arroyo into the forest!"

Kenyon nodded silently. "I'll kill him and bury
him there under the leaves," the distracted man plotted,
as he followed. He almost laughed aloud. "And
Charley will think the Mexicans slew him if he ever
finds him!"

Unconscious of his impending doom, Maxan strode a
few paces. "I've got my horse hidden up there in the
forest!"

"Good!" said Kenyon, with a cheerful face.

Maxan busied himself at gathering dry leaves and
branches, and soon a fire leaped up with a bright light,
illumining the little cut, but not visible in the higher
level of the dense forest.

As soon as it was light enough to read, Maxan tore
open his letters. He read, and with a hollow growl of
despair threw them down. His head dropped on his

breast. "I'll follow her, by God, I'll—" his hoarse growl of defiance ceased as he realized that Kenyon had thrust a pistol in his face, and, holding out Milly Steele's picture, cried: "Pray, you dog! I'll kill you myself! *You stole my wife!*" El Jaguar, cool and fearless, gazed in his half-crazed enemy's eyes! A sudden inspiration seized him! "Shoot, Major!" he cried, "kill an innocent man! That picture! You found it in my pocket-book?"

"I did, you villain!" roared Kenyon. "It's my lost wife's. Oh! God! How beautiful!" He threw down the revolver at Maxan's feet and sobbed like a child.

Ramon was of the electric mind of great commanders. He eyed the cocked weapon scornfully as it lay at his feet. Handing Kenyon his own, he said: "Kill me now! Take this and then—*then*—you would never know the truth."

Young, fearless, resolute, his handsome face lit up by the flickering fire, Ramon Maxan looked like a dauntless demi-god. His words brought conviction to Kenyon.

"Tell me the story. I must be on my way. And you—you! Ah! My head is bad—bad!"

"That woman is now the wife of Senator Steele at Washington, the great carpet-bagger politician. She told me she was a widow. That her name was Smiley. That her husband died abroad. She and her rascal husband decoyed me down here to further their schemes. When I had done all I could, they planned my assassination as I knew of his corrupt frauds on the Government. It is God's truth! I see it all now!"

In a half-hour the specious tale was done, and Kenyon rode alone toward Charley's camp. He seemed sobered by the pretended revelation.

"Leave vengeance to me! I will **face them both!**

Be comforted! I will send Charley himself to you. Take my pistol also! Put your fire out. You might be surprised. You will hear ringing over the South the story of how I will punish them." He galloped away.

"Am I going mad?" said Maxan while he hid like a bear in his cave, waiting Charley's coming. "It seems my head will burst. So this half-crazed fool's wife was Milly Smiley! He may do a *part* of my work for me. Now, it is only vengeance! I will pull down the temple on the wedding feast. I can strike them all."

The letter from Milly Steele proved that his lying deceit was discovered. Panchita's story was now known.

"You never were true to even the passing moment. We are, in life and death, strangers now." The woman wrote, secure in her position: "Try to shake my influence over my husband! Your every interest is ruined. Dare to use this letter, and I'll have you hunted out of Mexico."

"The sly fiend! She has used another woman's pen. She would claim I forged this. And Mr. Chisholm! I am to look out for the trains of smuggled dollars from Saltillo, another great 'run in of smuggled goods from Havana.' I have it! Let every fiend of hell rejoice! I'll pay them yet in their own coin. Blood for blood! Lie for lie! Treachery for treachery!" He crouched in the dell till Charley dashed up.

"The coast is now clear. I had the boy and the woman dog the soldiers out of the settlement, and I have a dozen spies ready to bring me word of any descent. The boy will be here in a few minutes with a pack-mule, and I have brought your horse along. He's in splendid trim. Now, what can I do for you? You must leave at once!"

"Charley, do you want some money?" said El Jaguar temptingly. "How would £200 English Bank of England start you home?"

The emigrant sprung to his feet.

"If *I had that*, I'd drive my horses, packed, to Tampico, sell them, jump on the steamer (there's two a week to New Orleans), and when I got a gentleman's outfit and was trimmed up, I'd work the Mississippi River boats and live at home like a gentleman—*gambler!*" he prudently concluded silently.

"Now, listen to me," calmly said Maxan. "I have a powerful friend at Hidalgo, forty miles from here. He has a gang in the Sierras. I'll have them land me at Presidio del Norte. Now, if my horse does not drop dead, I'll ride in by daybreak. Can you take the open road and be, at sundown, at the market plaza of Hidalgo to-morrow night?"

"Yes; but what for?" Charley queried in mystified astonishment.

"To get a half-dozen letters which I will prepare and two or three telegrams. Also to get *the two hundred pounds!* I will give you the cut halves of two hundred *more* myself, and when you send back the registered receipts for the letters and telegrams, I'll send by the boy a sealed letter with the other half-notes to you. Can I count on it? Will you play fair?"

"Ramon, I'd sell my soul for half of it! I want to leave this cursed land forever. I have even thought of suicide. Go ahead! I'll meet you! I've brought all you need. Here's brandy and cigars. Stay! I'll send the boy on with you with my horse, and I'll come over on Kenyon's."

The servant appeared at the arroyo mouth leading a packed mule, as Charley spoke. "Let the boy wait in the market-place and meet me. You go cross country of course?"

"Certainly," said Maxan, who was now ready for departure. "I can count on you? You'll come for the money, anyway," sneered Maxan, as he mounted.

"Shake hands, Charley, once for luck!" he said kindly, and resolutely plunged into the forest.

Two days later, Alligator Charley was astounded when he read the addresses of the letters confided to him. "The President of the United States." "The Secretary of the Treasury." "The Secretary of War." "The Attorney-General," and several other dignitaries. The telegrams bore such names as A. R. Chisholm & Co. of New Orleans; Mark Manson, 18 Wall Street, New York City, and others.

"This is some important business broken up by my trouble at Zacate. I have been in secret relations with the customs and treasury departments," Maxan wearily said.

"Well! I will attend to all! Now, I'll make the quickest trip ever made to Tampico. I'll wager my life on this!" Charley was radiant. He had his money —a fortune to him. The means of return and a gambler's stake outfit. Looking around the obscure hovel in Hidalgo, where Maxan met him, for he would not take Charley to his lair, the messenger said, "And the boy is to come here to meet you?"

"Yes!" shouted Maxan in impatience. "They will bring him to me!"

Charley sprang on his horse. "Anything more I can do?" He had a sympathy for the hunted man! There were already official posters on the walls of the alcalde's house, offering a reward for "El Jaguar!"

"Yes!" said Ramon, struck by a sudden thought. "If you can get Kenyon to go over with you, do so, and turn him loose in New Orleans. He will go crazy here. I'll send a hundred pounds for him."

" I'll do it!" cried Charley as he gathered his horse.
" And you, old comrade, where do you go?"

" I go to the wilderness; to hell, for all I care!"
said Ramon, turning on his heel and striding away,
undaunted and triumphant. He watched the flying
steed bear Charley away. "It's done!" he cried, as he
drained his flask.

" I may win *on the double event!* Now, for
Comanche Land!"

When the column, escorted by Mejia's troop of
Lancers, reached the elm-fringed banks of the Rio
Grande at Ringgold Barracks, the two young men had
galloped on a mile in advance. As Colonel Ford noted
Katie Leavenworth's pretty head thrust out of the
ambulance impatiently, he suggested the getting ready
of a boat.

When the wagon drew up at the landing, without a
word Katie ran swiftly to the barge. The Mexican
Lancers gazed in astonishment. "Go ahead!" cried
Ford. "We will come over later." And while the
heavy boat swept slowly to the Texan shore, the fair
girl leaned her head on Jack Manson's shoulder and
burst into tears!

Colonel Ford was busied with crossing his now tired
men, and in saying adieu to the officers of the Mexican
escort who had borne themselves like good men and
true.

" Your men shall have a royal reward as well as a
father's thanks," said Ford, glad to see his own turbu-
lent volunteers safely on their way over the dividing
line. As the flat-boats pushed off, crowded with horsemen, the old colonel swung his hat and cried: " Boys,
take the town, hang out at the Post traders! Have a
night of it! Si Leavenworth will foot the bill in
Texan style." The happy colonel jumped into a skiff

and made his way to a light river steamer moored on the American bank.

It was one of the Rio Grande Company's light fleet. When he entered the cabin, Katie Leavenworth was being smothered in the embrace of a bevy of officers' wives about to embark for Brownsville. They had learned every detail of the romantic recapture of the Rose of San Miguel! Lovely Katie was carried away in triumph by the feminine coterie, and Jack Manson was left alone with the silver-haired ranger. Tom Bayard was already at the fort hastening an ambulance and escort. "Lady Bird, we will drive to Smith's Ranch before we sleep; for to-morrow night, please God, you will be in your mother's arms at home!" The grateful girl threw her arms around his neck and kissed him warmly, as he galloped away on a trooper's horse.

"Listen to this!" cried Manson to Colonel Ford, who was enjoying an immense cocktail brought by the officious head-steward. "It is beyond our hopes! McNally's men caught Ximenes hiding near Los Angeles. They found out the route of the other bandits from him, and, finding maps of San Miguel on his person, then hung him to a tree. Dispatching a courier to Buller at Las Cuevas, they cut off the rest of Maxan's hirelings, and have killed or captured the remainder of Caballo Blanco's band. It's a victory, a punishment, and a warning!"

"Glory!" cried Ford, starting to his feet. "Where's Lieutenant Buller?"

"Marching home here with his prisoners, and General Singleton has sent word he will send him to San Antonio with dispatches and permission to delay a week at San Miguel on his return!"

The old ranger's cup of happiness was full. "This

clears the border. There's but one thing now I ask for,"
he said joyfully.

"And that is?" queried Manson.

"*Maxan's death*," cried Tom Bayard, who had just
sprung on board.

"Even that will come. It is written in the 'Book of
Fate'!" said Jack Manson sternly.

Tom Bayard headed a visiting procession of officers,
ladies, and local notables who trooped down to welcome
the tender girl reclaimed from the awful perils of the
robber stronghold. Despite all the entreaty of General
Singleton, in an hour, a fleet four-in-hand team, hastily
made up, was bearing the rescued heiress, under the
escort of twenty bronzed cavalrymen, to the end of
the first stage of her homeward journey. Bonfire and
"baile," feasting and jollification made the evening of
Katie's return the red-letter day in the history of Ringgold Barracks! Far in advance, two breathless couriers
raced along under the starlight to announce the home-
coming of the captured maiden!

It was a month after the wild shout went up from
two hundred throats, as the rescue party drove up to
the broad porch of the mansion at San Miguel, when
Manson's promised bride awoke in her own lovely
home-nest. By her side a mother and sister smiled
through their tears!

"You have been very ill, my darling," cried the pale
nurse of love. "Do you know me now, my own little
girl?" tenderly said old Silas, clasping in his arms
the frail sufferer.

For it was a pale, white rose, not daring, laughing
Katie, who lay where the breath of the roses was wafted
in at the open windows. The fresh crimson came back
to her cheeks when, his face still drawn and ghastly
with the ravages of his wound, Jimmy Leavenworth

stole in, and silently led Jack Manson up to the tender-
eyed invalid. In the quiet of the sunny afternoon
Brother Jimmy placed his sister's then transparent
hand in his comrade's broad palm.

"For Life and Love!" he whispered, and left them
a few blessed moments together.

Time sped on golden wings, now that some strange
spirit of renewed life brought the blue-eyed little
frontier princess soon under the graceful shade of her
listening friends, the roses of San Miguel.

It was an exquisite season to the girl—this coming
back from the wan shade, hovering at the gate of departure, to be once more the spirited little autocrat of the
great domain! Gently pacing her familiar walks, leaning on the arm of her gallant lover, Katie Leavenworth's
eyes in their blue depths showed no shadow of parting
any more!

An unwonted bustle woke the echoes of San Miguel.
For in great detachments, like the advanced lines of an
army, hundreds of strong arms were now toiling on
the railway, in feverishly pushed construction.

But shadows, trials! A blackest thunder-cloud rolled
suddenly over the enterprise and its backers and pro-
moters! A bomb-shell had burst in the camp of the
Rio Grande Company hurled by a merciless hand.

Jimmy Leavenworth called Jack Manson aside

"For God's sake, do not bring matters to a crisis
about Katie now. Have you any telegrams? Father
is almost beside himself. He just showed me one in
cipher from New Orleans."

Look out for all! I have to get out to Cuba! Trouble somewhere! Steele in mortal terror. Discovery of private business.
Telegraph "Munoz," Havana. Will write.

                                        CHISHOLM.

And also another.

What is up? Everything against us here. Instruct me fully. No. 4. has drawn out! Danger!

This was signed "Steele."

"Now! I do not know all my father's old business, those war intrigues, cotton schemes, but he tells me that his mail contracts are stopped, and he is raging at heart."

"I am thankful," quietly said Jack Manson. "It is hard to be true to *both sides* of a question. But look at this, Jimmy. You and I are brothers now! I am afraid that your father has mixed in some dangerous ventures unknown to you. I will translate this cipher. I have not answered it! It is from my uncle." The lover read slowly:

Steele in disgrace with the President. Sweeping political changes on Rio Grande. Much excitement. Has affected bonds twenty per cent. Sensational articles in journals about Leavenworth. The Rio Grande Company attacked. Mrs. Steele coming here to see me privately. Our silent partner has abandoned us. What has happened? Is Silas Leavenworth playing fair? Answer. Strictly private. "Immediate!"

It was dated at New York and signed Mark Manson.

"Now, Jimmy, I have refrained from acting the spy as well as representative agent, for your sake, 'for Katie's sake.' I fear there are border mysteries you and I know nothing of. I will do this. I will answer, 'nothing unusual here. All satisfactory here. Silas is square in every way,' and after that Mark can use other special agents. I can't break a man's bread and spy on the host whose roof covers me. Let us swear brotherhood. Tell me all. I will work as if *your* father were *my own!*"

"You are a true man!" cried Jimmy. "I fear my

poor old father has something to conceal. Mother and the girls know nothing, but they are alarmed. Meanwhile, tell me all you can, in honor."

The feverish bustle of San Miguel for a week later exceeded any previous excitement even of the war. Nordenskiold, Blucher, Tom Bayard, Beriah Mott, the Collector from Brownsville, arrived in converging parties, with bad news and vague rumors, which blackened the clouds on old Silas Leavenworth's haggard brow. Riders and messengers kept the roads in dust-clouds, raised by flying hoofs.

"The whole military force on the border is re-arranged, the Customs Inspectors have been transferred, and a special session of the Grand Jury is called," whispered Jimmy, when he found Katie sobbing in Jack's arms. "There is some deviltry up!" said the open-minded Texan.

"I fear dear old father is going mad!" sobbed Katie, and Mary Leavenworth, with Alice's advice, sent a rider, post-haste, for Colonel Tom Bayard.

El Jaguar's letters had reached their destination, and he was far away safe in the fastnesses of No Man's Land. Revenge had won the first trick. The Rio Grand Company was ruined!

CHAPTER XV.

A NOTABLE ABDICATION—"WHAT! BOTH!"—"JIMMY ALSO"—A CAPTIVE KING—ON THE PECOS—THE TALKING WIRE—THE PEON BOY'S GRATITUDE— AT THE PAINTED CAVES—THE JAGUAR AT BAY— YOUR LIFE OR MINE—MY SON JACK.

WHILE discontent and gloom hung like a pall over San Miguel Rancho, the efficient working parties, sent

over from New Orleans by Mark Manson's skilled contractors, were rapidly laying down the first third of the
new railroad. A firm of veteran contractors, under the
old capitalist's personal orders, were simply throwing
up foundation enough to drain the track, as the initial
hundred miles was the very gentlest prairie inclined
plane. Time hung heavily on Jack Manson's hands.
Old Silas denied his confidence even to his son, and the
ladies of San Miguel were careworn and anxious.

"I can not press my heart demands in these days of
trouble," thought the lover. "I'll get Jimmy as his
father's representative, and inspect the undivided
ranches and the stock thereon. It will leave Katie free
to regain her mental quiet, and I will perfect my knowledge of the regions toward the Pecos and the Nueces."

"It is a grand idea!" cried young Leavenworth. "I
wish to arrange some business at Bayard's ranch. I am
determined to establish a running guard against horse
thieves, Indians, and desperadoes sweeping down from
the Northwest, for their day of rule between the Gulf
and Laredo is over. Even now our supply parties and
advance workmen, with the detail survey parties under
Major Blucher, prevent any sudden dash from Mexico.
The temporary telegraph is a wonder. As soon as it
reaches us we'll have a line run over to Ringgold Barracks. There we have the troops and rangers at call."

So, with only stolen interviews and a brief private
explanation to Katie, Jack Manson rode forth, glad to
relieve Silas of his presence, as it would give him time
for secret manœuvres. Manson's rapidly acquired frontier experience told him of a fatal undertow in the affairs
of the mysterious Company.

"Jack, it is better you should go away for a fort-
night," cried the loving girl, clinging to him in her
gentle sorrow. "Father and mother have long midnight

vigils of care, and I have heard her sobbing herself to sleep. Even Jimmy does not know the cause. It can not be danger! He would know of that. It could not be hidden from him. But it is some business trouble, and it must be grave. I never knew my father unnerved before."

The still invalid beauty could not know that Silas Leavenworth feared the open, honest glance of his gallant son. That he dared not tell all to the generous lover who had torn his daughter away from the arms of the kidnapper. She knew not that he feared Mark Manson's resentment at the imperilling of a great enterprise by the dark intrigues of hunting for "fool's gold." All the loyal daughter did know was that the strong man's heart was riven with silent sufferings.

Afar, in his lonely camp in the fastnesses of No Man's Land, three hundred miles away, Ramon Maxan would have been wild in a tumult of joy could he have realized how swiftly the shafts launched by him had sped; how his careful betrayals had crippled the "secret system" of his now hated confederates. For his telegrams to Chisholm and others had placed their unholy ventures where a sudden descent of the strong Federal arm had paralyzed every movement! The clear and daring letters to great Government officials had changed the Southwest policy of the administration! Revenue cutters, secret agents, army inspectors, and treasury officials were now eager to save their imperilled reputations, and be "in at the death" of the detected "Company's" illegal traffic. Alligator Charley had kept his faith. Raging in unrest, Maxan gathered desperate criminals around him. "Why not make a foray with renegades and Comanches down into the Nueces, sweep over the 'Big Bend of the Rio Grande,' and, leaving the band to divide the plunder, hang around for news of my revenge." The outcast pondered every chance and possibility. It was his Rubicon! "I will be months here before I can get news of unusual tumult on the lower Rio Grande." He dreamed of one wild raid, and then a *final disappearance* toward Sonora or Chihuahua.

"I would like to meet those two fools face to face! Or the old jackal, Silas."

His brow grew darker, and his devilish brain thrilled in every fibre with increasing plotting.

Manson and Leavenworth, for three weeks, guided by old Basilio, now as active as ever, though a shade more spectral-looking, scoured the regions where the broad virgin tracts of undivided land were covered with herds of cattle, sheep, and horses. Jaded, wearied, but freshened in heart and soul by the silent prairie voyage, the two friends rode down into Colonel Thomas Bayard's superb valley station, on the oak-fringed Nueces.

Before their steeds were at their corrals, the anxious ranch superintendent sought them with letters.

"Just arrived by express rider from San Miguel. I had orders to send out a party and find you," he said. When Manson opened his budget he saw a packet from his uncle, a bulky letter in the handwriting of the senator's beautiful wife, and a document franked by the statesman himself. He threw himself on a bench before the beautiful residence, now waiting its destined mistress, and began to read the fateful letters.

"Excuse me, dear old Jack," said Leavenworth, his voice shaky. "I only wish to confer a moment with you. My father writes me briefly that I must come to him as soon as horseflesh can bring me! Jones, here, will give me an escort and fresh horses. I know the road, and can do the sixty miles by nine o'clock

to-morrow morning. Of course, *I* am my father's main-
stay, his only confidant. *You* must have rest. Don't
mind if I leave you. Jones will send men on with
you to care for my horse and guide you. I'll leave you
Basilio. Can you read this mystery?"

"See here, Jimmy," said Manson, whose own brow
was clouded, "I will go with you. Let horses be made
ready. We will have some refreshment. Let us leave
Basilio to pilot our band in and bring on our two
beauties. There is grave trouble in store for all of us.
I will not hide from you; these letters are full of it. But
give me a half-hour to read all my letters, have a can of
good coffee, and I'm your man. I'll stand by your
father, by you, by all, for old times, and—for Katie's
sake."

There was a quiver in Jimmy's voice as he said, "God
bless you, Jack. You are true blue. It is as I feared.
Some estrangement of your uncle. It would break
down my father to have that enterprise stopped!"

"It must not be! Let me read and think." For the
first time since their college union of hearts, Jack's
honor forced him to have a secret from Jimmy Leavenworth.

Mechanically folding his letters, when he had read
them, he drained a huge measure of coffee, filled his
pockets with cigars, took a few turns around the beautiful enclosure, and said:

"Now for the road! We will get under way, and
when we have to breathe our horses, I'll tell you what
I can, and what I propose." The evening star was
sparkling in the east when they loosed their horses'
reins. It was well judged in Manson to wait until they
had covered twenty of the sixty miles, before he
evolved a plan to meet the issues presented by the letters which weighed upon his uneasy bosom.

Riding between their grouped escort, resting their horses changing from the "lope" to a shuffling walk, the engineer began: "I will ask you to hear all I have to say in silence, and think the situation over before you decide. I will try and spare you any pain, but, dear old boy, I do beg for your patience. I will indicate to you what your father can explain. I have here letters from my uncle, from Senator Steele, and a confidential one from his wife. There has arisen a serious juncture in my uncle's railroad and partnership affairs with your father. It means to me a change of my future. It may mean to you the loss of fortune. It might estrange me from your father and," his voice vibrated in emotion, "it might lose me your sister Katie's hand, not her love: of that, thank God, I am sure!"

Manson was gazing at the bright stars which Katie and he had loved to watch together. They spoke to him of her. The very night-breeze seemed to echo her voice.

"There has been a disclosure—a revelation—serious charges about some matters implicating your father!"

Leavenworth reined his horse across the road.

"Hold on, Jim! For God's sake, be patient!" Jack's voice was solemn. "You don't know what you may do if you give way to feeling. Chisholm has fled to Europe, by Havana. Steele is in the agony of despair. He is asked to clearly show his whole connection with these operations to the President. He is frantic with anxieties. Someone is dealing giant blows right and left! I know not whom they are aimed at. They reach your father, our railroad, all our plans. Uncle Mark is determined. I have an ultimatum from him. It is one your father *will not accept!* Only you and I, with your mother and sisters' aid, can prevent a final rupture. Steele has shown the white feather. He has his private and political short-comings to conceal from the President, who is aroused and demands a clearing up of all. Steele has thrown all his property interests into my uncle's hands. No. 4—the silent partner—has formally drawn out. Chisholm had his power of attorney—a proxy. He is silent—vanished. The books have been removed."

Jimmy Leavenworth dropped the reins of his horse. "Trouble I do not mind, but disgrace, dishonor, I'll not live to see it. It means that Gertrude Marshall will never place her hand in mine!"

"Listen, my brother!" cried Manson. "We must fight, you and I, for Life and Love, as we have, and that too, shoulder to shoulder. The only one who is cool is the senator's wife. In this strange muddle she seems to know more than anyone—to be able to point a way out, and to divine the black-hearted scoundrel who works to rob you and I of the women we love, as well as to overwhelm your father."

"It's Maxan!" shouted Jimmy, his voice trembling in rage.

"You are right," gravely said Jack, "and from what corner of safety does he strike back at us? But listen! I will not hold the truth back. I had made my mind up to telegraph my uncle that I threw up my trust. But I must go on. I will help you. It only places me where I would be cowardly to press for your sister's hand. I lived to win it like a man—not to ask a daughter's sacrifice. I'll tell you all; and you, your mother and sisters, and Tom Bayard must tell me what to do. But, I leave Texas—and—*alone!*"

"Go on, quick!" said Jimmy. "We must ride ahead."

" My uncle, you see, has the controlling power now

as well as responsibility. His orders to me are to demand the whole franchise to be assigned to him, to take the joint ranches and stock into my name as trustee, and to singly assume the entire charge of the railroad. He demands that your father retire from the open control of the Texan operations, or he will cease sending funds, and the result will be failure and further exposure."

"Exposure of what?" hoarsely cried the young Texan.

"Of various alleged operations, of a nefarious character, directed here on the border by your father and certain unknown associates. My uncle says that with this clear turn-over, Steele, secure in his financial support, can stop off all further investigation, save your father, clear his own record, and the properties and enterprises can be saved from utter ruin."

"My father will never consent! He will never yield under pressure! He will die first! It is horrible!" said Leavenworth. "It means ruin and heartbreak to us all!"

"And you, what do you propose to do?" said the Texan.

"I propose," said Jack slowly, "that the property referred to be transferred to you on the ground of your father's multitude of cares and business. That the railroad charter be turned over (as far as your father's interest goes) to Col. Tom Bayard, as trustee, and *thus* your family interests be saved. Uncle Mark has written your father, Steele has written him privately, and that wonderful woman has sent me a letter under the seal of a man's honor. It may help to save, but I can never tell its contents. But how to make your father consent? How I can handle Mark Manson? Even the senator's wife has imposed on his suspicious mind, and I can use the telegraph to her about this! Now, let us ride on, and when we have the journey under control, give me your views. If you and I should separate, *should quarrel*, Jim, it would only add a last pang to the bitterness of my departure. We can talk now, but once at the Rancho, if we lose our community of heart, and all is over."

"What do you mean by your departure?" said Jimmy Leavenworth.

"I will *not* do Mark Manson's bidding. He can select some other agent. I shall turn down the golden pages of my life and seek the Western plains once more!" Jack's voice rang as hard as the flints under his charger's feet.

"And Katie?" said the suffering young ranchero.

"Do you think she would ever listen to the name of Manson again, when Mark's cold measures have forced your unyielding father into a bitter contest, ending only in the family ruin? You do not know her *pride*, Jimmy." Manson was hopeless.

"And you do not know her *heart!*" said Katie's brother, as he spurred his horse onward. "Let us hasten forward."

Grim care rode behind the two gallant horsemen, and in the early gray of the dawn the friends looked haggard, as the sun showed them, two hours' ride away, the groves where Katie Leavenworth's graceful head reposed on a pillow the night before wet with bitterest tears. For her father's voice had been raised in the sternest malediction, and the old ranchero was ready to meet the wary capitalist in the struggle of greed and craft.

"Have you anything to say? What shall I do?" said Manson, with sympathy, as he entered the mansion.

"Let me confer alone with Tom Bayard. Let me

also talk with the ones who are dear to us both." Jack
Manson, glad of a pretext, sought his room, and slept
till the sun was streaming in through the western
windows.

His comrade, with delicacy, had stationed the colored
boy to await his young master's bidding. As Jack
opened his eyes, the valet gave him a little twisted
note. It was in Jimmy's writing.

I have had an hour with Bayard. I am now going to have a
long conference with father in the Den. It seems to me that my
mother is the only one who can draw from father every detail of
his cares. If she expresses a wish to permanently leave this
exposed rancho, and Katie knows your wishes, he may be led to
consent. But if you or I have to propose it to him, we will be both
thwarted in our dearest aims. See Katie. You will find her in
the garden! I only ask that you will not telegraph or write Mark
Manson until our plan has been tested. After that, should it
fail, I do not care what happens. I might as well go West with
you. But *we* must avoid each other. Mother alone can make
the proposition come from him so as to save his pride.

Jack read over the letters of the night before as he
drank a cup of coffee and broke a roll.

" Strange! " he murmured. " Steele held his head
high until trouble came. His wife now is the better
man! Old Silas has been an autocrat. His gentle,
patient wife and unworldly daughter alone can save him
now. Chisholm, Jimmy tells me, has left the protection of his vast interests to his wife, while he flees. And
from this letter of Milly Steele's, it is to her alone must
be given the task of swaying stubborn Mark Manson,
merciless in business diplomacy. Are the strong weak
or the weak strong? How few of the intrigues of life
which are not *guided by woman* after all! The subtle,
far-reaching, penetrating femininity of the modern
woman guides the hidden destinies of man and things."

"She is a gallant nature!" Jack admiringly said, as he read again Milly Steele's letters:

Telegraph me to the address I gave. I will go to New York and occupy your uncle's mind. I know No. 4 and his status in this hidden tangle. I know why Ramon Maxan has dealt this blow. Your uncle knows nothing of this. Now, I am with you to the last in our common cause. Steele is distracted. You alone can guide the Texan matters to save all interests. I can delay and placate here. But if any more fall away, the whole system falls inert. Each scampering away to save himself! Chisholm, to save himself, has secreted all damaging accounts and papers! Maxan is now an outlaw! His blow has been delivered; he can not strike again. Would to God some friendly bullet would relieve us of him! It is the whole future of Leavenworth, his children, and those projected marriages which hang on your prudence and steadiness now. Be patient, prudent, and calm the storm. *Think of me!* It is my very existence which is at stake! The war shadowed Northern homes, but it swept the whole social fabric away from under the feet of Southern women. Husbands, lovers, brothers, friends, homes, property, and all went down in the red wreck! One generation obliterated, and every tie that binds sundered! I deemed myself safe, secure in a future, and if I am saved, it is to you (the man I could have loved) I will owe the sheet-anchor of my tempest-tossed bark of life! Death is nothing to me. But I am too proud to submit to penury, obscurity, lonely age, and a future of vain adventure! For if Steele is a broken man, my last chance is gone! I will not have it! He must go down with his flag flying in honor! I have always craved peace, quiet, a home, and all that the sad war robbed me of when I was young and helpless. I have stumbled along life's path, been driven along by its storms, and I will owe it to you if I am spared being driven yet to the expedients which wreck women in body and soul! Steele has sacrificed all to maintain senatorial and political position. Without capital, if he loses prestige, and this crash throws all into Mark Manson's hands, I am simply offered up on the altar of Fate! My hopes, my fears, my heart are with you! Ah, God! how I could have loved a man like you, had I had a fair chance in life! For you, I prophesy all I would have died for! Life with the one your heart has chosen! Love met with Love! Life and

Love! Be it your prize! For you battle now "for Life and
Love!" Think of these words! My very soul goes out to you!
You are our savior or our destroyer!

"Poor woman!" sighed Jack, as he dispatched his
man to report the whereabouts of the family circle.
"From the dark depths of her nature, the home of black
shadows, the white aspiring peaks of noble impulse
rise toward God, robed in purity. Mysterious double
nature of woman! At once the toy and plaything of
man; slave and goddess; the hunter and the hunted;
her fevered dream of *what might have been* will only
cease when grim Death seals her pallid lips with his
unreturned kiss of icy power!

"And am I then the arbiter of others' fortunes? *I*,
who can not shape my own destiny?" He walked
down the stair and sought the one fair woman of the
world to him, who waited for her anxious lover among
her friendly roses. It needed not the thrilling shade of
sorrow, tingeing her dear eyes a deeper blue, to tell him
that she had shared her proud brother's burden of sorrow. He saw her standing, with graceful, drooping
shoulders, her fair hands clasped, and her delicate cheek
pale with the ashes of its own roses. Her head was
bowed. She was no longer the mutinous little beauty
of San Miguel. On her fair brow the lines of womanhood's cares were traced. "Child, child no more." A
loving woman battling for her own heart empire. It
needed but a glance to tell her lover that she knew all.
It was even so. James Leavenworth's heart was heavy
for the sake of the Greek-browed darling of Arundel
House. The gallant plainsman feared the calm glance
of Gertrude's mother—the woman who had faced
poverty and adversity with the unbroken courage of her
race.

Jack Manson drew the gentle girl to a seat in the covert bower. "You know of all our trouble, darling?" He spoke in pain, for even words seemed to be denied him. In a moment she was sobbing on his breast. The dear head resting on his bosom chased away his stoic mood.

"It is you alone who can save us all. No one else dares to brave your father in his wrath. I can find burdens in life too heavy for me. I will not be made the instrument of his humiliation, the bearer of a cold threat. I fear your father not! I fear my uncle less! But, with my hands tied, with duty and honor on the one side and my heaven on earth imperilled, if I lose you, I can not act. You must seek your mother. She alone has a right to the truth, and I will leave the field free then for Bayard and your brother to guard the fortunes of the women who will be tied to them by a happier fortune than my own. Jimmy has told you all?" he queried.

"All he knows. More than you fear," she whispered. "My mother is with father now! Alice and Jimmy have gone away with Bayard to leave them free."

"Then you must act at once, my poor darling. From this moment, look only at this fair home and the debt of nature you owe here. I must act to-day decisively, and I will wait for your victory or defeat. But leave here, I must. I will only wait to aid you as far as I can."

"You mean that you will *leave Texas?*" the loving woman cried, springing to her feet.

She never looked as beautiful even when hope led them on together under summer skies! A flash of sapphire light lit up the blue eyes fixed on her lover.

He bowed his head. "I shall not care for fortune. I shall not follow the call of ambition, for all the paths I cared to tread in life led me only to you! Now, I only care to go away. The farther from San Miguel, the easier it will be to walk alone."

There was a strange light in the eyes of the Texan heiress as she said: "And you would *give me up?*"

Her voice trembled, brave-hearted as she was.

"How could I demand your hand of your father as the price of my betrayal of my uncle's cold, egoistic money policy? If it is enforced I will be your father's bitter enemy. You know how he hates."

"I do," said Katie, with flashing eyes. "I know, too, how he loves. He hates and loves as I do, with all the heart's intensity!" Her bosom was heaving and her fearless brow was bright in the sunlight stealing through her roses and lingering around the beloved one. She cast one glance around at the princely domain, as she stepped out of the bower. Manson sat, his head bowed on his hands. He asked not for pity. He saw no escape from his duty or an immediate departure. There was an answer due the waiting Crœsus, whose treasured millions were now imperilled in the railroad.

She stepped back swiftly as a springing fawn. "Wait here! I will send Jimmy to take you riding while I am busied." Her light head rested on his shoulder.

"Where do you go?" he said, as he lifted his weary head.

"To my father," she quietly answered.

He saw that in her face which made his heart leap up in wild joy. There was a dreamy look in her eyes as she stood at the gate of her own paradise.

"It will be hard to leave all this, the dear old home," she said, as her reluctant feet lingered on the threshold. "Yet *it must come!*"

"Katie, what are you saying? Are you dreaming?

Do you not see the gulf between the frontier king's daughter and a wandering engineer?"

"It means," she said, softly speaking, as if indeed in a dream, as if timing her words by each throb of her heart, "that I will not give you up!" Raising her eyes she met those of her wondering lover. "If you go out into the world, wherever you go, you will find me *by your side!* Will you have me, Jack?" she said, the tears shading her lovely eyes. "Our compact was until death, 'for Life and Love'!"

The beautiful woman looked up smiling faintly from his breast as he caught her in his arms. "You promised me to be a Texan, Jack. A true Texan. They are all brave and—*generous!* Do not make me tell you more. Do not lead me on to say I love you enough to go out into the world hand in hand with you." She was smiling now through her tears. "If I do not win my point, then poor father's heart has changed toward me. Listen, my Jack! One thing you have not thought of. Father has not met Mark Manson for years. Now I know that some of these troubles come from this New Orleans banker going away. If we can persuade father to go at once to New Orleans, it will give him a chance to arrange matters there and learn all things now hidden or in doubt. He can take his lawyer. Then, if we persuade him that by going on to New York and acting with your uncle, that he can save all his Government business and his interrupted contracts, he will go certainly. There, at New York, your uncle and my father can agree on all. Brother Jimmy tells me that Mr. Manson has all the other interests in his hands, and Senator Steele's and this Mr. Chisholm's, too. Can you not see there are only *two* great interests left now in the whole thing—the Manson and Leavenworth?"

Jack gazed at the little financier in open-eyed astonishment. Katie was standing now ready to brave the old ranchero.

"We will tell my father it is absolutely necessary that mother goes with him, as he may have to stay six months, and, therefore, he must put the railroad matters all in Jimmy's hands. As Alice is all ready to marry Bayard he will give him the control of the ranch. Now this will satisfy your uncle. We can persuade father to leave it so. And, face to face, that quarrel will disappear when these two old men are together, especially if—if you write your uncle. It is only a fight between Love and Hate. Love will win! You *must* write him to-day!"

"Write him what?" said Jack Manson, who was dazed with happiness at seeing a way out.

"Why, that we are to be married, *you and I;* he can *then* trust my father, can he not?"

Jack Manson's outstretched arms caught only empty air, for the graceful girl had already reached the garden gate, in flight, to hide the burning blushes on the cheeks so lately pale with the shadowed cares of the upheaval. She smiled at his discomfiture and disappeared.

"I am only a stupid blunderer," thought Manson, as he caught his breath. "Katie is an angel! She would make a world-famous bank-president; but," he nodded confidentially to the roses, "she will make a peerless wife! The brave darling!" He walked up the path to meet her brother, who led him far out on the ozone-breathing prairie in a grand, swinging gallop.

"I will wager my head, Jack," said the Texan, "that Katie will have her way! *She always wins!* Let us wait on her now. I have a rider waiting to take your message. Do you wish to use the telegraph?"

"Yes!" said Manson. "I will stake my future on Katie's faith in her powers to bring your father into the only position safe for him and our whole circle. I will telegraph Uncle Mark, 'All will be arranged in a few days as you wish. Your partner probably coming to you at New York at once. I will represent you both in road. Answer, if satisfactory. All quiet here now.'"

"That's right, Jack," said Leavenworth; "it does not bind us all down. Now, my mother tells me that she has won him over to agree to Bayard's immediate marriage with Alice, and to give them the general ranch control for the present. We will wait for Katie now. Let us drop the whole thing till she has used her power."

The shadows were softly draping grove and hill as the two friends rode in and unostentatiously joined the circle at dinner. Few words were exchanged, but there was an infinite promise of victory in Katie's eyes, shining with happiness. Mrs. Leavenworth and Alice turned with glowing faces toward the young men as Silas Leavenworth, after a silent dinner, spoke to Manson.

"If you have dispatches to send, I am sending a man down to Corpus Christi. By the way, I have to go over to New Orleans and may go on at once to New York. You might mention that to your uncle. I will dispatch to him fully to-morrow from Corpus Christi."

Jack Manson managed to control his tell-tale face, for he knew that Katie had won the victory! He glanced at the little diplomate. She was looking straight to the front; her cheek was pale, and her lover saw the hand he had covered with kisses trembling as the old autocrat spoke.

"I would like to see you in the office an hour to-night, as I go down to-morrow evening," continued

Silas, addressing Manson. "I shall be away for some months."

"Most certainly, sir," said Jack, bowing. "When do you go North?"

"I will wait a few days at Corpus Christi for Mrs. Leavenworth," said the frontier king, "and then go over by New Orleans. As soon as I have done there, we will go on to Washington and New York. I have a vast amount of business at the departments, and I shall take Nordenskiold up with me."

Manson actually blushed, as he saw that the resolute Katie had "carried all the works in front of her!"

Silas Leavenworth's haggard face and tired eyes told of a mental struggle of no ordinary intensity. Noticing Jack Manson's preoccupation, he said: "Your affairs will not be interrupted at all. I shall leave my son in full control of the railroad matters and all my freighting and steamboat affairs. Colonel Bayard will manage the ranch and house business."

The engineer well knew the reason of the sudden rosy flush which made St. Cecilia Alice a glowing picture, as all eyes were turned upon her and the bronzed Confederate veteran, who actually looked sheepish.

The graceful author of these remarkable plans glided gently from the room, as Silas led his wife toward her favorite evening seat upon the portico.

Lightly as she moved over the dewy grass, her lover's swift strides overtook her before she reached the mansion.

"Did you speak to your father, Katie, for me?" Manson was eager and excited at his darling's wonderful success.

"About what." said the fleeing maiden.

"About our own affairs—*about our marriage!*" stammered Jack. She was another woman than the clinging

sweet one of the afternoon! Katie never turned her
head as she neared the porch, but calmly said:

" I have spoken *once* to-day for you; I think you
had better ask for me yourself, Jack!"

The lover paused. Her tenderness had vanished
with the far-blown cloud of trouble.

"Ah! I see!" muttered Manson. "Katie *does need
discipline* after all!" But as he watched her brave,
delicate face turned toward the matchless skies of evening, he could have knelt before her and adored the
unconquered spirit, the bright wit, and womanly fortitude of the ranchero's daughter!

" I would not have a feature or a thought changed,
were she to mount the throne as a queen!"

This was simply personal enthusiasm! But when he
realized that his strongest card was the announcement
to his uncle of this projected marriage, at once a guarantee and a safeguard, he realized that he must deal
with stern old Silas at once. He had seen the messenger dash away with his dispatch. Leavenworth was to
leave the rancho in the morning. He might not return
for months. Would it be safe to imperil the whole
settlement and union of interests? No! a few untoward
words between the wary millionaires might end all his
hopes!

So it was that after he closed the tedious hour of
business in the " Den " with the frontier king, he had to
face his duty, for when he returned to the parlors he
knew that Bayard and Alice were to be married at
once. Whether at Corpus Christi or the rancho he
knew not, but a sight of gallant Tom Bayard pleading with Alice at the farthest end of the stately portico,
told him that Mrs. Leavenworth would not sail for New
Orleans till Alice, as a budding young matron, could
replace the gentle mother, whose husband had practically " abdicated " in favor of his son.

Both the lady of San Miguel and her son looked inquiringly at the two men as they entered. There was a shade of disappointment on Mary Leavenworth's face. Miss Katie was seated, gazing aimlessly out into the starlit night. A Parthian glance from those eyes roused Manson to a sudden decision!

As Silas Leavenworth rose to follow his wife to her special haunt in the great room, which, by general consent, was named " mother's headquarters," the scene of her quiet labors in the long absence of her husband, Jack Manson rose respectfully. There was a grim resolve in his formal manner, as, observing Miss Katie Leavenworth about to save herself by flight, he said quickly, addressing the parents:

" Will you pardon me a moment? I have something important to say to you. Pray don't go, Miss Leavenworth," he added, with a glance of agonizing appeal. Miss Katie sank into her chair, perfectly unconcerned, and folded her pretty hands. " You are about to leave the State for a long period, Mr. Leavenworth. I could not see you and Mrs. Leavenworth go, leaving me here as a guest in your family, without telling you that I love your daughter Katie, and beg your consent to our marriage."

Jimmy Leavenworth sprang to his sister's side, for the dauntless Katie covered her eyes with her hands.

" *What! Both my girls!*" said Silas, as he dropped speechless into the nearest chair.

The frontier king's nerve was evidently shaken by his vigils. Mrs. Leavenworth walked gently to her daughter's side and stooped down to kiss her. The mother's kindly eyes beamed on Jack Manson, whose heart was thrilled in the suspense of the moment.

" What do you say, Katie? " slowly said old Silas, as the graceful maiden stole to his side.

By an impulse, Jack Manson joined her. The ranchero fixed his eyes on his daughter, who returned with her frank fearlessness, his steady gaze.

"For Life and Love!" she said, as she placed her hand in Jack's.

"And when did you propose to be married?" said Silas, who had caught a telegraphic verdict from his gentle wife's approving smile.

"When Colonel Bayard and Alice are married," said Manson, innocently, and suddenly realized that Miss Katie Leavenworth had transfixed him with one awful stony glare!

There was a silence. Brother Jimmy was on the verge of laughter, when Silas completed his son's discomfiture by saying quietly:

"Well, thank God, we do not *lose anyone* if you do settle at the ranch." The frontier king rose, and taking their hands, said: "You saved her life? Watch over her, my son! She has always been the apple of my eye!"

In the open doorway Colonel Thomas Bayard was standing, towering over Alice Leavenworth, at that moment the very happiest woman in Texas, when James Leavenworth resolutely approached his father.

"May *I* say one word, sir?"

"Is it about this marriage?" said Silas sharply, turning on his heel. "I have settled it. I suppose I might have seen the 'signs of the times' before, if I had been watchful. Everyone *else* seems to have been posted," remarked the ranchero dryly, scanning his resolute son's face.

All could see, however, that Silas was not seriously offended at Katie's spirited avowal.

"Not about *this marriage; another one*," said James Leavenworth, caballero and plainsman, looking his astonished father pleasantly in the face.

" Well, I thought *Bayard* and *Alice* were in thorough accord.   Your mother told me they would come in and be married at Corpus Christi before we sail!"

" We intend to!" was a smiling answer in happy chorus from the gallant Confederate and his promised bride.

".Well, then, whose marriage is it?" said Silas Leavenworth decisively.

"*Mine!*" remarked the young Texan, with a quiet glance at his mother.

"*Jimmy, also!*" said Silas, and, fairly overwhelmed, he gazed appealingly from one to the other of the two happy couples who smilingly watched Mr. James Leavenworth adroitly sailing on a flood-tide of good feeling.

" As the lady is not present, let me speak for her," said Mary Leavenworth, with a mother's dignity.   "It will be the happiest day of my life to see Gertrude Marshall the wife of my son."

" She is so lovely! Such a noble girl!" cried both the sisters of San Miguel, surrounding their puzzled father.

" If she is like her father, she will suit me," said Silas.   " Come here, boy!" He held out his hand, " I see that you have your mother and sisters on your side. That is enough!   When do you think of this union?"

"Not until it suits your business situation, and the railroad is finished. I do not wish to be away a moment while you need me, sir."

The thoughtful regard for his own interests touched Silas. He said kindly: "Jimmy, you've been a good boy to me.   I want you to marry next spring. When you will be, if I live, member of Congress and president of this railroad; you can then hold your head up with the best of them at Washington. Thank God! I have given you what I never had—an education!"

Silas Leavenworth, with a meaning glance directed to his now overjoyed wife, said: "I presume you young people can find ways to kill time without us. I wish to talk these family changes over." If ever mortals realized a perfect satisfaction in the anticipation of an unclouded future it was the circle of merry-makers in the lonely Texan mansion house.

Manson was sensible of a slight shadow upon his happiness. One or two chilling remarks by his promised bride upon the subject of "hasty weddings" led him to believe his own marriage would NOT be solemnized on the same happy day as that of Alice and Bayard.

"I am in no hurry," Miss Katie remarked to her sister, in a tone of hauteur evidently intended to impress Jack Manson, "besides I always dreamed of being your bridesmaid. We can wait."

"How long, may *I* ask?" humbly questioned Jack Manson, as he saw Bayard and Alice, gaily smiling at his woe-begone face.

"Oh, probably until next year, *until the railway is finished;* and it will be soon enough when Gertrude is here!"

The demure manner with which Katie insisted that her "sense of duty" would not permit her to be married until Gertrude Marshall had thoroughly won Mrs. Leavenworth's heart, seemed to afford infinite amusement to all but Jack Manson.

"You feel sure that you are willing to be married *sometime?*" persisted the Knight of the Rueful Countenance.

"Most certainly!" calmly answered the blue-eyed mutineer; "but the day and date is by no means certain. I must think of that."

It was only alone, when in the shadows, Jack folded her to his breast, that Katie said: "The curse is lifted now. When my father's cases are ended, when your uncle has given his approval, you may ask me to fix the day. But," she whispered, as he kissed her a last " good-night," " you may write your uncle and let this news precede my father's arrival. Pray God it will bring them and us together!"

Late into the night Jack Manson toiled, with Jimmy's aid, and covered every point of the business in careful dispatches to his uncle. He weighed every word of the announcements of his proposed marriage, and claimed the confidence of the capitalist in his judgment and in the security of the alliance.

" That's grand!" said Jimmy, as he read the last page. He had toiled over letters to Mrs. Marshall and Gertrude which unbosomed his whole soul to them.

" Now, Jack, in order to have no possible shadow of detection of our assistance in this general plan, I'll send old Basilio off at daybreak with these letters to Corpus Christi. He can rest a few hours at Corpus Christi, and ride back before midnight, and he can easily avoid my father on the road. He knows the team and outfit, and can let them pass him unseen. I would never wish my father to know how we have guided him unseen away from a final rupture with your uncle. Katie's fine genius has found a way which is easy, natural, and final in thwarting the bootless revenge of that villain! I wonder where he is now?"

The young man walked over to the men's camp, and the spectral Basilio noted a star on the blue heavens, and pointed to the position at which it would signal his departure. " Ready, aye, ready!" was the old scout's motto. An extra handful of tobacco, a few corn-husks for cigarette wrappers, fresh ammunition, and a box of matches were his only supplies, save a few yards of dried jerked beef in strings, and his canteen. He slept with his horse as a member of an adjustable Centaur organization. Basilio and his steed were only spoken of in the singular person. In the saddle a caballero par excellence, on foot as awkward as an eagle with clipped wings!

The night wind moaned around them cold and chill, as they stole back to the house. It was midnight. Jack Manson experienced a revulsion of the nerves. "There's something uncanny about the hour of twelve at night. The devil has a brief but mighty exercise of power. I have worn out my power of self-control in this maze of anxieties. It almost seems to me I am under some hideous spell."

"See here, old fellow," said Jimmy, as they stole upstairs. "Your night ride and these uncertainties have shaken you up. I'll bring you in a little bit of the old Henry Clay stock, and we will drink to our brotherhood. Then you can sleep as if fanned by angel wings!"

The future was fair before them, as the two tried friends drank to the loved ones, who waited, with rosy fingers on their smiling lips, in happier days for them both. There was bustle, but no final leave-taking the next day, when Silas Leavenworth drove quietly out at five o'clock. At Colonel Bayard's earnest solicitation, a private marriage with Alice would precede the departure of her parents from Corpus Christi.

"I will bring the whole family down in three days, and by that time all your legal papers will be ready for execution," said the expectant son-in-law.

The rapidly extending railroad was already at the once dangerous cañon, and a gap of only fifteen miles lay between Rancho San Miguel and the head of the line where five hundred men were at work. Disdaining escort, Silas Leavenworth drove away with only his

tried ambulance driver. Lingering over orders and
directions, the busied throng hardly noted the lateness
of the hour. There was work for all in the hastening
of the family hegira, and the wedding of Bayard and
Alice moved ahead in date by the practical "abdication"
of the great prairie magnate. Bayard was already
receiving the reports, and while at ten o'clock the stars
shone down on a gay reunion of the busy family circle,
Jack Manson sprung to his feet as the ranch foreman
rushed into the great parlors with a white face. His
lips trembled, but one motion to the new chief of the
domain told the story of disaster. Bayard looked won-
deringly at Manson and Jack, who followed the two
on the porch.

"Something wrong with the stock?" said unsuspecting Mary Leavenworth. "There is always unexpected
worry! I am glad Silas will have a rest from it
now."

While she spoke, her daughters listened with bated
breath, for the men had rushed toward the great fortress
storehouse. In a moment, the clang of the great alarm-
bell sounded on the night air. It had been rung but once
since the war. That was to signalize a sudden dash of
a few young Comanches, maddened with "tisan" drink
and their first warpath. They were killed to a man
almost in the very enclosure! *Now*, as the general
alarm pealed out, it brought a score of house attendants,
armed, around the frightened women, for Mary Leavenworth, her hands clasped, cried: "It has come at last!
My God! *Your father!*"

While the sound of shouts and hurrying hoofs proved
the rallying of the two hundred stout-hearted prairie
riders, Bayard, Manson, and Jack Leavenworth listened
to Basilio's story. His trusty horse, staggering to his
knees, lay dying with heaving flank and glazing eye.

" I was astonished," said the old scout, " not to hear along the line that Don Silas had passed down. I did not dare to show anxiety, for I thought he was only delayed. When I left the end of the railroad, I rode boldly out c 1 the main road, as I was sure the trip had been put off till to-morrow, and I wished to get in and report your letters. Half-way between the railroad and the outer ranch fence, in the little clump of cotton-woods we call 'algodones,' I rode on the remains of the team and ambulance. It had been overturned. The horses lay dead with their throats cut. There was no one there. Riding around in a circle, I found, a hundred yards up the road, the driver lying dead, filled full of Comanche arrows. But no sign of Señor Silas! On the side of the road, where the ambulance lay, the trail of twenty unshod horses. I galloped here break-neck."

" Your opinion?" said Bayard, as he shouted to Bronco Bill to send the horses for the three to the portico. A dozen willing hands were already preparing the arms and outfit of the three lovers.

" El Jaguar has watched the ranch, has laid in hiding and carried off Señor Silas, perhaps for ransom, per-haps *for torture!* "

Bayard sprang to his feet as a shout arose, " A cour-ier! a courier!" Dashing up to his very face, one of the ranch outriders gasped out: " Twenty-five Indians passed up the valley, headed toward the Pecos, three hours ago. They drove no stock, but several pack-horses. They chased me, with lances and arrows, but my horse was fresh and they turned back!"

" Here, Walton," said Bayard to the ranch superin-tendent; " do you move into the mansion till we return! Send an express of three men to Corpus for Nor-denskiold and Major Blucher to come and stay here. I'll get supplies from the nearest ranches and posts. Send a dozen men to examine the place of the attack, and let three of them strike up the valley on our trail. I'll *have your life* if you let anything happen here while I'm away. Inspect the men, give me fifty of the best. I'll get more as I rouse the country. Now, gentlemen!" He ran across to the house whence the sound of lamentation and wailing mocked the echoing mirth of an hour before. A hurried embrace, a rapid arming, and with a few last words, the three leaders sought their steeds, wild with eagerness and fretting on the lawn. As Jack Manson buckled on his frontier belt and settled his pistols Katie's arms were thrown round his neck. "My poor old father! It's that devil Maxan has carried him away! For God's sake, save him! and your own dear self. God be with you, Jack, my beloved! You must come back—back to me!"

His kisses rained upon her loving lips, as with one last embrace, he rode out on the trail of the fleeing savages. "I will meet that fiend face to face! May God defend the right!" The midnight premonition recurred like a blast from an open grave. His two men waited at the main gate as he dashed through, and it was half a mile before his matchless charger overtook the compact column swinging on in an elastic lope. Bayard briefly reported:

"I took ten men extra and sent three to Rio Grande, three to Fort McIntosh, and two to my ranch to turn out my extra men, get a pack-train of supplies to follow on our trail, and two more to find McNally's Rangers. I've got flankers out a mile each side, watching for the trail. Now, we must push on till the last man drops! It's the only chance to save Silas. If there had been private revenge alone, he would have lain dead by the ambulance. I can see it all. They shot the driver off his seat. The horses ran away. When the ambulance was upset, Silas was probably stunned. They found him and carried him away. It is money—a huge ransom—for it would not pay to take such risks to get a man merely to torture. There's but *one man alive* would do it, and Maxan has not had a chance to get around the upper posts, organize this raid, and come in here. It is some daring white criminal or deserter who knows of Silas' riches, who has put this scheme into execution!"

While he sought to bring conviction to Jack and the half-frantic son, their hearts were far away with the helpless prisoner and the sorrowing woman whose cup of happiness had been dashed away.

A scout came racing down the right-wing line. "We've struck the broad trail!" he cried. In a few minutes the pursuers were following it, preceded by their best scouts. Old Basilio's waving arm looked ghostly as he followed the wide swath with intuition. In grave silence the column rode till daybreak.

It was a killing pace! With two hours for breakfast, grazing and feed, the troop was moving ahead at the invincible wolf "lope" of the plains. The three lovers gazed in each other's eyes. There was no wasting breath in idle words. Every cool rider inspected his arms as the now broad trail might lead them on the Indians at any moment. "Jim," said Bayard, "you will need your mind clear. Now, Jack and I will divide these men in two bands. You leave the command to me. Our only chance is to run them down! I'll make it the hottest chase they ever saw. If we strike them, you look out *for your father*, nothing else! We will scatter the devils with a charge. You all know what we are on this trail for. I'll say no more!"

"For Life and Love!" said Jack Manson, leaning

easily over his superb racer, who moved as if steel springs guided his graceful bounds. "I'll save him for the last race."

By noon the trail left the grassy upper meadows of the Nueces and led out toward the dry, sandy desert, toward the Big Bend of the Rio Grande.

"My God! we've travelled ninety miles," said Bayard, as they drew up at a little spring, the last before crossing the dreadful sandy waste. All the men were hastily filling canteens, laving their necks and chests, and then every beast was well watered and mouth and nostrils sponged.

Don Basilio rode up from his scout's post on a sandy hill. "Two companies of men, here," he motioned to the right. "From your rancho and over there, the soldiers!"

Bayard shouted in joy. His express-riders had skimmed the prairie in a wild run, and the blessed "talking wire" had done its magic work.

"By heavens! *if it's Buller*, it would be too much luck. He's worth any dozen officers on the 'Bravo,' a born soldier; ought to have been born a Texan!"

"Jack, Basilio will lead you on. Take half the men. I'll wait till these fellows come up. I only want to give orders. I'll send my men off fifteen minutes after you, then they can take the lead when you rest."

With Jimmy at his side, Jack Manson pushed out on the blazing scoria and burning sands. His fiery ambition to win Katie's loving praise led him far to the front. By his side, silent, spectral, his dark face shadowed with grave concern, old Basilio moved as if a gliding shadow; and Jimmy Leavenworth, his gray eyes fixed on the winding trail, was at Jack's left flank.

The pace set by the Kentucky racer led them half a mile ahead. Jack Manson's keen eye caught a glimpse of a moving form behind a bush six hundred yards away. Loosening "Kentucky's" rein, he raced forward, when his companions reached him, he was guarding a panting fugitive prone on the sand. It was the spy-boy who had been wounded at the cañon fight! In an instant Basilio had the lad's hands bound. The frightened prisoner poured out a flood of Spanish, lost to Jack and Leavenworth in their excitement.

"Listen," said Basilio. "It is El Jaguar! Only two hours ahead. He has Don Silas, and is making for the Painted Caves, where he will rest! He knew he would be followed. He meant to hide till we had passed on, and get across to the 'No Man's Land' at night. Now, if we push on, they will kill Don Silas and scatter. I can lead you *ahead* so we will get in first! I used to be a 'contrabandista' there. I know the caves. Let us get on ahead. Take the boy along!"

"It's our only hope," said Jimmy, tears of rage in his eyes. "Now, Jack, give this boy your horse. We will leave two men here to warn Bayard."

"No!" cried Jack. "Ramon Maxan is *my foe!* You stay with two men. Guide Bayard on the trail. You watch over your father's life. Let Bayard command the attack. I will go on ahead with Basilio and the boy and ambush them."

"You are right!" the squad cheered, as with the prisoner mounted, Jack cried: "Now, boys, don't spare horseflesh. It's *speed now!* We can fight on foot, when we get there. We must be in first!"

All the pursuers knew now that the boy was afraid of being made a Comanche slave; that he had dropped off his horse in the night, and only ran because he feared some strange body of rangers might kill him, not waiting for his tidings; for the lad had kneeled on the sand and crossed himself, crying: "He saved my

life at the ranch! I had to run away; I was afraid El
Jaguar would kill me. Ah, tiger! Devil!"

"God bless you, Jack!" cried Jimmy, as Manson
threw up his hand and dashed away! Old Basilio in
front, like an avenging fury, rode steadily, swiftly, on
his mentally selected route, cutting off the detour the
robbers had made in the night. Shadow man and
shadow horse, they looked unearthly in the glare.

An hour later, re-inforced by the ranchmen and
keen-eyed Buller, Tom Bayard pushed hard on the
trail to save the father of the gentle girl he loved.

Jimmy Leavenworth silently pointed out every
yard to be saved, and Buller, his captain's double bars
now on his golden shoulder-straps, cried cheerily: "I
shall claim that Virginia Reel with Miss Katie soon!"
The lean, brown cavalrymen dashed along, eager to
show the peerless riders of Texas that "Uncle Sam's
troopers" were "Brothers of the Spur."

As the shades of evening fell, Jack Manson drew his
men together. Seven out of the twenty-five had
fallen out, exhausted in the fierce race, with orders to
pick up and come in as a reserve, but not till firing was
heard.

Manson's blood was boiling. In his excitement he
recked not of Basilio's warning whisper, "We have
ridden thirty-five miles in four hours!" The gallant
steeds with drooping necks inhaled the freshness of the
evening. There was yet an hour of light! And the
Painted Caves lay before them a quarter of a mile away!
An old bend of the river showed a limestone bluff, and
in later years the uneasy Rio Grande had cut a channel
on the other side. In these caverns of soluble limestone,
many a smuggler and murderer had hidden safe in the
connecting chambers whose windings were known only
to the Comanches. Rude figures traced with lance.

point, knife, or burning brand, gave them the name of the Painted Caves.

While Manson called his men together for last orders, Basilio riding ahead, screened by a fringe of cottonwoods leading up to the foot of the bluffs, indicated, as he rode away, how Manson could bring his men under cover.

At any moment the murderers might now wind down the long arroyo leading up to the plains they had crossed at a sharp angle. Hastily giving Bronco Bill half the men to lead, Manson cried: "We'll know in a moment if they are here yet. If they are, we will fight on foot and hold them till Bayard comes up. If they are not, we must take our station in hiding and attack in ambush. I'll only keep five mounted men with you, Bill, to single out old Silas. Dash in and surround him! Leave the other fighting to me. *I'll attend to Maxan myself!*" Jack Manson's voice rang like the thrilling note of a charge. Every Texan knew that he would fight under the spell of the sparkling blue eyes of the girl he left behind him.

Basilio had dismounted, and crawling forward like a snake, left his horse behind a knoll, its bridle thrown over a cactus. His two heavy revolvers, the huge knife, and the Winchester impeded the old man's movements.

It seemed an age! Every heart was beating wildly. Suddenly, the old phantom stood up and waved his arms. In five minutes, Jack Manson's men were hid in the shadowed arches of the caves. Behind a clump of trees fifty yards away, sat Bill, revolver in hand, another slung to his saddle-pommel by a rawhide thong. The other horses were sent around the bend into the willows where the rushing river would drown any sound! It was a supreme moment. Jack Manson, on

beautiful, quivering "Kentucky," was screened by a tangle of vines. He was as silent and stern as a bronze statue.
Five dismounted men in front, lying behind bushes, lay
silently, Winchesters in hand. An awful thrill passed
through Manson's nerves as Basilio, touching his arms,
said simply: "Look! They come!"

Jack passed the word. "Remember, not a shot till
they are in pistol range. Wait my word! Bill, then
ride straight for the old man!"

Straggling down in twos and threes, a squad of
twenty horsemen were pushing toward the caves. A
half-dozen were grouped around a led horse, guided
by a lariat on either side. The four hundred yards
dwindled to two. The Texans could almost hear their
bounding pulses throbbing in the wild impulse to spring
out. As a lithe horseman rode out in front, calling to
his band and made straight for the cave. Jack Manson
saw his foe before him. *"It's your life or mine, you
dog,"* he thought, as he one flash of a blessing hovering
from afar. "For Katie's sake!" Driving the spurs
into Kentucky, he yelled, *"Now, boys!"* and rode
straight at his mortal foe. A withering volley rang
out, wild yells rose on the still evening air, as Bronco
Bill's men rode down the surprised Indians, who fled
like frightened wolves!

Wheeling his horse to gain freedom of movement,
El Jaguar snatched his pistol and fired point-blank at
Manson. Jack's teeth were set as the great Kentucky
horse crashed into Maxan's tired steed. He leaned
easily to the right and fired three bullets, with lightning
rapidity, into the writhing body of the prostrate villain.

Wheeling his faithful horse, Jack saw in the outstretched arms and staring eyes that Death had set his
eternal seal on Ramon Maxan's handsome face! Up
the gorge the evening shadows were now lit up with the

sudden flashes of the heavy revolvers. As the firing
began, the reserve, dashing down the bluff, cut off the
fleeing Comanches. Bill had been faithful to his chief!
His body-guard had sprung on the confused group
around the captive frontier king.

As Jack Manson rode over, with the spectral Basilio
at his side, Bronco Bill was drawing out his flask. He
had poured half its contents down the ranchero's throat,
and the rescued Silas lay on the sward safe, his gray
head resting on a folded coat.

Manson sprang off the beautiful racer who had
borne him so bravely, and cried: " Bill, is he safe?"

" All right!" said the scout. " He's had the roughest
old trip of his life!" Stretching out a bony hand, he
said: " Cap, let me shake your hand! You're a Texan,
by God, every inch of you, and *I'm proud to know
you!*"

The gathered victors gave three rousing cheers, and
wearied Silas Leavenworth feebly opened his eyes. He
motioned. Jack bent over him. The indomitable old
ranchero closed his hand upon the young man's in tenderness. *For once*, the world saw old Silas unmanned;
it was when, with tears streaming down his cheeks, he
murmured:

" *My son Jack!*"

In half an hour a dozen camp-fires on the bluff signalled the victory. The dead Comanches lay in a silent
line. A herd-guard controlled the horses, and three
armed men watched over five living sullen red devils
lashed to as many trees. Sending out pickets and two
riders to lead in the main party, Jack Manson was the
happiest man in Texas when Jimmy Leavenworth
rode up, sprang from his horse, and threw his arms
around him. Happier still, when Colonel Tom Bayard,
with a sly glance at Buller (who, for once in his life,
missed a fight), said, with a crushing grasp of his hand:

"Jack, I guess Miss Katie will make no objection to our being married *on the same day now!*"

Manson hardly heard Buller's remark about "that Virginia Reel," for before him lay his implacable foe, dead in his sin, and one avenging bullet had pierced his very heart through neglected Panchita's picture! The Jaguar was cold and still, and Love had won at last!

CHAPTER XVI.

THE BRIDES OF SAN MIGUEL—SENORITA PANCHITA —THE CONGRESSIONAL ELECTION—AT ARUNDEL HOUSE—A FALLEN STAR—FROM THE DEAD— MILLY STEELE'S VISITOR—A NUECES BRANCH OF THE RAILROAD—UNDER THE SOUTHERN CROSS!

THE long vigil of the Creole's sleepless revenge was over. By the light of the flickering camp-fire, his nameless grave was hollowed. The painted Comanches slept in a common fosse under the mèsa, at some distance from the red mound where El Jaguar lay alone. There was not a word spoken, no woman's tear, no solemn voice of priest, as the pale face of the dead bandit was shut out from mortal gaze. By some common impulse, the rangers heaped a cairn of stones above Ramon Maxan's lonely grave. With happy hearts the troopers and ranchers made hurried preparation for the morrow's march. Side by side, Silas Leavenworth and his gallant son slept, guarded by their faithful men, on the prairie, while the stars swung away to the west in peaceful silence. The last thing Jimmy noted, as he laid his head upon the drifted leaves, was Jack Manson standing, uncovered, by his foeman's grave!

It was even so! In the silence of the night, broken only by the howl of the prairie wolves chasing down the wounded ponies of the Comanches, Katie's lover thanked God that the release had come, that the future showed no haunting terror, and breathed a manly prayer for his misguided and fallen foe.

Thanks to the sudden dash and the completeness of the ambush, not a man of Jack's brave band was missing. But one rider was absent; it was Bronco Bill! Even as Jimmy was embracing his father, in rapture at his safety, Jack Manson thought of Mary Leavenworth's agony, of the sisters in their tears!

"Bill," he said, "fill your pouches; take my flask; I want you to ride like the wind to San Miguel. You know what to say. We start home to-morrow early. Take the best horse in the camp!"

"All right, Cap!" said Bronco Bill, as he quietly took Kentucky's rein.

"What do you mean?" said Jack in surprise.

"I am following *your orders.*"

Jack Manson laughed, even in his anxiety. The bold rider was right.

"God bless you, Bill! You're a rough diamond, but a gallant fellow. Now, use him like a man."

Bill was in the saddle; he bent over the pommel: "I know the news I'm taking; but Miss Katie—"

"*Give her this,*" he said gravely, handing Bill the picture of Panchita, with its fatal sign, where the heavy ball had crashed through it into Maxan's heart.

"Tell her from me she can *sleep in safety now!* And, Bill," his face softened as he said, "tell her I am, at last, a Texan, and her father called me ' My son Jack!' Say that I'm coming home, for Life and Love. You can also tell her, Bill, to pick out the best horse in the ranch herds and give it to you *herself!* I'll see you have him saddled in style, if the Chihuahua jewelers can do it!"

With a convulsive hand-grasp, the wild ranger leaned forward lightly, loosed the rein, and Kentucky bounded on over the cool plains. The noble steed knew well that Bronco Bill's ride would live long in border story, and his patrician nature longed for the crowning honor of his life—a waiting honor—for far beyond the weary miles his flying hoofs must cross, the sweetest woman in the South waited to throw her arms around his arching neck and kiss the white star in his forehead!

By peep of day the merry victors rose with shouts from their grassy beds! The dew lay on the grass as they rode on homeward, and Silas Leavenworth was able to mount an easy steed.

"We will find an ambulance waiting for you at Comanche Spring," said Manson, as he grasped the ranchero's hands.

"What shall we do with the Indians?" said Tom Bayard, as the cavalcade moved off in triumph.

"I will take them down to Ringgold," said Captain Buller, who was humming his regimental march as he inspected the troopers filing by. "It will give me an excuse to swindle General Singleton out of a trip to San Antonio, for the commander of the department will send these 'studies in copper' to Dry Tortugas to listen to the thin-lipped Yankee missionary girls. I will get in a week of fun at Headquarters and be back at San Miguel, in time to dance that Virginia Reel. Is it a bargain, Jack?" said the trooper, for Bayard, Buller, Leavenworth, and Manson were now a sworn quartette, "brothers evermore!"

Jack Manson mounted his borrowed steed and turned away to hide his blushes.

"Don't worry him! He is not sure of his nuptial

arrangements. I am all right," laughed Colonel Bayard, " but *Miss Katie is a little capricious.*"

" I think she will be willing to yield a point *in this case*," said Jimmy, as he rode off to join his father.

The last man to ride out of the lonely valley of death was Manson, who gazed in silent adieu upon the grave of a man born to a better fate.

In the hour of triumph, even with Katie's open arms strained toward him, Jack Manson's brow was grave as he thought of the blood upon his hand!

" He fell in fair fight, God help him! It was his own doom!" the lover said, as he left his foe lying in the silence, where only the rippling river murmured of life.

Alone in life, alone in death, Ramon Maxan was at last sleeping the sleep which knows no waking.

No frontier crisis ever brought such a horde of horsemen hurrying up the valley. When the long reaches of the burning desert were traversed, Silas Leavenworth found the chiefs of the border waiting at Comanche Spring to welcome him. There were feasting and revelry, and in every direction couriers sped away to spread the good news and turn back new-comers.

Not even to his son would the proud old borderer speak of any incident of his brief captivity. He sought the cover of the waiting carriage, and conversed in low tones with his son.

One night's camp on the grassy billows of the Nueces was the prelude to the home-coming. By the fire Silas assembled Bayard, Manson, and his heir in a private conference.

" I have fought this border fight long enough," he said simply. " My sons, I shall make these business changes *permanent!* I will take my wife North and give her a few peaceful years. We may even go out into the great world beyond the sea. Jack, you may telegraph your uncle that you will handle the whole joint business in future."

"When do you think of going?" said Manson respectfully.

"I shall leave as soon as these marriages are over," replied the ex-prisoner. "*Everybody seems to be getting married!* I think," he said dryly, turning to Jimmy, "I can get down at New Orleans, and with Mark Manson, in time to see Miss Gertie Marshall and find out if she will make a good daughter.

"Yes, Bayard and Jack, you can fix it all up with Jimmy. You will not be lonely, and he can come up to Arundel House as soon as he can get an invitation from Virginia."

That invitation was ready at that very moment. In royal procession the old frontier king approached his own kingdom for the last time.

When the mansion house of San Miguel was seen at last, nestling in its gardens, shadowed by the masonry citadel, Jack Manson became strangely uneasy. There was a family reunion to unite the severed hearts! He seemed to have no exact place of refuge in the affecting scenes. His tired eyes roved over the grand domain with its princely sweep of billowy green, covered with bands of wild-eyed cattle, dashing madly away with tossing, spreading horns, as the pickets on every hill announced the return of the prisoner by firing their repeaters. The herds of graceful cattle raced away to mingle with the last of the "mustangs," warily circling in mad career in the open plain, stretching far toward the treacherous wood where the Comanches waited their victim.

In some pretended accident to his horse, Jack Manson found time to fall behind, for the ambulance was now speeding along to the portico of Silas Leavenworth's home. It was delicate in " Bronco Bill" to dash out, leading the peerless charger which overthrew man and horse when Ramon Maxan went down like a falling star!

"I thought you might want to *ride Kentucky in, Cap!*" said Bronco Bill, who was mounted on Silas Leavenworth's best personal charger. "He's fit to race for a world to-day."

Jack leaped from his faithful substitute and bounded on Kentucky's back. His boy caught the abandoned road-horse. The beautiful racer threw up his lean, delicate head and, bounding forward in a swift swallow stride, raced for the house where a happy group was hovering in general excitement.

Bill kept by his side with ease.

"You ride pretty good stock," said Manson, good-humoredly. He had to break the current of his thoughts or go mad, for something seemed to gather at his heart.

"I'm playing to high luck, Cap," said Bill simply. "Miss Katie gave me her father's own horse and this gay and festive riding rig! I had to fight hard to keep her from giving me the whole ranch! I'm to be a sort of major-domo on double pay and half work!"

Jack's eyes were dim and he only heard half the scout's babble, for, as he drew up at the door, a gentle, gray-haired woman, dressed in black, glided out from the opened doorway of the mansion.

Her arms were around his neck, her grateful tears fell on his bronzed cheek as she kissed him, and Mary Leavenworth whispered to the new son of her heart:

"Down there in the garden!"

Jack's heart throbbed with an infinite bliss as he strode down the well-known path where the scattered rose leaves lay under his feet. His blue eyes gleamed tenderly under the crisp curls shading his glowing face. There was no one in sight, no rustle of any robe, no footfall waking the silent, rose-shaded alleys.

"Ah!" he gasped in one deep-drawn heart-throb, for the shading rose-vines showed him, in his own chosen retreat, the maid who "needed discipline" standing with outstretched arms and a light he never had seen before in the deep-blue eyes!

"My darling!" he cried, as he clasped her to his breast. "Look up!" For the little sunny head lay lightly on his breast! He felt her heart beat against his own, and as their lips met, she whispered, with her arms around his neck:

"Never to be parted any more."

The sparkling eyes grew suddenly dreamy, and it only was her lover's burning kisses which called Katie Leavenworth back to "Life and Love!"

Hand in hand the lovers slowly moved up the garden an hour later, and entered the drawing-room, where the family circle was united in tender reunion. There was an expectant silence as they entered, until Silas Leavenworth motioned to his best-beloved child. Katie stood waiting, with throbbing heart, before the abdicating King of the Border! He gently placed her hand in Jack's, and said: "My boy, I *owe you nothing now!* A life for a life!"

Katie's eyes were strangely shy as she said submissively to Jack Manson, standing by her side: "I must do as my father bids me!"

Colonel Thomas Bayard broke the spell by saying in a voice breathing an unwonted happiness: "I do not approve of haste, but a minister whom I know will be here to-morrow, and the opportunity may not occur for some time again!"

No voice was raised in protest, and a welcome

diversion was made by dashing Captain Buller, who had been ushered in. He gazed fixedly at the expectant bridegrooms, and said to the Rose of San Miguel: "I beg to ask the honor of your hand for the Virginia Reel at your sister's wedding!"

"Captain, I do not know if brides dance," said rebellious Katie, with a flash of her old spirit.

"*You* are going to be married to-morrow also?" said her military tormentor in mock astonishment.

Katie glanced furtively at the tall lover by her side. "I do not know! I *think so!*" she remarked doubtfully.

"I am *sure* of it!" said Manson, with an air of cheerful resolution, which settled that question forever.

It was late in the afternoon when the whole party rose from an impromptu feast.

As Captain Buller departed to leisurely inspect his troopers, who were enjoying a carte-blanche merrymaking, he said: "Nearly everyone I hear of is going to be married. Now, Señora Panchita will be a bewitching widow and I think I will ride over in a few months!"

"You need not go so far, Captain," said the happy Katie, who had now recovered her semi-defiant manner. "That lady is coming in a few days to be my guest for a month."

"Ah!" said the gallant soldier, turning, cap in hand. "In that case, I may look in here then, on my return from San Antonio. I believe in military promptness!"

"You are welcome as long as a blade of grass grows on the ranch, Captain," said Silas heartily.

"Even with my blue coats?" said hardy Buller.

"Yes, bring the whole Yankee army!" said the overjoyed old ex-rebel.

"That's a game and gallant fellow," said Silas, as

Buller was heard cheerfully whistling, "Then you'll remember me," as he sprang on his steed and rode away.

"*Gentlemen!*" said Silas, as his wife's wearied eyes gave him a mute signal. "We owe something to these anxious and wearied ones. I have sent for Nordenskiold already to come and bring all our friends from the bay. He can arrange the law-papers here. So I will leave all the business in your hands. There will be plenty of time for Jimmy to arrange all as he goes North with me. We will leave at once after the wedding."

The stars shone tenderly down on the lovers that evening wandering in the garden, when Katie whispered in, good-night. "God keep and bless you! My own darling, I am yours. But you must be a Texan forevermore!" The compact of Jack's naturalization was sealed with unnumbered kisses.

It was a strange circle which gathered in the great parlors when the sun had sunk to rest the next evening and the white, glittering stars swung up from the blue Gulf. Stalwart men, whose names were famed in border life, watched the gathering throng, which filled even the great porticoes. There were few women present, save Pastor Sunderland's wife and the wondering maids who followed the two sisters to the hall-doors. But in the throng, hawk-eyed, aristocratic Nordenskiold, jolly old Major Blucher, the stern, revengeful Hodges, and all the available local dignitaries of Corpus Christi marked the loveliness of the Brides of San Miguel.

Silas Leavenworth and his patient wife were the objects of profound attention, when the fateful words were spoken which gave them two noble sons to close up their family circle.

While Jimmy Leavenworth clasped his new-made

brothers' hands, there was a thrill of astonishment as
jaunty Captain Buller, in a wonderfully neat impro-
vised, half-dress uniform, saluted *both* the brides with a
kiss, murmuring archly " military promptness!" Old
Colonel Ford gravely kissed the girls' foreheads,
simply saying: " This is the happiest day of my life.
May the Lone Star shine always on your happiness!"

St. Cecilia Alice, in stately loveliness, led her
strangely gentle sister Katie up to the brother who had
tenderly watched their girlhood, and whispered, as she
kissed the gallant fellow, " For Sister Gertie." And
it was late that night before Captain Buller led that
never-to-be-forgotten Virginia Reel with lovely Katie!

Before the train rolled away, four days later, which
bore Silas Leavenworth and his overjoyed wife to the
shores of the Gulf, Jack Manson, beaming with happiness, was glad to announce, in full dispatches, to his
uncle the lull in the passing storm.

For Mark Manson's cipher had flashed to him these
fateful words:

The great border movement has been abandoned. Steele and
I are in accord, but you must direct and reorganize the whole
line of operations. We look to you to save everything.

It was with a thankful heart Jack Manson read the
return to his own dispatch announcing the double
wedding:

You have my full authority to control the future of the Rio
Grande Railroad, for you own half my interests there.

It was indeed a royal wedding-present!

In these busy days the happy sisters were not alone,
for a graceful woman, in black, whose wonderful eyes
shone tenderly on them, wandered in Katie's garden.
It was Señora Panchita!

Strange to say, the tall Dane hovered around her every movement, and the musical Castilian tongue of their dialogue guarded some weighty matters of secret import. The legal papers were finished, and a volunteer escort awaited the departing ranchero—king no more, for his sceptre had passed to others.

Before an astonished circle, Olaf Nordenskiold led Señora Panchita up to Silas Leavenworth. " It is only just to inform you all that this lady, in seeking a shelter with friends, has found a *father !* "

There was a happy wonder in the eyes of the beautiful brides, who never begged their lovely visitor to unfold all the sealed pages of that life-mystery !

" Mr. Manson," said Nordenskiold, when the carriages were ready, as he drew Jack aside, " I have a few private words for your own ear." Walking up and down the lawn the Dane astonished the happy Benedict.

" I must go on with Silas, for he has a flood of business at New Orleans. We have been friends for a quarter of a century; we are both men of a border type soon to disappear. I am his lawyer, his father-confessor in things mundane. You are now his son-in-law and representative. Do not be astonished at any things touching his past life which may come to you ! You are now one of us—one of the mystic circle which, guided by self-interest, has controlled the great advance on Mexico! Silas has been like all of us, *a soldier of fortune,* a creature of circumstance, and, guided by self-interest only, his bravery, nerve, and plotting brain have built up a border empire for a thankless future generation! Be charitable in your judgments." The old lawyer paused. " I shall leave Panchita here until I have saved Silas Leavenworth every possible annoyance from that dead brute's treachery. I will not disguise

that we were bound together by gain and pride
of control. We had to direct every interest here,
and our record is not clear! Jimmy is a noble fellow.
He knows *nothing* of the dark side of the Rio Grande
Company. His mother and sisters have shared the
anxieties, not the *profits*, of these hidden adventures.
Now, you must spare all their feelings! I have instructed
Rudolf Harbeck, Beriah Mott, Collector Rains, and
Chisholm's factotum at New Orleans to post you fully
through my chief clerk, whom I leave with you here.
A number of men will come here on business from
Brownsville, Matamoras, Indianola, perhaps from
Havana and San Antonio, timorous fellows frightened
by this noise. All you will have to do is to refer them
to me later! I know the law's delays," said Norden-
skiold, with a sneer.

"I shall first smooth up Chisholm's affairs so he can
safely return. Then, clearing up all clouds between your
uncle and Silas, bend my energies to induce Senator
Steele to resign and go abroad in a diplomatic position.
We control the courts here. Steele is a fool, though
crafty. I want him out of the way. Chisholm is a genius.
The President will not be able to hold Steele up longer
as a great party leader in the South. General Grant is
loyal to his friends, but he has a noble soul. The pressure brought on him to press forward on defenseless
Mexico and conquer the Free Zone has been gigantic!
But Maxan's annoying disclosures have made a frontier
quarrel impossible. It will be only a peaceful commercial
and railroad advance which will throw us on to the halls
of the Montezumas, not a cowardly and unnecessary
war. I have kept in the inside of the whole intrigue.
It will yet be written in letters of gold on Grant's tomb
that, though he gained his laurels by the sword, he was
at heart a man of peace—peace-promoting and peace-

loving. The great onward movement has failed! The day of 'irregular operations' in the border is passing. Your railroad is the great civilizer. Now, take up your burden with Bayard and Jimmy. Live an honorable and clean life. Build up the State you are doubly tied to now. And when Silas and the man who speaks are lying with our heads under the prairie grass, remember that, *in our place,* you and your comrade might have drifted into the same questionable ways!"

"I shall close my professional career with this last service to Silas. I have enough—too much, in fact, for peace. Money beyond reasonable needs is *only a source of daily care!* I shall return to open the closed leaves of life's book, simply to be loyal to old clients. As for my future," he said, with a glance of his steady, gray eye toward the beautiful Panchita, "I have found that there is one thing sweeter than sin, dearer than the pride of life or the joys of passion!"

"It is," said Jack, in wonder at this touch of tender feeling.

"A manly atonement for the past!" said the lawyer, as he grasped Jack's hands and whispered: "You can use my cipher through the clerk. Rely on him; he is skilful and quiet. Let nothing reach Jimmy's ears to cloud his future." He joined the waiting ranchero.

So, with a triumphal escort, Silas Leavenworth went forth to rest in peace after the storm-tossed days of a life of intrigue on the wild border.

That most bewitching of young matrons, Mrs. Jack Manson, began to rivet up the golden chain of her supremacy, the guiding thrall of her husband-lover, by complaining artfully of "neglect," "his great attention to business," etc.

The days were not long enough now for Manson and Jimmy, who was preparing to seek the shades of Arun-

del Manor.   One local scheme interested the Bayards
and delighted Katie's heart.   A sudden vacancy had
caused a special congressional election.   By common
consent of the Western magnates, the name of James
Leavenworth was decided upon to be used in his
absence upon the wedding tour.

It befell later, that the absent candidate received
every vote in the district, save three, which were cast on
a principle of "personal honor " by three Federal office-
holders, who were escorted to the polls by a Mexican
band playing " Dixie's Land! "   The gallant plainsman
indeed received a "Texan majority," practically, the
whole vote!

Mrs. Katie, a picture of happiness and dangerously
liable to become a source of "grave future trouble," in
her loving mastery of the man who held her heart in fee,
rode out several times with Jack to see the railroad now
crawling up to the very ranch gates.   An impromptu
race, witnessed by a thousand cheering workmen, gave
Manson a chance to display his gallantry.   Mrs. Katie
won the canter by a length!

" You dear old humbug!" said the beauty, as Jack
swung her from the saddle.   " You *know* Kentucky
can beat my darling just one length in a mile.
You held him in, sir.   You do not race fairly.
Jack," said Katie, as she walked gayly along by
her husband's side, flicking off the prairie flowers with
her riding-whip, " do you remember the day when you
asked me at Arundel House if I could ride? "   Her
ringing laughter made the sons of toil pause and gaze
admiringly as they leaned on pick or shovel.

" I do! " said her husband humbly.

" Well, sir, I will confess now I had already made
up my mind that I would show you how I could ride,
and continue the exhibition for many, many years!

You were *doomed to be a Texan* from the first day I met you."

" I am satisfied," said Jack; " and to show it I'll give you a prize you won in this remarkable equestrian competition. It comes from Uncle Mark, but you can credit it to me. I kept it until you were unusually worthy of praise and *now* I will reward you for your frankness."

" Oh, Jack!" said Miss Katie, in an ecstasy of delight, as she gazed on a magnificent set of diamonds which Mark Manson had forwarded as a firstling of his generous approbation. " You will have to take me sometime to Saratoga or Long Branch to exhibit these," the beauty cried, for it was in the golden days of those Vanity Fairs.

" You are best fitted to shine *at home* here on the ranch!" said Jack severely.

" Never mind!" cried his lovely wife; " I will be like the moon—go around the world and *shine for all!* "

" Not till Mr. James Manson has become a slave of the golden lamp, like me!" answered Jack. " Then we may do a bit of world-wandering, but only when the railroad is all done, and you have also given Gertie some of your sage advice about life in Texas."

" If she finds as easy a road to happiness as I have," cried Katie, " she can spare my advice. I will leave her future happiness in Brother Jimmy's hands."

The young men toiled in Silas' den with Bayard, and received deputations of leading citizens, affected by the new regime, or curious to meet the winsome brides of San Miguel. Colonel Mejia, while looking for new matters to busy his hard-worked adjutant, yet found time to send to Madam Katie the complete trousseau of a bride, and these splendid garnitures were prepared in Paris and sent complete to Mexico.

Katie Manson's happy laughter brought all the

dwellers in the mansion to feast their eyes on these wonders, for the daughters of Mexico, in their womanly pride, were as richly furnished forth often as an arch-duchess of Austria. The boundless wealth of the hacienda aristocrats of Mexico gladdened the far-off Parisian merchant's heart.

"So thoughtful! and a soldier too! Who would have fancied that he could be so delicate in this princely gift? *So timely!*" It was remarkable, for several sets of robes for every possible occasion, with the remotest detail, were spread out when the great cases were at last emptied.

" They have these outfits entire in the great marts at Matamoras," said Brother Jimmy. " But how he was enabled to suit them to you, I can not divine." All eyes were turned on the brilliant bird of paradise, for Katie had re-entered the great rooms arrayed in one of these marvels.

" I must confess," said the dark-eyed Panchita. "I was secretly charged by Colonel Mejia to furnish the measures which your maids gave me. And let me now complete the offering," said Panchita, for the madcap Katie had donned a rich evening toilet. The lovely Spaniard clasped a superb necklace of Gulf of California pearls around the beautiful wife's neck.

"Not *his!*" she said, with a shudder. There were shining tears in Panchita's eyes as she whispered, "*My mother's!* I was told to give them to you by the father I have found at last."

There were serious labors waiting to occupy the three young men at the "Den." For Silas Leavenworth was now at New Orleans, and the temporary tele-graph of the railroad, now at their very door, was busied with cipher messages from the wily Danish lawyer. The property and vessels, the seized goods and con-fiscated moneys of the associates were bonded, released, or by some mysterious processes placed where, in the sluggish course of investigation and nerveless litigation, they would finally return to the partners. Manson alone understood all these manœuvres. The men embroiled in these troubles were forced to go on and finish their plans!

But grave governmental changes had occurred. Several Cabinet officers had been transferred or resigned! A new set of customs officials suddenly appeared, and all the journals were now strangely reticent as to the movements of that great statesman, Senator Steele.

Jack Manson understood a brief note from Olaf Nordenskiold traced in his own hand:

All is safe now; Chisholm can quietly return. The mail and other contracts are saved. One of our associates in power had to do this to save himself, but I think that Senator Steele will resign and accept a foreign mission. The best news is that Mark Manson seems to feel very well—by wire. My next will be from New York. Meanwhile, my clerk has reported that you are a man of both energy and prudence! Look out for any straggling, revengeful desperado. Guard your lines everywhere. Silas is safe at last in name and pocket.

Manson marvelled at Nordenskiold's success. He never did know the agonizing efforts of the mysterious No. 4 who was *obliged* to save Senator Steele public disgrace. Only Milly Steele ever knew the real identity of the hidden agent who, as No. 4, had schemed to throw a great people in arms upon a weak sister republic! There was such an ebb-tide of fallen statesmen, drifting away after the abortive " Greeley campaign " that no one surmised who the great man was, who owed his own ruin and the balking of a desperate enterprise to Ramon Maxan's insensate love for Katie Leavenworth.

Conjecture was vain! The mantle of silence has never been lifted! The all-seeing journalists only knew that a new spirit breathed along the Rio Grande; that the arrival of cavalry corps, heavy trains of munitions, artillery movements, and secret planning had been mysteriously diverted, arrested, or countermanded!

The three lovers laughed when a scrawl from Silas reached them from New Orleans. It was through Harbeck, the confidential book-keeper. It was laconic.

Rudolf, what ready money have I on hand in my private account? I need fifty thousand dollars to go to Europe. Will there be anything left for Jim? If not, show him this and tell him from me to *sell some cattle*. Telegraph your answer!

"Well, old man," said the expectant bridegroom, "can my father go abroad in peace and not worry about me?"

"You need not sell any cattle!" said the old German, with a quiet smile, "I suppose you will wish to draw liberally, on your marriage." He gazed respectfully at the young heir.

"By Jove! boys," laughed Jimmy, "I had my mind simply fixed on getting away for the Virginia trip. I forgot all about any money."

"You will need money," said Tom Bayard gravely, as he reflected that he was married longer (by five minutes) than the careful Manson. He was the ranking "family man!"

"Is that your experience?" roared Jimmy, with sly reference to the hidden glories of Bayard's Nueces Valley mansion, which Alice had not yet examined. "I'm told that you emptied the New Orleans shops."

"I have a whole lot of new things," admitted the now thoroughly tamed ex-rebel, in manly confusion. "I hope that they will please my wife," he finished in a doubtful tone.

"Well, I'll not break your bank, Rudolf," said Jimmy, "you can hold, however, twenty thousand dollars subject to my order. So telegraph my father it's all right.

"The fact is, gentlemen," said James, in a modest tone, "I shall have a little look around and then bring my wife (he smiled faintly) back here and economize!"

"That's right!" said Manson; "and be sure first to *get the wife*, then you can come here and economize all you wish! For Katie proposes to give a rather ambitious reception or two in Uncle Mark's old palace on Gramercy Square. She will just set off your economical fit in the annual balance-sheet."

"Seriously," said the young plainsman, "I have a little special business at Arundel House, and father and mother will be there waiting me soon. I feel that this little estrangement with Mark Manson will yield to Nordenskiold's experience and tact. Now, Tom," said Leavenworth, turning to the genial Confederate, "the border was never as quiet. Buller's dashing troopers, McNally's Rangers, and our own stock riders and railroad men make an invincible ring of faithful guardians around San Miguel. I can go away with a clear conscience as to responsibility. You two can run a dozen situations like this. Keep Bronco Bill and old Basilio moving. If you should both leave, send for Colonel Rip Ford and let him act as generalissimo. He never sleeps on guard, the dear, old, gray fox. Look at the changes of the last four years! Cortina is out of power, a prisoner far away. Caballo Blanco is dead! Mauricio Portugal was shot all to pieces in Matamoras Plaza the other day. Poor John Wesley Hardin, too, was captured in Florida the other day. He will chafe out his life at Huntsville prison. The Freedmen's Bureau and Reconstruction Government shams are at an end. There is no disturbance now. I feel that the era of the knife and six-shooter is

over. There is every promise for the future, and I
look forward to the day when Texas will be grid-ironed
with railways, these plains covered with smiling homes,
and all our land under fence. That is the epoch for the
final disappearance of the cowboy."

"You may be right. God grant you are a sound
prophet," said jovial Tom Bayard. "But what will
you do with Bronco Bill?"

"Oh, he is so proud and lazy since he rode Kentucky in with the good news, that I think he will 'get
religion' and become a popular exhorter. Katie has
already spoiled him, Jack, as she is rapidly spoiling
you!"

"Look here, young man, it is about time for you to
pack your kit and march toward the Potomac. I
think we can let him go now, Colonel?" said Manson,
appealing to the ex-rebel.

"Vayase V. con Dios!" remarked Bayard, exhausting
his Castilian flourishes.

"Very good," cried James Leavenworth, and it is
a matter of history that he embraced his lovely sisters
and rode away to the Gulf, drawn by the magnet of
Love, and one of the first bits of astounding news he
heard, after that wedding which revived the olden
glories of Arundel House, was that he was a Congress-
man in spite of himself!

Winifred Marshall was happy once more in the
friendship of Mary Leavenworth. The ranchero's
steadfast wife, gentle and placid, fitted admirably the
quiet dignity of the home-life at Arundel. Silas
Leavenworth, under the astute counsels of Nordenskiold, had met Mark Manson in peace, and the broad
plan of the final development of their great properties was left to the younger men. The old New
York financier, in earnest of his renewed friendship,

made a pilgrimage to Arundel House, and beamed upon the marriage with approving eyes. In view of the recent dignity conferred upon the young ranchero, he purposed an early return to San Miguel.

"You will have a delightful opportunity to meet the picturesque constituents of your husband," said Mark Manson to the happy Gertrude. "From the private reports of my nephew, there are certainly some remarkable people on the Rio Grande! You are an exception, my dear young lady, to the general rule. I have heard it.said that it is peopled only by those who are wanted *in no other place!*" He smiled benignly, in hinting at the Texan welcome already in preparation by her sweet sisters of the heart.

"I have a little commission for you," said the old Crœsus. "Will you kindly bear this little reminder to Mrs. Bayard and accept a similar token for yourself?" The jeweler's art had been taxed to provide the exquisite parures of gems offered as a token of peace.

"I regret that I can not visit the great rancho myself, but we seniors have one bit of final diplomacy to finish at Washington, and *then* Mr. Leavenworth can proceed in peace to Europe."

It was in fact to "efface" Ezra Steele, as a responsible statesman, and see him wafted to some foreign clime, that Nordenskiold, Leavenworth, and Mark Manson labored in unison. Steele was pompous, obstinate, and crafty, and vain of the public mention of the journals. The acute Dane well knew that Chisholm (now returned), Manson's railway venture, and old Silas' reputation were not safe while the "carpet bagger" cumbered the floor of the Senate! After two weeks' careful intrigue at Washington, aided with the persuasion of the Senator's anxious wife, the change was effected. Several little dinners, with séances in the

Turkish smoking-room, made the three veterans of intrigue admire the wisdom and persistency of Milly Steele. She foresaw the inevitable downfall of the carpet-bag government.

"I would sooner, gentlemen, see my husband peacefully translated to our foreign diplomatic service than go down to ruin with the wreck of his party-faction in the South, but he seems so fond of public life."

"I think that I can influence him," said Nordenskiold. "Mr. Leavenworth's son-in-law, Colonel Thomas Bayard, is coming North with his bride to pass a few weeks at Saratoga, and he can see our friend Mr. Chisholm at New Orleans. Now I know Chisholm can do much with Senator Steele. I'll ask Colonel Bayard to come here and bring a private letter from Chisholm setting up certain matters of which you naturally know little!"

The lawyer ceased as he noticed a ghastly paleness grow on Milly Steele's face. "I beg pardon. You are agitated!"

When the three gentlemen left, Milly Steele stood alone before her glass, a quivering, cowering woman.

"Colonel Thomas Bayard coming! My God! Steele *must* go abroad! Bayard knew me as Florence Mortimer!"

The sudden thought of her knowledge of the identity of No. 4 flashed over her mind. That personage still had influence, even in retirement. He held locked in his breast secrets which were of moment to the country and party, even if he no longer administered a high trust.

The next day a graceful, deeply veiled woman entered the abiding-place of the retired statesman who had been Steele's shadowy partner. In a half-hour, seeking her coupé, she was swiftly driven home by a roundabout route. Her head lay helpless on the cushions, but she whispered, "Saved! Saved!" for the hidden influence needed was at hand.

A brief note next day called Olaf Nordenskiold to her side:

I have good news for you. The Senator was sent for from the White House to-day. Following the advice of party leaders whom I do not know, he has decided to resign, and one of the South American republics will be selected for his entry into the diplomatic service as Minister.

" Is this *sure?* It seems too good to be true!" said the doubting lawyer.

Milly Steele turned a worn and wearied face toward him. "I had much to do to reconcile Mr. Steele, but his resignation was forwarded to his Governor to-day, and he will call to-morrow at the Department of State."

"This is glorious!" said Nordenskiold. "The Senator's interests in Texas will be our joint care. Mr. Mark Manson and Silas Leavenworth will both recognize your valuable assistance ! The fact is, my dear madam, that the intrigues of this dead robber Maxan—"he started in astonishment as Milly Steele strode up and down, wringing her hands and crying:

"I know ! I know enough ! *Too much !* Spare me ! I only wish to go quietly abroad ; that is, I am quite reconciled," she said artfully, as she noted the lawyer's wondering look of amazement.

" Bring your friends to-morrow evening; I will give them the news so you will know just how to handle my husband. So Colonel Bayard's services will not be needed," she said smilingly.

" True, but he is already on his way!" said the lawyer, as he bowed his way out.

"Maxan's name seemed to affect her," mused Nordenskiold, as he sauntered to his hotel. "It's a queer
world! I wonder if they ever were allied in heart!"

While he speculated, Milly Steele, with trembling
lips, thanked God that she could never meet Maxan
again! "Not on this side of the grave!" said the
beautiful woman, as she drained a glass of cordial, for
she knew now that her lover had fallen by the hand of a
man she could have madly loved.

The momentous interview of Senator Steele at the
White House was wrapped in diplomatic secrecy. His
visit to the State Department was less confidential.
Received by a suave Assistant Secretary he was blandly
informed of his appointment as Minister to Peru.

"It will be a delightful voyage, a charming post of
duty, important natural interests, and a great future for
you diplomatically, sir," said the official.

"Ah! I should like to see the Secretary of State
personally and confer upon this important charge," said
Steele, thrusting his hand in the bosom of his Prince
Albert. He was already a budding Metternich, with
strong ambitions to be recognized later as a Talleyrand!

"Quite unnecessary, Senator, quite unnecessary; the
Secretary reposes *every confidence* in your tried states-
manship. Your instructions will be sent to you at
once. You are aware that you have six months in
which to proceed to your post. Your drafts will be
honored for your salary for that period in advance as
usual!"

"Ah!" said Steele; "in that case I may spend a few
weeks at Saratoga. Public service has worn greatly
upon me!"

"Certainly, certainly, sir," said the Assistant, bowing
him out. "Report your address, sir; we will forward
all your instructions."

As Ezra Steele drove away, the official smiled. "The President has pastured that old fool abroad to get rid of him, I suppose. Well, we will only hear from him quarterly, that's one blessing of the situation."

The newly-made Minister, whose resignation as senator would naturally be eagerly accepted, drove away in high good-humor.

"There are valuable interests; nitrate beds, islands of fertilizers, and railroad schemes. I should make some money down there." He smiled and dreamed of a golden future, as he drove home and announced the news to his wife. "We will pass a few weeks at Saratoga, and then close our affairs here. You will be charmed with Peru, so courtly and hospitable are the Dons, our Secretary tells me."

Steele was already satisfied, as he had his eagle eye fixed on the "nitrate beds."

"If they *are there* when I arrive, I will have some local interest before long. I will find the way!"

So the Foreign Service was reinforced by a representative ripe and polished statesman "going abroad to shed lustre on his country."

Ezra Steele never knew how he was bodily moved away into strange and devious paths, to protect the wreck of the secret Rio Grande cabal, by Chisholm's frantic appeals to the mysterious but still powerful No. 4. The mysterious partner was a fallen star, sweeping in brightness in the train of the one great national luminary, and, in his sudden extinction, had cast the crafty, narrow-minded "carpet-bag" Senator out to wander as a poor, fading asteroid, his little sparkle quenched in the darkness of South American revolution and uncivilized obscurity!

A month later Milly Steele walked alone by the shores of Saratoga Lake. Her face was as wondrously fair as ever, and her heart was happy and light. For, in going forth to his late apprenticeship in the great world beyond the sea, Silas Leavenworth had arranged the most substantial guarantees of income for the now ambitious Minister. Steele was absent at Washington, as he was closing their private affairs, the Russian Legation renting the superb residence for a period of years.

Mark Manson, in parting, had frankly told her: "I am under an obligation to you, which I can never forget! You have been earnest, prudent, active, and your husband has been saved complication and disaster by your powerful influence for good in his career! He will at least have a name and position, and when his confreres of the 'carpet-bag' order are forgotten, this dignified exile will shield him. Besides, your income is assured! We will take care of that. I have a warm admiration of your efforts to get a solid foothold under you in life, and you will have peace at least."

"Peace! That is all I pray for!" said Milly Steele, grasping the old financier's hands. There were few secrets between them now!

" *Think of me kindly*," she said, " if you do not see me again! Think of me at my best!"

"You can test my memory of your bright and friendly assistance by calling on me from your distant home for anything in your interest," said Mark heartily, as he announced his departure for a long tour.

"Better than the world would have her be—better than many another of Eve's daughters would have been in her place! I pity, I admire, and I wonder," mused the old man, "is there any one who *must* say I forgive?"

It was of all these things that Milly Steele thought on the eve of her departure from Saratoga, as she wandered alone by the lovely lake. She had walked down to its shores, leaving her carriage at some distance.

"I am only too glad to go!" she murmured. "I fear not the future; I only wish to go out in peace, away from the haunting memories of old days. It is strange," she mused, "that I have not met Colonel Bayard here! Would he remember the girl-wife he so gallantly aided in her sorrow if he met me? Alice, his sweet wife, knows me only as Milly Smiley. No! Time has brushed me away from Memory's picture, and there is no one now to speak of Florence Mortimer! Bayard did not come here, and Robert Kenyon rests in an unknown grave."

Alas, for the shortness of human vision! Thomas Bayard had hidden his new happiness from public gaze at the romantic Lake House, avoiding the already vulgar crowds of the "Springs," for it was in the days of flaming "petroleum" and rampant "shoddy" millionaires. Milly Steele looked out on the exquisite shores of the placid lake smiling at her feet! Not a ripple roughened its calm beauty. The passionate woman drank in the charm of the still hour, the glassy, mirrored waters and their fringing shores.

"Peaceful, calm, yet below lie yawning depths, black caverns, jagged rocks. Yes! like the false life of the broken butterflies of fashion—we poor smiling women—looking forward with no thought of anything, save to smooth the pathway under our feet. To look back over the road our weary feet have travelled would be horrible. Beneath our calm lies often the dark agony of the past! My God!" she shrieked, for, pale, haggard, unkempt, with a strange gleam in his eyes, Robert Kenyon strode out from the shadows and roughly grasped her by the arms. He bitterly hissed in her very face: "Florence Mortimer! *You she-devil!* What have you done with my life? Where have you hidden all these years?"

The pallor of death was on Milly Steele's face as she gasped: "Back from the dead. Back again!"

"Tell me!" shouted the maniac. "I've tracked you here from your splendid home. I've watched you for weeks till I could meet you face to face. Now! By the God who made me, we will *die together!*"

He dragged her toward the rocky bank. Despite his attenuated frame and homeless wanderings, he had the strength of frenzy. Ramon Maxan's revenge was at last to be glutted. It was his curse hovering over her! Her stormy life passed before her as she strove in the energy of despair. "Robert, have mercy!" she screamed. "Help! Help!" The woodland echoes rung as the demented husband of her youth strove with the desperate woman.

In a moment more her loosening grasp would have finally yielded. Shrub and clinging vine gave her help, and inch by inch Milly Steele fought for her life as the hot breath of the demented wanderer swept her cheek.

With a last superhuman effort, she freed herself as he stumbled over a rocky ledge, in his mad fury falling backward. She ran with the swiftness of a deer, and the pursuing madman's grasp was almost on her shoulder, as a breathless man leaped between them, crying "Hold!"

With one wild shout, "Bayard!" the poor waif of years glared at the woman now clinging to the tall Texan, and, rushing to a jutting point, threw himself into the dark water under the shade of the gloomy pines! The woman glided from her savior's arms and fell senseless on the turf. Tom Bayard, darting to the rock whence the maniac had sprung, saw only a few widening circles on the shadowed black waters. There was no sound, no ripple, and the dark depths of the mountain tarn never gave up the body of the worn and wasted soldier. Kneeling by her side on the turf, Bayard saw the eyes, which had once looked on his men going forth to battle as he rode at their head, open in amazement.

"*You here!* At last! Over the world my fate has hounded me down!"

"You must try and rise! You must let me help you away from this place! For God's sake, let me bear you to a place of safety!"

In desperate resolve, the half-fainting woman struggled on Bayard's arm to her carriage!

"Your mistress has fainted. I will accompany her home. I am Colonel Bayard," said her guardian, as he lifted Milly Steele bodily into the Victoria. "Drive rapidly!" he cried. "Can you bear up?" he whispered to the Senator's wife. "You must. It is your life's salvation!"

An hour later Colonel Bayard left the darkened room, where Milly Steele lay safe in her hotel, with the echoes of the madman's voice still ringing in her ears.

"Tell me but *one thing*," he said, when the grave-faced physician had gone. "You always believed him dead?"

And Milly Steele was honest, as her trembling lips faltered: "Yes, I never heard but of his death. He made no sign in all these years!"

"Then your secret sleeps in the lake. If there shall be any inquiry, let me bear the burden. I can say an insane man attacked you, and in sudden frenzy threw himself in the lake. I will come to you—alone! It is well that you should not meet my wife."

An opportune telegram of the Minister, now anxious to personally verify the glories of his new position, enabled Bayard to quietly escort Milly Steele from the scene of her last life crisis. In silence, with grave kindness, Colonel Bayard said: "Go forth and look forward to a new life beyond the Andes, for my lips are sealed." The graceful woman pressed his hands, and as her tears fell on them, whispered: "May God be with you and yours always!"

There was no public comment as the ex-senator passed out on the ocean to his new post. He was a very dim asteroid now in the national firmament! He only marvelled at the shadows on his fair wife's brows, who gazed steadily forward to the new world of her future, her chastened heart imploring "Peace."

"I learn that Mrs. Steele has been at the Springs and sailed for South America," said happy Alice a few days later to her husband. "I am glad I did not meet her here, for, beautiful as she was, I always feared she had a secret in her life."

"Be gentle in your judgments, Alice, my darling," said the tall Texan, raising his eyes, which had been anxiously sweeping the broad lake. "Whatever her secret was, it is hidden forever now! Let us not speak of her again."

When the happy circle was finally reunited at San Miguel, Thomas Bayard told Jack Manson of the strange happening at the lakeside.

"I know not if it was really Maxan's plan to set the demented husband on her trail to effect her murder in revenge," Jack answered. "Mejia's indefatigable adjutant traced both Kenyon and Maxan to the same camp. But it is a wonderful story. Let us drop the dark memories of that fiend and his futile plans. It is strange!" said brave Jack Manson, look-

ing at his beloved Katie, whose fair face was lit with
happiness as she saw the heart-brothers returning from
their walk. "It seems providential that, in the end,
where Hate and Love struggle to the death, Love
wins! Love is unsuspecting, hate is crafty and plotting, yet in all Ramon Maxan's devilishly cultured
schemes, each careful snare laid for others failed at
last!"

"Do you know it is stranger than even you say,
Jack, in this very case? Nordenskiold is now dividing
up some lands. I asked him what he was doing so
for! 'I owned them half in half with poor Bob
Kenyon,' he said, 'and I have set *my* share aside for
Panchita, who will be married next month to Colonel
Mejia. The other interest should be Bob Kenyon's
widow's. He left a will which was proved here, for
he had sent it on from Atlanta, where he married a
lady named Mortimer.' When I told him *who she
was now*, the old man said, 'Well, the lady will have
a hundred thousand dollars for pin-money!'"

"I always thought Captain Buller might marry
Panchita!" said Jack, musing on what he had heard.

"Buller's marriage is gazetted, sir, as well as his staff
majority. He has captured a senator's daughter, and
has got an extra grade with *military promptness!*"

"Come here, you wanderers!" cried Mrs. Katie.
"We are all going to drive over to your Nueces ranch
to-morrow, as Alice is at last going over to take possession! Father will bring mother home soon, and we
have decided that *three brides* are too many for San
Miguel!"

"Then we must build a Nueces branch of the railroad soon," cried Colonel Bayard; "the travel will be
immense!" a proposition heartily joined in by Jimmy
Leavenworth and fair Gertrude, dashing up on their
return from a ride.

"Do you like building railroads in Texas, Jack?" said Katie Manson, with a flash of her old spirit.

"I have found a new life and a true love under the Southern Cross!" said Jack, as he stooped and kissed her rosy lips.

www.ingramcontent.com/pod-product-compliance
Lightning Source LLC
Chambersburg PA
CBHW031058110726
47900CB00003B/971